*Dedicated to*

*My mom for inspiring me*
*My dad for understanding me*
*My big brother for believing in me*
*My husband for supporting all my dreams*
*and also dedicated to*
*My babies for giving me a reason.*

*When demons knock on your door, throw it open and show them*
*what you're made of.*

*Tricia Warnock*

# Prologue

Don't Leave

*Tricia Warnock*

4

Comfort and peace. I was curled up on my bed, enjoying the warmth of his body curled behind mine. It was not so long ago that the feeling of someone's breath on the back of my neck would have made my skin crawl and make my heart pound to the point of causing real pain. My lips curled into a contented grin. Finally, I felt at ease in my own skin.

I survived a war, with battle scars to prove it and finally, I was allowed to come home. The flashbacks would haunt me for the rest of my days and certain sounds would
always bring me to my knees. My history would never be left on the shelf long enough to build a layer of dust, that was a certainty.

For now, I would bask in the contented intimacy with a man who loved me regardless of what happened before him. I knew he entertained a few theories, some of which he felt compelled to share with me. In the beginning, I was afraid that if I divulged the truth, he would look at me in fear, thinking he had become involved with a mentally deranged woman. He might even bring me to a doctor where I would have one hell of a time trying to explain myself. Now, I wasn't so sure the outcome would send me to an institute.

There was a reason my mind had drifted to the fears I hid in the beginning of our relationship. He was running his fingertips up and down the three raised scars that ran diagonally under my left breast down across my rib cage and the fourth more shallow line I had added to it. When my ordeal drew to an end, I ran a razor across my skin to blur the meaning of having three very distinct scars. I shivered from the softness of his touch against the sensitive skin.

"Sorry." He whispered, laying a light kiss on the back of my neck. The rough stubble on his chin tickled the nape of my neck making me giggle and pull my shoulders up to break the contact. I felt his lips curl up into a knowing grin against my shoulder blade.

He raised himself on an elbow to lean over me. "Don't like my kisses? That's kind of rude you know." He stuck out his bottom lip in an exaggerated pout. I raised a hand to run my fingers against his cheek and he took the opportunity to pounce. Straddling me and grabbing both of my hands to hold over my head, he touched the tip of his nose to mine. "It's on now lady!" When I squirmed, he kissed me under my earlobe, forcing more giggles to escape. The kisses around my neck did not stop until tears rolled down my cheeks and both of us were out of breath.

He plopped back down beside me and his smile melted my heart. Slowly I watched as his smile faded and a serious expression replaced it. Worry filled my chest, unsure where his thoughts had gone.

"I love you Paisley."

I was lost. Completely caught off guard. I sat up, holding the sheet to my chest, trying to buy time to catch my scattered thoughts. He sat up beside me, running a hand gently down my back.

"It's okay, you don't have to say anything. I just wanted

you to know." He didn't need to add that he was hurt. The forced smile he was giving me quivered and I was certain his heart ached as much as mine did.

"Look Connor, you know I love you too." He moved to pull me into his arms but I held up a hand, stopping him in his tracks. He covered the hand I held on his chest with his own and looked at me, more hurt than before and silently pleading. He thought he knew where I was going with this but he could not have been more wrong. I would not be the one to end any hope I had to a happily ever after. It would be up to him. He would have a decision to make and the only prayer I had left was that he had meant it when he said he loved me.

I took his hand and used his fingers to trace the scars on my body. His eyes softened and though he was still confused, the fear had subsided.

"Do you want to know what ruined me before we met?"

"You're far from ruined. You're perfect." He kissed me and the guilt in the pit of my stomach did a somersault.

"Connor you need to listen to me. I'm going to tell you a story and when I am done, you won't see me the same way." His grip on my hand tightened and I returned a gentle squeeze. "I need you to keep an open mind and know that the past 6 months, has done more to heal my soul than any kind of doctor could have."

"You don't have to tell me anything. Some people face traumas and spend their lives fighting the demons that those traumatizing moments leave behind. I get it. I love you and I want to help you fight your demons moving forward."

"You think you love me but... you don't *really* know me."

I stood from the bed and went to my closet to retrieve a box I kept hidden under a pile of blankets. Butterflies filled my stomach as I sat back on my bed facing Connor, holding the box tightly against me. Taking a deep breath, I removed the lid. Inside were notes I had taken while I was still able, pictures my parents had taken to document the progression of my 'ailment' and a battered copy of the Holy Bible that I only recently stopped sleeping with.

I placed a picture of me prior to my ordeal in front of Connor. The second picture was one my mom had taken of my distended stomach, swollen like a woman who was moments from going into labour. Healed bruises in a sickening shade of green and fresh purple bruises covered the mound like a child's painting. The third picture was a close up of my battered face. Dried lips with 2 deep splits on both sides of my bottom lips. One eye was swollen shut but the other was just black with a sliver of white circling it. My cheeks were turned up into a smile of sheer delight. The last picture I placed in
font of him was a picture of me climbing a chain link fence upside down. My matted hair hung by my face. My mother took the picture from the other side of the fence, capturing the evil look on my face. The last picture made my skin crawl. My hands were wrinkled, swollen and broken, my feet were bare and my toes clung to the fence like a second set of hands. I was smiling in the picture, rotting flesh left exposed between my teeth. The sides of my mouth were cracked open, making my smiling mouth unnaturally wide.
"What the fuck is all this?" Connor leaned away from the pictures like the subject would jump out at him.
"This is Braxeus. A demon who took over my body for a year and a half." I dug a little further in the box and pulled out a research paper with a black and white picture of a demon who had a striking resemblance to the one of me on the fence. He took the sheet of paper to have a closer look at Braxeus.

He looked up to make eye contact, searching my eyes for more answers.

"You're not kidding." He concluded and I shook my head. He put the paper back on my bed and took a moment to work through his thoughts.

I watched him pick up the pictures and put them back in the box before closing the lid. He leaned over and pulled me into his arms before laying us both back down on the bed. He held me close and I felt his lips on my forehead.

"I love you Paisley." He said again and the tears of relief flowed freely down my cheeks.

"I love you too Connor." He kissed me before taking my hands into his and giving them a reassuring squeeze.

"Now, from the beginning Paisley, tell me how it started."

"Well, I don't know the exact moment it happened but a lot of doctors seem to think it started when I was really little. I'll start there and let you decide whether or not they are right." I looked into a dark corner of my memory, a place I avoided like the plague. Without any difficulty, things I had been trying so hard to forget, all came flooding back.

*Tricia Warnock*

# Chapter One

## Ugly little Coleman Girl

It's so ironic. At eleven years old, I had perfected the resting bitch face. People didn't approach me unless they were left with no choice and that's just the way I liked it. The irony laid in the fact that in reality, I was a weak, terrified little girl who was lost in a world that just couldn't be bothered.

I had no control at home. None. You could be damn sure that outside of the house, I had full control. The other kids at school feared me, shit, even some of the teachers did. Nobody needed to know that they only got a small taste of the terror I felt when I got back home.

I walked through the main entrance of my elementary school. The bell had yet to sound but I made my way to my cubby to drop off my things. I waited on the benches outside of my classroom. My body was stiff from sleeping under my bed the night before. I was not a runt. I was as tall as the boys in my class and my shoulders were just as wide. I was far from being a butch. My nearly black hair hung just below my bottom and my dark eyelashes framed matching eyes. It was braided that today, I liked when it was braided because I liked running the tied end along my face. The soft touch was what I craved against my cheek.

I concentrated on the darkness behind my eyelids as I mentally prepared to face another day. I fought with a couple older girls the day before, I didn't let them get the best of me but I would have to face my punishment. No outside play for me. Detention during recesses was what awaited me for the foreseeable future. I was thankful they didn't call home and just sent a letter to be signed.

The morons actually thought I showed that shit to my parents? As if. I'd been signing those stupid forms since I'd learned how to defend myself. I doubted they even knew what my mother's actual signature looked like.

The sound of the bell went off above my head on the speaker. Seconds later, kids came barrelling in from the front door and the other end of the long hallway. I took a deep breath and went to stand. Halfway up, a hand reached out and shoved me back down.

"Well, well, well, look what we have here, the ugly little Coleman girl." Shit. Natasha, Gladstone public school's number one princess. My tussle with her the previous day obviously hadn't been enough to knock her down a peg. The day before, it had just been Natasha and her ever-present Shirley. They were joined by two girls I hadn't crossed paths with yet.

I smirked and gave her my best holier-than-though look. "You broke my nail yesterday, Natasha. I take it you came to say you're sorry?"

One of the other girls leapt forward and grabbed a hold of my braid, giving it a solid yank, pulling me from the bench. I landed hard on my knees; the tiles provided no cushion against the impact. My scalp stung; my knees throbbed but my lips curled up into a satisfied smile. My switch went off. Logic went to the wind and all I cared about was the anger induced adrenaline pounding in my veins. I put my hands on the floor while I moved my feet underneath me to stand up. The girl holding my braid lost her grip as I jumped forward, tackling Natasha to the floor. I heard the wind shoot from her lungs as we both slammed to the ground. I straddled her waist and for a moment, our eyes locked. The fear in her eyes lit the match on my anger. The smirk on my face stayed in place when I raised my fist behind my ear. For added effect, I held a fistful of her shirt and waited a couple of heartbeats before I let loose. My knuckles connected with her face several times before Mrs. Hamlet yanked me from Natasha. Innocent little Shirley ran to tattle, as per usual.

As I sat outside the office, the fury was gone but I was riding a new wave of adrenaline. This time I was filled with nothing but pure terror. They had me sitting out there while they phoned my parents. I prayed no one was home. No one home meant no one would answer.

"Oh no, not again. Paisley what did you do?" My sister rushed to sit beside me. Her eyes were filled with the same fear that had been eating away at me for the past five minutes. Her arms wrapped around me as the tears began falling.

Shella was the only person in the world who understood. She knew the person underneath the mask. She was my only ally in this shit world we were brought into. Though I was also close to my little brother, John, he and I didn't see eye-to-eye. We were just different people. Shella was my rock. I could tell her the truth and she wouldn't judge me because she lived the same hell I did.

"He's coming." I forced out between hysterical hiccups. She pulled away just enough to look me in the eye but kept her arms around me. "How do you know?"
"I knocked Natasha's lights out and they're on the phone with him right now."

"No... no no no. *Shit.*" She cursed before biting her bottom lip. I could tell by the look in her eyes that she was desperately trying to find a way to protect me like she always did. "Maybe he won't be home. Maybe he's still at work. Maybe she answers and doesn't tell him."

"Shella, she ha-has to this time. I-I'm being sus-suspended." Shella's shoulders dropped in defeat. There was no escape. She squeezed me close.

"I gotta get back to class before Mrs. Masterson realizes I'm not back yet. Be strong. I'll see you at home." She patted my back and got up to leave. She didn't look back as she walked away, knowing it would just set me off again.

I took a deep breath and awaited my fate. This was the worst part. Waiting. The blood pounded in my ears, meeting the ticking of the clock beat for beat.

What felt like a lifetime passed before the door to Mr. Finch's office opened up.

"Your mother is on her way Ms. Coleman. I hope you spend the next two weeks reflecting on your actions. Upon your return, I expect you to be on your best behaviour. I won't be so lenient a second time around." Mr. Finch stated without an ounce of sympathy. If only he knew that he just signed my death warrant. Scratch that. If he knew, he would have signed it a long time ago.

The door clicked closed again as my chin connected to my chest. She was coming. Tik tok, tik tok. I filled my lungs and slowly let the air out through my nose. Repeatedly. Each time, letting it out slower and slower.

By the time I heard heels clicking on the linoleum, the exercise had left my chest aching but at least I hadn't psyched myself into hysterics. I looked up to see my mother quickly approaching me. Not a hair out of place, not a wrinkle in her pencil skirt. Though her makeup was light, she would never leave the house without her pink lipstick and a thick layer of mascara. She was the kind of woman who
didn't need any makeup and when she did her face up for a night out on the town, it detracted from her natural beauty.

She reached a hand out for me. Once I placed mine in hers, she rapped on the office door.

"Yes?" Mr. Finch's irritated reply came through the closed door.

Opening the door, my mother stepped into the office, pulling me in behind her. When he looked up from his desk and spotted us, the balding man slid his glasses from his nose and presented my mother with his brightest smile.

"Mrs. Coleman," He stood and circled the desk, pulling a chair out for her to take a seat. She released my hand so she could hold her skirt against the back of her thighs as she sat, always mindful of preventing undesirable pleats. She sat on the very edge of her chair, crossing her feet at the ankles.

Mr. Finch, the disgusting pig, leaned his bottom on the desk right in front of her. Leaving his legs wide and forcing her to be at eye level to his crotch. He slowly crossed his arms across his chest, his eyes slowly travelled down my mother, all the way to her black pumps.

"I'm sorry to have to disrupt your morning, Mrs. Coleman but your daughter here has decided to act like an animal in my school." I watched as my mother's soft lips tightened the slightest bit. Enough that I knew, she would not take any of his shit.

"Are you calling my child an animal Mr. Finch?" She asked calmly. Without waiting for a reply, she continued. "Do you think maybe I raise barn animals at my house?" Her index finger moved up and tapped against her chin as she pondered sarcastically. "Or maybe you think I run a zoo and keep wild animals in cages somewhere in my basement."

"No, most certainly not Mrs. Coleman. I was simply stating that Paisley was *acting* like an animal." He was flustered. He had aimed to impress my mother and instead scrambled to gain the upper hand.

"Mr. Finch, I have raised all three of my children with impeccable manners. Though they are children and have stepped out of line from time to time, *never* have any of my children ever acted like *animals*." She said animals with a sneer, still seated calmly in front of the very uncomfortable Mr. Finch. "If this is the kind of behaviour you are faced with, perhaps the issue is not my child but rather the lack of supervision in your school. Maybe this isn't the best school to send my children to. Maybe I should discuss alternatives with the very kind ladies at my church, I'm sure they would love to hear all about my *animal*." My mother had a very solid reputation at St. Columban's Church. All the women there, flocked to her and hung onto everything she said. She was like the head cheerleader, only at church.

"Well now Mrs. Coleman, that won't be necessary. Paisley here just needs a couple of days to reflect." He stood from the desk and went back to his side to retrieve a sheet of paper.

He applied white out, blew it dry and then wrote what I assumed was the adjusted length of my suspension. He slid the paper across to my mother who reached forward to retrieve it before taking my hand again. We left without another word.

She led me to her parked car. When we are both seated, her in the driver's side, me in the back passenger seat, she met my eyes in the rear-view mirror. The fear she had disguised was now written clearly in her beautiful blue eyes. We sat staring at each other for a moment before she took a deep shaky breath and blew it out through her lips in a long, terrified sigh. The fingers on her right hand tapped against the steering wheel as her other hand pulled out her cigarettes from her handbag. It was evident by the way her hand shook when she lit her smoke, that she was barely holding herself together.

"We have to tell him. It will be worse if we don't." Her fingers continued tapping on the steering wheel and she blew out a steady stream of white smoke before quickly pulling another drag. "We can pretend to send you off to school every morning with Shella and John but what will you do all day? You can come home after he leaves and then hide when he comes home for lunch but that would be a huge risk. If he found out..." Her words trailed off but we both knew what was left in the silence. Her wheels turned as she desperately tried to figure out our next move.

"I'll tell him when he gets home from work mom. Better if it's just me than both of us." She broke eye contact with me in the mirror as she looked at her lap. I didn't miss the shine of tears in her eyes or the drops that fall to her skirt.

She started the car and pulled out of the parking lot and we drove home in silence. The fear was still present but pushed to the back of my mind as I was filled with numbness, accepting my fate.

I spent the rest of my day sitting on the front porch steps, watching cars drive by. Mom came out twice to sit with me while she had a cigarette and brought me a sandwich for lunch. We didn't talk, just sat quietly. By late afternoon, I watched the corner my siblings would take to get home. Eventually, Shella and John turned the corner, John following behind, his nose buried in a comic book, as always. I wait, eyes glued on my sister. Halfway to our house, she noticed me sitting on the step and our gazes locked. She knew. I didn't have to say a word. We both knew it was going to be a very long night.

Later, we were sitting at the dining room table with our homework spread out in front of us, waiting for the front door to open. John had already finished his school work for the night and was reading across from me. I pretended to work on my book report, staring at a blank sheet of paper, holding a pencil. My mind was somewhere else entirely. Shella had erased the same word several times on her worksheet, letting out a frustrated sigh every other minute. The smell from the kitchen made my stomach rumble, my hunger did nothing to appease the nausea. I happened to glance at the clock right at 5:15 and the front door swung open.

He stood in the entryway, wiping his feet on the mat before bending over to untie his boots. I knew he was tall; I had seen him around other men and he always seemed to be just a bit taller. He wasn't a big man but he was lean and very strong from years of hard manual labour. His dark hair and eyes were the same as mine but his moustache always seemed to have a hint of red in it. He was a handsome man, all the ladies in the neighbourhood turned their heads when he was around and were always extra nice to Shella and I in hopes of turning his.

He spotted us all seated at the table and his eyes stopped on mine for a split second before I jumped and turned my attention back to my task.

"Hello to you too, guess it hurts to greet your old man." Without looking at him, it was hard to tell if he was trying to instigate a reaction or making a sarcastic remark. I braved a glance. He was smirking. Thank God. He was in a good mood.

"Hi dad. Good day at work?" I asked carefully. It was a narrow line to walk with him. Anything could turn that smirk into a fierce scowl.

"It was all right P-Baby. How was your day?" My heart went to my throat. I loved when he was like that. I could almost forget that there was another side of him. It made me feel like a normal girl who could adore her daddy. At the same time, my heart broke because I knew that I was going to ruin it all too soon.

"Not so good. I need to talk to you about something daddy." His steps toward me came to a halt. The expression on his face turned to confusion as he looked at me. There was no doubt that he could read the fear and sadness on my face.

Without warning, he dashed toward me and grabbed me from my chair. He threw me over his shoulder like a sack of potatoes, his free hand tickled my side mercilessly. I squealed and mom came racing from the kitchen to see me cracking up on dad's shoulder. She stood frozen; mouth open. These moments were too few and far between. When they happened, everyone took notice.

He set me on my feet and led me to his chair, patting his lap for me to take a seat.

"All right kid, what's eating you up?" He asked as I sat down and curled into his lap. I rested my head against his chest to soak in the affection while I could get it. Tuck it into my memory bank for a dark day. "Out with it,"

I took a deep breath for courage before letting it all out. "I beat up a girl at school today and got suspended." I felt his hands tighten on my waist but he said nothing. Thump, thump, thump. My heart pounded in my ears.

"You gonna explain why, or was it just because you felt like it?" Shocked, I lean back to look at him. His elbow is on the arm rest and his forehead rests against the palm of his hand, waiting for me to continue.

"A girl named Natasha and her friends are always picking on me, shoving me around, calling me the ugly little Coleman girl. Today one of her friends pulled me to the ground by my hair." His hand squeezed tighter against me and though I could no longer see his eyes, I could see red flush into his cheeks as his temper began to flare. I couldn't take it back now. "I got mad, so I tackled her to the ground and I... I punched her in the face. One of the teachers pulled me off of her and took me to the office." The last few words were choked out through the lump in my throat. Thump, thump, thump.

Finally, he looked me in the eye. He was angry but there was something else there too. Something I had never seen before and couldn't tell what it was.

"And did this Natasha girl go to the office too?" He asked between clenched teeth.

"No, she was crying and told the teacher I was crazy and someone should put me in juvi." The hand
that was cupping his forehead curled into a fist. With white knuckles, he pressed the fist against his mouth. I sat very still, waiting for him to decide my fate.

When he pulled me tighter against him and placed a kiss on the top of my head, my heart stopped. What. The. Hell. He really was going to kill me, wasn't he?

He pulled my face up to force me to make eye contact with him. The anger was gone and his eyes were bright as he smiled at me.

"That's my girl. Don't take any shit from those bitches at school. She deserved getting clocked in the face for calling my P-Baby ugly."

Mom stepped up beside him, tears of relief in her eyes as she laid a hand on his shoulder.

"What did the principal say about all of this?" He asked her.
"He called our daughter an animal." The anger flashed back into his eyes.
"But mom sure put him in his place too. Didn't you mama?" I looked up at her and she smiled.
"Bet your ass I did."

Dad stood and put me on my feet before wrapping his arms around mom, lifted her off the floor and gave her a loving kiss.

"My girls are pretty bad ass if I do say so myself." He said against her lips and grinned as he kissed her again, making her giggle.

When he put her down, he ruffled my hair and walked into the kitchen. The four of us let out a breath of relief and smiled at each other happily. I guess it wouldn't be such a long night after all.

"I'm starving. Is supper ready? OUCH! FUCK!" He hollered, obviously he dipped his finger into something on the stove. "Yes sweetheart, have a seat. I'm coming." She laughed and followed him into the kitchen.

Supper was spent in peace. I sat listening to their small talk. Though I felt lighter knowing that I dodged a bullet, I struggled to swallow a sense of unease. I was out of the rain but the storm clouds still dwelt outside, waiting patiently to unleash their booming thunder.

Dad pushed his empty plate off of his place mat and leaned back in his chair. From his breast pocket, he pulled out his cigarettes and lighter. He lit a smoke and while it dangled from his lips, he undid his belt, sliding it from the looks on his jeans. Once free, he swung it over his shoulder.

"Supper was good Johanne, thank you." He smiled charmingly at my mother, cigarette still between his lips. He rarely removed a lit dart from his mouth, the ash was so long that it threatened to fall. Even then, he sometimes just let it fall.

"You're very welcome, dear." She rose dutifully to clear the plates and rinse them off in the sink.

I watched as dad's gaze slid down her back and landed squarely on her butt. My stomach turned.
I knew what the look on his face meant. It was time for Shella, John and I to scram before we witnessed something that would burn a hole in our brains forever. I nudged Shella with my elbow as subtly

as I could and motioned towards our father with my chin. Before she turned back to me, she stood from her seat.

"May we be excused?" She asked and we were dismissed with a distracted wave towards the archway leading to the living room.

Shella pulled John from his chair, though he didn't know what the rush was, he knew not to dawdle. I managed only to kick the back of Shella's feet three or four times as I rushed to follow them from the kitchen

I grabbed my shoes while Shella helped John slip his on, not wasting time tying the laces. Something hit the floor in the other room and we all froze.

"Donald! Just gimme a second! My hands are--" The rest was muffled but Shella swung the front door open and we all rushed outside. We heard faint cries from behind the closed door but we didn't stop to give it any thought.

My sister and I had been told not to stick our noses into the affairs between a man and his wife. We were taught at school that it is wrong for a man to force himself on a woman but no one clarified whether or not those rules still applied when the woman was married to that man. We never asked either.

"What do you guys wanna do?" John asked, lifting the collar of his shirt into his mouth. He often chewed on it when he got nervous, which was why most of his shirts had a neck hole big enough to fit around his waist.

"Let's go to the park by Ryssa's." Shella suggested, taking John's hand.

"TEETER TOTTER!" John screamed, dropping the shirt from his mouth. He loved the teeter-totter, the board that swings up and down with a kid on each end. The idiot didn't realize that because he was so scrawny, we just sat on the other end while he bounced around trying to get his side back down.

I followed behind them while we walked the two blocks to the park. My arms were crossed in front of me and I subconsciously watched for the cracks in sidewalk and stepped over them. My head wandered as I thought about the other kids in our neighbourhood. I wondered if they got to sit in their dad's lap every night and watch TV together as a family. Maybe their dads tucked them in and hugged them good night before bed. I envied the kids who had dads that played outside with them on their bikes on weekends. The ones with dads who walked with them to the park so that they could push them on the swings. Envy was an emotion I knew well. If those kids had a dad like mine, they would cry like the little pussies they were.

It was dark out and the three of us shivered as we stood at the edge of the park, unsure whether or not it was safe to go back home. Shella and I looked at each other to see which one of us was going to make the call.

"I'm sleepy." John moaned, leaning against Shella. She squeezed his hand between hers and tried to rub warmth into his littler one. "Let's go, we can listen outside the door and if it's quiet we'll go in. If we hear him, we can just wait on the porch a little bit longer." I suggested, trying to keep my teeth from chattering.
"Yeah, pretty much the only choice we have I guess."

We made our way home. As we got closer, we could see someone sitting on the front steps, the glow of a cigarette as they took a puff. Mom. She came outside to get away from him sometimes, she said it was because she needed to breathe.

"Hey guys, what have you been up to?" She asked as we headed for the steps. One of her eye lids is drooping slightly. She would have a nasty bruise in the morning.
"We took John to the park to play for a bit." Shella said, looking down at the grass as we all stopped in front of her, waiting for our cue to go in or pretend we hadn't come back yet.
"He's asleep in his chair. Why don't the three of you get upstairs. Brush your teeth quietly and get to bed." She tried to smile at us but it didn't hide the sadness in her eyes. We all nodded and one by one

headed to the door.

Shella slowly turned the knob and gently pushed the door open. She poked her head in and listened for a second before opening it the rest of the way. We took our shoes off as quietly as we could and made our way up the stairs. Shella stopped at the bathroom door and motioned for John to go in first. We both waited as he brushed his teeth. When he was done, Shella took him to his room while I took my turn. When I left the bathroom, Shella was waiting. I hugged her goodnight and headed to my room.

I quietly shut my door and crept to my bed. Within seconds of my head hitting my pillow, I was out cold. One side effect of stress was complete exhaustion. Sleep was a welcome escape. Sometimes.

The week flew by. It was supposed to have dragged by in misery, hiding and licking my wounds. Instead, it was spent eagerly waiting for my dad to come home for lunch. He would sit with me, telling me stories about the guys at work. Mom clucked her tongue at him, saying it was inappropriate to tell a young girl those types of things. I didn't care. Even though I didn't understand what blue balls were or why Phil's wife was so good at making balls blue, hearing my dad laugh as he talked to me was the only thing that mattered. At the end of the day, we at dinner as a family and everyone seemed to get along. I never pushed my luck. After supper, when his eyelids started drooping, I made myself scarce. John didn't see it the way I did. He stuck to our father's side from the moment he came home until mom announced it was bed time. I was surprised it lasted as long as it did.

That Saturday, Shella went down the road to hang out with her friend Ryssa, not bothering to bring me along. I decided I was bored enough to play hockey in the driveway with John, who was ran around, setting up the nets as I was leaning on my stick. He looked back and forth between the two nets, trying to decide if they were far enough apart and directly across from one another. Once he was satisfied, he put the ball down by his stick and began passing it from side to side, watching and waiting for me to make a move. I grinned. He was always trying so hard to beat me at everything we did. It was like the two years I had on him was a punishment and he needed to prove he was better than his older sister. Obviously, his need to beat me, fed my need to put him back in his place.

He was so focused as he approached me, his mouth pressed into a determined line, eyes shining with hope. Part of me took pity and I contemplated letting him get the first goal. As he got closer, I saw his smirk and the pity evaporated. I flicked my stick forward, throwing his out of the way and letting the ball roll out of his reach. I beat him to it and slapped it down the driveway, right into his empty net.

"Paisley you're such a jerk! I could have had a beautiful shot! You always have to ruin it!" He whined, swinging his stick around and stomping to retrieve the ball.
"Oh, quit acting like a baby." I rolled my eyes and threw him a cocky grin, feeding his competitive nature. "It's not my fault I'm better than you."

An hour. I mopped the floor with him for an hour, barely breaking a sweat. I didn't have to; John's temper did all the work for me. After my twenty-third goal, John let out a frustrated growl and turned to his net to drag it back behind the house. I smiled at his little tantrum and brought my stick along with me back into the house. I stored it in the back of the coat closet. Once I had my shoes off, I looked up to see my dad napping on his lazy boy chair. I met my mother's eyes where she sat at the table, reading her new romance novel. She pressed her index finger to her lips in a silent plea for me to keep quiet. I tip toed through the living room to the kitchen, getting myself a glass of water.

I returned just as John was coming through the front door, still fuming. I prayed he would look up and look at me so I could warn him but he didn't. He was too busy grumbling to himself as he kicked off his shoes. My heart pounded so hard against my chest that it actually hurt.

*Shut up John, Shut up John, SHUT THE HELL UP!*

I looked at my mom. She lost all colour in her face. She was still as she watched my father sleeping. More than likely praying he didn't wake up.

John threw the closet door open and blinded by his foul mood, tried stuffing his stick through the coats unsuccessfully. It snagged in a pocket but he continued trying to force the stick in. The force on the coat pulled the pole holding the hangers up. Everything went crashing to the floor.

Mom and I held out breath as dad let out a snore before turning his head. Before we could relax enough to remember to breathe, John threw his stick to the floor. With the loud slap, dad bolted upright. I couldn't see his face but the look on John's told me he did. His red cheeks drained and understanding hit him. His eyes darted around as he processed his panic but then he made a terrible mistake. He ran.

"John! *NO!*" I screamed. My hands fisted in my hair helplessly. Running only made it worse.

In no hurry, dad rose from his chair and went to retrieve the forgotten hockey stick before following John through the kitchen. It was like watching a snake hunt for its prey. Cold, dead eyes fixed on its victim. Slithering up to the helpless animal as it cowered, shaking while it awaited its fate.

With dread, I went to the threshold into the kitchen. I could see John through the door to the laundry room. He squeezed himself between the washer and dryer, vibrating with fear when dad spotted him. Shaking hands gripped my arms. Mom gently pulled me behind her. I knew she was trying to limit the damage by protecting me, knowing that if dad saw me while in that state, I would more than likely be punished just for being there.

"Come out of there you fucking pussy. Take it like a man." Dad warned coldly, standing in front of John, squeezing the stick in his right hand.

I could hear John whimper and my heart bled for my little

27

brother. If I stood up for him, it would only make it worse for John. Dad would blow a fuse if he needed *a girl* to protect him.

"I SAID GET OUT!" Dad yelled and even I could see the vein in his forehead bulge from where I stood.

The hockey stick went up and with a precise downward swing, it connected with the back of John's head. He had his face buried between his bent knees. Mom let out a sob before she could stop herself and cover her mouth. I pulled on her arm to turn her towards me and away from the gut-wrenching sight. I buried my face in her shoulder and we waited for dad to run out of steam. We both jumped every time we heard the stick make that horrible thud against John's flesh. What was probably less than three minutes, felt like an hour before the stick dropped to the floor. Dad stomped past us through the threshold to the front door. We waited a few seconds after it slammed shut before rushing to John.

When I saw John crumpled up on the floor, I had to swallow hard to prevent bile from leaving my stomach. The left side of his face was pressed against the washer, leaving the right side exposed. I knew he wasn't dead because his chest moved as he struggled to catch his breath. His right eye was the size of a golf ball and sealed shut. A cut above his eyebrow wept streaks of blood down his face. A garbled moan came from John as he tried to move.

"Help me get him to the car Paisley." Gone was my whimpering mother, in her place stood a calm and composed woman on a mission.

She managed to pull John out with only a few pained cries from him. She put her arms under his arm pits and waited while I struggled to get a good grip on his legs. We carried him through the house and without even putting on shoes, we loaded him into the car. I ran back for her purse while she secured him in the backseat. I watched her pull out of the driveway and race down the street, wondering what bullshit story she was going to tell the triage nurse.

I was still alone when the sun went down and the stars came out. I was sitting at the kitchen table in the dark when Shella walked in and flicked on the lights.

She screamed so loud it felt like my ear drums vibrated.

"Jesus Paisley! What the hell are you sitting in the dark for?" She looked around to see if I was alone before asking, "where is everybody?"
"Dad beat the shit out of John with a hockey stick and mom took him to the hospital. God only knows where dad went." I explained, emotionless and drained.

Shella knew. If mom brought John to the hospital, it meant it had to be really bad. Mom didn't take those kinds of risks for a scratch or a few bruises. She quietly came and sat beside me at the table. She held my hand to offer a small comfort while we waited.

It was past midnight when the front door opened again. Mom came in, supporting a very pale and heavily bandaged John. Most of the right side of his face was covered by white gauze and around his neck was a sling holding his right arm. To say this was the worst punishment dad had ever given would be a lie. Shella and I had both been in John's place and none of us could tell you what had been done to our mother before we were born and old enough to understand. Mom had gotten drunk once and told us she would hide us in her dresser when we were little. She would empty a drawer, stuff her clothes under her bed to lay us down in it with our blanket.

"So, what fairy tale did you tell them this time, *mother?*" Shit, Shella was pissed. "Did your little boy go horseback riding and get stomped by a horse? Or did a ghost decide to use John as a fucking punching bag?"
"Shell, I am far too tired to argue with you." Mom warned as she helped John settle into dad's chair.
"I'm sorry mom." Shella's voice oozed sarcasm as she glared at our mother in disgust. "You're right. Covering for him must be *exhausting.*"

Mom's terrified face when John was facing off with dad's

anger, flashed in my mind.

"Shella..." I pleaded.
"Oh, don't give me that shit. She's just as fucking guilty as he is."
With that, Shella stood and stormed out of the house.

Mom fell to the couch, covering her face with her hands. I didn't bother consoling her. I pitied her but she chose him. We didn't. I went to John and kissed him gently on the cheek, wishing him well before going up to bed.

The next morning, I woke up to a quiet house. John was still asleep on the chair, covered in a blanket. Mom was sitting at the table, pale and with dark circles around her eyes. I doubted she slept at all. She didn't look at me as she continued smoking her cigarette and staring off into space.

"I tried leaving once." She said quietly. I sat across from her and waited. "He found me. He beat me so bad they told me I was lucky I could still walk. I was pregnant." She let out a humourless laugh that sent chills down my spine. "I lost the baby and didn't think I would ever be able to have children after that. I was barely recovered from that when he got me pregnant for Shella. I went to my father for help but all he said was that I chose to marry Donald, I wasn't his problem anymore." She took a sip from her coffee cup. "There was no leaving after that. I had no where to go and if he found me, who's to say I would be lucky a second time? He was so kind during my second pregnancy. He treated me like a doll." She smiled sadly at the memory. "He took me out, showed me off. I felt like I was the most important thing in his world and I fell in love with him all over again. Then Shella was born and he was such an amazing father. He adored her. He went back to treating me like shit but he doted on Shella. Then I got pregnant with you and the loving husband returned. He would rub my feet and wash my hair. Same end result. He was smitten with you and threw me away like yesterday's garbage. I was okay with how things were. As long as he was good to you girls, he could do whatever he wanted to me. The first time he lost his temper with Shella, she was four. She had a fat lip for a week and her poor little bottom was black and blue." Her face was blank, no emotion. She was telling me her story like she was a voice

recorder and it all meant nothing to her. "That only happened when he was in a bad mood and you girls misbehaved. Otherwise, he was a great dad. He *is* a great dad. He just has a bad temper." She looked at me and her mind was set. She was convinced we were looking at our situation with eyes
half open. That our father's temper was only a fraction of who he was. "We mean everything to your father and he works hard to support his family. He is a good man." She went back to staring off into space before she whispered, "And I love him."

As if summoned, in walked the man himself. He looked worse than mom did. Clearly wherever he went, he did not sleep. Mom sprang across the room and wrapped her arms around him like she hadn't seen him in several days instead of only one.

"Oh Don, are you all right sweetheart?" She asked searching his face for signs of distress. It was disgusting to me that she could worry about his welfare when she spent the night in the hospital with her son because of him.

"I'm fine darlin'. Where's John?" He held her hands away from him and looked around her for John. Once he spotted him, he kissed mom gently before moving to the chair.'

He ran a hand down John's good arm gently, his eyes glistening with unshed tears. His Adam's apple bobbed as he looked him over, assessing the damage he had done.

"He has a fractured clavicle. Twenty-two stitches at the back of his head and eight in his eyebrow. The rest is bruising but no other major injuries." Mom explained.

Dad hit his knees beside John, grabbing his hand and holding it against his face as the tears he was holding back broke free and streaked down his face. His chest hiccupped with suppressed sobs as he looked at John's beaten face.

A few minutes later, John must have opened his eyes because he jumped and cried out from the pain of his sudden movement. Dad was on his feet in the blink of an eye.

"Don't move buddy, keep still. I'm so sorry. What do you need? What can I do? Are you thirsty? Want some milk? I can get you a bowl of cereal. God I'm so sorry."

Watching my father fret over John fuelled my own temper. Before it got me into trouble, I got up from the table and followed Shella's lead from the night before. I stormed out of the house.

It took a long time for John to get better. Eight weeks later and he still couldn't raise his right arm higher than his shoulder but otherwise, he was back to his old self. Irritating the hell out of me and following me around. Life at home had been quiet but we all knew that the quiet was only temporary. Shella spent more time at her friends' houses than she did at home. I barely saw her and when I did, she never had time for me. She was distant and I kept waiting for her to snap out of it. It hurt that she seemed to have put our relationship aside in favour of her friends. I couldn't blame her. If she could ignore our home life and find happiness elsewhere then I should be happy for her. Not jealous. I *was* jealous though. I had friends of my own but I never had the nerve to open up to any of them. I let them believe that my family was the same as theirs. The only thing they found odd was that I never invited them over. I just brushed it off by saying my dad worked nights and I wasn't allowed to have friends over. It was easier to avoid than to explain or make excuses. Knowing they would compare their home lives to mine and remind me of things I was already well aware of. I didn't need them feeling sorry for me. All I wanted was to feel normal outside of the house. I didn't want to have to live through it at home and then relive it when I was with them. I *needed* them to be separate. Shella shared everything with her friends. They knew we lived with a monster.

I was laying in bed late one night. Thinking of nothing in particular, just waiting for sleep to take over. I heard the front door open and someone come stumbling in. They weren't steady footsteps, more like a step followed by two quicker ones. Step... step, step. He's drunk. *Oh God no.* Silence. I knew mom had already gone to bed, hopefully he would just pass out on his chair and that would be the end of it.

No such luck. After hearing nothing by my heart beating for several minutes, I jumped out of my skin when a foot stomped on the first step up the stairs. I was so glad I managed not to scream. I waited, counting the steps he took. Twelve, thirteen, fourteen... At twenty-two he reached the landing. I felt my throat tighten as he past by my bedroom door. He moved down the hallway and I realized I was shaking. I held my blanket tightly to my chin and squeezed my eyes closed. The only way out was to fall asleep.

I jumped again when his bedroom door flew open and slammed against the opposite wall. *Shit, shit, shit.*

"Donald?" My mother sleepily called out. "What are you doing?" No answer. "Donald, answer me." Again nothing. "What. Are. You. DOING?" Panic. She was scared.

I heard his angry growl before I made out the familiar sound of a slap. Followed by another one and another one.

"Donald, what's going on?" Mom cried.
"You think I wouldn't find out?" Slap. "Make me look like a fool and think I wouldn't find out?" Slap.
"What are you talking about?" She pleaded.
"James. I'm talking about you spreading your fucking legs for James!" Slap, slap.

Another door flew open. Shella. *No.* Before I could process what was happening, I was running to my door and tearing it open just in time to see Shella running down the hall to our parents' room.

"You get your fucking hands off of her!" She screamed, flying into their room. "You're a coward. A wife beating coward! Keep your fucking hands to yourself or so help me God, you'll be planning my funeral or sleeping with your eyes open." Never before had I seen Shella so angry. It scared me. Not because I thought she would hurt me, but because she looked just like *him*. He was the only other person I knew who could be completely swallowed by his anger.

It worked. He stood completely still, staring at his twelve-year-old daughter like she was off her rocker. No one spoke. No one moved. We were terrified of how he would react to being confronted.
When he turned and left the room without another word, we looked at each other, lost for words. Her temper must have poured ice water on his. We waited but he didn't come back. Mom pulled back the covers on both her sides and Shella and I snuggled in on either side. We spent the rest of the night curled together, dozing in and out of restless sleep.

That was the one and only time standing up to him worked. I never had the nerve to try. Shella did. The only thing she succeeded in doing was turning his wrath onto herself. That didn't stop her though. If Shella was home, she would interfere and walk away with bruises she didn't earn. John hero worshipped her for her bravery. I didn't. Her lack of self preservation pissed me off. I found myself getting into more and more trouble when Shella was around. I knew deep down that I was punishing her in my own way. I needed my sister back, not a fucking martyr.

# Chapter Two

Truth be Told, I'm Alone

*Tricia Warnock*

Self confidence. Something all fifteen-year-old girls struggle with. They're coming into womanhood, learning about makeup and popular hairstyles. Boys were cute now. Crushes were the hottest gossip in the hallways at school. If Friday night rolled around and you didn't have a date, *everyone* was talking about it Monday morning. It was a new world for me. I was now in high school, I left the pig tails and braids behind, opting instead for high pony tails or loose and wavy. The training bras were long gone, replaced by push up bras that made my mother cringe. *There's no reason for a young girl to wear something that is meant to flaunt their breasts like prostitutes.* Every time she went on her rant, I would just roll my eyes and walk away.

Cliques. Though they had started in elementary school, they were in full swing in high school. Shella was part of the jock crowd. She played basketball and hockey and she excelled at both. It took me two weeks to decide I didn't really give a shit. I didn't care for sports. My grades were all right but I wasn't the least bit interested in devoting myself to my studies like the nerdy kids. The popular girls could kiss my ass. They spent more time looking in the mirrors hanging in their lockers than talking to each other. The punk kids pretended like they didn't care what everyone else thought about them. Then they went out of their way to stand out and draw attention to themselves with their spiked hair and jewellery. No thank you. No point talking to the potheads. Sentences longer than three words were too long to keep their attention. I fit nowhere and I couldn't be bothered to try. There were four of us who didn't fit the mould and we stuck together.

Laurie was my very best friend. We had all the same classes and we were glued at the hip. For the first time in my life, I had someone who understood me. Her home life was a lot like mine and in the beginning, we were drawn to each other because we both hid bruises and shied away from the spotlight. We always said our souls recognized each other in the darkness and pulled us together. I envied her auburn hair and fair skin. She envied my dark locks, freckled nose and full chest. It was her and I against the world. Gemma and Claire were another pair of best friends who joined us at our lunch table the first week of school and never left.

Shella had tried to push me to join extra curricular activities but I had no desire to join the drama club or debate team. I did my mandatory time under that roof. Nothing more. Shella saw it as an excuse to spend more time away from home but just because I wasn't at school, didn't mean I was going home.

"Hey Pais! What's up gorge?" Laurie came strutting toward me as I stepped off the bus in the loading zone.
"Hey, I missed you! How was your weekend?" I asked, hugging her close. She had spent the weekend away at her grandmother's cottage.
"Ugh, you don't even want to know. Nana's breath could kill a healthy bull." She made a show of exaggerated gagging.
"Gross, stop it. I'm getting a sympathy whiff and I haven't seen your Nana in ages."

"It's worse now. She has a rotten molar that she calls the black abyss. That shit is rancid my friend." She hooked her arm through mine and we made our way to the entrance.

"Hey bitches! Just gonna ignore me?" Gemma called out as she jogged from the parking lot, cigarette bouncing between her lips. She took once last drag and tossed it aside as she joined us.
"Never! Only psychos ignore beautiful girls." Laurie grinned, holding her other arm out for Gemma.
"Where's Claire?" I asked, curious as to why Gemma would have walked to school alone.
"Sick. I think she's still sore because Cody ditched her at the movies last night."
"Say what?" Laurie nearly screamed.

"Yeah, we went on a double with Cody and Jake. Cody's buddies showed up and they decided to take off midway through the movie. Didn't bother to say by to her or nothing."

"Wow, what a dick." Laurie and I said at the same time.

"Tell me about it. She would have definitely given him head too. She told me so before we even went out. She's been wanting to hook up with him for ages." Gemma and Claire were both heavy into the experimental phase with boys. Neither of them were virgins and both of them were hornier than most of the boys we knew. Which was why they often dated seniors. Claire once explained to me that boys our age were too immature to handle her or Gemma. Older boys were more fun and had the added bonus of knowing how to drive.

Laurie was seeing a guy named David, who was sixteen and had trouble finding jeans that weren't torn. She adored him and for what it was worth, he seemed smitten with her too. Everyday there was a note stuck in the vent on her locker when she got to school. She would blush and stick it in her pocket to read in homeroom. I didn't mind sharing my best friend with her boyfriend. He made her smile and I wouldn't dream of making her feel guilty about spending time with him that she used to spend with me.

I was the only one of our group who has never had a boyfriend. Not for lack of interest. I had become very adept at declining offers from the opposite sex. Though Gemma and Claire could not wrap their heads around my refusal to date, Laurie understood.

"So, what about you Paisley? What did you do this weekend? Join a convent?" She leaned forward to see me on the other side of Laurie

"Convent?" *What?* I was so confused.

"You know, since you don't wanna date boys, I figured you aspired to become a nun." She explained with a mischievous grin plastered to her face. I could see Laurie biting her cheek in an attempt to stop a giggle.

"I hear so many horror stories about boys from you and Claire. Why the fuck would I want to put myself through shit like being left at a movie theatre?"

"You know, this is exactly the kind of sick prank God would play." This time Laurie and I both looked at Gemma, waiting for her to elaborate. "The girl who makes all the boys turn their heads wants nothing to do with them. Meanwhile, us mortal girls have to bend over backwards to make them bat an eye. It's a fucking pity." She let out a mocking sigh of disappointment as she smiled at me.

"I do not turn heads." I denied, frowning as I paid attention while we walked through the hallway. Now that she had pointed it out, I did see a few pairs of eyes following me.

"Don't kid yourself darlin', you're the star in many wet dreams." I don't think my face could have gotten any more red.
"She's not wrong lovey." Laurie squeezed me against her in an effort to ease my discomfort.
"Doesn't matter anyway. I want none of that shit. I don't need some ass-hole toying with me." I shrugged Laurie's arm off me and went to my locker.
"Well, there's a beautiful girl." Jake shouted from halfway down the hallway and Gemma was off, running to him like an obedient puppy.
"Shoot me now." Laurie mumbled beside me as she spun the dial on her lock.
"What, not into everyone's leading man? He does play on the football team you know." I poked at her.

"Ugh, don't remind me. God, he gets on my nerves." Jake was all right. He was a friendly guy. Cocky but friendly. I just laughed off her comment. "So Paisley, you know I love you like crazy, right? You're my bestest friend and I would do anything for you."
"Oh no, where's this going?" I asked, the feeling of dread climbing.
"Well, I know we were just talking about you not wanting to date but I was wondering..." She trailed off, struggling to find the best way to ask me whatever it was she wanted to ask.
"Spit it out Laurie."
"Well, you remember me telling you about David's cousin who was constantly getting into trouble?"
"Yes."

"Turns out his parents sent him to live at David's place. They think he needs to get away from the crowd he was hanging around with and start fresh, ya know?" She picked at the corner of her binder while she slowly made her way to the point. Whatever it was, Laurie was sure I was going to shoot her down. She was usually very direct, borderline bold. The only time she built up her argument was when she was certain she wouldn't get her way.

"I don't understand what David's family has to do with me Laurie. He's not *my* boyfriend. You're talking in circles and I am not following you whatsoever." She let out a frustrated huff and closed her locker so she could look me in the eye.

"David's parents don't want him going out with me and leaving Thomas behind. They want him to include him, show him around and make him feel at home. Either I go out with both of them or I lose my boyfriend." *Oh man.* She was trying to guilt me into offering myself up for David's cousin. "It really sucks." She pouted. Of course I was going to help my friend out. I just wasn't going to make it easy for her. If it was too easy, it wouldn't be the last time. I kept my mouth shut and waited. She looked at me, hoping I would fill in the blanks and offer her a solution so she wouldn't have to ask.

"Sounded to me like Claire was free." I said, deadpan. She groaned out of frustration, clearly not appreciating my humour.

"I'm not asking fucking Claire! I want to *enjoy* some time with David, not watch her teach Thomas her *moves*." She gyrated her hips to bring home her point. "I told Dave I would ask you to go out on a double date with us Friday night. I let him know that it wasn't very fucking likely but that I'd ask. So there. That's it." She turned toward our homeroom, giving up and the assuming that I would never agree.

"Oh Laurie, of course I'll help you out. Do you seriously have so little faith in me?" She whipped back around. Shocked.
"Fuck off, you'll come?"
"Yes, I'll come but I'm raiding your closet."
"Eeeeeek!" She screeched and jumped at me. "You're the greatest!"

She planted a sloppy kiss on my cheek. "God, I love you!"

It was still a house rule to have dinner together at the table. If we were home, we were expected to be seated by five thirty, even if we were sick. We discussed our grades and our father had a way of knowing if there was something you were leaving unsaid. Like a bloodhound, he could sniff it out and once locked on, there was no way to dissuade him. Today seemed to be a good day for him. He was looking back and forth between John and I, waiting to see which of us would be the first to crack.

"I got a ninety-two percent on my English essay this morning. Mrs. Barker was thrilled." Shella boasted sitting up straight and smiling brightly.

Shella had been getting under my skin more and more lately. Her kiss-ass attitude made me crazy. She lived the same life I did, there was no point pretending she was any better than me or any one else for that matter. I no longer felt guilty when I saw her disappointment with dad's lack of interest. Dad wasn't one for academics. As long as we weren't failing, he didn't care.

I stuffed my mouth with mashed potatoes to prevent a giggle from escaping. It didn't work. Dad's eyes caught my smirk but he said nothing as he stared me down. *Shit.*

"And, the basketball team is voting for a new captain. Coach Bennett thinks I'll for sure get the spot!" This was something Shella was genuinely excited about. Her butt practically wiggled in her chair.

"Good for you Shella. Hard work pays off." Dad praised her with his eyes still pinned on me, daring me to speak. "Don't think your mom and I have been to one of your games, guess we'll have to fix that."

Shella's mouth dropped open.

"That would be awesome dad! I'd love for you guys to see me play." If her smile were any bigger, her cheeks would be in her damn ears. "What about you P-Baby? Any teams scouting out Shella's little sister?" He asked sarcastically.

"Nope. I'm still teamless." I took another bite of my food, building up my nerve. "I do have a date Friday night though." I couldn't look at him. He was fine with Shella dating so there was no reason for me to be so afraid. I was nowhere near expecting the booming laughter my announcement evoked.

"With a boy or a girl?" More laughter. "You just said you were teamless!" This time Shella and mom joined in with their own fit of giggles.

"A boy." My face was burning. I was embarrassed but more than that, I was angry. I watched my fork as I moved the rest of my dinner around on my plate.

"Oh P-Baby, don't get your panties in a twist. Your mother and I were wondering when you would start dating. We just assumed you were a rug muncher is all." He didn't bother wiping the amused grin from his face before bringing my sexual preferences into question.

"No. I like boys. I just couldn't be bothered. Laurie asked me to go on a double date with her boyfriend and his cousin."
"Well at least it's a double date. Now I know the little shit will keep his fucking hands out of your skirt." My cheeks were burning even more.
"You wouldn't have had to worry anyways. I'm not Shella. I have no desire to take my pants off for anyone." *Eat that, Bitch.* Dad's laughter kicked in again.
"What about you son? What's got you all in knots?" He was still smiling when he turned to John, who instantly lost all colour.
"Well um... At recess today, I uh... well Lucie and I, well uh..."
"Come on, get it out."
"Lucie asked me to show her my penis so I uh... at recess I... We hid behind the bleachers and well..."

"You showed a girl your dick?" Dad filled in, completely shocked.

"Yes, but she showed me her crotch too and another kid caught us and told the teacher." Silence. Mom and dad looked at John, stunned beyond words. John squirmed, terrified of the repercussions he knew had to be coming. Mom recovered first.

"John, maybe you should head up--"
"That's my fucking boy!" Dad shouted, jumping out of his chair.

Dad went around the table to John. He was *proud* of John. Thrilled that his son had shown a girl his dick. *What the fuck?* He patted John on the back before placing a noisy, wet kiss on his forehead. Dad spent the rest of dinner smiling between mouthfuls. No one dared break the spell so the rest of us ate in silence.

I was just making my way to the front door to meet up with Laurie, Claire and Gemma when the phone rang. I debated leaving it for someone else to pick up but my conscience kicked in.

"Hello?"
"Hi, can I speak to Paisley please?" *Who the hell was this guy with the super cute voice and why was he calling* **me?**
"Uh, this is Paisley."
"Oh, hey. This is Tom, Dave's cousin. I hope it's okay that I asked him to get your number for me."
"Sure, I don't mind." He sounded so sure of himself while I struggled to form a sentence.
"How are you Paisley?" He asked and hearing him say my name made my stomach flip.
"I'm all right. How about you?"
"I'm excited now."
"Now?"

"Yeah, I wasn't so sure about this blind date idea. Now that I hear how sexy you sound, I'm excited for
Friday now. A girl who sounds like you could not be less than gorgeous." *Holy shit. He was smooth!* I let out a nervous giggle. "Oh my, don't do that sweetheart. You'll stop my heart."

"Wow, you sure now how to make a girl blush." I debated flirting back but truth be told, I had no clue how to do that. He chuckled.

"I just tell it like it is Paisley. I hear something that I like, Imma say so. What do you think about being set up on a date with someone you haven't met yet?"

"If we're going to tell it like it is, I haven't given it much thought. Laurie asked me to help her out. I'm going to help her out. I like David so I figured you couldn't be all that bad." Silence. When a few seconds passed without a reply, I started to get nervous. Did I already mess this up? That must be a record. "Hello?"

"Yeah, I'm still here. David and I are very different Paisley. I love him like a brother but I'm not a good guy like him." He sounded sad and it pulled on my heart strings.

"What do you mean by that?"
"I just mean that he and I are different. It may not be a good idea to get involved with me."
"So, you called tonight to warn me? Maybe convince me not to go out with you Friday?"

"God no. I don't wanna miss my chance to meet you. Just putting it out there. I don't want you expecting a guy like David and then being disappointed when you get me." A smile curved my lips. I liked him already.

"I said I liked David. I didn't say I *wanted* David. Who knows? Maybe it's you who shouldn't get involved with me." He laughed again and my heart rate spiked.

"We'll just have to wait and see about that sweetheart. I gotta get going. Gonna have myself a nice cold shower. Can I call you again tomorrow?" *Nice cold shower? Who the hell liked cold showers?*

"I'd like that, Thomas."
"Great. Looking forward to it. Good night Paisley."
"Good night." We both waited. I giggled again and heard him sigh before hanging up the phone.

I smiled the whole way to Laurie's house. We often met up at Laurie's place on Monday nights while her parents went out for their date night. It was never anything exciting. Often just hanging out, talking, calling boys or watching a movie. It was nice to get out of the house, spend time with my favourite people, outside of school.

The three of them were sitting on the front porch when I walked up.

"Hey girlfriend! Nice of you to finally show up!" Gemma yelled to me.
"Bitch, some people have lives that don't revolve around you, you know."
"Get a phone call?" Laurie asked with a mischievous smile.
"No. Was I supposed to?" Her smile disappeared, replaced with confusion.
"Well, David said his cousin wanted to call you. Feel you out to see if he wanted to go out Friday night."
"Oooooh, *that* phone call. Yeah, Thomas called." I grinned.
"And?" She was sitting on the edge of her seat, dying of curiosity.
"What? Hello? What the fuck is going on Friday night?" Claire asked. Totally lost and looking frustrated with being left in the dark.
"Paisley and I are going on a double with David and his cousin. Now, shush! Go on Paisley. Tell us what he said."
"*Paisley* is going on a *date?*" Gemma's eyes went wide.
"YES! Shut up! Paisley?"

"He seemed really nice. He told me he wasn't sure about Friday night. --"
"He didn't!" Gemma cut in.
"He did. Then he said because I sounded so cute, he was excited to go now."
"Thatta girl!"

"Yeah, I think I'm really going to like him. One thing that was weird, he said he wanted to go have a nice *cold* shower. Who the fuck *likes* cold showers?" I wanted to know if they thought it was weird too but they all burst out laughing. Gemma even laid back, clutching her middle. Claire was laughing so hard, tears were streaming down her cheeks. "Why's that funny?" They couldn't get anything out past their guffaws. I waited, annoyed while they got it all out of their systems.

"Oh Pais. He had a boner!" Claire said, using her palms to wipe the moisture from her cheeks.
"Shut up. He did not." I smacked her thigh, thinking she was pulling my leg.

"She's telling the truth. Guys take cold showers to get their dicks to sit back down." Laurie explained, still smiling. I waited to see if she would start laughing again. If she did, it meant she was lying. She didn't laugh.

"Why would he tell me that? Seems kind of private." God, I knew nothing about boys.
"He told you that to get you going. Probably trying to see if you would play along." Gemma explained. "Some guys like talking dirty on the phone."

"Well fuck." I was mortified. If he was testing me, I failed. Why the hell would he want to go out with a girl who was clearly clueless.

I waited close to the phone the following night. I felt stupid hanging around, waiting for Thomas to call me. I didn't even know him. Why I felt the need to wait for him to call me, I had no idea. At 9:30, when Nathan called for Shella, I gave up and went up to my room. It bothered me that he didn't call when he said he would but then again, he didn't know me. He didn't owe me anything. I didn't get much sleep that night. I was hurt and unsure how to deal with it.

The rest of the week past in a blur. Nothing outside of the normal everyday monotony. School and boredom. I never heard from Thomas again but Laurie's excitement was contagious and I couldn't keep myself from looking forward to our big date. We walked to her house together after school so she could treat me to a 'makeover'. I acted like the thought irritated me but in reality, I was thrilled to have Laurie dress me up.

"Are you even sure Thomas still wants to do this? He hasn't called me again or anything..." I didn't want her to think I would be disappointed but I was too afraid of being stood up to wait and see.

"Yes, I'm sure. David and I have been talking about it all week. He probably didn't call because he's been too busy settling in. Don't stress about it. He'll be there. He is our ride after all." She wiggled her eyebrows at me like him being old enough to drive was enough to make me drool.

"David could have driven." I pointed out.
"He could have but he's bringing us beer to drink at the drive in." She now had a little skip in her step. This was all news to me.
"Beer? Where the fuck did he get beer?"
"Thomas has friends who bought them a case."
"How old is Thomas, Laurie?" I couldn't believe I hadn't asked before. Old enough to drive, friends who were old enough to drink. I was nervous he was a lot older than I expected.
"He's seventeen. Well... almost eighteen."
"And does he realize I'm only fifteen?" *Shit, what did you do Laurie?*
"He is well aware how old we are. Don't be a weirdo." She smirked.
"Jesus. Why didn't you tell me he was eighteen? There's no way he's going to want to hang out with me." I was filled with dread. When he saw me, he was going to hightail it right back home.

"Calm down Pais. That's what makeup is for, it'll add a couple years. Then we get you in a top that shows off these bad boys." She turned to poke my boobs. "And there's no way that boy will be able to keep his tongue in his mouth."

"Fuck Laurie. Why do you do this shit to me?" It was a rhetorical question. She hooked her arm with mine and kept the extra bounce in her step the rest of the way to her house. She had a plan. I had no choice but to follow her lead.

Laurie wasn't kidding. When she was done with me, I definitely looked a few years older. She worked magic with her makeup. I had a beautiful smokey eye that brought out the deep chocolate tones. My lips were bare but with a coat of gloss. The black tube top did wonders to push up my chest.
She insisted I leave the bra behind, stating the shirt was snug enough to hold them in place while leaving a little room for a sexy bounce. She loaned me a pair of tight black jeans with tears in the knees big enough to expose my knee caps and a studded belt. My hair was left loose and the whole outfit was set topped off with a jean jacket.

"Shit bitch. You look stunning." Laurie stood back to admire her handy work.
"You think he'll like what he sees?" She gave me her famous 'are you stupid' look.

"Girl, if he doesn't like what he sees, he's gay." She turned to her vanity and ran the brush through her hair. We were pretty much dressed the same but her top was in a royal blue colour and she wore a silky black jacket. "I know David's gonna shit bricks when he sees my ass in these jeans. Betcha ten bucks he grabs it before we even make it to the car." She smiled at me through the mirror.

We heard a car pull into the driveway and we locked eyes. She was up and grabbing my arm before I made it to her bedroom door.

"Nuh-uh. You gotta make em come to the door. Then you make em wait five minutes before you're *ready*" She went back to her vanity and kept brushing. When the door bell rang, she stayed where she was.

"You make David wait for you every fucking time?" I asked, appalled at her lack of manners.

"Pfft. Not anymore. This is for your benefit." She pointed the brush at me. "You make that boy wait for the first couple dates. If he's patient, he gets to keep coming around. If he's a dick about it, he's not worth your trouble." *Huh. That was actually a smart approach. Test the waters before jumping right in.*

"All right. They can wait." I grabbed a magazine from her bedside table and sat on her bed, flipping through it.
"Girls! David and his friend are here!" Laurie's mom yelled from the bottom of the steps.
"Be there in a minute!" Laurie answered, taking her time applying her lip gloss.

Those five minutes took *forever.* When Laurie finally stood up, fluffed up her hair and smoothed down her jacket, I was moments away from a nervous break down. She went to her door while my butt stayed glued to her mattress. She looked at me, waiting for me to follow.

"Come on Pais. Love awaits." She smirked mischievously. I let out a loud groan before managing to stand up.

I wiped my sweaty palms on my jeans while we went down the hallway. At the top of the stairs, I kept my eyes glued on Laurie's back, knowing the boys were waiting for us at the bottom. I wanted to puke.

"There's my girl." David smiled brightly when he spotted Laurie coming toward him. He met her on the last step, lifting her off her feet to plant a loving kiss on her lips while she giggled.

Moment of truth. I looked up and what I saw made me lose my footing on the last couple of steps, crashing into the love birds. *Fuck. He's gorgeous.* His dirty blonde hair was bordering on shaggy, curling at the top of his ears. He had a very masculine jaw with a day's growth shadowing it. Full lips and gorgeous honey-coloured eyes smiled at me, clearly amused with my near fall.

"Hey Paisley. It's nice to finally meet you." He stepped forward, offering me his hand. I placed my hand in his and shook, not failing to notice how his nearly swallowed mine.

"Hi." Despite the makeup Laurie put on me, the red in my cheeks still burned bright.

"Let's get this show on the road kids." David said, wrapping his arms around both Laurie's shoulders and mine, leading us out the front door.

On my way past Thomas, I saw his jaw tense as his eyes locked on David's arm on me. *Odd.* I didn't think much about it while we walked to the red sedan parked behind Laurie's mom's van. David opened the front passenger door and gestured for me to hop in before opening the back door for Laurie. Thomas slid in beside me and I smiled shyly at him when he looked over at me. He shook his head with a smirk before starting the car and pulling onto the road.

"So, ladies, how has your night been so far?" David asked from the back. He was seated in the middle, glued to Laurie, with his arm draped around her shoulder again.
"Oh, we spent the afternoon getting ready and talking about these cute boys we know," Laurie flirted.
"Oh yeah? I know these cute boys? Might have to knock them out. Lucky fuckers probably don't even know what to do with a pair of gorgeous girls like you two." David smiled.

David was hot. His dark hair hung to the bottom of his ears and he was always running his hand through it to get it out of his face. He had a panty smile that stopped girls in their tracks. If the smile wasn't enough, he had dimples to go with it. The cherry on top was that he was super nice. He always made me feel included when the three of us were together, making sure I didn't feel like the third wheel.

"Oh babe. You're the only cute boy worth my time." Laurie leaned into him. Giving him a kiss. The kind that heated up really quick.

I avoided the rear-view mirror, a little uncomfortable with their PDA. I looked at Thomas who looked back at them and chuckled.

"Looks like you're stuck with me. Sorry I'm not one of those cute boys you and Laurie were talking about." He was fishing for information. *Was he worried I was interested in someone else?*

"I guess you'll just have to do for now." I tried to flirt. From the frown on his face, I wasn't doing a very good job with it.

"We don't have to do this you know. We can drop them off at the movies and I can drive you home." He looked at me and he seemed annoyed.
"I was just kidding." I hurried, placing a hand on his arm. "We were talking about you." He looked at me, still unsure. "I want to go out with you tonight but I'm not going to hold you to it." I sat back in my seat, deflated. "You can just drop me off. It's still early enough to salvage some of your night."

He didn't answer me right away, just kept driving. Laurie and David were too wrapped up in each other to notice the awkwardness up front.

"I live on Augustus. You can just stop at the corner and I can walk the rest of the way." I said in barely more than a whisper.
"You're even more beautiful than I expected." Surprised, I looked up at him again. The irritation was gone, replaced with a flirty smile. *Whoa.*
"You're pretty handsome yourself." Blushing. Again.
"I couldn't get your voice out of my head all week."
"Why didn't you call back?" I asked, dying to know.
"What?"
"You said you would call me again. Why didn't you?" He focused on the road, flicking his signal light on.
"I punked out."
"What? Why?" Not at all what I expected to hear.

"Well, you sounded so sexy the first time, I couldn't get my nerve back up to call again. I dialed your number a dozen times but always hung up before it rang." This time, his cheeks flushed with colour.

"Huh. You seemed so self confident. I never would have thought you could be shy." He reached over and took my hand in his.

"I'm not usually such a pussy. I've never had a hard time talking to a girl before." He laced his fingers with mine and flashed me another smile that I returned.

Thomas pulled into the drive-in, paying for the four of us. David and Laurie had come up for air in time to help pick a spot to park. We all got out and the boys went to the trunk to grab some blankets and their cooler. They spread out two blankets and made themselves comfortable. Laurie quickly curled up beside David, helping herself to a can of beer. Thomas reached out a hand to me and gently pulled me onto his blanket. I sat beside him, leaving enough space between us to fit another person. He reached over hooking an arm around my waist to pull me close to his side.

"I don't bite sweetheart." He whispered against my ear. "Hey Dave! Pass us a couple drinks." Dave tossed him a beer then a second one.

He cracked open my can, handing it to me before opening his own and taking a long sip. I'd never had alcohol before. Though I wasn't comfortable having any now, I didn't want to come off as a prude. I took a tiny sip, enjoying the bitter taste. Thomas was grinning at me knowingly.

"First time?" He asked.
"That obvious?"
"Well, not very many drinkers look terrified of it." He took another healthy sip before leaning back on his elbows.

I felt compelled to follow his lead. I emptied a third of the can before leaning back on my own elbows beside him. I looked over to see David and Laurie sharing secret whispers. Thomas followed my gaze.

"I'm kinda jealous of what they have." He shared and I looked at him surprised.

"Really? I didn't think boys cared about that kind of stuff."
"What do you mean?"

"Well, I didn't think finding a girlfriend and falling in love was important to boys. I always just figured it was all about sex for them." I took another sip of my beer, curious about what he was going to tell me. He chuckled.

"Of course, we care about love. Probably just as much as girls do. What kind of person *wouldn't* want to have someone to share everything with? Someone to talk to at the end of the day, share all their dreams with? Have *sex* with?" I smiled, melting even more.

"Good point."
"Hey, can I ask you something?"
"Of course."
"Do you think you and I could have something like that?"
"I... Well I... I'm not sure. We just met. I suppose it could be possible." I stumbled over my words, struggling to find the right thing to say. The irritated look crossed his face briefly but he hid it with another smile.

"I think we should try." He reached up and ran a finger down my cheek. I felt warmth heating up my chest and the beer was already going to my head. I drank the last of it and set the can aside.

Thomas stood and went to the cooler to get me another drink. Opening it again and handing it to me when he sat back down. We watched the movie for a few minutes. His hand brushing against mine every now and again. I was very grateful for the effects of the beer. It seemed to be mellowing me out quite a bit. When Thomas leaned over and placed a kiss lightly on my shoulder, I didn't even flinch. When his lips moved to the side of my neck I shivered and tilted my head to the side giving him more access. He hooked a finger under my chin, pulling my face to look at him.

"Can I kiss you Paisley?" He asked, eyes on my lips.
"You already did." I laughed, sipping my beer.
"Can I kiss these?" He ran his fingertip across my lips. I sucked in a breath, feeling his touch in the pit of my stomach.

"Yes."

I waited while he slid his hand behind my neck, tilting my head enough so that he could put his mouth on mine. My heart was pounding more than I ever would have thought possible. When his tongue swiped my bottom lip, my lips parted on their own. His tongue flicked against mine, tasting me. Teasing me. He leaned in, forcing me to lay back onto the blanket. Most of his body was on top of me and one of his long legs was pressed between my mine. I felt his stiffness against my upper thigh and I could feel moisture building in my panties. I was in way out of my depth. His hand ran up my hip and just when I thought he was going to touch me, he broke off the kiss.

"Holy fuck. We keep this up and I'm going to make an ass of myself." He laughed, running a hand through his hair.
"What do you mean?" He looked down at his dick pointedly.
"Pre-cum's gonna make it look like I pissed my pants." I covered my mouth to hide my giggle. I could play along.

"Well, my underwear probably looks like I dropped them in a toilet." I smiled. His eyes went dark and he groaned before flopping on his back beside me. He crossed his arm over his face.

"You are killing me."

"Oh, I'm sorry." Boldly, I reached over and lightly placed a hand on the bulge in his jeans. "Does this hurt?" He gasped, looking at me in shock. I gave him a bright smile before getting up and getting us another drink.

When I sat back down, he took my drink from me to open it. After opening his own, he clinked it against mine.

"To everything I want us to be." He toasted.
"To finding love, sharing dreams and sex." I replied to which he groaned again before chugging the entire beer.

He wrapped his arm around me and we quietly watched rest of the movie. When the credits started rolling, Laurie and David were tangled up, groping each other and sucking face. I shook my head at the two of them, lost in their own little world.

"Hey fucker! We getting out of here or do Paisley and I have to wait for you to bust a nut?" Thomas threw an empty can at David's head. Without looking up, David flipped him off. Laurie started laughing and pushing at his chest.
"Come on babe. Let's go to the docks." Laurie suggested.

"Aw, but things are getting so good." David pouted. Kissing her under her chin, tickling her with his teeth. She started giggling and pushing him off. "I fucking hate you Tom. Goddamn cockblock." Though he was cussing Thomas out, he was smiling.

David stood and helped Laurie to her feet before folding up the blanket. We packed up the car and waited for an opening in traffic to exit the theatre. Thomas rubbed my thigh as he drove, giving it a light squeeze every now and again. His touch was burning me up. When his pinky went high enough up on my thigh to brush against the zipper, I thought I would combust. He smiled at me slyly, knowing our friends were clueless as to what he was up to.

We split up at the docks. David and Laurie going down by the water, while Thomas and I walked down one of the docks to sit on the edge. We started out talking about school and lighter topics but it wasn't long before the conversation became deeper.

"How many boys have you been with?" He asked, running a thumb across the back of the hand he was holding.
"You mean boyfriends?"
"I mean sex." He locked eyes with me, waiting for my answer.
"I haven't..."
"You're a virgin? There's no fucking way." His brows dropped in disbelief. Looking at me like he was waiting for the punch line. That stung
"I'm still a virgin. Why do you say there's no way?" I asked, a little insulted.
"Wow. With the way we were going at it at the drive-through, I would have bet money on you having slept with *someone*." Now I was insulted which lit my temper.

"Well maybe it was the beer you fed me." I accused, standing abruptly and turning back toward the sidewalk.

"Paisley wait! I didn't mean is as a bad thing!" He shouted but I kept walking.

I was halfway back to the car when he caught my arm and pulled me against him. He held me close and kissed me softly.

"I'm sorry sweetheart. I didn't mean to hurt your feelings. I was just caught off guard."

"Well how about you? How many girls have you been with?" I asked, still a little hurt.

"I've had 3 girlfriends. I've slept with 4 girls." He answered honestly and I didn't know how to feel about it. "What about boyfriends?"

"No boyfriends."

"You haven't even had a boyfriend?" Stunned, his arms fell to his sides. "What kind of boys go to your school? Are they really that stupid?"

"I was just never interested in dating any of them. I just stayed clear of boys." I wrapped my arms around myself protectively. He looked down at my arms then up at my face before wrapping his arms back around me.

"Does that mean I shouldn't get my hopes up because you aren't interested?"

"Oh, I'm very interested. I've never met anyone like you before." I looked him in the eye and leaned in to kiss him. He reached up and cupped my face in his palms, deepening the kiss briefly before leading me back to the car.

For the next three months, Thomas and I spent all our spare time together. Sometimes Laurie and David joined us but more often than not, it was just the two of us. He would pick me up from school and we would spend a couple hours together before he would drop me off at home for supper. After dinner, if he didn't pick me up to go back out, he would call me and we would talk on the phone for hours. He had very quickly become the centre of my world. Laurie didn't seem bothered that I had less time to spend with her, she was often with David anyway. Gemma and Claire were getting a little annoyed with me but figured the newness of our relationship would wear off and I would go back to having time to spend with them. If Laurie was upset, it would have bothered me. Gemma and Claire didn't really concern me, they had blown me off for boys too many times to have a right to be upset.

It was a Wednesday afternoon and Thomas had convinced me to blow off school after lunch to
hang out with him. When the bell rang, I rushed to my locker to grab my bag so I wouldn't leave him waiting too long. Laurie caught up to me on my way to the side door.

"Where the hell are you off to?" She asked, eyeballing my bag.
"Thomas is picking me up."

"Girl, they're gonna call your house if you don't show up to classes after lunch." She warned, knowing that there would be hell to pay if my dad found out.

"Don't worry. My mom is out with her friends this afternoon and my dad is working, even if he was home, he wouldn't answer the phone anyway." I brushed off her concerns.

"Pais, I don't think it's a good idea." She pleaded with me.
"Laurie. He's waiting. I'll see you later, ok? Maybe we can go out just the two of us this weekend?"
"I'd love that. I miss girl's night" She squeezed my hand, knowing there was no convincing me to stick around.
"Me too. I'll see you later." I kissed her cheek and rushed out.

Thomas was parked in the lot with his window down and music blaring. When he spotted me, he turned the music down and waved.

"There's my gorgeous girl." When I got into the car he leaned across the console and kissed me, squeezing my hip and teasing me with his tongue.

"How are you?" I asked, smiling at his eagerness.
"I'm so much better now." His own smile matched mine. "I missed you baby girl."
"You saw me yesterday." I laughed.
"Yesterday was a long time ago." He kissed me once more before putting the car in drive.
"Where are we headed?"
"There's a carnival in the fair grounds. Thought we could go and hit up a few rides and play some games. What do you say?"

"I'd like that." I slid my hand in his and held it while he drove. He pulled my hand to his mouth and kissed my knuckles, melting my heart.

We parked across the street and walked over to the carnival. We were having a blast. Our stomachs hurt from laughing on the rides and we our cheeks ached from all the smiling.

"Smoke break babe." He pulled me to a bench and pulled out his cigarettes. He lit one and leaned back against the bench, taking a deep drag. "You are amazing, you know that?" He asked and what could I say to that?

"Can I have one of those?" I sometimes smoked with him, enjoying the head buzz it caused.

He handed me the one he had lit and got out another one for himself. I took a puff and held it in, instantly feeling the light headed feeling. We sat in silence, smoking and watching the people around us. When I was almost finished, a hand gripped a handful of my hair at the back of my head. I looked
to Thomas for help but he was looking past me at whoever was behind me. I was barely able to turn my head as whoever it was hauled me to my feet. I caught a glimpse of the man pulling my hair. Dad.
"Isn't Wednesday a school day Paisley?" He asked accusingly. He

was livid. I felt his hand shake in my hair and there was no mistaking the look in his eyes. "Isn't that where you should be right now? Not out fucking around with boys?" He shoved me to the ground and spit on my shirt.

Worried Thomas would try to interfere, I looked at him, ready to ask him to stay out of it. He hadn't moved from the bench. He sat there and watched as my father shoved me around. My heart squeezed in pain. He clearly didn't care enough about me to defend me. For the first time in a very long time, tears streaked down my face.

"Get your fucking ass to the truck." Dad stood there and waited for me to stand and head to the parking lot.

He followed behind me, knowing it would intimidate me. He didn't say a word on the ride home. When we pulled into the drive way, he walked into the house without looking back to make sure I followed. He knew I wouldn't make him wait.

I wasn't even through the doorway when he was on me. The back of his knuckles connected with my cheek and I fell to the floor. When I looked at him, his teeth were bared and spit was sliding down the side of his mouth. I whimpered. He leaned forward and grabbed a handful of my hair, using it to pull me back to my feet and onto the tips of my toes. He held his grip in my hair and he used his free hand to backhand me across my other cheek. I was momentarily blinded by bright spots. Another slap before he let go of my hair and I crumpled to the floor. I could hear the buckle of his belt as he pulled the metal tooth from the leather hole. It made a jingling noise as he slowly pulled the belt from the loops on his jeans. I knew that he was prolonging the process to allow my fear to build and build it did. I was so overrun with terror that there was a metallic taste in the back of my mouth because my teeth punctured my cheeks.

Fifteen times. He whipped me fifteen times before his breathing grew ragged. He finally tired himself out. I waited while the final blow was delivered. When the metal buckle hit me across my lower back, I tightly clenched my teeth, knowing that he did it to make me cry out and beg him to stop.

"Get the fuck out of my sight." He shoved me out of his way with his foot as he headed to the living room.

I stood up as quickly as I could manage with my back in agonizing pain. As I stumbled up the stairs, he reminded me what happened to girls who skipped school to fuck around with boys and if he were to catch me smoking again, it would be even worse.

Thomas didn't call that night. The next morning, mom helped me cover the bruises on my face with makeup. When Laurie saw me the next day, she could tell I got caught by the way I sat at my desk and walked through the halls. I was very stiff; I made the least number of movements possible because everything hurt. She didn't ask and I didn't offer to tell. That's why I loved her. I didn't *have* to explain.

At the end of the day, I got on the bus without checking the parking lot for Thomas's car. When he called me that night, I didn't answer. I didn't answer the next night either.

Friday, Laurie and I walked to her house after school. It was time for a well over due girls' night
with just the two of us and I was looking forward to spending time with my best friend. After eating pizza for supper, we were both laying on her bed watching a romantic comedy when her phone rang.

"Hello?" Laurie answered the handset beside her bed. "Hey babe, what's going on?" "Pais and I are just watching a movie in our jammies." "Well, we were planning on just having a girl's night." "I'm not too sure she wants to see him right now." "I don't know, she hasn't said anything." "David, I don't think that's a good idea." Her tone became firm. "No. If he can't get a hold of her, she obviously doesn't want to talk to him." "When she's ready to speak to him, she'll call him." "Aw, babe. Why are you doing this to me?" "Fine, I'll ask her." I looked at her, waiting.

"Thomas wants to know if he can talk to you." I felt guilty. There was no reason to put my friends in the middle.
"Fine." I held my hand out for the handset while she told David I

would talk to Thomas.

"Yes?" I asked with ice in my voice.

"Baby, please." His voice was thick with emotion. "I don't know what to say. I'm so sorry. I didn't think it was my place to interfere. I didn't know what to do, if saying something would make it worse. I can't get arrested." He stopped and I could hear him breathing heavily through the phone. Clearly, he was trying very hard to keep himself under control.

"It's not your problem Tom. It has nothing to do with you." I was losing my resolve. It bothered me that it was so easy for him to get his way with me, make me forgive him.

"Sweetheart, don't do this to me. I can't handle the cold shoulder from you. What did you expect me to do? Should I have taken you away from him? Where would we have gone? I'm living at my aunt's house; I can't really take you here. That would have pissed him off even more, right?" He was getting desperate.

"You're right. It would have aggravated the situation." I was relieved that I was able to disguise my feelings. I was able to sound detached when I just wanted to ask him to come and get me.

"Please, baby. Please. You mean the world to me. I need you." I heard him take a deep breath that shook with his hurt. "I love you Paisley." I was speechless. Those words from him tore me wide open. I was done. Completely his.

"I love you too Thomas."

# Chapter Three

Hate is A Grown-Up Word

*Tricia Warnock*

Thomas rarely came over for dinner. It made him uncomfortable and I didn't blame him. I often felt the same way. Tonight, he would be joining us. It was my sixteenth birthday and though I told him it wasn't important, that he could skip it, he accepted my mom's invitation. It made me happy. It was him I wanted to spend my birthday with anyways. I would have skipped it, if it were an option. No such luck. Mom always insisted on cooking our favourite meal on our birthdays and baking a cake with candles and the whole nine. Like our births were something to celebrate. What a joke.

As if having to spend my 'special' day at home with my family wasn't bad enough, Nathan was coming. Shella's boyfriend was a creep who made my skin crawl. I couldn't stand that boy and wasn't shy about making my dislike known. All my encounters with him ended with Shella pissed off with me. He always stared at me. Not just spacing out kind of staring. Staring at me as though I were naked and he was the only one who could see me. It didn't matter who was around and no one else seemed to notice or pretended they didn't. It pissed me off and I'd become very good at avoiding him or being in the same room for more than a brief moment or two.

I was up in my room reading when the doorbell rang. I stayed put, assuming Nathan would be the first to arrive. When I heard Shella rushing down the hall towards the stairs, I knew I was right with my assumption. *What a loser.* When five thirty came, I was sitting at the table as was expected. I was also disappointed that Thomas had not shown up like he told us he would be. I was confused and hurt that he would do something like this to me. I swallowed the lump in my throat as I cleared off his place setting. Mom made up our plates and I made a point of ignoring Nathan and his probing eyes.

"Here you are baby girl. Happy birthday." Mom gave me a big smile, placing my plate of spaghetti in front of me.

"Thank you, mom. It looks delicious." I tried to smile back at her and hide the fact that I was hurting. She kissed me on the forehead before moving on and serving everyone else.

"Sixteen now. You kids are growing up way too fast." Dad said, shaking his head. "Happy birthday P-Baby. Love you."

"Thanks dad. I love you too." It was rare for him to say those words so when he did, I cherished them.

"Happy birthday P-Baby!" Nathan said, raising his glass to toast me. Dad's eyes locked on him. He clearly did not like Nathan using his endearment.

"You call her Paisley. Not P-Baby." Dad's tone was sharp, cold and unforgiving.

"Sorry sir. Won't do it again." Nathan apologized, shrinking into himself and avoiding my dad's eyes.

"Don't take it to heart babe. No one's allowed calling her that. Only dad." Shella rubbed his back, trying to ease the sting from being scolded by our father.

"I'd prefer if you didn't call me anything, if we're all being honest."

"Paisley, don't start." Mom warned. While I felt my temper starting to simmer, a knock sounded at the front door.

I placed my fork down beside my plate as calmly as I could before standing from the table.

"I'll get it." I offered.

I went to the door and when I opened it, my foul mood disintegrated. Thomas was standing there, holding a shiny present and a sad smile. He didn't get a chance to greet me before I was jumping into his arms.

"I'm so sorry baby. I couldn't get out of work on time." He apologized, burying his face in my neck and holding me close. "I tried to get out early but an older lady came in with the tow truck and she was hysterical." Thomas worked at an auto repair shop as a junior mechanic, working towards becoming a licensed mechanic.

"It's okay. You're here now." I gave him another squeeze before taking his hand to lead him to the dining room. "Thomas made it." I announced.

"Oh good. How are you, Thomas?" Mom asked, standing from her chair to make him a plate.

"I'm great Mrs. Coleman. How are you? The food smells fantastic!" Mom giggled and placed a plate in front of him along with the cutlery I had put away. "Good afternoon Mr. Coleman." Thomas shook hands with my dad before coming to sit beside me.

"Glad you made it. Thought P-Baby was going to start crying a few minutes ago." Dad said flashing me a teasing smile while my face burned.
"I was not." I pouted.
"I'm sorry, Paisley." Thomas apologized again, pushing my hair behind my ear gently so I could look at him and see the sincerity on his face.
"I know, it's okay." I smiled at him, relieved that he had come and saved my birthday from certain disaster.

Dinner was great. I was happy and held hands with Thomas under the table while everyone chatted. I was so wrapped up in Thomas that I paid no attention to Nathan and his crude leering. I noticed Thomas getting tense but I assumed it was just from discomfort. When his hand started squeezing mine under the table, I looked at him and saw that he was angry. I squeezed back and he looked up at me. He was more than angry, he was *pissed.* My eyebrows lowered, confused. He read my expression and shook his head.

"All right Paisley. It's time for your presents!" Mom clapped her hands before reaching down beside her to pick up the gift bag she had sitting beside her on the floor. "Here you are sweetheart."

"Thanks mom." I pulled out the tissue paper and pulled out a beautiful leather jacket. "Oh wow, Mom, this is gorgeous! I love it!" I stood up and put it on right away and it fit like a glove.

"I knew it would look good on you." Mom was beaming, she loved giving gifts. Oddly, so did dad. He was smiling at me from across the table, watching me model the jacket.

"My turn." Dad stood and went out to grab a box from the laundry room. He handed me the slim box and kissed me on the top of the head.

"Thank you, daddy." I ripped the colourful balloon paper. Inside the box was a silky emerald summer dress. It was beautiful short sleeve dress with a flowing skirt that reached just above my knees when I held it up against me. I was speechless. It was probably the most beautiful dress I had ever seen and very grown up. "Wow dad. It's... It's so... I don't even know what to day other than, wow." I went around to give him a hug.

"When I saw it, I couldn't resist. Green is definitely your colour."
"I can't wait to see you in it." Thomas put in, heat simmering in his eyes. I smiled at him before giving him a wink and sitting back down.
"Here Paisley. Happy birthday." Nathan handed me a small rectangular box. I looked at it for a moment, knowing whatever was in it was going to make me very uncomfortable.
"Thank you." Manners took over and I took the box he offered. Inside was a silver bracelet with a small flower on it. In the petals, there looked to be tiny diamonds.

"Whoa man. Talk about splurging on your girlfriend's sister."
Thomas said, disguising the jab with a chuckle.
"I had no clue what to get her." Nathan shrugged.
"This is too much. I can't take this." I closed the lid and tried
handing it back.
"I bought it for you. Just enjoy it." His smug grin sent shivers down
my spine.
"Paisley, don't be rude." Dad said, clearly unhappy with the way I
was reacting to the gift.

Everyone was quiet, unsure how to get over the awkward
atmosphere. Leave it to Nathan to make everyone feel weird. *Dick.*

"Well now I feel like a jerk." Thomas laughed, picking up the
wrapped box he had come with.
"Why?" I asked.

"Another guy just gave my girlfriend a bracelet. This isn't even close
to measuring up." He dropped the present in front of me, looking
like he regretted whatever he had chosen to get me.

"Oh babe. If it's from you, I'll love it." I reassured him, ripping into
the paper. A bag of reese minis, a tub of my favourite body butter
and a framed picture of Thomas and I were all laid in a box. "Aw,
this is the perfect gift, Thomas! How could I not love a box of my
favourite things? Chocolate, lotion and you!" I leaned over and
kissed him, not caring that my family could see. "Thank you."

"You're welcome." His smile returned and he wrapped his arm
around my shoulders. At that moment. I was very happy. It was by
far my best birthday to date.

We sat around and chatted some more. Everyone in a great
mood and laughing. Dad was enjoying a beer and surprisingly, so
was mom. Thomas kept his arm on me and I leaned into him,
enjoying his warmth. John was the first to ask to be excused so that
he could go up to his room and finish some homework. Shella and
Nathan didn't look like they were going to leave any time soon.

"Mr. Coleman, would you mind if I took Paisley out for a bit?"

Thomas asked during a lull in conversation.

"Sure. You kids go have fun. No school tomorrow."

"Great. Thank you." He stood and turned to me, offering his hand. "Shall we?"

"We shall." I took his hand and after saying our goodbyes, I followed him out the front door.

When we got to his car, he opened the passenger door for me before going around to the driver's side. The first few minutes passed and he said nothing. I didn't mind the quiet until I looked at him and saw that the anger was back on his face, then I was confused.

"What's wrong?" I asked. He didn't answer right away but his hands tightened on the wheel. I decided to wait until he was ready to talk. It took him a couple minutes but eventually he seemed to have calmed down enough to share.

"What the fuck is that loser's problem?" He growled through clenched teeth.

"What loser?" I was lost but thinking back to dinner when the look made it's first appearance, I realized who he was referring to. "Nathan?"

"Yeah *Nathan*. You two got something going on that I should know about?" He looked at me, seething. "You fucking your sister's boyfriend?"

"Are you kidding me? You know how I feel about that creep!" Now, I was pissed.

"Yeah, Paisley. Pretending to hate someone is a good way to try and hide the fact that you're cheating on your boyfriend."

"Bring me home." I demanded.

"Sure. I'll bring you home. Maybe he'll still be there and you can suck his dick before bedtime." He sneered.

"Fuck you, Thomas. I wouldn't touch his dick to save my life." I crossed my arms to hold myself back from slapping him.

"Guys don't stare at girls like that if they don't want to get in their panties, Paisley. He was eye-fucking you the whole time I was there. Then he gives you a fucking diamond bracelet! There's no way he drops a couple hundred bucks on a girl who hasn't given him a taste of her pussy." My hand shot out, slapping his cheek.

He whipped the car to the side of the road and when he yanked the gear shift to park, I got out of the car. My body shook with my fury. I couldn't believe he had the nerve to accuse me of hooking up with Nathan. Just the thought of Nathan made me sick. I didn't make it very far before he caught up to me and spun me around. His hands curled in the front of my shirt, lifting me onto my toes.

"Don't fucking walk away from me Paisley." He pulled me closer so that our noses almost touched. I was too mad to be afraid. "You wanna be with other guys then at least have the balls to end things with me." He paused, waiting for me to tell him I was done. "If you're mine, you're all mine. I. Don't. Share. Do you understand me Paisley?" He shook me. "Did you fuck around with that asshole? Huh?"

"I didn't fucking touch Nathan. I cannot stand him." I shoved against his chest. "I'm not the kind of girl who fucks around on her boyfriend." I slapped at his chest, losing whatever hold I had left on my self control. I was insulted. I felt dirty. I was disgusted with the way Thomas was acting. "Let go of me Thomas. You want to act like a fucking dickhead, go ahead but I'm not going to hang around and let you treat me like this." I pulled at his hands on my shirt.

We stared at each other, both of us breathing heavily. I wasn't willing to bend and I could tell his wheels were turning. He was trying to decide whether or not he should believe me. Suddenly, his mouth smashed against mine. It was an angry kiss but it was the most exciting kiss we've shared. His arms wound around my waist, pulling me into him. He spun us around and backed me up until he was pressing me against his car. He held his hands against my cheeks and pushed his tongue through my lips, kissing me like he was starving and I was his next meal.

He ground his hips against mine, pushing the bulge in his pants against me. My head was swimming with sensation. I squeezed my thighs together to ease the throbbing between my legs. When he felt the shift, he rocked his hips to tease me further. He pulled away from the kiss and looked into my eyes. He watched me while one of his hands trailed down my neck, over my nipple making me shiver and down even further. My stomach knotted when his touch brushed across the hem of my shirt. He looked just as turned on as I was when his lips parted and he ran his tongue across his bottom lip. Briefly his touch disappeared and I gasped when he cupped me where I was desperate for relief. He rubbed against the denim of my jeans, increasing the wetness that was building there. I was soaked. When he squeezed me in his palm, I let out a moan. He started rubbing me through my pants and a foreign sensation started to build in my most private place. I felt my nipples stiffen and I pushed my chest against his, wanting him to feel the effect he was having on me. He groaned and kissed me, continuing to give me the pressure I craved. The pleasure built and eventually my whole body tensed. I moaned into his mouth and the muscles inside my entrance pulsed. I rocked against his hand, riding out the sensation. I had never felt anything like it before.

"Did my girl just get off?" Thomas asked, smirking at me, clearly pleased.
"I do believe I did." I panted. He groaned again and made a fist in my hair, pulling my face back to put his mouth on mine.
"Come." He commanded after breaking the kiss.

He pulled me from the side of the car and opened the door for me. He jogged around the car and when he hopped in, he grabbed my hand before pulling away from the curb. We drove for a few minutes before he pulled in behind an old diner. There were no other cars and we parked at the back of the building where a line of hedges ran along the other side of the car, keeping us hidden.

Thomas turned off the car before leaning over and running a hand through my hair stopping behind my neck. He pulled me toward him and kissed me softly then rested his forehead against mine.

"Paisley, I need you to help me out." He whispered. The question and tone made me nervous. Not for the first time, I was in a situation with Thomas that reminded me I was out of my depth.

"What do you need help with?" Part of me knew the answer but I wasn't ready to go all the way. It was something Thomas and I had already discussed and he seemed to understand.

"Watching you come... Was the sexiest thing I have ever seen in my life. I'm so hard it feels like my dick is going to explode." He explained, squeezing himself to emphasize his need. Seeing his hand on hard on made my mouth water.

"Thomas, I'm not ready to have sex." I told him; afraid he was going to get upset with me.

He let out a frustrated growl but reached beside him to pull the lever, laying himself back. He watched me as he reached down to undo the button on his jeans. He slowly pulled the zipper down and out sprang his erection. He wasn't wearing any boxers. He kept his eyes on me while he wrapped a hand around himself, squeezing and stroking his gorgeous cock. Soon his hips were lifting from his seat to meet the movements of his hand. His free hand reached out, grabbing the front my shirt and pulling me towards him. He pulled me until my mouth landed on his, plunging his tongue between my lips, not bothering to ease into it. I pulled my legs under me, kneeling on my seat and pouring myself into the kiss. I was on fire again.

"Baby, please. Please help me." He begged and I melted. He looked over my face, knowing he had me where he wanted me. "Put it in your mouth?" He requested.

I didn't answer. I reached down to pull his hand off to replace it with mine. I felt the smooth skin on his shaft. He was too big to wrap my hand all the way around. I watched my hand move up and down his length, looking up at him when he moaned softly. His lids were half closed and he was watching my hand playing with him.

"Yeah Paisley. Squeeze a little harder." His hips were moving again, meeting the strokes of my hand.

I ignored him. Instead, I leaned farther over and placed my lips around the head of his cock, running my tongue along the slit to taste him. His body shook and he pulled he pulled in a sharp breath.

"Oh, fuck Pais." He pulled my hair aside so he could watch and rested his hand on the back of my head.

I slowly slid my mouth down, taking more of him. When I felt the head push on the back of my throat, I fought the urge to gag and pulled off. I stopped at the tip and gave it a suck. I held the base with my hand while running my tongue from sack to crown. When his hand grabbed onto my hair, I knew he was desperate for his release. I began to really move. I sucked him down, using my hand to stroke the part of his shaft that I couldn't reach with my mouth. Out of curiosity, I reached up with my other hand to feel his balls. I ran my fingertips over them, gently scraping them with my nails.

"Fuck..." He moaned, bucking further into my mouth, forcing the crown further down my throat. I tried to hide my body's rejection but my gag set him off, his hips started to pump, fucking my mouth. I concentrated on breathing through my nose. He was panting and moaning, clearly enjoying the feel of my mouth.

"Babe, I'm gonna come. Can I go in your mouth?"
"Mhm." I gave him permission without taking my mouth away.

It wasn't long before his hips started fumbling and I could feel his shaft throbbing against my tongue.

"Fuck yeah. Fuck yeah. Ah babe." He was mumbling before his hips pushed forward and his orgasm fired off deep into my mouth. I swallowed quickly, afraid of the way my gag reflex would react to the warm fluid invading my mouth. When he let go of my head, I leaned back in my seat, wiping my mouth with the back of my hand.

Thomas laid still, breathing heavily, not bothering to cover himself. My head was spinning. I was struggling to wrap my head around the fact that I had just given my first blow job. I started feeling self-conscious. I knew it wasn't the first time for him. Other girls had used their mouths on him. I knew he enjoyed it; I swallowed the proof but I couldn't help wondering if I measured up.

"You're fucking incredible Paisley." He sat up, leaned over the consoled and kissed me. "You blew my goddamn mind, you know that?" He asked with a satisfied grin before sitting back and doing up his pants.

"Was it okay? I wasn't too bad at it?" I asked, twisting my hands in my lap. He looked at me like I was crazy.
"Are you kidding me?"
"No, I know you've gotten head before..." I trailed off looking down, too embarrassed to make eye contact.

"Paisley, that was by far the most amazing blow job I've ever had." He assured me, making me smile. He looked at me thoughtfully for a few moments. Just when I was about to ask him what was on his mind, he spoke. "That was your first blow job, wasn't it?"

"Yes." I answered truthfully.

"I'm sorry Paisley. I didn't like Shella's boyfriend looking at you while we were having supper. I wanted to punch him in the face. I shouldn't have taken it out on you." He reached over to take my hand and place a loving kiss on my knuckles.

"It's okay. I get it. That guy pisses me off too. I was ready to punch him before you got there." He smiled at my admission.
"I love you Paisley." I pulled him over to kiss him.
"I love you, Thomas."
"I should get you home before your dad hunts us down." He started the car and backed out from behind the diner.

It was Friday night. The girls and I had been sitting in a booth at Billy's Pool Place, waiting for our drinks. Gemma's older brother supplied us with expired licenses from girls who looked enough like us to get us into bars, not that getting into Billy's was very hard in the first place. Only one of the four bar tenders ever asked to see our ID.

Gemma was already feeling the effects of the alcohol and was openly flirting with the boys sitting in the booth behind us. The three guys were soaking it up, talking over each other to get her attention. They were probably the same age as Thomas and were good looking. Laurie and I sat across from her, laughing at her antics. The girl didn't have a filter when she was sober, alcohol definitely didn't make it better. She was currently asking about their favourite sexual position. I groaned, embarrassed for her.

"Why don't you tell us yours, sweetheart?" The blond one in the baseball cap asked with a smirk.
"Oh darlin, I like being on top. Nothing better than watching a man lose his mind while I get myself off on his dick."
"Oh, shut up Gemma. Quit acting like a slut." Laurie laughed, tossing handful of peanuts at her.
"Thanks, Lo, love me some nuts." Gemma smiled seductively, picking up a peanut from the table and popping it in her mouth. Claire, Laurie and I broke out in a fit of laughter.

We were still laughing when the bartender placed our drinks in front of us. I took a sip from my bottle and nearly choked when I saw who walked into the bar. Fucking Nathan.

"Shoot me now. I'll pay you." I sighed, sinking down in my seat. The three of them peeked over to the door.
"Oh fuck." Claire said, rolling her eyes. "Of all the fucking bars to go to, he has to come to this one."
"Who Nathan?" The guy with the pierced eyebrow in the other booth asked, watching Nathan approach. "He's a buddy of ours." He lifted an arm to wave Nathan over.

"As fucking if." Gemma said to him, not bothering to disguise her irritation. "I cannot believe I just wasted a half an hour trying to get into the pants of a friend of Nathan's." She mock gagged before turning her back on the boys and sitting back down.

"Come on now baby. I'd ditch Nate for you in a heartbeat." The blond leaned over the back of our booth to coax Gemma.

"Fuck you ass-hole." Nathan had reached his friends and pulled off his bomber jacket. Before sitting next to the guy who had waved him over.

"Oh, come on now Nate. Look at her and tell me you wouldn't jump at the chance."

Nathan's eyes landed on me and a creepy grin curled his lips. I flipped him off before chugging the rest of my drink.

"Sorry Chris. I'm not used to girls that gorgeous giving you the time of day." His eyes never left mine when he spoke. The loser was talking about *me*. His friend looked at me too and smiled.

"Yeah, she hasn't said a word to me. I was referring to her girl Gemma here." He reached down to run a hand through Gemma's hair. "Wanna dance with me beautiful?"

"I guess I can spare you a song." She stood and let him take her hand to lead her to the tiny dance floor by the speakers.

Gemma had barely left her seat when Nathan plopped into it. Sitting right across from me without invitation.

"That's spots taken." Laurie told him, lacing her words with attitude.

"I'll give Gemma her spot when she gets back. I just wanna talk to Paisley here for a minute."

"Well Paisley doesn't want to talk to *you*." Claire put in, squeezing herself against the wall, trying to be as far away from him as possible with him sitting on the same bench.

"I just said I wanted to talk to Paisley. Not you two." Nathan's tone was cross as he spared them both a
dirty look before putting his eyes back on me. "How are you doing P-Baby?"

"Do not fucking call me that." I could feel my ears burning with my rising temper.

"Oh, I'm sorry. Does it get you all hot and bothered?" He asked with a smug smirk plastered on his face.

"It makes me want to vomit." I shot back with a sarcastic smile, which he ignored and lifted a hand to flag down the bartender. He didn't say anything as he watched her approach.

"What can I get you?"

"I'll have a Canadian and the ladies would like another round of Smirnoff ice please." He ordered, passing her a fifty-dollar bill. "Keep the change." The twenty-dollar tip put a smile on her face. "Coming right up," She turned, making her way quickly back to the bar to get us our drinks.
"So, you finally decide to ditch that scumbag of a boyfriend?" Nathan asked when he turned his attention back to me.
"Oh sweetheart. Are you jealous of Thomas because he knows how to treat his girlfriend?" I asked with overly sweet voice. He chuckled. *Ass-hole.*

"Paisley, that boy doesn't know how to handle a girl like you." He was completed comfortable sitting there while my friends and I glared at him. He clearly could not take a hint.

"Oh yeah? I suppose you would know how to handle a girl like me right?" My answer was exactly what he wanted. Leaning forward he put a long over mine of the table. Before I could pull it away, He tightened his grip.

"Baby, I could make you scream my name and beg me to stuff my cock into that tight pussy you keep locked away in those girly little panties of yours." Something told me he knew what my panties looked like and the thought chilled me to the bone.

"You're fucking disgusting. What the fuck my sister sees in you, I'll never know."
"Come to the bathroom with me and I'll show you." He winked. I was able to pull my hand free and quickly put it on my lap with the other one.
"In your fucking dreams Nathan. Get the fuck away from me." My anger was boiling.
"Come on baby. There's no need to pretend you're not into me. Thomas doesn't even have to know."

"Even if I was single, I wouldn't be interested. I would fuck another woman before you." Again, he just laughed. He was acting like everything I was telling me was a joke. Like this was all some kind of fucked up foreplay.

"Hey girls, Chris and I are gonna head out. I'll catch you all later." Gemma told us as she led Chris to the door.
"Nate, wanna go out for a smoke?" Eyebrow piercing asked, patting Nathan on the shoulder.

"Sure." He stood but before following his friends he reached out and ran his fingers over my hair. "I'll see you later beautiful. Don't miss me while I'm gone."

"Don't worry. I'll be thrilled not to have to look at you." When they walked away, I slammed my fists on the table. "I'm going for a piss and then I'm going home. I don't want to be near that fucker." I stood and stomped my way to the bathroom.

After using the toilet, I washed my hands and stood by the sink trying to calm down. I shook my
head at my reflection unable to wrap my mind around Nathan and his fucked-up antics. I could see why my sister was attracted to him. He was good looking. The blond hair and blue-eyed type but his personality was abhorrent. The longer Shella stayed with him, the more respect I lost for her. Who in their right mind would waste time in a relationship with such an ass clown?

Just then the floor flung open and made me jump in surprise. Nathan came strutting into the ladies' room with a cocky grin.

"What the fuck are you doing? Get out!" My anger reignited but underneath it was ice cold fear. He wasn't in here for a good reason.

"I saw you come back here from the window and I knew you were signalling me." He stepped up to the counter beside me, leaning his ass against it.

"Are you fucking ill? I had to pee. This is where normal people go when they need to empty their bladder." My heart pounded. Clearly Nathan was mentally unstable, there was no way I was *signalling* him.

"I asked you to come back here so I could show you how I would take care of you, then you come in here all alone. Girls don't go to the bathroom by themselves, Paisley. Not unless their waiting for a guy to join them." He reached out to touch me but I smacked his hand away. "Don't play coy with me Paisley. It only turns me on more." Before I could get around him, he had his dick in his hand and was moving to trap me against the counter. "Come here baby, touch it." He leaned into me with eyes closed and lips puckered for a kiss.

I couldn't stop myself. I had enough of Nathan and all his bullshit. I cocked my fist and planted my knuckles right into his nose. He cried out, clutching his nose which was spewing blood down the front of his shirt. Hitting him felt too good not to do it again. So, I did. I put everything I had into the punch I landed right to his left eye. I don't know if it hurt him as much as I had hoped but I was satisfied with the shock or pain on his face. I threw the toe of my shoe into his crotch just to be sure.

I grabbed my things and left him on his knees, cupping himself. On my way out, I waved to Laurie and Claire before heading out the door. Shella was going to lace into me when the jerk tattled but it was worth it. The thought of Shella set my guilt off. I hated Nathan even more for putting me in such a shitty situation. I was going to have to tell my sister that her boyfriend was a cheating dirt-bag. Who the fuck comes onto their girlfriend's little sister?

When I walked into the house, John was sitting on the couch watching his stupid shows while mom read. Clearly dad was still out with his buddies and if Shella wasn't with them in the living room, it meant she was upstairs in her room.

"Hey mom," I said racing to the stairs.
"Hey Paisley, thought you were staying at Laurie's tonight?"
"Changed my mind." I didn't stop to explain.

I stood outside Shella's room, trying to decide how to approach the conversation. I couldn't think of a way to bring the topic up kindly. My only solace was knowing that Shella would surely dump
him. With that, I decided to just rip the band aid right off. I knocked on her door before poking my head in. She was sitting at her desk,

working on some assignment or other.

"Got a minute?" I asked.
"Sure. What's up?" I walked to her bed and took a seat and she turned her chair to give me her full attention.
"Ran in to Nathan at Billy's." I threw out there to see how much she knew of her boyfriend's plans.
"Billy's?" Clearly nothing if she didn't even know what Billy's was.
"The bar down by the pop shop." I explained.
"What in the hell were you doing at a bar Paisley?" Mrs. Goody-Two-Shoes was annoyed.
"That's not what I came here to talk about." I rolled my eyes.
"Well, you shouldn't be going into bars. You're only sixteen." She crossed her arms as she scolded me.

"Shella, I appreciate your concern but it is far from the first time and it will not be the last so just get over that part. There's something more important we need to talk about."

"All right, all right. You ran into Nathan there?" She circled back to where I started.

"Yes. He was acting really weird. Even for Nathan." I probably could have gone without the jab, especially when Shella's eyes narrowed at me. "He hit on me." There it was. Time to face the music.

"Hit on you?" She laughed like I was out of my mind. "Nathan wouldn't hit on you Paisley. You're not at all his type."

"I'm telling you, he told me he would make me scream if I let him have sex with me." I couldn't bring myself to repeat exactly what he had said to him.

"You had to have misunderstood him." Excuse number two. She wasn't going to make this easy.

"Okay, so even if I misunderstood his vulgar pick-up lines, he followed me into the bathroom when I went for a pee. He showed me his penis and tried to kiss me."

"Paisley. I'm not stupid. I see the way you act around him. If anyone hit on anyone, it was you who came onto him." I was stunned.

"Are you fucking kidding me Shella? He's a fucking creep! There's no way in hell I would hit on him."

"You have *always* been jealous of me. It only makes sense that you would want my boyfriend. I'm not surprised, Thomas is a loser with no future. Nathan has his shit together and a ten-year plan. There's no contest." Shella smirked, thinking she held all the cards.

"Right. No contest. Thomas loves me and treats me like I mean the world to him. Nathan treats you like shit and will more than likely give you a venereal disease. Good luck with that." I stood and went to her door but before shutting the it behind me, I turned back to my sister. "I can't believe I was worried about telling you. You definitely deserve him." I slammed the door.

The next night, I was sitting outside on the porch waiting for Thomas to pick me up for our date. I was as excited about spending time with Thomas as I always was. It didn't matter how often I saw him; it was never enough. That excitement withered when a familiar sports car pulled up to the curb in front of the house. Prince Charming was here. *Just my fucking luck.*

He got out of his car and when he spotted me, he smiled like nothing had happened the night before. I was happy to see him with a nice black eye. At least I left him with a souvenir. I ignored him as he walked up in front of me, determined not to let him ruin my night.

"Hey there beautiful. Miss me?"
"Like a bloody hemorrhoid."
"Aw no need to get feisty sweetheart. I'm just trying to make conversation." He leaned forward with his palms against his thighs.

He was right in my face and I could smell the gum.

"Get the fuck out of my face before I give you another shiner." I warned.

"Got a problem with my girl buddy?" Thomas had appeared behind Nathan, looking very angry at the scene in front of him.

"Not at all. I was just telling her how beautiful she was today." Nathan turned his smile on him, daring him to make a move.

"Oh wow. What happened to your pretty mug? Piss of another girl's man? Glutton for punishment, aren't you?" Thomas taunted.

I stood and went to Thomas, taking his hand and leaning into him. When he looked down at me, I smiled brightly.

"No, that was from me. Surprised he doesn't have a broken nose to go with it." Thomas cocked a brow at me.

"Oh, my baby get into a scrap with the little bitch?" Thomas spared a grin in Nathan's direction.

"You two can fuck right off." He mumbled before stomping off to the door and walked right in like he owned the place.

"You seriously gave that fucker a black eye?" Thomas asked, pleased.

"Ass-hole hit on me at Billy's last night. Punched him in the nose and then the eye before kicking him in the balls."

"That's my girl!" He squeezed me in a side hug, obviously very proud of the way I handled the situation. "Wish I could have seen it."

"Well, he clearly didn't get the message if he was back at it again today." I sighed, following him to his car.

"If he pulls that shit again, you tell me." He was serious, the humour was gone and the look in his eyes was murderous.

"Aw, you gonna defend my honour?" He grinned, opening my door for me and giving me a kiss before
I got in.

"Can't people think that I let my girlfriend fight all her battles without me."

"Where are we going?" I asked when he sat behind the wheel.

"Mom's." *Oh God.*

This would be the first time I meet his mom. During the first few weeks of our relationship, he admitted that he hadn't told his parents about me. From what I understood, he didn't really get along with his parents but he never explained why. He told me he wanted to keep me to himself for a little while and avoid being interrogated about us every time he spoke to his mother. It bothered me at first, all I wanted to do was talk about him when he wasn't around so I couldn't wrap my head around the fact that he didn't. I wondered if my feelings weren't reciprocated. I refused to dwell on it. We were great together, why let one little oddity dampen what we had.

I was nervous. I knew what my parents could be like and the only other reference I had were Laurie's parents. Laurie's mom was drunk eighty-five percent of the time and her dad never paid attention to what Laurie and I did. I barely even heard the man speak. At least I could sure they couldn't be any *worse.*

The drive was way too short for my liking. I hadn't had enough time to psyche myself out. Thomas parked the car and unbuckled himself. When he noticed that I hadn't made a move to get out, he turned to me and waited. I was frozen.

"Babe?" He took my hand and squeezed, searching my face. "You okay?"
"I'm nervous." I was irritated when he chuckled.
"Nothing to be nervous about. Mom's going to love you and dad does whatever mom says." He assured me
"Well then why have you been avoiding this?"
"*Because* my mom's going to love you. If we didn't work out, she would have kicked my ass." I looked at him and he was smirking.
"You're such an ass." I shoved at his shoulder.
"But I thought you loved this ass." He poked out his bottom lip in an exaggerated pout.
"I do love that ass." I laughed and kissed him before taking a deep breath and getting out of the car.

He laced his fingers with mine and led me to the front door. We made it inside and had our shoes mostly off when an older version of Thomas came out of a room down the hall.

"Tom! Nice to see you, my boy!" The man was clearly happy to see him. He hugged Thomas and patted him on the back. "Who's this little lady?" He asked, reaching a hand out to me.
"This is Paisley, my girlfriend. Pais, this is my dad, Phil Shaw." I shook Mr. Shaw's hand and Thomas smiled at me cheerfully. It was nice seeing him this at ease. I assumed it would be awkward for him too, considering his living arrangement.

"Nice to meet you Paisley. Glad to know there's a girl out there willing to put up with Tom's shit." He grinned mischievously and the resemblance between father and son was adorable.

"You boys get out of the way! Let me look at 'er!" A woman came bustling out of the kitchen to my left. "Oh, she's gorgeous Tommy!" She wrapped me in a bear hug. I loved her immediately.

Thomas's mom was short, couldn't be much more than five feet tall. She was a ball of read-headed energy. She wasn't thin, she was a little more than healthy. The only thing Thomas carried of hers was her beautiful honey eyes. She was perfect and her joy was contagious, I caught myself smiling from ear to ear when she let me go.

"Mom, Paisley would probably like to breathe." Thomas pulled his mom away from me and distracted her with a hug and a kiss on her cheek.

"Oh, you cheeky little shit." She laughed. "I'm not that bad."
"This is my mom, Julia Shaw." He wrapped his arm around her shoulders, giving her a squeeze. "Mom, this is the girl who has be tied up in knots." This had his mom holding her heart and smiling at me.

"I am so glad you could make it hon; I've been dying to meet you." She hooked an arm through mine and led me into the kitchen. Thomas and Mr. Shaw followed, talking in whispers.

"Sit. We can chat while I finish up dinner." She pulled out a chair for me before going back to the stove and stirring whatever she had in her pot. "Thomas tells me the two of you met on a blind date?"

"We did. My friend Laurie is dating David."
"Oh! My David is such a sweet boy."
"He is a very sweet boy. He treats Laurie like a princess. I love him for that." Thomas caught my eye. He was watching me and he did not look happy.

"You love him huh?" He asked, not quite disguising his displeasure.
"Oh, you stop that, Thomas." His mom stepped behind him and swatted him behind the head. "She doesn't mean it like that."
"How do you know? Doesn't *everyone* just love David?" The question dripped with sarcasm.
"Tom, come on now buddy. It isn't a competition." Mr. Shaw put in calmly from across the table.
"Whatever." My mouth hung open at Thomas's attitude. "Where's Tanya?"
"She's over at Holden's place." Mrs. Shaw pulled out the seat beside Mr. Shaw and sat down with us.
"Who's Tanya?" I asked.
"Tanya is Thomas's younger sister." Mr. Shaw explained, looking at Thomas, confused.
"She's another one who is loved by all." Thomas added, standing to go to the fridge. He filled his arms with five beers before returning to his seat. He passed them out, leaving two in front of himself. His parents didn't even blink at his choice of drink.

"How did you and Mr. Shaw meet?" I asked, desperate to find a topic that might distract everyone from Thomas's rudeness.

"Julie, please. I'm not my mother-in-law." She requested. "In the girls' bathroom at the courthouse!" She got out between fits of uncontrollable laughter.

"Oh Julie, why do you tell people that? Can't you make something up instead?" Mr. Shaw was clearly embarrassed, though I'm sure it was far from the first time his wife had shared their story.

"I ain't a liar Phil!" She was still laughing, wiping tears from her cheeks.

"Well, you can't just leave me hanging now!" I couldn't help but laugh along with Julie.

"Aw fuck, here we go." Mr. Shaw grumbled, leaning back in hair chair and drinking his beer.

"Well, I was feeling pretty good, a bottle and a half of wine will do that to a girl." She began with a wink at me. "I had to use the toilet so I went off to the ladies room." She stopped to get her laughter under control. "I opened the door and there's a man standing against the sink. She looks over his shoulder and he looked so confused to see me there." More laughter. "He was gorgeous but when I got closer, I saw that he had his manly parts in his hand and was relieving himself in the sink!" Off she went, struggling to breathe through her roars.

"In my defence, I was drunk and sure I was in the men's bathroom. I thought I was going in a urinal." Mr. Shaw's face was red but he was chuckling.

"If that was the urinal, where in God's name were you planning on washing your hands? The same urinal?" She challenged, still smiling.

"I hadn't gotten there yet."

"How did you get from seeing him peeing in the girls' sink to dating?" I asked, curious.

"Well, I died laughing at the poor fool but we spent the rest of the night together. We've been together from that day on." She explained, smiling at her husband before he leaned over and gave her a kiss.

The two of them proved that true love existed. Not the kind my parents shared. The healthy kind, where both parties adored and respected each other. The fact that Thomas came from people like Julie and Mr. Shaw, assured me that he was capable of loving someone the same way. I reached over and took his hand, giving him a smile. My smile disappeared when he jerked his hand away and curled his lip at me angrily. He was still brewing. I quickly looked at his parents and was thankful that they hadn't seen Thomas's actions. They were still looking at each other lovingly.

"I hope you like pork chops with mashed potatoes and gravy hon. It's what Tommy requested" Julie stated, getting up to pull plates from the cupboard.

"I'm very easy to feed." I told her and she smiled.

"Glad to hear it. Drives me nuts when girls refuse to admit that they eat like normal people."

Julie started plating food so I got up to give her a hand serving. She seemed surprise with my initiative at first but handed me the full plate.

"That's for Phil."

When we were seated, Thomas and his dad picked up their forks. I was flattered that they had waited for us to join them before eating. The rest of dinner was filled with small talk. I adored his parents and couldn't believe I was nervous to meet them. I wondered why Thomas had always been so distant when talking about them. If they were mine, I would brag about them incessantly. With the mood he was in, I wasn't about to ask. He had four beers polished off and was halfway through the fifth when Julie pulled an apple pie out of the oven.

"I hope you like apple pie. I've been told mine is amazing." Julie said, placing the dessert in front of Phil so he could cut it while she got the forks and plates.

"That's because no one has the balls to tell you it tastes like soggy apples and cardboard." Thomas sneered before emptying his beer and going for another one.

"That's rude Tommy." Julie frowned, trying to brush off his comment but there was hurt in her eyes.

"I'm sure it's delicious Julie. The smell alone is making my mouth water." I smiled at her, eager to bring back her jovial attitude. Thomas counteracted my efforts with a sarcastic laugh.

We sat in awkward silence while Phil passed out pieces of pie. Thomas pushed his to the side and slouched in his chair with his beer. Phil and Julie didn't seem surprised with Thomas's surliness and it broke my heart that this was clearly a regular occurrence with the three of them. I wanted to slap Thomas and snap him out of it but my history with angry men told me that confronting him was a bad idea.

"I'm going to watch the game." Thomas announced, grabbing a couple more beers on his way to the living room. I let him go, deciding to stay at the table with Phil and Julie.

"I'm so sorry hon." Julie said when he was out of the room.
"It's not your fault Julie, it's his own fault for acting like a baby."
"You're right Paisley. Boy is spoiled." Phil said, getting up and grabbing a beer for the three of us. "We might as well get another one in before they're all gone."
"Thanks, dear." Julie tried to smile at her husband but she was still bothered.
"Why don't you tell Paisley about the time Tom brought your undergarments to the front yard for a yard sale?" Phil suggested with a mischievous smirk.
"He did what?" The picture I visualized had me laughing hysterically which brought a real smile to Julie's face.
"Oh, little five-year-old Tommy, saw the neighbours having a yard sale and decided he wanted to have a store in his yard too." Julie started, grinning at the memory. "Except little Tommy didn't want to sell his toys so he went into my dresser and found some bras that he thought I had no use for and some of my old ratty underwear. He brought them outside and laid everything in neat rows. He used spider man stickers for price tags." By the time she was finishing her story, she struggled to speak through her giggles.
"Oh my god, you must have been mortified!" I said but laughed with her. I could picture a little Thomas setting up a yard sale with his mother's intimates and not having a clue why she would be embarrassed.

"Julie wouldn't look any of the neighbours in the eye for weeks after that!" Phil chuckled. "I had to run and pick up all the gotchies from the lawn because she wouldn't go outside. Try explaining to a five-year old that he can't sell his mom's panties!"
"He always was a naughty little shit." Julie shook her head, smiling as she reminisced.

Phil and Julie told me stories about Thomas for almost an

hour when I realized it was getting late and I should probably start my walk home. Thomas clearly hadn't thought about how I was getting home when he decided to get drunk.

"I should head home. Good thing it's still warm, great night for a walk." I stood and pushed my chair in.
"I can drive you home." Phil offered kindly.
"Oh no, it's okay. I don't mind. Gotta work off that apple pie anyway."

Julie and Phil walked me to the door. I debated finding Thomas to wish him a good night but decided against it. I preferred ending the evening on a good note.

"It was really nice meeting you. Thank you very much for supper, everything was delicious. Thomas is very lucky to have such sweet parents."
"It was our pleasure. Thanks for coming Paisley. Don't be a stranger, we loved your company." Julie leaned in and gave me a tight squeeze.
"Don't let Thomas's grumpiness bother you sweetheart. He'll come around. If he doesn't, I'll kick his ass for ruining a good thing." Phil wrapped an arm around me in a half hug.

I smiled and waved before walking out the front door. I went to the sidewalk and started on my journey back home, going over the evening in my head. I was pissed that Thomas would treat his parents so poorly. He witnessed my dad's temper; it should have made him realize how blessed he was. His lack of care was part of the reason it bothered me so much. I was jealous and he was throwing away something I envied.

I was deep in thought when I heard someone running up behind me. I didn't have time to turn around and see who it was before someone grabbed my arm. I jumped and tried to yank my arm away before I realized that it was Thomas. I gave my arm another sharp yank, dislodging his grip. Under the street lights I was able to see the fury on his face.

"Where in the fuck do you think you're going?" He demanded

through clenched teeth.

"Home. Where the fuck else would I be going?" I spit back then turned to keep walking.

"Didn't think about saying bye to me? Huh? Maybe letting me know you were leaving so I could drive your bitchy ass home?" He followed close enough behind me that I could feel his hot breath on the back of my head.

"Why would I bother saying bye to you Thomas? You ended our evening hours ago."

"No." Again, he gripped my arm. He spun me around to get a hold of my other arm before getting into my face. "You put an end to our evening not ten minutes into it. You come to *my* house to meet *my* parents and don't see anything wrong with telling us all that you love *David.*" I could feel his fingers digging into me as he tightened his grip.

"Quit being such a jealous ass-hole. I love David with Laurie. I'm not *in* love with him. I'm not interested in him like that." I shoved at his chest, attempting to put space between us. I could feel my heart pounding in my throat and not in a sexy way. In that moment, I was afraid of Thomas. If he crossed that line, there would be no way for us to recover.

"I wouldn't be a jealous ass-hole if my girlfriend wasn't such a self-centred slut!" His grip tightened a little more and brought me up onto the tips of my toes.

"Wow Thomas. I never knew a virgin *could* be a slut." I blocked out the throbbing in my arms where his fingers held me, focusing on my anger instead.

"Virgin maybe. Doesn't mean you haven't sucked a lot of dick" He argued. When I rolled my eyes at his lack of confidence, his resolve wavered.

"One. Yours." I told him, my voice dripping with condescension. His hand dropped away like my skin burned him.

"With how often I see guys staring, I didn't think there was any way you'd be so inexperienced." A faraway look came into his eyes.

"Get this, yours is the first dick I've ever touched. Imagine that?" I threw out in an overly friendly tone and a fake smile.

"Seriously?" He was completely blindsided by this new information and I was frustrated that he thought so little of me.

"Yes. Don't worry though. After this, it'll never happen again." I shoved my finger into his chest to be sure he understood how serious I was. "I won't ever let myself lose control with a guy who treats his parents and girlfriend like shit." Poke. "Fuck you, Thomas. Fuck you for making a fool out of me tonight. Fuck you for making me believe that we had something special. Most of all, fuck you for taking away the little bit of hope I had that I would find a happier future for myself than what my parents have." Again, I turned away from him, determined to get away.

"Paisley." He wasn't following me this time. "Paisley wait. Please!" I just kept walking. I didn't look back, just held my head high and focused on the road in front of me.

I was gutted, completely broken. The confrontation with Thomas reiterated something that had always scared me. Women often married men who reminded them of their father. I saw that truth in Shella with Nathan. I was so sure that Thomas was nothing like my father. That he cherished me more than that. I believed deep down that he would never lay a hand on me but the bruises on my biceps proved that he would. No, he didn't strike me but he did leave marks. He didn't cross the line but he had stepped on it with both feet, leaving very little room for trust that he would land on the right side. He lost his temper with me so easily that it was hard to wrap my head around his reasoning. It hurt. I had given him the power to hurt me when I swore to myself many times, before Thomas came into my life, that I would *never* allow another man to have that kind of control over me. I was sure I had found someone who was worth the risk.

I cried into my pillow that night. I didn't want to share my pain. I wanted to wallow in it and punish myself for being so stupid. The second night I was on my bed in the fetal position, trying frantically to hold myself together, my body shaking with my sobs. I bit down on my knuckles, muffling the sounds coming from my mouth.

On the fourth day of my self-imposed imprisonment, there was a knock on my door. Thus far, I had appreciated the fact that everyone had left me alone to suffer in peace. I knew it wouldn't last forever but I wasn't ready to be interrupted yet.

"P-Baby?" I would have bet it was mom. I might not have been surprised if John came to my room. I would have been less caught off guard to see *anyone* but dad.
"Yeah dad?" He had his head poked into my room but when I sat up, he came the rest of the way in.
"What's going on baby girl?" He asked, sitting on the edge of my bed, searching my face. *Was he worried about me?*
"Just boy trouble. I'll be okay." I gave him a smile but my lips quivered as I tried to hold back a wave of fresh tears.
"I kinda figured as much. That boy has been calling here relentlessly."
"Next time he calls tell him to go fuck himself." It was the first time I had ever used that word in front of him. I didn't care. Apparently, neither did he because he chuckled.

"I've always been extremely hard on you kids." He began, serious again. "The world I grew up in was no place for a child. Love and affection were non existent. When we could walk, we were left to fend for ourselves. I didn't want that for you guys but I needed you to be strong enough to face anything. Especially when I'm no longer around. My temper always takes it to the extreme and that's not an excuse, just a fact. You kids are the greatest gift God could have ever given a man like me." He patted my leg lovingly and I could see moisture in his dark eyes. "You know, Shella and John are so much like your mother. Same light hair, same blue eyes, same temperament. They're your mother's through and through. You,

Paisley, you're all me. When you first came into the world, you stole my breath because I was so proud and there was no doubt as to who fathered you. Even watching you grow into the young woman that you are, I still see so much of myself in you. That probably pisses you off because I've been such a shit dad." He smiled sadly at me. "I don't mean it as a bad thing. You're so much stronger than I ever was. So independent with a good head on your shoulders. You make me proud P-Baby. Don't tell your brother or sister." He gave me a wink. "The only thing I want, is to see the three of you happy. Last week, you were happy. That boy made you smile more than you ever have before. Now, that happiness is all gone and it's breaking my heart to see you like this. Whatever happened between the two of you, is it really worth throwing it all away and making yourself so miserable?" He asked and when I didn't answer he continued. "Maybe you could just talk to him. Hear him out. Let him apologize. See if you two can work things out. I'm sure whatever it is, it's eating him up just as bad as it's eating you." He stood from my bed and pulled me to my feet to wrap me in a hug. He held me close for a couple moments before kissing me on the top of the head and leaning back to look me in the eye. "And Paisley?"

"Yeah?"
"Take a shower kid, you reek." He smirked and left my room, leaving the door open behind him.

# Chapter Four

## Being a Witness

Talking with my dad eased a lot of my pain and resentment where Thomas was concerned. I didn't immediately jump at the idea of forgiving him but I was headed that way. I got into a routine without him, determined to regain some independence. I was consistently getting stronger and bouncing back to my old self in the two weeks that followed the end of my relationship. I was in a much better state of mind and ready to jump back in.

Thomas continued calling daily. Twice on Saturdays and Sundays. I had to give him credit for persistence. I wont lie, I did wait a little longer than I had planned, wondering if he would give up. He didn't. The fact that the calls kept coming convinced me that there had to be something special between us.

On the third Friday, I was ready when the phone started ringing at the usual time. I waved my mother off when she came in from the kitchen to answer it. I let it ring another three times before picking it up.

"Hello?"
"Paisley?" I caught him off guard. He obviously hadn't expected me to take his call, let alone be the one to answer it.
"Thomas." I kept emotion from my voice even while my heart pounded in my throat.
"Oh God Paisley." He breathed, his voice thick,
"Is there a reason you're calling?"
"Christ, I miss you baby." I could hear the relief when he spoke. I let the silence hang in the air. "Are you still there?" My heart ached knowing he thought I would hang up on him. *Forget it Paisley, he did this to himself.*

"I'm here."

"How are you? What have you been up to? Have you thought about me?" He was spitting out questions, trying to get them all in while he had the opportunity. "Do you hate me?" The last was asked in barely more than a whisper but the emotion was loud and clear.

"I'm better now. I haven't been up to much aside from school and hanging out with Laurie and the girls. Of course, I thought about you Thomas." I took a deep breath before answering the last one, purposely making him wait for it. "I don't hate you. It would help if you would apologize but I don't hate you."

"Of course, I'm sorry. I've never regretted anything more in my life Paisley. I was such a dick and you didn't deserve that." I couldn't be sure but it sounded like he was crying. "I was never a jealous guy. With you, it's like I can't control that side of me. Like I'm waiting for you to realize I'm not good enough for you and you'll eventually meet some lucky ass-hole who is." I heard him sniffle, further proving that he was shedding tears.

"Thomas, you need to trust me. I told you I loved you and I meant it."
"Loved, as in past tense?"
"Love isn't an emotion that disappears dickhead." I heard a soft chuckle through the line.
"I love you Paisley. So much that you ignoring me has been torture." He sighed. "I even drove by your house a dozen times trying to get a peek at you." Another chuckle. "Didn't have the balls to actually knock on the door but I did drive by." I wasn't sure how I felt about his admission. Part of me melted but part of me was weary.

"Are you planning on driving by again tonight?" I hinted.
"No. I won't do that anymore. Sorry if it's weird." He didn't catch on.
"Well maybe you should."
"I should?" He was lost.
"Yes, you should. Maybe this time I'll be on the porch."
"Oh! In that case I'll be driving by in about ten minutes." I could hear him rustling around.
"All right. I'll see you then."
"Can't wait."

"And Thomas?"

"Yeah?"

"Make sure to stop." I smiled, excited to see him.

"Don't have to tell me twice. Paisley?"

"Yes?"

"Can I kiss you when I stop?" The hopefulness in his tone gave me butterflies.

"I'll think about it." Then I hung up before he could reply.

I took the stairs two at a time. Ten minutes. I rushed to my room and changed my shirt to the black tube top I had worn on our first date. I was hoping that he would notice and see it the same way I did, a chance to restart. I had to dig around for the jean jacket and was thrilled when I found it at the back of my closet. I quickly brushed my hair and bounced back down stairs.

"Mom?"

"Yes dear?" She answered from the kitchen.

"I'm heading out for a bit." I told her when I poked my heard through the threshold.

"All right, have fun and don't be out too late." She smiled at me from the counter where she was thumbing through one of her cookbooks.

"I won't. See ya later!" I called, already making my way to the front door.

I sat on the top step and waited. My body felt like it was vibrating from excitement. I forced myself to sit still and keep my cool. I didn't want Thomas thinking he had the upper hand. I needed to keep some of the control this time.

Looking down the road, I could see a man stumbling down the sidewalk and a voice in the back of my head told me who it was. He was clearly very drunk and that was never a good sign. The most brutal beatings began with dad walking home drunk. Alcohol left him without a fuse. The only way to avoid his wrath would be to remain quiet and out of sight. If we were unlucky enough to catch his eye, it would inevitably lead to a severe assault. No one was safe. Goosebumps covered my body and I prayed that Thomas would get here before dad did. The closer dad got, the more my stomach twisted in terror. I was out in the open, it was already too late to run inside and hide. I kept my eyes locked on dad and when he was passing the neighbour's front yard, Thomas's car pulled up from the opposite direction. He stopped in front of the house and I bolted to the car before he could step out.

The second my door was closed, I hit the lock. I looked up to see my dad standing on the sidewalk, eyes burning holes in my head. His fists were already clenched and there was no doubt in my mind that mom was in for a very long night. She would be wearing bruises in the morning but hopefully there wouldn't be any broken bones.

"Babe? Are you okay?" Thomas was worried, he hadn't noticed my dad.
"Just go, please. Just drive." I begged, not feeling safe while he was looking at me. Thomas pulled away from the curb and when he turned the corner, I could finally breathe.
"What's going on?" Thomas asked again, looking over at me.
"Dad's drunk. He was on the sidewalk when you pulled up."

I had never given Thomas many details about what happened at home behind doors. He had seen dad haul me away once. He knew that my father used physical discipline but that was about it. I never felt comfortable explaining everything to him and part of me didn't want him to pity me. There was nothing he could do to change my home life so in my mind, there was no reason to make him feel helpless.

"Well, that wasn't really how I pictured our greeting." He grinned at me, attempting to relieve some of the tension.

His grin hit me right in the stomach. He was so handsome. The time away had done nothing to tame my desire. Admiring him took my breath away and my heart swelled with our reunion. Being this close now, reminded me of why leaving him had hurt so bad.

"I missed the hell outta you, you know that?" I turned in my seat and leaned against my door to look at him.
"Then why the fuck didn't you take my calls?" He asked, still

smiling at me.

"I needed some time to re-evaluate."

"Re-evaluate?" His brows lowered with his confusion and he pulled into an empty parking lot and turned off the car.

"I want a healthy relationship, Thomas. I don't want to be with someone who makes me feel like shit. That night, you made me feel like shit and I was done."

"I'm so sorry Paisley. I don't want to make you feel anything but happy with me." His smile was gone, he looked broken and it tore me apart.

"I know that." I crawled over the centre console and sat myself across his lap. He wrapped his arms around me and buried his face against his neck. "I forgive you Thomas. I do but... if it happens again, I won't come back a second time."

"I won't let it happen again baby. Trust me, I can't go without you again." He didn't lift his head, he just snuggled closer and breathed me in.

"Are you gonna give me that kiss or what?" I teased, nudging him with my elbow. He looked up at me, happy and relieved.

"Bet your sexy ass I am." He said before cupping the back of my neck and pulling my lips against his.

The kiss started sweet but quickly caught fire. Everything we had missed in the last few weeks was poured into it. I pushed up against him, desperate to get as close as possible and his hand around my waist pulled me closer like he wanted the same thing. His tongue dipped between my lips to taste me. A low growl escaped the back of his throat, instantly making the flesh between my legs throb with need. I sucked his bottom lip between mine and ran my fingers under the bottom of his t-shirt. He had a thin trail of hair from his belly button down into the waist of his jeans. That little bit of hair made me crazy, I knew where it led and right then, I could feel the stiffness digging into the back of my thigh. I couldn't stop myself; I adjusted my hips and a moan escaped when it provided pressure where I needed it most. He broke the kiss and looked at me with hooded eyes. His lips hung open and his breaths came in short bursts. His hips started to rock up into me and the sensation was incredible. I gripped them hem of his shirt and pulled it up over his head, wanting to feel him. As soon as I tossed his shirt onto my seat, his lips came crashing back to mine. I could feel his fingers working the button on the front of my pants. When the zipper was down, he pushed his hand into my panties.

"Baby, you're so wet." He said, sounding surprised. "You're so ready for me." He panted and I froze. I grabbed his hand to stop him. "I'm not ready for that." I told him, scared. I was ashamed that I hadn't used my head. I was being a tease and it wasn't fair to lead Thomas on.
"Don't worry about it, babe. Let me take care of you." He said against my mouth. When he kissed me again, I let go of his hand.

I felt his middle finger slide down my centre, circling around the small nub that was aching with need. I pulled my mouth away and rested my forehead against his, unable to concentrate on his kiss while his hand was doing such wonderful things between my legs. I moaned and my nails dug into his shoulders. The pleasure was climbing and I was squirming against his hand. My eyes squeezed closed but I felt his on me, felt his breath against my cheek.

Just when I thought I couldn't handle it any longer, he plunged a finger inside me and I gasped. I leaned back, giving him easier access, my head falling on Thomas's shoulder. His finger slid in and out slowly, giving my body a chance to adjust to its intrusion. When he added another one, I bit my bottom lip to block a scream of pleasure. He started to really build momentum and within moments, I was coming undone. I felt my body contract around him and heard myself moaning his name.

"Did you like that?" He asked with a cocky grin.
"Not one bit. Worst experience of my life." I answered, generous with sarcasm. Thomas laughed, poking me under the ribs and forcing a giggle to escape.
"You're such a brat." He said before planting a firm kiss on me.

I wiggled out of his lap and back into my own seat. I reached for the front of his jeans and squeezed gently. When I got a hold of the zipper, Thomas's hand fell onto mine, stopping me from pulling it down.

"What's wrong? It's your turn." I asked, confused. Starting to feel the sting of rejection.

"No time baby. Mom wants us to head over. She's been nagging me since everything went down. She asked me to stay with them until I started feeling better." A blush darkened his cheeks.

"You were sick?" I asked as a poor attempt at softening the seriousness of his statement.

"Not exactly." He didn't smile. Instead, he turned the key in the ignition and avoided eye contact.

"Thomas, is there something I should know?" His reaction was unsettling, I silently willed him to look over and reassure me.

"I didn't handle what happened between us very well Paisley." He stayed focused on the road ahead of us, not even sparing me a sidelong glance.

"Are you going to elaborate or just let me think you did something completely crazy?"

"No, I didn't do anything crazy. I *went* crazy." Still, no eye contact.

I didn't push anymore. I watched the traffic glide by through my window. It was
something that we would have to discuss eventually but right now, I was willing to wait. The rest of the ride past in silence.

When we pulled into the driveway, Thomas finally looked over at me and the smile on his face was unsure. His self confidence was sexy but there was no way any straight woman could resist this new, shy side of Thomas.

I took his hand and gave it a squeeze before smiling and opening my door. I made my way to the front door. I didn't have to look behind me to know that Thomas followed. Before turning the knob, he took my hand into his and led me inside.

"Mom? Dad?" He called from the entryway.

"Oh, you're back!" Julie came rushing from the living room at the end of the hallway. When she saw me, her smile was blinding.
"Paisley!" She hugged me so tightly that breathing was difficult.
"I'm so happy to see you, hon!"

"I'm happy to see you too Julie." There was moisture in her eyes and it made my heart clench. I never considered the fact that more than just Thomas and I would be affected by what had happened between us. Thinking they remained neutral was incredibly naive. Thomas was their son, of course they would be impacted. "I hope you're not upset with me." I feared that she would resent me after the breakup.

"Oh no hon. I'm not upset with you. I'm..." She looked thoughtful, searching. *"Relieved."*
"Relieved?" Had she used the right word?
"Yeah, relieved." She hugged me again as if to reassure herself that I really was standing in front of her.
"Well. I'm not sure what to say to that." A nervous laugh slipped out.
"Well, Thomas has been miserable to be around lately. We couldn't even talk--"
"Mom..." Thomas cut in; his voice thick with warning.
"It's not a lie Tommy. You have been unbearably churlish. I avoided leaving my own room at times."

Her admission put a knot in my stomach. It was wrong for a mother to hide from her own son, in her own home. Thomas must have seen it on my face because he reached out to squeeze my hand. I didn't squeeze back. I couldn't shake the uneasy feeling I was left with.

"I was struggling Paisley. I was hurt and confused. I couldn't figure out how to process it." He explained, needing me to understand.
"He's right, he was in a world of pain. You are definitely the light of his life. I hope he apologized for the way he acted and that he grovels for a little while." She smiled again and it pushed the rest to the back of my mind for later inspection.

She put an arm around my waist and led me into the kitchen to sit at the table. She grabbed us all a beer and sat across from Thomas and I. There were shadows around her eyes that hadn't been there the last time I saw her. I didn't ask. Instead, I remembered that I had a favour to ask her.

"Julie, do you think I would be able to stay here tonight?" I asked, nervous about how she would react. It was common knowledge that letting your son's girlfriend stay over usually meant that they weren't going to keep things PG. I had limited options. Either I ask her or go home and face the monster I knew awaited me.

I caught her off guard, her lips parted in surprise but she didn't show any other emotion. She looked to Thomas, who wore his shock plainly on his face. Realizing that I hadn't discussed staying over with him, her brows lowered in confusion and she searched my face.

"My dad was drunk when Thomas picked me up. He's not really a friendly drunk." It was vague but she seemed to catch my meaning. "Has your dad ever put his hands on you?" She asked, worried but clearly very uncomfortable asking.

"Mom, that's not really any of our business." Thomas stated, looking at her like she had asked what colour panties I was wearing.

"It's okay Thomas. Yes Julie, my dad has used his hands on us. He's a firm believer in corporal punishment." I didn't elaborate. She didn't need to know that the punishments were not always justifiable. That sometimes, it went to extremes, which resulted in broken bones or concussions.

"Just punishment Paisley? Never... Sexually?" She pressed. The thought pushed bile to the top of my throat.

"Oh God no. Our dad is very tough on us but in his mind, he's doing what's necessary to raise good kids." I explained.

I felt oddly defensive of my father. It was the first time I had ever entertained conversation about what went on at home. I didn't like it. I didn't like that Thomas and Julie were both looking at me with pity, like they knew that I was downplaying it but didn't want to push me. They didn't know, they weren't there, in my mind, that meant that they had no right to judge my dad. He was my dad and he loved me in his own way.

"He's a good man. He takes care of us and makes sure we are all comfortable. I just don't like being around him when he's been drinking so I thought I would just stay out tonight." I polished off my bottle, trying to calm my nerves. "It's not a problem. I can just call Laurie and see if I can go there. Do you mind driving me there if she says it's okay?" I asked Thomas.

"Don't worry about it sweetheart. You can stay here, I don't mind. I can make up the couch for you and Thomas can keep himself in his own bedroom." She looked at him with a no-nonsense mom-look.
"Yes mom, I will lock myself in my room to protect Paisley's virtue" He rolled his eyes.
"Thank you, Julie. I really appreciate it."
"Do you need me to call your mom and let her know?" She offered.
"No that's okay. She knows I'm out and doesn't usually wait up for me." It wasn't completely true. Mom would be relieved, one less child to worry about. Not to mention, she was probably already licking her wounds.

"Hello?" Phil yelled from the front door before we heard the door close behind him.
"We're in here dear. Thomas talked Paisley into coming for a visit!" She called back to him.

He came into the kitchen, a smile already painted on his face. I wondered if there was anything that could put Phil in a bad mood. Him and his wife always appeared happy. Being around such a pleasant man was a foreign feeling. Not having to worry something would set him off meant that I felt safe in his presence, which was new for me.

"Hey Phil!" I greeted him happily.
"Hey kid gimme a hug!" He was coming towards me with his arms already open. I stood and let him wrap me in a warm fatherly hug.
"Missed you Paisley. Good to see you," He gave me another squeeze before letting me go. "I see you all got into the beer without me." He laughed, leaning over to give Julie a kiss before getting us all another round.

"How have you been doing Paisley?" Phil asked, settling into a chair beside his wife.
"I've been all right. Kept myself busy." I gave him a small smile. "I didn't realize how much I missed out on by spending so much time with Thomas. Two of my girlfriends are headed overseas for a whole month this summer. My friend Laurie got us weekend passes to the music festival in two weeks and that's going to be a blast, I can't

wait."

"Good for you kid. Sometimes taking a time out can be refreshing." I didn't miss the scowl Thomas sent his father.
"It really was. It was hard at first and of course I missed Thomas but I am better for it."
"Better for leaving me?" Thomas asked, his eyes were dark. If I didn't know him, I would think he felt nothing. But I did know him and to me, it was easy to see that there was anger but there was also hurt.

"Yes, I needed to leave you. After the way you treated me, I couldn't stay. I proved to myself that I would not settle for someone who would think it was okay to hurt me. I deserve more than that."

"Phil, you wanna take me to Billy's? I'll let you buy me a drink and play a game or two of pool. These two need to talk." Julie stood and held her hand out for her husband.

"I just got home!" Phil complained half-heartedly. Julie leaned over and whispered in his ear. "What the hell kind of man would I be to turn down an offer like that?" He stood abruptly and followed his wife out of the room. I laughed at their antics. It warmed my soul to witness a love so pure.

Alone, neither of us spoke. We sipped our beer, both waiting for the other to break the silence. We looked at one another, him unsure, me patient. After a while, Thomas stood and went to the cupboard above the fridge. He pulled down a bottle of spiced rum and two shot glasses before coming back to the table and sitting across from me. He poured us each two ounces of rum and slid one in front of me. We clinked out glasses and swallowed the alcohol. I could feel the burn down my throat and settled in my chest. When the bottom of the glasses touched the table, Thomas refilled them just as quick. I didn't hesitate, just emptied the glass. Again, he refilled it.

"Are you trying to get me drunk?"
"No. I'm trying to get myself drunk. It's only polite to refill your glass when it's empty."

"Ah, manners. Just being a gentleman? No ulterior motives" I asked with a smirk.

"Of course not. I mean, if you got drunk with me, I wouldn't be upset." He gave me a mischievous grin.

"Oh Thomas, what ever will I do with you?" I leaned back in my seat, enjoying the way his eyes slid down to my chest, full of heat.

"I have a few ideas." His Adam's apple bobbed.

"Yeah? Care to share?" I slid my glass over to him to be filled.

"Rather just show you but... it hurt Paisley." The hunger was still on his face but there was a shadow of pain with it.

"What hurt?"

"Hearing you tell my dad that you were glad you left me. I was here, losing my mind. Miserable. Knowing you were happier without me... it hurt." His eyes were full of moisture, the thickness I heard in his voice on phone was back.

"I wasn't happy not being with you Thomas. It wasn't the ideal situation but I took advantage of the time alone." I reached across the table and gripped his hand. "Seeing how persistent you were showed me how much this relationship means to you too and I needed that reassurance."

"Of course, I couldn't just let you go. I would have done anything to just talk to you." He turned his hand over to hold mine.

"I'm feeling pretty fuzzy." I laughed, tired of the seriousness. The boyish smile I loved so much covered his face.

"Me too." He topped up our glasses and held his up to tap against mine again.

This time, when I put my glass down, I stood and circled the table. He turned in his chair to watch my approach, curious. I straddled his lap and wrapped my arms around his neck while his hands instinctively went to my hips. He was eager for my closeness; the proof was pressing into my bottom. His lips parted as I leaned in to press mine against them. I gave him several teasing kisses before leaning back and pulling my shirt over my head. He sucked in a breath as his eyes drank in my breasts, barely hidden behind a lacy black bra. I reached down, grabbed the hem of his t-shirt and ripped it off. I wanted to feel his skin against mine. When I kissed him again, his hands roamed up my bare back, making me shiver. When his fingers landed on the clasp of my bra, he looked me in the eye to gauge my reaction, ask my permission. I nodded, excitement building at the bottom of my stomach with the thought of being bare in front of him. He undid the hooks and his eyes followed as it slid down. His gaze stayed locked on my chest while the bra fell to floor. Seeing his reaction, how he stared at me like he was starving, made me feel like a goddess. I ground my hips against him, sealing his lips against my own, panting, unable to get enough. Feeling the hair on his chest against my overly sensitive nipples made me crazy. When his hands slid up my rib-cage to the sides of my breasts, I moaned into his mouth.

The sound I made must have set him off because he stood abruptly, holding my thighs around his waist and lifting me with him. His lips barely took a break while he carried me up the stairs and to his room. A coherent part of my brain was shocked that he was able to carry me so effortlessly. Mostly, I was too focused on wanting Thomas to care. He laid me down on his bed and settled himself between my legs, rocking himself against me and the pressure produced another moan.

"Babe, you keep making those sounds and I'm going to lose it." He warned, nibbling my neck, just below my ear.
"What if I want you to?"
"What?" He leaned up on his elbows, looking down at me in disbelief.
"What if I want you to lose control?" I teased, wrapping my legs around his hips and squeezing into him, frustrated that our jeans were keeping us apart.
"Paisley, stop. You're not ready for that yet." He squeezed his eyes closed, struggling to keep himself in check.
"Thomas. Please." I begged, reaching for his zipper.
"Paisley..." His voice shook with the last remains of his resolve but he didn't stop me.

I unbuttoned his jeans and slid the zipper down. I used my feet to pull his jeans and boxers down his legs then kicked them to the floor. I gripped his shaft and squeezed him lightly. He groaned and his hands shook while he worked on my pants. He got to his knees to pull my bottoms off then ran his hands up my legs and between my thighs. When he reached the apex, my hips bucked against his hand with a will of their own. He cupped me and rubbed a finger across the nub that throbbed at my centre. When I moaned again, one of his fingers slid home, stroking deep into my warmth.

"I love that you're always so wet when I touch you. So ready for me. So..." He paused, leaned forward and ran his tongue over my clit, keeping his eyes on mine while he did it. "fucking sweet." He growled and the sound vibrated against me in an amazing way.

"Oh Thomas."
"Tell me what you want." He demanded, taking another taste.
"You." I whimpered.
"You have me. Be more specific." Another lick.
"More. I need more."
"More of my mouth or..." He straightened and wrapped a hand around his erection, stroking slowly.
"Anything! Please, just get me off." I pleaded, unable to think straight.

Thomas stood from the bed and I wanted to cry. I reached down to try and ease the ache myself when he turned. His eyes locked onto the hand I was using to pet myself.

"Hands off. That's mine." He ordered through clenched teeth. The irritation and hint of jealousy threw me off. I always assumed men enjoyed watching women masturbate.

"Then take care of it!" I whined petulantly, removing my hand and squirming on his bed.

He retrieved a packet from his dresser and handed it to me before crawling back onto the bed beside me. When I realized what it was, I had to swallow a lump in my throat. Reality cleared my lust fogged brain and my nerves set in. When I looked back at Thomas, there was no turning back. Succumbing to my cold feet would be utterly cruel.
If he noticed the shift in my focus, he kept it to himself.

"Put it on me." He requested in a husky voice.

I was surprised that my hands remained steady while unwrapping the condom and sliding it down his shaft. No sooner had my hands left when he fell on top of me, reclaiming my mouth. His hands were all over me, his patience gone and setting me on fire all over again.

When I felt him line up with my opening, butterflies celebrated in my stomach.

"Babe, this time it'll hurt for you but trust me, eventually it'll feel really good for you too."

He didn't wait for an answer or give me a chance to process what he said, just forced himself deep inside of me. Tears sprang to my eyes when my body protested the intrusion, my most private place felt like it was on fire.

My discomfort didn't slow him down. He kept pounding into me, seeking his own release. The pace aggravated the stinging so I but down on my lip to hold back my cries. When I felt him jerk and stiffen against me, I breathed a sigh of relief.

I was lost. I couldn't understand why my body was so eager during foreplay, craving sex when it was so excruciating. I was so grateful that I was wet beforehand or I may not have been able to stand it.

He laid down on top of me, satiated and breathing heavily while I wept in silence. My innocence was gone and the pain between my thighs felt like a punishment. When Thomas nuzzled the side of my neck, I was not comforted by his tenderness. After several minutes, he lifted onto his elbows to look down at me and I was thankful that my eyes were dry.

"I'm sorry I didn't last very long. You were so tight, there was no way I could stop myself." His hand came up to rest on my cheek before he leaned forward to kiss me.

"It's okay." I didn't know what else to say. In my pain, it felt too long, whereas to him, it hadn't lasted long enough. I wasn't going to share my thoughts with him, worrying that it would hurt his feelings.

"Will you stay with me tonight? Let me hold you while we sleep?" He asked, rubbing my cheek with his thumb.

"Your mom told me to sleep on the couch." I reminded him, not wanting to disappoint her when she was kind enough to let me stay. He chuckled, rolling beside me to remove the used condom before turning to me and pulling my back to his front.

"By the time they come back, she won't remember."

"Still, I can't disrespect her."

"Paisley, she wanted to keep up separate to stop us from fucking." He gestured down our naked bodies with his hand. "It didn't stop us so there's really no point now."

I was torn. Part of me wanted to spend the night feeling the comfort of his warmth, the other craved isolation. Goosebumps covered my body when Thomas trailed his fingertips over my hip and along my rib-cage then back again. I didn't have the chance to decide, my eyelids grew heavy and I quickly fell into the darkness of sleep.

Over the next few weeks Thomas and I spent every spare moment together. He would pick me up at school and bring me home with enough time to shower, get ready for bed and before falling asleep, he would call to wish me a good night. No one seemed bothered by the little time I spent at home or how greedily Thomas consumed my attention.

Aside from the first time, we did not have sex. I was too afraid and when he pressured me, my aversion to the idea grew. At the beginning, he seemed to just assume we would every time we were alone. Then he started hinting that he wanted more than a kiss or a touch here and there. The hints became more forceful, more demanding. We were now deep into passive aggressive territory and it was making me insane. I contemplated giving in to him but I knew that if I did, he would want more and so, we were at a stalemate.

From behind me, Laurie started tapping on my shoulder to get my attention. I turned in my seat to see her smiling at me.

"What do you want? Other than to get me a detention slip?" I asked, matching her contagious smile.
"I was wondering if you remembered my name?"
"Of course, I remember your name, Anne-Claude Van-Fuckelton."
"Ha-ha, fucking hilarious, bitch." She threw back sarcastically.
"Ms. Coleman, Ms. Stanley, something you ladies need to share?" Mr. Lotty asked, as irritated as always.
"Not at all. Paisley just asked if I had a tampon to spare. She's cramping and feels as though she may start leaking from her lady parts any second now." Laurie explained without an ounce of shame and a face full of forced innocence.
"Would you ladies mind discussing this out in the hallway?" He asked with a face a deep shade of red.
"Happily." She stood without hesitation and led the way out of the classroom.

Once in the hallway, she hooked her an arm through mine and smiled gleefully. We made our way towards the girls' bathroom, taking our time.

"So, tell me, where in the hell have you been? Too good for me now?"
"Of course not. I'm sorry, I know I've been a shitty friend."
"You really have." Laurie agreed, never shying away from complete honesty.
"I've been so... wrapped up in my own little world."
"I get that. It was like for David and I when we started seeing each other. Could never get enough."
"I don't remember that."
"Well, that's because I never shut you out, Pais. David understood that I needed my best friend and always encouraged our bond, didn't

want to come between us." She explained and for the first time, I saw how hurt she was.

"Laurie, I really am very sorry." I pulled her in for a tight hug, overcome with shame. "I hope you know that you mean a lot to me. I've always needed you too. I've been so selfish." Regret burned a hole in my throat.

"Don't sweat it babe, moving forward, I'll be harder to ignore." She pulled away to smile at me.

"I'll hold you to it."

"Now that we've discussed our need for more time, my parents are away this weekend and I have decided to have a small get together. Can I expect to see my best friend?"

"I'll be the first one there." I promised.

"And I suppose you can bring your boy toy." She added, feigning reluctance and making me laugh. For the first time since getting back with Thomas, I felt lighthearted.

I stood on the sidewalk after classes, waiting for Thomas in our usual spot. It was odd that he wasn't already parked at the curb when the bell signalling the end of classes sounded. I pulled out my history notebook to study while I waited.

I watched the last yellow bus leave the loading zone. Only a handful of cars were still parked in the lot and worry was steadily building in the pit of my stomach. We spoke the night before and he never mentioned anything about being late or unable to pick me up. I didn't want to leave, fearing he would show up the moment I left. I sat on the curb, leaning forward on my knees and resting my cheeks in my palms.

When my stomach started to protest in hunger, I decided to give in and make my way home. I had mixed emotions. If he stood me up, I would be hurt, furious but I was worried that something bad might have happened. It was a long walk home, by the time I got there, I was late for dinner. I had to decide between quietly heading upstairs to my room or face sitting at the table, late. I chose the former, closing the door behind me as gently as possible, not wasting time to take of my shoes. I made it four steps before I his voice stopped me in my tracks.

"Care to grace us with your presence Paisley?" *Fuck.*

After a deep breath, I turned and went into the kitchen. Not a peep was made when I crossed the threshold, except my stomach which decided then was a good time to growl loudly. Mom, Shella and John were all very tense, a clear sign that dad was not in a good mood. My ears burned as my nerves swirled in my throat. We all waited for the outburst that would surely accompany my lack of respect and not following the house rule for dinner time. To our surprise, dad seemed to ignore me. Instead, he picked up his fork and returned to his meal. Nothing happened until mom stood and went to the stove.

"You make a plate for her Johanne," She froze. "neither of you will sit comfortably for a month." Dad threatened. She returned to her seat obediently and glanced at me with pity. Obviously, it wasn't over, he was just making me wait for it.

I waited while everyone ate. My stomach grumbled more than once and I was annoyed that I couldn't hide the fact that I was hungry, that he knew I was hungry. When he pushed his plate aside and leaned back in his chair, he looked over at me. His eyes were dark and soulless. I hated when they looked empty, they scared me.

"What are you doing here Paisley? On the rag and can't fuck your boyfriend? Or did the boy finally sprout a brain and get bored with you?" He pried cruelly. I didn't have an answer, just bit my lip to deflect the pain in my chest caused by his words. "One day you'll understand that spreading your legs for some loser isn't as important as your family. Let's hope that you figure it out before you end up pregnant or with a rotten pussy." Standing, he grabbed the back of his chair in one hand and flung it in my direction. I managed to dodge the air-born chair but it crashed against the wall behind me, breaking apart, wooden pieces scattering across the floor.

The rest of us were frozen while he stormed out of the kitchen. No one moved for several minutes, unsure what was expected of us. Eventually, mom stood and filled a plate, placing it in front of me.

"Eat up quickly kiddo." She insisted, glancing between me and the entrance to the kitchen, both of us praying he stayed away.

I shovelled food into my mouth while she scurried around, picking up the remains of dad's chair. My siblings rinsed off their plates then John escaped out the back door while Shella went up to her room. Once mom had the floor tidied, she went to the sink to start washing the dishes. I managed to finish my food and hand her the empty dish without incident.

I leaned against the counter beside her, trying to avoid going through the living room to get up to my room. I knew he was in there, sitting in his lazy-boy and waiting like a tiger ready to pounce.

"The longer you wait, the more you torture yourself." Mom said, not taking her eyes off the post she scrubbed.
"I know. I'm just being a wimp." I sighed. "Thanks mom." I added sarcastically.
"Don't be sassy with me Paisley. It isn't my fault you were late to dinner." Her excusing his behaviour made me fume.
"Nope. It's definitely my fault he's a fucking lunatic." I spit out, leaving before she could retaliate.
For a second time that evening, I only made it up a few steps. Someone knocked at the door, halting my retreat. Thinking it might be Thomas, coming to beg forgiveness, I hurried to pull the door open, only to end up grinding my teeth at who stood in front of me.

"Paisley, my God it's good to see you."
"I'm not going to pretend the sight of you gives me any pleasure."
"I can't stop thinking about you, even if you were a bitch the last

time I saw you."

"*Excuse* me? *I* was a bitch? You have got to be fucking kidding me."

"It's okay. I forgive you. Show me your tits and I'll never mention it again." Nathan's vile face cracked into a suggestive grin.

"Go eat a bag of dicks you fucking sleazy ass-hole." I slammed the door in his face.

My fury was doused quickly when a hand gripped the hair at the bottom of my scalp. The hand turned my head and I was nose to nose with a raging bull.

"You think it's acceptable to treat guests at *my house* with such language?" Spit sprayed from between his teeth as his voice boomed in my eardrums. I was tempted to swipe the moisture away on my sleeve but I didn't dare make any unnecessary movement. "You think you have *any* say in who is or is not allowed into *my house?*" His grip on my hair tightened and I could feel strands ripping from my head.

He shook me violently, making me stumble over my own feet. Taking his hand out of my hair, he held onto my chin. His fingers were long enough to dig into my cheeks leaving me no choice but to face him.

"Understand something little *girl*." He said as though my gender alone made me inferior to him. "You are *nothing* in this house. You do what you are told when you are told to do it. You follow *my* rules. You have no right to treat company like shit." When his hand let go, my cheeks stung from the relief of pressure from my teeth.

I saw nothing but darkness for one heart-stopping moment when the back of his hand smacked the side of my face. The force of the blow brought me to my knees. I looked up at him, slightly dazed. I barely registered the fact that his hand was cocked when he hit me with a closed fist for the first time. I didn't feel the second punch that knocked me over or third because my head was swimming. My breath whooshed out when his foot swung into my stomach. I rolled away from him, curling my arms and legs into my stomach. Turning my back to him was a mistake. His foot continued its attack, pounding relentlessly. The pain was unbearable and thankfully, I blacked out.

I didn't know whether minutes had passed or hours before I came to. I could hear ringing and it exacerbated the throbbing in my head. It was only when it stopped that I realized that it was the phone. I pulled my knees under me slowly, testing the severity of my wounds. Nausea swirled in my chest so I waited before pushing myself any further. Ringing. Whoever was calling was persistent. Persistent. *Thomas.*

I crawled to the living room. The house was quiet and I wondered if I was alone. When I reached the end table where the phone was kept, I used it to pull myself to my feet. Again, I had to wait for nausea to subside. The phone was quiet but I didn't care. It didn't feel like anything was broken, just severely bruised.

I cried out when the phone rang again and startled me, making me jump. I breathed through the pain and picked up the receiver.

"Hello?" I asked, barely recognizing my own voice.
"Paisley?" Thomas asked, concerned. "I've been trying to call you for over an hour."
"Good for you." I didn't bother trying to disguise the bitterness in my tone. I didn't want to hear any of his bullshit so I replaced the receiver and made my way upstairs. When it rang again, I ignored it and locked myself in my room.

Ice pressing against my face woke me from a deep, dreamless slumber. I tried opening my eyes but only one would open and only part-way. I hurt everywhere. I groaned, wishing I could go back to sleep and not feel anything.

"Good morning sweetheart." Mom held the ice pack against the eye I couldn't open.

"Good morning." I whispered.

"How are you feeling?" I looked at her with my good eye, thinking she had a sick sense of humour but she wasn't smiling.

"How does it look like I'm feeling?" I snipped. "Wait, let me guess, I look like I'm having the time of my fucking life and you're confused."

"I was asking to find out where you were hurting most." She explained patiently.

"How about I tell you where it doesn't hurt?" My gut burned with resentment. "My toes feel fantastic."

"I'm trying to help Paisley."

"It doesn't matter mom. I mean nothing so just fucking leave."

"Of course, you mat--"

"LEAVE!" I screamed, the pressure pushing blood to the bruising in my face and making me whimper, bellying my demand that she leave.

"Calm down Paisley, getting mad isn't going to help."

She went to put the ice back on my face but I grabbed it and threw it at the wall. Her need to care for my wounds after her husband beat the shit out of me did nothing but fuel my desire to lash out at her.

"Leave me the fuck alone." I didn't raise my voice but the threatening tone was worse.

She turned and shut the door quietly behind her, not looking back. I breathed deeply, trying to calm myself down. I wanted to scream out my frustration. If reincarnation were real then I must have been a horrible person in my past life.

"Hello?"

"Paisley. Please don't hang up." Thomas pleaded.

"I won't."

"Where have you been? You disappeared on me."

"Home."

"And you didn't miss me enough to return my calls?"

"Of course, I did, I've just been... sick." I lied

"For two weeks?"

"Yeah, real bad stomach flu." The bruises on my face were almost gone, only a hint of yellow where they used to be dark blue and purple.

"Oh, I'm sorry baby. If I'd have know, I would have brought you soup or something."

"I wasn't exactly up for soup or something." I laughed without humour.

"What are you up to later? Want to hang out?"

"I'm still pretty weak Thomas..." I didn't want to see him just yet; afraid he would notice the discoloration.

"Tomorrow then?" He nearly begged.

"How about Saturday?" I offered.

"But that's three whole days away!"

"I'm aware." I laughed at his pouty tone. "I'm sure you will survive."

"Listen lady, I survived this long. It's a damn shame you're making me wait even longer." He teased.

"You're such a good boy." I mockingly praised him.

"Don't be a jerk. I gotta get to work. See you Saturday then?"

"I'll see you Saturday." I agreed.

"I miss you gorgeous."

"I miss you too." I was smiling when I put the receiver down.

"Well, isn't that a sight for sore eyes." Dad commented from the front door and my smile instantly disappeared. "I suppose I don't deserve to be graced with such a beautiful smile." He admitted, looking guilty and ashamed.

"I'm nothing remember? If I'm nothing then my smile doesn't matter." My heart softened, seeing him so bothered by what he had done to me but I refused to let it go.

"I say dumb shit when I lose my temper P-Baby, surely you know that I didn't mean it?"

"Just because you didn't mean it, doesn't mean it didn't hurt dad."

I went back upstairs to my room, leaving him to wallow in his own self-hatred. No one would question whether or not he deserved my cold shoulder. Least of all, him.

The next three days were uneventful and I looked forward to my date with Thomas. I took my time getting ready, doing my makeup and picking the perfect outfit. I wasn't sure what he had in mind but as long as I could spend time with him, I would be happy. I stayed in my room to wait for him to pick me up. I sat at my desk, going over my notes but struggled to concentrate. I was getting impatient, wondering what was taking him so long. It felt an awful lot like the day he didn't show up to pick me up from school. No way was I going to stick around and be forced to sit through dinner at home.

I grabbed my jacket and let mom know that I was walking to Thomas's house in case he showed up looking for me. The sun was just starting to set and it wasn't cold enough for my jacket yet so I wrapped it around my waist and enjoyed the gorgeous weather.

I was glad to see Julie's car parked in the driveway when I got there. At least the journey wouldn't be a complete waste. Thomas's car wasn't out front but that could mean it was either in the garage or he was stuck at work. I didn't mind visiting with his mom until he came home. I knocked on the front door and Julie was quick to answer.

"Hey hon, in the neighbourhood?" She asked, her usual smile was strangely absent.

"I had a date with Thomas tonight but he never came to pick me up so I thought I would just walk over and see what was holding him up." She looked uncomfortable and I began doubting my decision to walk over.

"Oh Paisley." She let out a sad sigh and held the door open for me.

"It's okay Julie, if you're in the middle of something I'll just go home and Thomas can call me later." I
offered, a sinking feeling in my stomach.

"No, no hon. Come on in. You're always welcome here."

I entered tentatively, wringing my fingers. She didn't lead me to the kitchen like she normally did, just slowly closed the door and stared at the carpet, deep in thought. She was struggling with something and by her demeanour, I guessed it wasn't going to be something small and petty.

"What's wrong Julie?"

"Do you know someone who could pick you up?" She prodded, making up her mind but whatever it was, it bothered her a great deal.

"Oh, if it's weird for me to be here without Thomas, I really don't mind walking--"

"Do you know someone who could drive you somewhere?" She interrupted me, clarifying her question.

"Yes..." I trailed off, confused.

She went down the hallway and came back with a cordless phone, handing it to me. After I called Laurie and she agreed to come and get me, Julie seemed to have settled down a little.

"Do you know that bridge over Joseph's creek?" She asked. I wrestled with the reasoning for the question, unable to figure it out.

"Yes." I answered, hoping she would elaborate.

"Get your friend to drive you there."

"Why do I need to go to Joseph's creek?" I was trying to hold on to my patience, wishing she would just spill it out and give up the pointless treasure hunt.

"I can't tell you Paisley. It's something you need to see for yourself." She pulled me in for a comforting hug that felt an awful lot like a good-bye.

"Okay." I relented. "I'll wait for Laurie outside." I added, eager to get out of the house.

Laurie made it in record time, pulling up in her dad's grey tundra. I rushed to the passenger side and hopped in.

"What's going on? Is something wrong?" She asked, surely as confused at I was.
"I don't know. Can you take me to the bridge on Joseph's creek?" I asked and she threw the truck into reverse.
"Okay..." She answered, looking at me like I was nuts. "Not to like, jump off or anything right?" She asked, knowing it was a ridiculous assumption but trying to ease my tension.
"I have no fucking clue what's going on." I filled her in on my visit with Julie.
"That's so messed up." Laurie always had a lead foot but we were on a mission where we didn't know the outcome. With the unknown urgency, she seemed to put more pressure on the accelerator. I wasn't going to ask her to ease up.

When we went around the last bend and pulled into the parking lot for the public trails, I could see a couple wrapped in each others' arms toward the middle of the bridge. The sinking feeling came back with a vengeance. I had a feeling I knew who was on the bridge and if I was right, all hell was going to break loose very shortly. Laurie came around the front of the truck, pocketing her keys and staring down at the same place I was.

"That better not be Thomas." She warned.
"I'm willing to bet you it is." My voice was a lot steadier than I was.

Side by side, we made our way onto the bridge. Halfway to the couple, it was clear that they were doing a lot more than kissing. The girl's skirt was up around her hips and the buckle on his belt was hanging against his thigh. A few steps closer and the side of his face became visible. It was Thomas, balls-deep in some chick who certainly wasn't me. They were so caught up in themselves that they didn't hear us approach. A few feet away, I stopped and pulled Laurie beside me to lean on the guard rail of the walking bridge. Pretending to be nonchalant in a devastating situation. I crossed my arms for added effect before interrupting the lovers.

"Well, looks like our date is going really well." I said loudly enough to startle them.

They jumped apart, her scrambling to pull her skirt down and cover herself, Thomas stuffing himself back into his jeans and quickly zipping up. When his eyes landed on me, panic set it.

"Paisley, baby. You weren't supposed to see that." He sprinted over but before he could put his hands on me, my hand shot out and slapped him. Feeling Laurie at my side, vibrating with her own fury put the steel I needed in my spine.
"You selfish prick. I wasn't supposed to see that? Who is she? How long have you been fucking her?" I was beyond livid. I could have torn his balls off and still burned with rage.

"No baby, she's just a way to let out tension. I know you don't want to have sex so I fuck her to get it out of my system." He explained, expecting me to understand because he had a valid reason to cheat.

"To get it out of your system." I repeated, unable to suppress my chuckle at the lack of sensitivity and utter stupidity of the situation. "Hear that, Laurie?"

"Yeah, almost like the idea that if he didn't use it, he would lose it." She answered in a cold tone, full of hatred.
"Baby come on; you know I love you." Thomas changed tactics, assuming he would win me over with charm.

To my utter shock, the dumb bitch Thomas was caught with, walked up beside him, wrapping her arm around his waist. I don't know how I managed to control my temper when he didn't push her away but I did. He just stood there, begging me with his eyes, while his slut had her arm around him.

"Thomas, I don't ever want to see you again. Enjoy stuffing your bimbo, I'll be spending my evening with Laurie. Who knows, maybe I'll find some other ass-hole to satisfy my needs, you know, *get it out of my system.*" I was gratified when he flinched as though I slapped him.

"Paisley, stop. You don't need to be like that." He said, using a condescending tone. The fact that he was getting past the poor me attitude made it easier to hang on to anger.
"Babe, forget about her. You don't need some bitch making you feel bad." The slut told him, rubbing her hand on his back.
"Oh, she knows how to talk?" I mocked surprise. "Who'd have thought she knew how to use more than just the fish flaps between her legs?"
"I definitely didn't. Scared the shit outta me when her upstairs lips moved." Laurie answered.
"Fuck you, you're just jealous that Thomas wanted me more than you."

"No hon, I'm just grossed out that he would fuck you, he could have paid a little more and at least got decent pussy. Maybe you should ask your pimp to fork over some of your tips to get yourself a new face." I suggested. Thomas had the nerve to laugh and my eyes zeroed in on him. "Why you would find that funny is beyond me. If you were worried before about losing it if you didn't use it, I would *really* worry after sticking it in that hole. I hope that shit gets gangrene and falls right the fuck off."

"Oh please, there's no need to get all pissy because some of us enjoy sex." The slut haughtily stated, crossing her arms and looking down at me.

My control snapped and I pounced. Her eyes registered her surprise but her arms didn't have a chance to uncross before I had my hands in her hair. I didn't fight cattily, I used her hair as a handle, pulling her face down while my knee raised, connecting with her nose, creating a sickening crunch. She dropped to the ground and I straddled her, feeding my fists into her bloody face.

Laurie came up behind me, pulled my arms behind my back and hauled me off of the bloody mess of a girl. When Thomas came to stand in front of me, I pulled all the saliva in mouth onto my tongue and spit in his face.

"Fuck you, you lying piece of shit. I hope it was worth it. I pray one day some bitch has the balls to castrate you, you fucking worthless ass-hole." Laurie continued to hold on to one of my arms while I screamed in his face. I loved her for it but I was glad she hadn't pulled me out of range and I managed to plant the toe of my shoe between his legs, hard enough that he could probably taste his testicles.

I kept my word. I went out with Laurie that night. We drank so much that I slept with my head in the toilet and my best friend in the tub beside me.

# Chapter Five

## If I Could Run Away

I held on to my anger. Catching Thomas with his fling was a visual that stuck in my head, making it easy to stay bitter. I spent the majority of my time with Laurie or Gemma, going to Billy's or hanging out at one of their houses. Laurie never mentioned what happened with Thomas, she knew I didn't want to talk about it and respected my need to avoid the topic. I didn't know what she told Gemma but she never brought it up either and I was thankful for the small reprieve.

"Hey ladies, what are we doing tonight?" Gemma asked, leaning against my locker where she waited for Laurie and I after our last class. "We gonna doll ourselves up and hit the new joint down on Guinness?" She suggested.

"Think our IDs would work there?" I asked to which she grinned. "Shouldn't be a problem, I'm dating the bartender." Her grin widened into a self-satisfied smile.
"Seriously? You lucky bitch!" Laurie exclaimed excitedly.
"Oh yeah and just you wait till you see how gorgeous this guy is. He'll scorch your eyeballs."
"Can't be that good looking if he's settling for you." I jabbed at her,
"Wait, you'll see. You'll be licking the floor when you see him." She warned me.
"Looks like we're going to scope out Gemma's new man tonight." I said to Laurie.
"I'll bring David she he can hold me back." She smiled. "We going to my house now?"

"Sure." I grabbed my bag from my locker and stuffed the books I needed into it. "You coming too?" I looked at Gemma who slanted her head, pretending to weigh her options.

"I guess, haven't got anything better to do."

"Oh, well I'm glad you're willing to allow us to entertain you." Laurie smirked.

"You know how it is Laurie dear, gotta keep your bitches close when boys come sniffing around. You girls are like my prick sniffing dogs, you sit pretty when you the ass-holes." We laughed, knowing Gemma had an affinity for jerks. I had some doubts after my recent escapade with Thomas but I didn't let thoughts of him dampen my mood.

When we entered the bar, the three of us were dressed to turn heads. I let them dress me up like a doll, paint my face and twirl my hair in some kind of curly half up style that used an ungodly amount of bobby pins. I felt pretty and seeing older guys turn their heads for a better look, did wonders for my confidence.

Before we found a booth, a guy standing by the bar raised his arm to wave us over.

"Oh, there's Travis." Gemma smiled and pulled Laurie along beside her to meet up with him. Laurie made a grab for me but she was out of reach and I wasn't in a hurry, just wandered along behind the.

I felt a hand grip mine from behind and my first thought was that drunk boys were very bold.

When I turned to see who it was, my jaw dropped. Of all the places he could be, of course I would run into him here. I ripped my hand free and used it to shove him away.

"Keep your fucking hands off of me." I snarled.

"Paisley, you shouldn't be here. Let me take you home." Thomas offered and I couldn't tell if it was concern I heard in his voice or something darker.

"Where I go, is none of your goddamn business."

"When you show up in a bar dressed like slut, it's everyone's fucking business." He raked his eyes meaningfully over my outfit. The skirt was shorter than I would normally wear, stopping mid thigh and the sleeveless blouse only showed the top of my cleavage, normal people would not consider my outfit shamefully revealing.

"Don't sweat it Thomas, I'm perfectly capable of deciding whether or not I want to fuck some guy I met at a bar." I turned away to join Laurie and Gemma but his hand wrapped around my forearm. His grip was tight, biting into my skin.

"I don't share." He stated quietly, his lips barely moved but I could feel the heat in his hand, his blood was boiling.
"I'm not yours to share."

"The fuck you aren't." He gave my arm a solid yank making me fall against him. Before I could pull away, his free arm wrapped around my back, locking me in place. He leaned in close to my ear. "You gave yourself to me the second you spread those legs and let me be the first to fuck your needy little pussy. You told me you loved me and that those feelings don't just disappear so stop playing hard to get baby, we both know how easy you really are." I was so flabbergasted by his words that I couldn't even feel angry.

"I'm easy? Then why did you have to fuck some other chick when we were together?" I spit the excuse he used on the bridge back at him.
"So, I fucked up, get your snobby ass over it. You're not better than me just because I made a mistake."
"I don't have to get over it, Thomas. You need to get over the fact that I'm done. Go call Miss Skank, maybe she has the time for your bullshit."

"Hey man, I think it's time for you to call it a night." *Holy shit.* The guy was a fucking drool inducing God. His hair was dark, shaved on the sides and longer on top, hanging just above the darkest blue eyes I had ever seen. Thomas stared at the hand on his shoulder like he wanted to tear it off of the guy's arm.

"Walk away." Thomas warned.

"I'm just trying to help you out buddy, people are looking at you weird, I think the couple in the booth behind you are thinking about calling the cops." The gorgeous God held his hands up in surrender in an attempt to dissuade an altercation. It worked because Thomas's hands fell back to his sides as he looked around the room, noticing several people glancing at us curiously.

"Fine." He turned back to me and spit on my shoes. "Fuck you bitch. This conversation isn't over. I'll be seeing you." Then he walked away, shoulders tense with wound up energy.

"You, okay?" The God asked, looking me in the eye, a frown on his beautiful full lips. All I could think about was how those lips would feel. They looked so soft. When the frown crept up into a knowing grin, I realized that I had been staring at his mouth and my cheeks instantly burned. "I'm Connor." He held out a hand.

"I'm mortified." I shook his hand, unable to hold in the embarrassed giggle.

"That's a fucked-up name for such a beautiful girl." He laughed, his hand lingering on mine.

"Paisley's my real name. It's nice to meet you Connor and thanks for rescuing me from my psychotic ex." I smiled, stunned stupid by his gorgeous face. To save myself from further humiliation, I headed in the direction I last spotted Laurie and Gemma.

Both of them were still by the bar, watching the exchange with Thomas, sharing the same look of disgust.

"What did that ass-hole want?" Laurie asked when I was within earshot.

"To drag my ass outta here for looking like a slut." I accepted the cocktail Travis handed me. "Thank you. I'm Paisley." I introduced myself.

"So I've heard. First time I've had to hold two chicks back from trying to claw out some dude's eyeballs." I laughed, knowing he was telling the truth.

"Yeah well, it probably won't be the last time. We take turns. There may even be a time where you'll have to hold all three of us back, you ready for that?"

"As long as you guys aren't aimed at me, I'll manage." He had perfect white teeth and movie star dimples. I could see why Gemma liked him.

"No promises." Laurie put in, clinking her glass against mine.

"Here, here." Gemma agreed, taking a swig of her drink.

"So, who's mister sexylicious?" Gemma asked, tilting her glass towards the God who had joined a group of guys at the other end of the bar, his eyes still locked on me, full of charming mischief.

"That Gemma, is the Pussy-God." I dubbed him.

"Pussy-God? I feel like I'm the gay friend in a girl gang." Travis pouted, emptying his bottle and signalling the bartender on shift for a refill.

"Oh, don't worry, you're the Wet-Panty king." Gemma reassured him with a kiss on his cheek. Laurie smacked her on the arm.

"Gem! That's private!" I laughed along with her when Travis flushed.

"Next time, get your own damn drink Trav, I'm not your bitch." The bartender smiled at us, emptying his tray filled with a fresh round.

"Thanks, handsome." Gemma smiled.

"No need to thank me, just gimme your friend's number and we'll call it even."

"Well, this one's taken." Gemma poked Laurie in the ribs. "And this one is crazy." When she poked me, I laughed out loud. The bitch knew I was ticklish, she did it on purpose.

"I like crazy." He winked at me before going back to work before the crowd got jealous with the attention he gave us.

"Wow, Thomas, Pussy-God and now the bartender. Jesus Pais, you're on a fucking roll!" Gemma teased. "You should let me play makeover with you more often!"

"You're always gorgeous my friend." Laurie told me, wrapping her arm around my shoulders and planting a kiss on my cheek. "Don't ever change," She added in my ear.

For three days I couldn't shake the feeling of being watched. The feeling ceased when I was in class but would resume the minute I stepped out of the building to catch the bus. The hair at the back of my neck was constantly standing. I could no longer change in my own bedroom, I felt exposed. I didn't tell anyone what I was feeling, it felt like if I shared my concerns, it would make it more real. I kept telling myself I was just being paranoid and to calm down. No one had the time to follow my boring ass around.

Unfortunately, when the fifth day rolled around and my unease persisted, I was slapped with the first piece of evidence proving my instincts were spot on. I was stepping onto the bus when I noticed a black truck with heavily tinted windows parked right outside the loading zone. I'm not sure what drew my gaze to the truck, aside from the fact that I had never seen it before. Something told me to pay attention to it, so I did.

I checked the window on the emergency exit at the back of the bus regularly throughout the ride home. The truck never strayed farther than two cars behind. Turning every time the bus did, stopping whenever we came to someone's stop. For the first time, I wished that Shella took the bus with me.

I wanted to cry with relief when I got off the bus and the truck stayed behind it. I even laughed at myself, feeling stupid. The uneasy feeling of being watched had also disappeared and I chalked it all up to an overactive imagination.

I was in a great mood for the rest of the evening. I called Gemma after supper, sharing some gossip and laughing with her until it was time to get ready for bed. I took a hot shower and forced myself to get dressed in my room. I was wrapped in a towel and rummaging through my dresser for some pyjamas when I felt the need to look out my window. Outside, parked by the curb right across the street was the black truck. My heart stopped. I tried telling myself it was just a coincidence but there was no way I could calm down. I ran to the linen closet and pulled out the darkest sheet I could find, navy blue. Standing on my desk chair, I hung the sheet in my window, making it next to impossible to see into my room. I fell asleep under my window, curled in a ball.

My eyes opened the next morning and the darkness in my room threw me off for a moment before I remembered the sheet. My heart pounded against my rib-cage, terrified to look outside and see the truck still parked on the road. My glowing alarm clock told me it was six in the morning. I stood on my knees and peeked under the sheet. The truck was gone. I could breathe.

I took my time getting dressed, dragging my feet to the kitchen. I considered playing sick and staying home but I couldn't give in. I had to keep going. If the black truck was following me, whoever it was, wasn't going to see anything exciting and the sheet was staying in my window. I didn't taste my cereal but I emptied the bowl anyways. I sipped my coffee in silence, unable to enjoy it the way I usually did. I didn't say a word when dad left for work or when Shella skipped outside to hop into Ryssa's car. John was always the last to leave, it was only a ten-minute walk.

I grabbed my bag and slung it over my shoulder, making my way down the road to wait for my bus. I only had to wait a few minutes and when I took my seat, the truck was not in pursuit. At the next stop, I didn't bother looking. I knew it was there, the hair on my neck stood at attention. My shoulders slumped, heavily weighed down.

Everywhere I went, the truck made an appearance. When Laurie and I went to Billy's the following Saturday, it was parked out front, the driver staying behind the wheel.
"Have you noticed that truck following you around?" Laurie asked, watching it curiously from our booth.
"Yeah."
"Who is it?"
"I have no idea."
"What the fuck? How long has this been going on?"
"About a week." I refused to show her how much the truck's presence impacted me. Part of me still thought that denial was the safest route.
"And you never thought to mention it?" She was annoyed with my

lack of reaction. "Paisley, this is serious!" She insisted.
"He hasn't done anything worth worrying about. Nothing I can do about a truck following me around. Whoever it is, will get bored soon enough." I assured her even though I had my doubts.
"So, you're just going to wait until he does something? Maybe kidnap you or rape you?" She looked at me like I was off my rocker. "Are you seriously that stupid? I should fucking slap you!"
"When I first noticed it, I thought I was just paranoid. Then I didn't want anyone to think I was crazy."
"Paisley, you could have told me. I'll always have your back. Even if no one was following you and you were crazy, I'd go to the nuthouse with you."
"How the fuck do I deserve you?" I was genuinely blown away by her doubtless loyalty.

Laurie smiled at me and squeezed my hand across the table. When the waitress passed us, she raised her hand to catch her attention.

"Can we get four shots of tequila please?"
"White or gold?"
"White."
"On it."
"Four shots of tequila? Are you kidding me?" I asked.
"Liquid courage my friend."
"Oh God, what do we need courage for?"
"We're gonna confront stalker boy."
"Could be a girl."
"Doubt it."

The waitress came back with the four shots and lined them up on the table with lemon slices. Laurie slid two in front of me and grabbed the other two.

"To fucking shit up." She held up both shots for me to cheers.
"Ditto."

We took our first shot, quickly followed by the second before the alcohol had time to burn in
our throats. Neither of us could stomach biting into the lemon so we

squished our faces until the alcohol settled.

"Lemme know when the room turns fuzzy and we'll head outside."
Laurie giggled.
"Shit, the room was fuzzy twenty minutes ago." She laughed out
loud.
"Fifteen for me!" She onto the table, cramping.
"You're such a dork." I snickered.
"Let's do this." She ordered, barely keeping herself contained.
"If you say so."

 I forgot my reservations, caught up in Laurie's energy. We
hooked arms with each other, confidently striding to the door. We
pretended to stroll past the truck but our attempts were unnecessary,
the driver's window was open. Thomas sat behind the wheel, looking
at me like he expected me to be thrilled to see him.

"What in the fuck are you doing?" I yelled. "Why are you following
me?"
"Just waiting for you to figure your shit out."
"Figure my shit out?"
"Yeah, eventually you'll come crawling back." He smirked,
overflowing with confidence. I laughed and his smirk faltered.
"Are you ill?" I planted my hands on my hips, gifting him with a
look filled with revulsion.
"Not even a little bit." He answered, undeterred.
"I'm not going to take you back. What you did to me is
unforgivable."
"I don't give a shit if you forgive me Paisley. You just need to get
over it and stop acting like a spoiled brat."
"Thomas, I am only going to say this one more time. Fuck. You." I
added my middle finger for emphasis.
"You can't get rid of me."
"What's that supposed to mean?"
"It means I'm going to be everywhere you go, watching everything
you do. I'm going to make sure your life revolves around me, even if
that means trying to avoid me or praying, I go away." His smile was
evil. "Eventually, you're going to break. When you do, I'll get what I
want."

"You're fucking psychotic. She'll be getting a restraining order."

Laurie warned him, holding onto my arm and pulling me away from the truck. He laughed and it was an ominous sound.
"You're so fucking stupid Laurie, a piece of paper isn't going to help."

We turned and went back into the bar to use the phone. I wanted to go home and hide under my bed for the rest of my life. When the cab pulled in front of my house, Laurie offered to stay with me but I declined. I wanted to be alone and she didn't deserve to be pulled into my mess.

I silently shut the door behind me, making sure to turn the deadbolt. I took a step towards the kitchen to get a glass of water but stopped dead in my tracks when I saw dad sitting in his chair watching one of his old movies. *Not tonight. Of God, please not tonight.* His eyes turned toward me and his face scrunched in confusion.

"What's wrong with you P-Baby?" I let out the breath I was holding, he was sober.
"Oh dad, everything's a mess." I answered vaguely. He flicked off the TV with the remote and sat up in
his chair, looking troubled by my answer. He jerked his head towards the couch beside him, signalling me to have a seat.

I flopped down and let the tears slide down my cheeks, deflated. The run in with Thomas had zapped away my drunken state and I was drained.

"What's going on?" He asked, gulping Pepsi from the 2-litre bottle he kept by his chair.

"Well, I caught Thomas having sex with some other girl a couple weeks ago." I began and everything poured out. I laid it all out for my dad, my first confrontation with Thomas in the bar, not caring what he thought about me being there underage, the truck stalking me and the way he reacted when Laurie threatened him with a restraining order.

"Has he hurt you before all this?" He asked and I noticed he was trying to keep his temper under control.

"No." I assured him, leaving out the bruises Thomas left on my arms the first time we broke up.

"Paisley, there's something wrong with that boy." He warned.

"I know dad. Trust me, I figured that out the hard way."

"Listen, wait it out. Chances are, some other girl is going to turn his head and he'll lose interest. If he doesn't, let me know. I'll take care of the little punk."

"Thanks dad." I stood, ready to collapse in bed but dad grabbed my hand before I left the room.

"I mean it Paisley." His eyes burned into mine. "If he's still pulling this shit by next weekend, tell me." He insisted.

"I will." Completely out of character, I leaned over and kissed my dad on the forehead lovingly. "Thank you, dad."

"Love you P-Baby." He rubbed his thumb across the back of my hand before letting it go.

Monday morning, the black truck made its regular appearance behind the bus. I rolled my eyes, irritated now that I knew it was Thomas. I went about my routine, less afraid of the invasion. Knowing who drove the truck eased my fear of the unknown. I knew what Thomas was after and I was sure I would be able to handle it. I hoped dad was right and that some girl would steal his attention. I felt bad for whoever it would be but I didn't concern myself with the idea.

When Thursday rolled around, I was almost able to forget the black truck existed. After school Laurie, Gemma and I were walking around the mall, ducking into a store here and there mostly using shopping as an excuse to hang out together.

The three of us were laughing at something stupid Gemma was saying when I looked across the mezzanine and locked eyes with the God. His smile flashed and he held up a hand in the universal signal to wait.

"Shit, the Pussy-God is here." I informed the girls.

"Oh, where is he?" They both looked around, trying to spot him.

"On his way over." I nodded to where he was making his way to us.

"Don't worry Pais, you're looking cute as hell." Gemma assured me.

"Hey beautiful girls." Connor greeted when caught up to us.

"Well thanks but we all know you came to check Paisley out." Laurie grinned when he didn't even flinch.

"I won't deny that. I couldn't help it." He focused on me. "You didn't give me a chance to get your number last time."

"Connor..." I scrambled to find words that wouldn't hurt his feelings.

"As you saw, I just had a nasty breakup. I'm not ready to jump back on the horse." *Fuck. Not the right words, dumb-ass.* He smiled.

"Well, I can leave you my number and when you *are* ready, I wanna be the first guy you call." He offered.

"I don't think--"

"Of course, she'll take your number." Laurie interrupted, handing him a pen and her notebook.

"We'll make sure she's *back in the saddle* as soon as possible." Gemma added with emphasis on the double entendre. I jabbed her with my elbow. "Don't be feisty, we all knew what you meant." My friends laughed along with the God while my face caught fire.

Connor wrote down his name and number on the paper from Laurie, adding a couple hearts beside his name, making me smile. He gifted me a gorgeous smile when he handed me the ripped-out piece of paper.

"Hey Con! Let's go man, I'm starving!" One of his friends yelled over to him. Connor flipped him the finger before leaning in and leaving a gentle kiss on my cheek.

"See you around beautiful girl." He made his way back to his friends, glancing over shoulder at me once more before joining them.

"Shit girl, if you don't ride that horse soon, I'm gonna kick your ass." Gemma threatened, staring at the group of guys as they walked away. I shoved her playfully, my cheeks still flushed.

"I'll hold her down for you Gem." Laurie offered.
"Fuck you." I laughed.

I didn't think about the truck again until I was walking home by myself. Laurie's mom picked her up and Gemma stayed behind to wait for Travis. I checked over my shoulder and didn't see it trailing me but that didn't seem to be enough to ease my nerves. I pulled up the hood on my sweater and slouched my shoulders in a sad attempt to disguise myself. I picked up my pace, earning a few curious stares with my determined speed-walk.

I could see my house down the street when the terrifying rumble showed up behind me. I heard myself whine. He had never stopped the truck this close to me before. He usually stayed within eyesight but with enough distance to avoid drawing the attention of bystanders. I regretted my decision to walk home alone.

I screamed when he grabbed me from behind but there was no one around to hear me. I put everything I had into trying to wiggle free but it was useless. He dragged me to the open passenger door and bent me over the seat, pulling my arms behind my back. He wrapped a thin piece of hard plastic around my wrists and when I heard him pull it tight, I knew it had to be zip ties. He over-tightened them and the ties dug in, any movement made them tear skin. Next, he stuffed a rag into my mouth before hauling me up into the passenger seat. I kicked out and managed to catch him in the stomach. He bent over to recuperate but stood in front of the door, blocking my escape. When he straightened, he delivered a blow to the side of my head, making my surroundings go out of focus. He grabbed a rope from the floor of the truck and tied it around my ankles, looping the end around the bottom of the seat. I had no idea how I was going to get myself out of the situation I was in.

When he pulled into the driveway at his parents' house, I breathed a sigh of relief. There was no way Phil or Julie would allow this to continue. I just had to wait until they showed up. Thomas parked the truck in the garage and hauled me onto his shoulder carrying me into the house through the side door so neighbours wouldn't see him. I was confused when he passed the stairs and went down the hallway. When he opened a door, I realized that it led into the basement and my heart sank. Basements freaked me out. Once at the bottom, Thomas dropped me carelessly onto a bed. I looked around and saw that the basement had been converted into his bedroom. I went berserk when he pulled his shirt off, assuming he was going to force himself on me.

"Calm the fuck down Paisley. I'm not going to fuck you until you beg me to." Bare chested, he grabbed a pair of scissors from his end table before joining me on the bed.

With a quick snip on the zip tie at my back, my hands came loose. I barely had time to check the rawness of my wrists before he grabbed a hold them, retying them in front of me. Laying down behind me, he pulled me close, spooning me but leaving a gap between my ass and his hips.

He pressed his face into the back of my neck, inhaled deeply and groaned. His hand drifted from my waist and over my hip before it disappeared. I waited, certain he planned to grope me but he didn't. The breaths against my neck became heavy and the bed started to shake. When he began to moan in time with his chest jerking against my back, I realized what he was doing and bile rose in my throat. I remained stiff as a board, even when he finished and I could feel warm moisture on the seat of my pants. Sated, he roughly pulled me against him, eliminating the space in front of his groin. My stomach rolled when I felt his softening dick against me.

"You smell so sexy." He said, taking a deep breath through his nose. I could feel his hand snaking over my waist. Steadily it crept across my stomach and upwards towards my chest. He didn't touch my breasts but his thumb made it between their mounds, rubbing back and forth and grazing the inside of their fullness. "You're so fucking soft." Unsatisfied, his hand made it's way down and this time he squeezed me intimately between the legs. "I miss this perfect pussy." He rubbed two fingers my jeans, applying enough pressure to be sure I felt them through the fabric of my pants and underwear. "I bet it's soaking wet right now."

"Get your fucking hands off of me or I swear I'm going to tear you into pieces, you psychotic prick!"

His hand shot to my head, balling in my hair. He yanked, forcing me to bend my neck and see the violent temper on his face.

"You think it's smart to threaten me?" His voice was frighteningly calm in contrast to the look on his face. "I can do whatever the fuck I want to you right now. You're fucking lucky I haven't used those scissors to cut your pants off and fuck your brains out." Steadily his hand pulled harder on my hair and my scalp was stinging in protest. "You probably let that dickhead from the mall bury himself inside you. Why do you keep pretending you don't want it?" His lips curled against his teeth. His own words infuriating him even further.

"Fuck you, Thomas. I can sleep with whoever the hell I want and you sure are shit are not on my list." I stated defiantly.
"Keep talking Paisley. You're only making things worse for yourself." He warned.
"There's only so much you can do before your parents get home."
"You're right." He smiled but his eyes were dark. "Luckily, there's a lot I can accomplish in four days."
"Four days?" *No, no, no!*
"Mommy and daddy went on a little trip. We have the house to ourselves for a few days, *babe.*" He added disdain to the endearment.
"You don't think my parents will come looking for me?"
"Who gives a shit if they do? They come to the door and I just have to tell them I haven't seen you since we broke up." He grinned when the true gravity of my situation hit me. "What's wrong Paisley? Where'd that smart mouth go?" He taunted.

I didn't bother engaging him for the rest of the night. I laid on his bed silently while his hand petted me like a cherished family dog. I focused on detaching myself from the situation and hoping that an opportunity to run would present itself.

On the third day, I felt disgusting. Thomas hadn't permitted me to shower and my hair was so greasy it fell in clumps around my face. I sat up in his bed and stared off into space while he was away at work. I learned about the locked door the first day and didn't bother trying to haul myself up to the window again, the third time I tried, I rolled my ankle when I lost my grip. I always thought I was strong but when I woke up that morning, my fight was gone and I was ashamed of myself for losing hope so quickly.

I heard something moving around upstairs. It was too early for Thomas to be home. I tried to keep my excitement under control, fearing I was losing my mind. I didn't rush to the door, thinking maybe Thomas left work early. I could taste copper in my mouth, my teeth were digging into my cheek as I listened intently for more noise. The door knob jiggled and I could hear someone muttering when they found it locked. I was halfway up the stairs when the door swung open. Phil's eyes landed on me and he froze in his tracks. All colour melted from his face and I wondered if he was going to faint.

"Julie!" He bellowed. "Julie! Get over here!" I heard her feet clacking hurriedly toward him.

"Tell me she's not down there." She demanded, flustered. He didn't say anything, simply pulled her in front of the stairs to look down and see for herself. Her hand flew up to cover her mouth as a heart shattering sob left her lips. "Oh no. Oh God honey." Tears overflowed from her eyes as she raced down to wrap her arms around me. "What the fuck did he do?" She demanded, utterly devastated. Seeing the normally upbeat and loving woman so defeated, incited tears of my own. She pulled me up the rest of the stairs and I could feel her body shake with her sobs.

At the top, Phil hugged me close and I heard a faint sniffle beside my ear. Then her first words replayed in my head. *Tell me she's not down there.*

"You came back early. Did you know I was here?" I asked, searching Phil's face for a clue.
"Your dad called the shop while Thomas was out on lunch. He threatened to burn the place down if they didn't get him on the phone right away so they gave him my cell phone number."
"My dad called you?" I couldn't believe what I was hearing. *My dad* was looking for me? God must truly hate me if he was sending me home to face my pissed off dad after the last three days.
"Yeah, he was in a panic. Told us Thomas had been stalking you for

weeks and he couldn't find you. He demanded to know where he was and threatened knock my lights out if I didn't tell him."

"We didn't believe that Thomas would do something this stupid but would never have forgiven ourselves if we didn't find out for sure. Thank Christ we did." Julie said through bouts of hiccups.

"I better go and call him." Phil rushed to the kitchen, out of earshot.

Julie sank to the floor beside the open basement door and buried her face in her hands. I sat across from her, weak but feeling revived after being locked away.

"I am so sorry Paisley. I can't believe he did this to you." Julie whispered, raising her face just enough to look me in the eye to apologize.

"It's not your fault Julie." I assured her.

"He's my son." She looked at me, struggling to understand why he would do something so horrible.

"Your son has a mind of his own." I wanted to comfort her but part of me was bitter. Thomas abused *me*. I shouldn't have to try and make his mother feel better.

I stayed rooted where I was, thankful that Julie stopped talking and let me breathe in peace. My dad must have raced over because it wasn't very long before the front door flew open, admitting a frantic man I barely recognized. His eyes searched everywhere, passing over me the first time before realizing I was sitting in the hallway. He came charging toward me. In his state of panic, he grabbed my arms and pulled me to feet, not realizing that he was being too rough.

"Are you okay? Did that little fucker hurt you?" He asked, looking over my face and feeling down my arms before spinning me around to make sure all of my parts were still attached.

"I'm okay dad." He made a strange sound at the back of his throat before he grabbed me in a bear hug. Though I wondered if his arms were going to snap my spine, no hug had ever felt better.

Phil turned the corner and stopped when he saw my dad holding me. Dad paid him no attention, holding me at arms length to check me over again, needing to be certain that I was in one piece. I watched in fascination as his face morphed from concern to blinding anger. He turned to Phil and pointed his long index finger in Phil's face.

"You tell that piece of shit son of yours that I'll be driving my daughter to and from school from now on and if I catch him anywhere near her, I won't hesitate to tear off every one of his limbs, including the part of him that's supposed to make him a man." He warned Phil, who stared at him in shock. Fear covered his face and I had no doubt that Thomas would get the message. As quickly as the anger had appeared for Phil, it returned to softness when he looked back at me to take my hand. "Let's go baby girl." In that moment, my dad was my hero.

Dad kept me home from school for a week. Hovering around me like I was going to disappear again. I knew what happened with Thomas had been traumatic for my parents so I did my best to be patient.

By the following Monday, I had enough. I got ready for school and sat at the table for breakfast. I enjoyed every sip of my coffee and counted down the minutes until I could leave. I hopped up when the oven clock read 7:55 and grabbed my bag. When I walked through the threshold to the living I halted. Dad stood at the front door, blocking my exit.

"What's it gonna be P-Baby? You gonna let me drive you without an argument or are you staying home today?" He asked, clearly braced for a confrontation.
"I don't mind you driving me to school dad." I informed him, wondering why in the hell he thought it would bother me.
"Seriously?" He asked, testing me.
"Why would I care if you drove me to school?"
"'Cause I'm your dad."

"Uh, pretty sure I already knew that." I replied sarcastically.
"Huh." Was all he said before opening the door for me.

Dad kept his word and drove me to school every morning
and though he wasn't supposed to, he parked in front of the buses in
the loading zone at the end of the day. I was surprised with how
much I enjoyed riding with him, spending the extra time together
was special and knowing he was doing it to protect me made it even
better.

It was at the end of the day on Thursday. Heavy clouds
darkened the sky and rain started to fall. I split with Laurie quickly
so she could run to her mom's car before she got too wet. I smiled
when I spotted dad's truck waiting at the front of the line. I hurried
jogged the truck and hopped up beside dad.

"Hey P-Baby, good day?" He asked with a smile.
"Boring as ever." He chuckled at my response.
"Yeah, school always put me to sleep." He replied, pulling out of the
loading zone. "Probably why I got the boot in grade ten."
"You got kicked out of school?" I asked, surprised with the new
information. He looked at me through narrowed eyes.
"I did. You get kicked out and I'll break your fucking leg." He
warned good-naturedly.
"Nah, if I wanna live in a tent, I gotta graduate." I explained,
deadpan. He looked at me with one brow raised and my straight face
was gone, breaking into a fit of giggles.

When we turned right at the first set of lights, I wanted to
puke. A black truck was pulled over
just ahead. I watched with rising panic as we got closer. As soon as
we passed, I spun in my seat to see if the truck pulled out behind us.
I let out a whimper when it joined traffic after the little red car
behind us. Dad glanced at me and seeing my face, he frowned.

"What's going on?"
"The truck is back." I whispered, keeping my eyes glued to it.
"You have got to be fucking kidding me. That kid must have a death
wish." He didn't use his signal light, whipping the truck over to the
side of the road and putting it in park.

His eyes fixed on his rear-view mirror, grinding his teeth when the truck crept up behind us. He waited, watching to see what Thomas would do next. I watched the driver's side door on the black truck swing open and Thomas hop out without a care in the world. He strode confidently around dad's truck, headed for my door. Before he could reach me, dad was out and stomping up to him.

He grabbed the front of Thomas's shirt with both hands and slammed him up against the truck. He got right in his face, not even an inch between their noses.

"You got a problem *boy?*" Dad spit out, slamming him against the tuck again, knocking the wind out his lungs.

He didn't wait for an answer, it didn't matter. There wasn't anything Thomas could say to alleviate dad's need to pound flesh. Dad tilted his head back and quickly threw his forehead against Thomas's nose. Dad didn't stop when Thomas fell to his knees. From above, dad's fists hammered into his head. Thomas reached up and gripped dad's shirt, attempting to trying futilely to hold himself up. With the bottom of his shoe dad shoved him off and to the ground. From my window, I could see dad's leg cock back and pelt into Thomas's stomach, his ribs, his hips.

"Stay." Kick. "The fuck." Kick. "Away." Kick. "From my daughter." He bent down and pulled Thomas up by his hair. "Didn't your daddy tell you what I would do if I saw you?" When Thomas kept his mouth shut, Dad gave his hair a violent yank. "Did he not?""

"He did." Thomas squeaked.
"Are you stupid?"
"No."
"Are you mentally impaired?"
"No."
"I'm about to fix that." Dad delivered a series of quick punches before a couple of men ran out of the house beside us and pulled dad off of Thomas.
"You disgusting piece of shit!" Dad slung a mouthful of spit into

Thomas's face.

"I think you should get out of here boy." One of the strangers advised Thomas.

"That little prick kidnapped my daughter!" Dad bellowed.

"Beating him out here in the street isn't worth going to jail Don."

Dad shrugged out of the man's hands and watched Thomas scurry away with a murderous glare. With battered knuckles, he struck the bed of his truck, leaving a dent in the metal. By the time he came around the hood of his truck and sat beside me, his anger had faded.

"Who was that man?"

"A guy from work." He answered, starting the engine to continue our ride home.

Life fell back into a somewhat normal routine. I went to school and I came home, nothing more. I joined my family for dinner but otherwise my time was spent locked away in my room. There was no desire to be around other people, I was barely able to stand my own company. I couldn't look at myself in the mirror, the sight of my own face brought me nothing but heartache. I was ashamed and didn't understand why and because of my fruitless shame, I couldn't force myself to look anyone in the eye. No, my mom, not Shella or Laurie. No one.

# Chapter Six

## Meeting the New Me

For a while I thought I would snap out of it. I would wake up one morning and remember who I was. As it stood when I first opened my eyes, I looked forward to bedtime. Sleep provided relief from days spent pretending to give a shit about *anything*. Keeping myself engaged in conversations was a chore and I only brushed my hair when my mom complained that it looked like a rat's nest. Most people grew uncomfortable when trying to talk to me because I didn't always contribute my thoughts or opinions, I often didn't have anything worth adding or didn't want to. With me avoiding eye contact and remaining silent, it proved difficult for even the closest people to be around me and I couldn't be bothered to fix it. Laurie stopped calling everyday but would pass me a letter in class every now and again to remind me she still cared. In the beginning, I would reply but as the weeks went by, I ran out of words.

The last letter I had written was a request for her to stop wasting her time for her own sake. Of course, Laurie ignored it and kept writing to me twice a week. Mostly she told me about gossip or mundane day-to-day stuff. Every letter ended with her reminding me that she cared and would be there to listen whenever I was ready.

I felt empty and alone. I *wanted* it that way. The alternative was to capsize under the weight of my weaknesses and inability to heal. I didn't confide in anyone. I couldn't bring myself to burden them with my ridiculous self loathing. Mom thought it was just a phase, dad believed it was some form of PTSD. Neither of them disclosed their diagnosis to me directly, I just happened to overhear a discussion between the two of them late one night. In any case, I didn't give it much thought, I just wanted to go to bed.

And so went life for several weeks. Winter was fast approaching and I embraced the biting cold. I spent more time on the front porch, feeling the sting of the wind against my cheeks. I stayed there until my fingers went numb and the moisture in my eyes disappeared, then I would return to my room. Most nights I skipped supper. There weren't any repercussions, it was pointless when the repercussions were meaningless.

I lost weight. My cheeks were sinking and there was barely enough meat on my stomach to pinch between my fingers. I tried to pay more attention to my diet but without an appetite, I often forgot to eat. I had little energy, barely able to make it through the day without my eyes getting too heavy to keep open. I usually skipped third or fourth period to hide in the supply closet and nap. It didn't matter how much I rested; I would never feel refreshed. Always drained, tired. The fatigue led to impatience, irritation and a very short fuse.

Leaving homeroom one morning, I accidentally bumped into a girl whose name I couldn't remember. I turned to apologize and the snotty look on her face set me off.

"Are you blind? Watch where the fuck you're going." I used both hands and shoved her.
"You're the one who walked into me you dumb raw-boned bitch."
"What did you just call me?" I stepped into her bubble to intimidate her.
"I called you a dumb. Raw-boned. Bitch. Are you deaf too, slut?" I laughed without humour before I curled my fist and smashed it into her face. Her hand covered her tender cheek and her eyes went round with shock.
"Did you just hit me?" I didn't answer, just curled my lip into a snarl and fed her another one. Her face flushed with anger. "You got some balls!" She yelled, grabbing a handful of my hair and using her second hand to deliver a blow of her own, splitting my lip.

Adrenaline vibrated through my veins and it felt exquisite. For the first time in forever, I felt *something*. I fought back just enough to keep her going. Every time her knuckles pummelled into me, it was like some of the darkness leaked out with the blood. I laughed in exhilaration and she froze, looking at me like I was insane. She pushed me away, freaked out by my reaction. I wasn't finished yet, I tackled her like a football player and I could have sworn her feet lifted off the ground before she landed on her back with me on top of her. I only managed to get in a shot or two before someone hauled me off of her. I looked over my shoulder and saw Mr. Tanns's angry face.

He set me on my feet, a safe distance from my opponent but held onto the collar of my shirt like a misbehaving child. He half dragged me through the hallway to the principal's office. He tossed me onto the bench outside of the office door and pointed a finger at me in a silent warning to stay put while he spoke to Mr. Schaeffer. I wasn't nervous like I used to be while waiting for the principal in elementary school. This time I didn't care. I was too focused on the idea that I found a sliver of relief through pain.

I didn't listen to a word Mr. Shaeffer said and it aggravated the hell out of him. None of his usual scare tactics held any weight, which left him at a loss. Frustrated, he yanked up the receiver of his phone and jabbed some buttons.

"Hello, Mister Coleman?" "This is Dominic Shaeffer, the principal at Laurentien Valley High School. I have Paisley here in front of me." "No, nothing like that." "I beg your pardon?" "Of course not, I don't make it a habit to raise my voice with the students in my school." "She hasn't said a word." "Listen Mister Coleman, the reason I'm calling--" "She hasn't listened--" "Mister Coleman, please. If you would just--" He held the phone in front of his face, staring at it, taken aback.

"He's on his way. Told me to send you outside to the loading zone in five minutes." He explained, oddly tranquilized by whatever my dad told him.

"What did he say?" I asked, bizarrely curious.
"That's none of your concern." Mr. Shaeffer snipped petulantly.
"Whatever." I mumbled, shrinking back into myself.

I didn't go back to my locker, leaving my jacket and

bag behind while I went to wait outside. I went out the front door, taking the long way to the loading zone. A couple of younger kids stood by the sidewalk, puffing cigarettes.

"Can I have one of those?" I asked a boy who was staring at me like he had never seen a pair of tits before.
"Uh, ye-yeah of-of course." He stuttered, fumbling in his pockets to find his pack.
"Thank you." I put the filtered end between my lips. "Light." I leaned forward so he could light it for me. I had to turn it a few times before managing to produce a flame.

I took a long drag before forcing a smile for him and resuming in the direction of the loading zone. I leaned against the building before turning the corner, enjoying the rest of my smoke and the head-buzz it provided. When the cigarette was done, I flicked the butt aside and pushed myself off of the wall. I knew that if dad was already waiting, he would be able to see me blowing out smoke while I headed to his truck. I didn't care, part of me hoped he would lash out so I could test my theory and see if it would alleviate some of the emptiness in my head.

I was disappointed. When I hopped up beside him, he didn't say a word, barely even spared me a glance from the corner of his eye. If I got away with being sent home from school *and* smoking, it would be a miracle. There was no way his blood pressure would tolerate one of his offspring acting out so recklessly. I waited while he pulled away from the school. Waited while he drove in the opposite direction of home. I knew an outburst was building. The longer the delay, the worse it would be. Fear slowly flourished in my chest but the feeling wasn't unwelcome.

He drove out of the city limits, where houses were older and spread farther apart. I wasn't familiar with the roads this far out of town. What our destination was, I couldn't begin to guess. He turned down a dirt road, lined with pine trees on either side. It wound this way and the next, steadily up an incline. When the road flattened, we came into a wide clearing. A lake filled the centre of the clearing and the trees looked tiny on the other side. Dad parked the car and got out, shoved his hands in his pockets while he wandered to the water's edge. I hesitated before following him, unsure of his intentions but when I noticed that his shoulders weren't tense and he wasn't putting off angry vibes, I followed.

Up close, the water was breathtaking, clear blue, free from the ruin that so often followed human beings. Even the air smelled fresher and I drank in the peace from my surroundings. For a long moment, dad and I seemed to be in the same head space. When he looked at me, his eyes were overflowing with sadness and it hit me like a solid punch to the chest.

"You're a great kid Paisley. You take after me so much that it freaks me out sometimes except that underneath it all, you're *good.*" His voice was thick with emotion and the sight of my father, vulnerable, was disconcerting. "I spent a was shipped off to a boy's home when I was about fourteen. Your uncle Doug and I were too much for our mom to handle alone when our dad was working out west. The dean was..." He reflected, going back through his memories. "He was a heartless man. We had a class with him every afternoon and his room didn't have any chairs. We spent the hour and fifteen minutes, on our knees on the old cement floor while we listened to him *teach* us about how useless we were. He would walk around the room, between the rows of boys and if anyone squirmed or cried about their knees hurting, he would whack them across the back with his long wooden ruler." He rubbed a hand across his face, tortured by thoughts of his youth. "I would have chosen to be in his class all day, every day, to avoid being tutored by Mister Nelson." He coughed, trying to disguise an odd anguished noise. "He was supposed to tutor me in English. Instead, he taught me how to please him sexually." For the first time in my life, I saw a tear slide down my father's face. "It happened a couple times before I told my mom during one of our weekly phone calls. She told me I was full of shit. I only had a few months left before my dad would be home and she told me to be a man and suck it up." He swiped his tears away like they burned his skin. "I never trusted anyone again after that. I kept my shit to myself and tried to leave it in the past. The thing is P-Baby, I went to a very dark place when I got back home. I hated everything for a long time. I pulled away from people, locked them out." He looked me in the eye. "It took me a long time to find myself." He gestured around us. "I found this place and I truly believe it's what saved me."

"Jesus dad... I don't even know what to say to that." My eyes burned.

"I know that it might not do the same for you but I just need you to understand that it's not permanent. Things *will* get better." He pulled out his cigarettes and after lighting one, he held it out to me.

"Dad?"
"I'm not stupid Paisley, I know you smoke sometimes. Just take it." I took it from him and felt the tension start to melt away after the first drag. He pulled out a second one for himself.

Standing side-by-side on the water's edge, we smoked together in silence. We watched the ripples across the lake, listened to the birds chirping in the distance and enjoyed a well-deserved break from real life.

"Thomas didn't rape me dad." It felt like something he needed to know.
"I wondered if he had." Relief flashed briefly across his face.
"He didn't. I don't know if he would have eventually, but he didn't take it that far."
"He took it too fucking far even if he didn't." He muttered. "That boy deserves to be torn apart."
"I'm sure karma will have fun with him one day."
"God willing."
"Thank you, dad." I wasn't back to myself but part of the weight had been lifted.
"Thank you, kid." He replied, smiling lightly. "It's nice hearing you talk again. When you were a baby, you never shut up, lately, trying to get you say *anything* has been like pulling teeth." He chuckled.
"Yeah, I know."
"What happened at school today?"
"I got into a fight."
"And did the other girl's parents get a phone call too?"
"No."
"Why the hell not? Looks like she got in a few good punches." He stated angrily, indicating the damage to my face.
"Well, I'm easy to blame I guess."
"That mister Chafer is gonna get an earful." He said, purposely

mispronouncing his name. "Gonna sic your mother on him." He and I both chuckled. Though it sounded weird coming out of my mouth, it felt good.

A new bond formed between my dad and I that day by the lake. An understanding. He gave me the comfort I desperately needed without pushing me to change. He made me realize that depression was a battle I would have to fight alone. No one else could force it out of my head. I had to come to terms with my trauma and find a way to come back from it but that it would take time.

I stood in front of my mirror, staring at my reflection. I still didn't like the person looking back at me but I was slowly starting to be able to bear the sight of her. The first few times I forced myself to look, I cried. When the tears stopped, the angry frown set in. It took a bit longer to overcome the bitterness. Now, looking at her didn't provoke any strong emotions. Just distaste.

I bent my elbow and looked down at the inside of my forearm, just below the crease. The scab was starting to peel so I peeled it off. A thin line of blood formed where the fresh skin wasn't finished healing. Beside it, I ran the nail on my middle finger back and forth. Slowly, the tender flesh became irritated. When it started to feel hot, I kept scratching. I clenched my teeth against the burn as layers of skin started to collect under my nail. I still didn't stop. I wasn't satisfied until the wound was tomato red and pain radiated down my arm. It was slightly longer than the last one, just over two inches. I wiped the guilty finger off on my jeans and pulled down my sleeves. The fabric rubbing against the weeping sore, enhanced the stinging sensation. I breathed out a sigh of relief.

I ran a brush through my hair before going downstairs for supper. Dad and John were already sitting at the table while mom stood at the sink, pouring noodles into a strainer.

"Hey P-Baby. How was school?"

"Good. Getting ready for exams."

"Any tough teachers?"

"Just Mister Tanns. He's been an asshole since the fight."

"Oh? I need to make a couple phone calls?"

"Nah, he'll get over it eventually." I declined his offer, knowing that it would only make things worse for me.

"Okay, but if you fail that class because of him, I'm going to do more than just make some phone calls. I'll be going down to that school to have a few words with him." He threatened and his protectiveness made me smile.

Mom put our plates on the table and sat down across from me. I noticed that Shella was absent again for the fourth time this week. I found it odd because Shella rarely went out during the week, she took school very seriously.

"Where's Shella been?" I asked mom.

"She's been spending time at Nathan's with his parents." Strange, Nathan generally ignored Shella on school nights, calling her on Wednesday afternoons when she got home to 'touch base' but otherwise they only saw each other on weekends. How their relationship survived their bullshit rules was something I would never comprehend. Especially because Nathan was such a dick.

"Those two are weirdos." I mumbled and mom looked at dad, speechless when he chuckled.

"She isn't wrong." He explained, still smiling in amusement.

"Donald!" Mom chastised him.

"Oh, come on Jo, those two have a fucked-up way with each other. I don't know if they have it right or wrong but it's not *normal*." Mom just shook her head.

"I don't like him." John stated out of the blue. We all turned to him, surprised that he paid enough attention to Nathan to have an opinion.

"Oh, he's a nice young man." Mom defended.

"Yeah, it was nice of him to drive by with a bunch of guys and throw eggs and me and my friends while we were playing hockey." John said sarcastically.

"He did what?" I exclaimed, instantly furious with Nathan.

"Yeah, a few weekends ago, I was playing hockey with Josh and the guys. Heard someone yelling my name so I looked over and waved when I saw it was Nathan. Then they started pitching eggs at us and laughing like it was the funniest thing they'd ever seen."

"I'm gonna fucking break his face." I gritted through clenched teeth.

"Why did you tell us?" Dad asked.

"Because you all think he's *so nice.*" John pouted.

"You could have told me; you know I can't stand the douche bag." I shouted.

"I *did* tell you. You ignored me." John threw back, irritated.

I couldn't argue. Not that long ago, he could have told me the house was on fire and I wouldn't have reacted. I hated myself even more for not listening when John asked me for help. I was ashamed that I brushed him off when he confided something that clearly troubled him. I rubbed my aching forearm, feeling that I deserved the punishment.

"If Nathan pulls that kind of shit again, you tell me. Understand?" Dad demanded.

"I understand."

"Don, you know how boys can be, Nathan was probably just--"

"You can shut your mouth right there Johanne." Dad cut her off. "I don't give a shit if it was a game, a dare or someone else's dumb idea. That prick wants to date my daughter, turn around and treat my son like shit? He's going to face the repercussions." He glared at her. "You wanna defend him after he humiliated John? Huh?" He raised his fork to point at her face threateningly. His hand shook with his rising temper. "You're a fucking spineless bitch. I ought to show you the back of my fucking hand. You're his" Dad jabbed his fork in John's direction before returning it to point at mom, "mother. You should be on his side."

"It's okay dad." John told him with mounting nervousness. Dad's eyes spun on him.

"No. It is *not* okay." He countered. "Your mother seems to think that what everyone else thinks is more important than her children's feeling and it is *not* acceptable." His voice rose with each word. "Your *mother* is too hung up on her appearance, her *reputation* and what the fucking neighbour's will think." His reaction made it clear that this was an ongoing point of contention between the two of them.

"Donald, that's enough." Mom said, insulted.
"Fuck you, Johanne." Dad spit out at her. Throwing his fork down and standing abruptly. He stormed through the threshold.
"Where are you going?" She asked, keeping her voice calm.
"None of your goddamn business." He shouted before we heard the front door slam closed.
"Good job mom." I accused, pushing my chair back and leaving the table.

I found myself resenting my mother more and more lately. I could see her cracks and I didn't like what I found. I used to make excuses for her but suddenly I came to realize that she didn't deserve them. The more time I spent thinking about everything that happened inside those walls the more I came to realize a lot of things I didn't before. Like the fact that mom would defend Shella to dad but when it was me or John in the spotlight, she would turn her back or look away. She never stood up for her two younger children. Though she was always quick to point out dad's tendency towards violent outbursts, her temper ran hot too. There were several times when dad came home from work and she ran to him with tales of what one of us had throughout the day to earn a spanking, inevitably sparking dad's fury. She instigated some of the arguments with him that quickly blew out of proportion. She threw us under the bus. She hid our bruises. She spun stories for teachers and doctors. She put up the front that our family was perfect when it was far from it. I couldn't understand her and I wasn't sure if I would ever be able to look at her the same way after seeing a side of her, I was blind to in the past. It was irrelevant nonetheless; she was my mother and that wasn't something I could change.

I wanted to drink but I didn't want to reach out and

invite anyone to go out with me. After briefly weighing my options, I made the questionable decision to walk over to Billy's alone. The parking lot was scarce and I was glad that I wouldn't be brushing elbows with strangers.

I stepped into the bar and parked my bottom on a stool near the door. The bartender was cute so at least I would have a nice view while I drank. He wore snug jeans and a button up shirt, rolled to his elbows and open at the collar. Every time he bent down for a glass below the counter, my eyes were blessed with the sight of a gorgeous butt. He must have noticed me checking him out because when he came back to get me a refill, he wore a cocky grin.

"Darlin', you keep looking at me like that, I might not make it through the rest of my shift." He laughed.
"Gonna go home sick?" I teased.
"Yeah, that's what I'll tell my boss before hauling you over my shoulder and taking you with me" It was my turn to laugh. He was full of confidence and I loved it.
"Might want to warn him now then because there's no way I can stop looking." I warned, quickly swallowing the drink he brought me.
"Wow, you don't mess around, do you?" He grabbed a bottle from the shelf behind him and filled my glass.
"I don't have the patience to beat around the bush anymore." I told him. He raised a hand and waved someone over.
"Ryan, I'm taking my break, will you cover the bar?" He asked when the other man joined him behind the counter.
"Sure."
"Wanna come outside with me?" Sexy bartender asked, coming through the swinging door.
"Love to." I answered, emptying my glass again before hopping down from the stool and taking his offered hand.
"We'll head out the back door." He led me through the bar to the emergency exit.

Outside, he pulled a pack of cigarettes from his back pocket and held the open packet out for me. I took one and leaned forward so he could light it for me.

"Thank you."

"Names Dimmy."

"Dimmy? That's different."

"Short for Dimitri." He explained with a smirk.

"Oh, nice to meet you Dimmy. I'm Paisley. Short for nothing."

"Oh, darlin' you are from nothing." He said, his gaze taking a lingering stroll down my body then back up again.

"Keep talking to me like that and I'll tell your boss you're sick so I can drag you home." He groaned longingly.

"You're gorgeous *and* a tease. That's quite the combo." He remarked.

"Except I'm not teasing." He groaned again and leaned his back against the brick wall.

He pulled a medicine bottle from his pocket. Shaking out a pill, he popped it into his mouth, swallowing it easily with nothing to flush it down.

"What's that?" I asked, noticing that it didn't have a label.

"It's uppers. You want one?" He offered.

"Uppers?"

"Yeah, they make you feel good." Without realizing it, he offered me a pill that would ease all of my mental anguish.

"Where'd you get those?"

"My supplier." He answered vaguely.

"Can I buy some from you?"

"Here." He handed me the bottle. "I got more in my backpack."

"I'm not sure I can afford this much," I worried he would take them back when I badly wanted to keep them.

"Consider it a gift." He shrugged.

"Are you sure?" I asked, full of doubt.

"Of course. They're yours. If you need more just let me know." He smiled warmly.

"Thanks. Again." I popped the bottle open and fished out a tablet. I put it on the back of my tongue where it stuck and I had to fight against the urge to gag as the taste hit me. After swallowing several times, I was able to dislodge it.

"It wont take long till you start to feel it." He explained. "I assume it's your first time?"

"Yeah."

"You're gonna love it. It makes you feel amazing."

"I'm pretty sure you could have done that without the pill." I flirted.

"Paisley! You're killing me here." A laugh bubbled out.

"Sorry, I'll rein myself in."

"Please don't. I'm not complaining."

"Good." I smiled.

"Come on, let's get back inside before we get busted with our pants down. Literally."

Dimmy hadn't been exaggerating when he said the pill would make me feel incredible. I couldn't get enough of the euphoria that hit in a matter of minutes after swallowing the tablet. I met up with Dimitri on a nightly basis, either at the bar or at his apartment. Being with him was refreshing. We spent most of our time laughing and riding the high. He seemed to have a bottomless supply of pills. He always shared and when the first bottle he gave me was empty, he sent me home with another one. I didn't often use when I wasn't with him but when the days at school were long, I would have one to get me through it.

There was always intense flirting between us but neither of us seemed willing to rock the boat by going any further than that. We both seemed to silently agree that what we had, was enough. I learned a lot about Dimmy. His mom gave him up when he was just two years old leaving him to grew up in the system. He formed a close relationship with his high school basketball coach who opened his doors to him when he was sixteen and quickly became Dimitri's role model. Four months after his twenty-first birthday he moved into his own place. He was now settled in and loving life as a bartender.

"So happy-cheeks, you want a beer?" Dimitri asked from his kitchen. He had taken to calling me happy-cheeks because he said my cheeks were rosy when I smiled and I loved the endearment.

"Yes please." I pulled my legs up under my butt, comfortable on his old second-hand couch.

"Feel like watching a movie?" He asked when he came back into the living room, handing me an open bottle and taking a swig from his own.

"Sure." I agreed.

He flicked through Netflix, neither of us finding anything we wanted to watch. We probably scrolled for half an hour before he turned it back off and flung the remote beside him on the couch.

"Fuck that." He cursed, irritated.

"You in a grumpy mood?" I asked, looking closely at his face.

"No, I'm just restless. I met girl the other day." Well, this was unfamiliar territory, we did usually talk about that kind of thing. We usually just brushed around it.

"Oh yeah? At work?" I asked, wiggling around, uncomfortable.

"Yeah, she came in with a group of girls and we seemed to hit it off."

"Why do you sound so unsure about it?" I had no idea where he was going with this conversation.

"Well, she gave me her number but she always says she's busy and can't talk or has plans and can't go out." He wanted my advice and I didn't know how I felt about it.

"Was she super drunk when you met?"

"She was tipsy but no completely out of it."

"She do something embarrassing?"

"Not that I know of."

"Huh. Weird." I was stumped. I thought about it for a minute. "Did her friends seem kind of weird? Like standoffish? Not really talking to you?" He thought about my question for a moment before answering.

"Yeah, kind of. One of them was nice enough but the other two barely said two words."

"I think she might have a boyfriend." I suggested.

"What makes you think that?"

"She wouldn't have given you her number if she wasn't interested but it's easier to turn someone down over the phone. She would have put her friends in a very awkward position by flirting with another guy when she's already seeing someone. I'm not saying she's definitely in a relationship. I'm just brainstorming. Like she doesn't want to shut you out all the way just in case things don't work out with her boyfriend."

He was quiet, pensive. He seemed to be mulling over my suggestion. Everything seemed to be falling into place in his brain. What I told him made sense and he could see the mixed signals for what they were.

"That fucking blows. I can't believe it. Why are girls such bitches?" His ignorant statement stung and I glared at him. When he saw my face, he backtracked. "Not you happy-cheeks. Never you. You're perfect."

"Right. Way to kiss ass Dimmy." I said sarcastically, crossing my arms across my chest. He sighed, defeated.

"I'm not kissing ass Paisley." He finished his beer and walked off to the kitchen to grab us fresh ones. When he sat back down, he guzzled half of the new bottle, still wearing the look of defeat. "You *are* perfect Paisley. You're sweet and considerate. You're funny and you are so easy to talk to." He looked at me, filled with a sadness that confused me but quickly hid it behind a lascivious smile. "And that body." He let out an exaggerated groan of appreciation. He scooted closer to me and ran a finger down my cheek. "But this beautiful face is what kills me the most." I could feel myself blush under his appraisal. "Can I tell you something weird?"

"Sure." Was all I could manage.
"I've jerked off thinking about you." He looked me in the eye while he made his confession and it made the moment that much more intimate. "A lot." He added with emphasis.

I looked down at my crossed legs, unable to think straight. The image of him touching himself was seared in my brain, creating an ache between my legs. The fact that he was thinking of *me* while he did it, set me on fire.

"I'm sorry. That was fucked up, I shouldn't have told you that." He was embarrassed and I felt for him.

"It is kind of fucked up. One minute you're telling me about meeting a girl at work, the next you're telling me you fist fucked yourself to thoughts of me." It was my only defence against the desire in the pit of my stomach.

"I know. I'm sorry." He ran his hand roughly across his face, filled with regret. "I don't know why I told you about Tracie. I was just hoping things would go somewhere with her so that maybe I would stop wanting you."

"Why is it so wrong to want me?"

"Because we have something amazing right now. You're my best friend and I haven't even known you that long. I just feel so connected to you and I don't want to ruin that by giving in to my dick."

"You're right, we do have a pretty fantastic friendship." I smiled at him. "You're dick just wants in on it too." I laughed and he smiled at me.

"You want a pill?" He asked, probably in an attempt to change the topic.

"Sure."

He lifted his hips from the couch so that he could reach into his pocket to retrieve his ever-present medicine bottle. When his hips were up, I couldn't help but notice the bulge under his zipper. He was clearly well endowed and the sight made my mouth go dry. I squirmed a little, trying to relieve some of my discomfort. He looked at me curiously, catching me wiggling in my seat.

"You got an itchy butt or something?" He asked with a laugh, handing me a tablet and taking one out for himself. I swallowed the small pill with a mouthful of beer.

"Just trying to adjust, if you catch my drift." I explained with a mischievous smirk. His brows furrowed.

"I can't say I do. I thought only people with penises needed to adjust."

"Well, when you tell a girl she makes you so horny that you have to jerk off, it tends to create throbbing pussy syndrome." He coughed out beer making me laugh hysterically. When he caught his breath, he joined me in a fit of laughter.

"So, you're telling me, you're turned on at the thought of me masturbating?" He asked after catching his breath.

"I'm telling you that thinking about you masturbating turns me on." I agreed.
"And you still made me feel like an ass-hole for telling you?" He asked, pretending to be offended.
"Yes." I was still giggling.

The hysterics returned when he pounced on me. He had already discovered that I was ticklish and he used that knowledge while he straddled me, poking me in the ribs relentlessly. I couldn't get in a full breath of air and I had a feeling that my face was an unattractive shade of red from lack of oxygen and laughter.

He eventually stopped and I could finally breathe again. I panted and he stared down at me with need. I pressed my fingers under my eyes to wipe away the moisture. He slid back to his spot on the couch, letting me to sit up. He picked up his bottle of beer and stared at it thoughtfully for a moment before emptying it and setting it on the end table beside him. When he looked at me again, his eyes were full of heat. They stayed glued on me but mine followed his hands as they reached for his belt buckle. I watched him undo his jeans and slide down the zipper. My breath caught when I saw that he wasn't wearing underwear and his dark pubic hair was exposed. One of his hands reached down the front of his pants to pull his very stiff cock free from the denim. I watched in a daze as his hand wrapped around his shaft and start stroking it with a firm grip. I swallowed so I wouldn't drool. When I managed to tear my gaze away, I looked at his face to see his lids had lowered, his lips parted slightly and he seemed to really enjoy having me watch him.

My heart pounded in my ears but I badly wanted to be on equal footing. I smirked, watching his eyes widen as I reached for my zipper. Once the front of my jeans hung open, I slid my hand into my panties. I wasn't brave enough to pull my pants down and show him the most private part on my body but with the sounds coming from somewhere deep in his chest, he understood what I was doing and it was driving him crazy.

"Fuck. You're incredibly sexy Paisley."

"I love it when you say my name." I moaned, stroked the nub between my folds.

"Does it feel good?" He asked, so focused on watching me that he seemed to forget about moving the hand on his dick.

"If feels *very* good." He groaned, squeezing his eyes closed to regain some control over himself.

"I'm dying to get inside you." With that, my hand froze. I quickly pulled it out and did up my jeans. When I stood, he looked at me in confusion.

"What's wrong? Why'd you stop?" He asked, tucking himself back in his pants.

"I don't want to have sex Dimmy."

"No one's forcing you to have sex Paisley."

"It's cruel of me to give you the wrong impression."

"You didn't. I wasn't going to push you for more. I was happy just doing what we were doing." He assured me, looking worried that I might bolt. "Are you a virgin? Is that why sex makes you nervous?" He asked, curiosity getting the better of him.

"I'm not a virgin." I admitted. "But sex is very painful and I have no desire to do it again." I explained, slightly embarrassed.

"Painful?" He sounded surprised. "Sex shouldn't be painful Paisley. Girls enjoy it just as much as guys do."

"Not in my experience." I answered stubbornly. He stared at me, turning something over in his head before shaking his head.

"I'm gonna bed you only had sex once."

"So?"

"Whoever that lucky fucker was, didn't do it right." He explained, looking at me with pity, which aggravated me even more.

"I'm pretty sure it's hard to fuck up sticking your dick into someone. It would have hurt regardless of who did it."

"No happy-cheeks, if the dude was selfish, he wouldn't have done it right and it would have made things a lot worse for you."

"Doesn't matter anyways. I'm not interested in a repeat performance."

"Which is what breaks my heart."

"Why? Cause you won't get to bury yourself inside of me?"

"Because you're missing out on something amazing." He genuinely looked upset for me while he pulled up his zipper.

I don't know what I was thinking, maybe it was the drug pushing rational thought from my head but I suddenly *needed* him to prove me wrong. I caught him off guard while he was struggling to do up his jeans around his semi stiff dick. Planting myself on top of him, with a knee on either side of his hips, I crooked a finger under his chin and pulled his face up so I could kiss him. I didn't hold back. I licked his bottom lip, asking permission to enter. He didn't hesitate and quickly took control. He cupped the back of my neck, holding me still while he invaded my mouth. I moaned at the sweet taste of his tongue. His other hand squeezed my hip and I could feel his erection come back in full force between my legs. My body had a mind of its own as my hips rolled against him, glorying in the pressure of his manhood rubbing against my eager clit.

The hand on my hip slid under the hem of my t-shirt, sliding upward. He gently pulled down the cup of my bra to free my breast for his hand to touch my skin. It was long before he couldn't deny himself anymore, he yanked my shirt up and devoured my hardened nipple with his warm mouth. I moaned, the tingling on my sensitive bud making the opening between my legs clench with the need to be filled. I pushed harder against him, needing the pressure. He breathed heavily against my chest, going to the other side to lavish my second nipple with the same attention he gave the first one. My hands balled in his hair, loving the feeling of his mouth on me.

I was disappointed when he leaned his head back and looked up at me. He was fighting an internal battle. I could see that part of him wanted to keep going while the other part remembered what I just told him about my reservations.

"Happy-cheeks, this is how you give a guy blue balls." He said with a grin.

"I want you to show me." His grin vanished and his face became very serious.

"You want me to show you what?" He asked, needing me to say the words.

"I want you to show me what it *should* feel like to be with someone."

"Paisley..." He groaned, torn. I pulled away, putting more distance between us.

"Listen, if you're not interested anymore, I get it." I assured him, knowing full well that he wanted me, especially with his erection pressed up against my happy place.

"You know damn well I want you. I made that pretty fucking clear." He growled hungrily, putting a hand behind my neck to pull me back against him. "I don't want you to do this just to prove a point Paisley."

"I know. I don't want to be afraid of sharing myself anymore. You told me it wasn't supposed to hurt and I believe you. I want you to show me what it's supposed to feel like."

"A girl's first time always hurts. Sometimes the second time is still uncomfortable but if the guy knows what he's doing, the discomfort goes away and the rest is... nothing but pleasure."

"Will you show me?" I persisted.

His answer was to kiss me senseless. I felt giddy when he stood from the couch, lifting me up with him. I wrapped my legs around his waist and placed kisses along his neck, smiling when they made him shiver. He smelled phenomenal, just soap and Dimitri. From over his shoulder, I spotted his jeans tangled up on the floor behind him where he must have kicked them off. I started to laugh at his eagerness but it caught in my throat when I realized that he was now half naked. I groaned with impatience. I reached behind me when he stopped in front of his door to turn the knob. He shoved it open with his toe. It only took a few steps for him to reach his bed and lay be down gently. I loved that his bed was always made and he kept his room tidy.

He followed me onto the bed, using his knee to spread my legs enough to settle himself between them. Softly, his lips traced my collar bone while his fingers gripped the bottom of my shirt to pull it over my head. The cups of my bra were still trapped beneath the breasts they were supposed to be supporting and Dimitri's eyes drank in the sight of them completely bare beneath him. He trailed kisses down the middle of my chest and kept going down my stomach. I gasped when he kissed the button on pants. He backed away just enough for his fingers to pull the button loose and slide the zipper down. I couldn't stop the moan when his lips landed on the front of my panties, right where my lips began. He smiled at me when he sat up on his knees, softly patting my hips so that I would lift them enough for him to pull my jeans off. I was mesmerized watching him strip me. He left my white cotton panties in place and I wondered if it was his way of letting me have a small barrier until I decided I wanted them to disappear. He crawled back and kissed me softly, teasing me and pulling away every time I tried deepening it. Just when I was getting really frustrated, he let go and his mouth scorched me. He was an amazing kisser but his hips grinding against me, rocking his hardness against the part of me that was desperate for more, set me off. I moaned into his mouth, surprised by my climax. He leaned back to watch my face as I got off. When I opened my eyes, my stomach tightened at the sight of him on top of me, wearing a cocky grin.

"That was the sexiest fucking thing I have ever seen in my entire life." He said before leaning down and taking my mouth in a quick kiss. "Can I taste you?" He asked.

"You already have." I laughed.

"No, I haven't. I want to taste you..." His hand slid between our bodies, rubbing over my moistened underwear. "Here." He finished. I moaned, bucking my hips into his hand.

"I don't want to wait any longer." I complained. "I want you now." He groaned at my words. I hooked my thumbs into the hips of my panties and shoved them as far as I could. He took the hint and peeled them the rest of the way down.

When he came back, he slid a finger between my legs. He toyed with the overly sensitive nub, making me squirm uncontrollably.

"Are you sure you want this?"
"More than anything." I whined.
"Oh happy-cheeks, you're..." I searched my face. "There are no words for what you do to me."

He pulled a condom from his nightstand and I watched as he opened it and rolled it on. He didn't dive right in, instead he returned his hand between my legs and tortured me with his fingers. When I was on the brink of another orgasm, he pulled his hand away and slid the head of his cock inside of me. Just the tip, while he waited for me to adjust to the intrusion. I hooked my feet around his hips and pulled him in further. He showed unbelievable restraint, waiting for my body to accept him. Slowly he added more and more until his pelvis was pushed against mine. He kissed me with such heat that I felt myself clench around him where our bodies were connected. He used his thumb and forefinger to tease one of my nipples, submerging all of me in unimaginable sensation.

"Dimmy, please." I begged.
"Please what Paisley?" He grinned knowingly.
"I need more, please. Oh god, please."
"Anything for you, happy cheeks."

He pulled his hips back and slowly pushed back in. Keeping at a cautious pace, making me crazy. I dug my nails into his bottom, desperate for him to follow me into mindless desire.

"Do you want more?" He asked in a trained voice.
"Fuck yes!" I demanded.

His hips pound violently into me once while he watched my face to make sure I was still with him. I could practically see the control disintegrate from his face. It wasn't long before I fell apart once more, losing my mind to the pleasure. A few more thrusts and he followed me over the edge. Panting, he collapsed with his head pillowed against my chest. We rested for several minutes in silence before he looked up at me.

"So? Did I prove anything to you?" He asked, with a mixture of confidence and a hint of uncertainty. I cupped his face between my hands.

"You definitely showed me how amazing sex can be and proved that Thomas was a selfish prick in more ways than more." He looked unsettled by my words.

"Please, it's fucked up to hear you say another guy's name when we're still basking in post-coital bliss." I laughed at his jealous comment.

"Oh Dimmy, compared to him, you are a God."

All the wonder from my night with Dimitri faded just as quickly as it has been discovered. Being unable to hold on to even a morsel of the pleasure I found with him added another cloud of darkness over my head. I was frustrated with myself for dwelling in my own prison.

For a week straight, I fought demons while I slept. I was plagued with terrifying nightmares that startled me awake several times throughout the night. They always began the same way.

I found myself walking towards a black door with bright light shining through the crack beneath it. Fear plagued me but I couldn't stop my feet from bringing me closer to it. I would cry as I reach for the doorknob but the door would swing open before I touched it. A scream would choke out as I came face to face with the evil looking old man who stood on the other side of the doorway. He was bald with elfish ears and his face was heavily wrinkled along his forehead. Dark bags hung heavily below his eyes; his grin stretched from the middle of one cheek across to the other side in a grotesquely unnatural way. Deep seated lines framed the creepy grin like ripples in water. His eyes were unsettling because they were dark with barely discernible pupils. They looked so much like my own that goosebumps covered my body when I looked at them. My feet would be rooted in place until he let out a foreboding laugh and it was at that point where I would jump awake, trembling convulsively in terror.

When the nightmares persisted into a second week, I started to avoid going to sleep. Staying hidden in my room until I was certain everyone else was fast asleep, I would creep downstairs into the kitchen. The coffee machine was well used late into the night. I consumed cup upon cup of the hot beverage until my eyes ached and I couldn't fight them any longer. More than once, I would awake from the nightmare, still sitting at the kitchen table.

Dimitri's pills offered a temporary solution. I discovered that I could last three or four days without sleep if I took one every time exhaustion hit me. The pills always came with a dreadful crash. When it reached the point where my body couldn't take it any longer, I had to give it rest. The dreams would come and I would jump awake to the usual tremors but my chest would hurt. I was never able to keep my eyes open for very long and I would slip back into a deep sleep where the dream would start over. It was a vicious cycle that lasted a minimum of twelve hours at a time. The crash was so brutal that I wouldn't be able to sleep the following night, unable to take another visit to the world in my subconscious and so I would take one of the magical pills.

I was on my third day, struggling through the end of my slumber-free time. The school was midway through exam week and I sat in my math class, anxious to finish the test and go home. I watched the teacher count out booklets and hand them out to those sitting in the front row. Kids would grab their test and hand the rest behind them. When everyone had their copy, the teacher checked the time before telling us to flip our papers over and begin. The only thing I could hear was the sound of pencils furiously writing and the grating noise of a sharpener.

I must have blacked out, staring blindly at the blackboard in the front of the room because I found myself walking down a dark hallway towards a black door. I whimpered, knowing what was going to happen but being unable to make it stop. The door swung open and there stood my tormentor. Oddly, this time, he reached out and touched the centre of my chest. I felt something in my hand and when I looked down, I realized that I was holding a pencil. In a desperate attempt to make the old man disappear, I drove the pencil through the hand on my shoulder. It went through because I felt it puncture my skin.

When my ears were assaulted with screams, my eyes flew open. The horrified face of my math teacher filled my line of sight. Confused I looked around and saw that blood dripped steadily onto my desk. My hand throbbed and I was stunned when I realized that I had stabbed my pencil through my own hand, into my chest and the blood on my desk was mine. Slowly, I withdrew the pencil, causing more screams from my classmates and a few gags.

Laurie was standing beside me, tears of worry streaming down her beautiful face. She pulled the sweater off of her seat beside mine and wrapped my hand before pulling me up and rushing me from the classroom. She led me to the front office and sat me on the bench beside the door before running in and yelling at the secretary to call an ambulance.

I knew I was falling but I couldn't stop myself. My eyes rolled to the back of my head and the last thing I could remember was the sickening sound of my head hitting the linoleum.

# Chapter Seven

Help Me.

After forty-eight hours of observation, the hospital released me into my parents' care stating I had suffered a mental break caused by stress. Making any kind of assumption about my mental state was ridiculous seeing as I had only seen a nurse twice the entire length of my stay and after dressing my wounds, the doctor spent a total of three minutes asking me questions. It was a lot easier for my parents to accept their explanation. With exams and my history of depression, it made sense to them that I finally broke down.

Leaving the hospital, I felt refreshed. During my stay, I had not one nightmare and I took advantage, rarely keeping my eyes open for more than a few minutes the entire time I was in the hospital room.

When we got home, my parents followed me to my bedroom. The first thing I noticed was that they had taken down the sheet that blocked my window ever since I saw the black truck parked outside. Light poured in and the brightness irritated me, I wanted my gloomy bedroom back. Second thing I noticed was the new bedding. A bright yellow blanket spread across my bed with matching yellow pillow cases. A meticulously arranged bouquet of flowers stood proudly on my vanity beside a teddy bear with my name embroidered across its chest. The sight of the stuffed animal made me unreasonably angry so I closed my eyes and took a deep breath. I couldn't afford to blow a fuse right then or my parents would probably bring me right back to the hospital.

I turned to my parents who stood just inside my door, waiting to see my reaction. I forced my mouth to curve into a smile, knowing full well my eyes showed my displeasure but I didn't have the energy to try and fix it. Dad scrutinized me while mom smiled happily, taking my reaction at face value. I couldn't bring myself to thank them. Instead, I used the excuse of being tired to get them out and closed the door behind them. I looked around my brightly lit bedroom and let my tears fall. I badly wanted to appreciate the happy vibes in the room but I couldn't.

My hand unconsciously slid to the scars along my forearm and began to scratch away the skin. When my nail drew blood, I forced myself to stop. The pain provided only a hint of the relief that it used to. The wounds took longer to heal because of my erratic sleeping patterns.

Annoyed, I pulled the unwanted blanket from my mattress and stuffed it under my bed. I curled under the sheet and sobbed into my pillow, lost and desperate for an escape from myself.

I returned to school three days later, secluded in the room across from the main office to finish the remainder of my exams. At first, it was easy to concentrate with the complete silence. Gradually, I started hearing strange noises.

It started with scurrying across the floor like a startled mouse trying to find a dark corner to hide. I looked under the desks but was unable to spot any rodents. Dismissing the interruption, I returned to my paper. Not long after, I could hear a scratching noise from right above my desk. I stared at the drop ceiling, half expecting to see the panel move out of place. It didn't. I shook my head, convinced that the silence combined with my exhaustion was the cause of my auditory hallucinations. I tried to turn my attention back to my task when I caught a movement from the corner of my eye and I froze, afraid of what I might see. The hand holding my pencil began to shake. I tried futilely to regulate my breathing. Hearing glass fall and shatter on the floor behind me, I whipped from my chair and turned. Nothing. My heart was pounding and I struggled to catch my breath. I waited for several moments before deciding it was time to pack up my things and leave. I spun back to my desk and screamed when the old man filled my line of sight. His creepy smirk cracked open as he cackled.

My bladder let go. Warm urine trickled down the leg of my pants. I couldn't move, couldn't find my voice. I was paralyzed with terror. The room spun briefly before the room went black.

I woke up freezing cold. I could see fog leaving my lips when I exhaled and my nostrils burned with the smell of rotting flesh and pee. I made it to my knees before nausea flooded my stomach and bile poured from my mouth with a wrenching heave. Even when it was empty, my body kept trying to expel vomit. I got to my feet and held my stomach as I hunched forward. I managed to grab my bag and make it out the door. Only once I passed the doorway did the queasiness subside. With a few hungry gulps of air, the sickness passed just as quickly as it had arrived.

The office door stood open and the secretary stared at me, confused. I didn't say anything, I just rushed to the exit. Walking home, I prayed that I would find comfort with its familiarity. Part of me hoped that someone would be home and part of me wanted to me alone.

Entering the house, I didn't even look to see if anyone else was there. I ascended the stairs and went straight to my room, curling up on the bed in my soiled pants and passing out cold.

For two days and two nights I slept, never opening my eyes. No nightmares, no brief moments of semi-consciousness, nothing.

On the morning of the third day, my eyes shot open and I gasped in a breath of air like I was coming out of a pool of water after an extended period of time. I sat up in my bed, holding my head when the room spun. I smelled disgusting and I wanted a shower more than anything else. I kept my mind blank while I pulled out a pair of comfy pyjamas and made my way to the bathroom to scrub the scent of stale urine and sweat from my skin. I filled the tub with only hot water, burning my feet when I stepped in. I ignored the pain, sitting in the water to soak. I took my time, scrubbing myself everywhere with the face cloth before adding more soap and repeating the process a second time. I still felt dirty when I stepped out of the tub but I dried myself off and dressed.

When I walked into the kitchen, everyone went quiet and stared at me in surprise. I went to the counter and helped myself to a cup of coffee before taking my seat at the table.

"Paisley, where have you been?" Mom asked, worry creasing her forehead.

"I just woke up." I answered confused.

"You were in your room?"

"Yeah..." I trailed off, wondering what the hell she was going on about.

"Where were you yesterday?" Dad pressed, sipping from his cup.

"I was at school yesterday."

"Paisley, there's no school on Saturdays." Dad stated cautiously, not sure if I was lying or nuts.

"Yesterday was Thursday." I argued and looked at dad then mom trying to figure out if they were screwing with me.

"Paisley, what's the last thing you remember?" Dad asked.

"I wrote my history exam then walked home and went to bed."

"That's it?"

"Yeah, I was tired so I went right up to bed. Slept like a log too."

"That means you slept for two whole days. It's Sunday." He explained, shocked with the discovery that I had been in my room the entire time.

"Why the hell didn't anyone try to wake me up?" I shouted, feeling like the ground beneath me was sinking.

"I went to pick you up at school Thursday and you never came out. I came home and you didn't answer when I called out to you so I figured you were out with that friend of yours again."

"Fuck..." Was all I could say and dad raised his brows at my foul language. I never swore in front of my parents.

I couldn't seem to get back on my feet after I lost two days. I couldn't trust my own head. If I could drift away for long periods of time, there was no telling what I would miss or whether or not I would come back the next time. It was one thing, trying to protect myself from the outside world. It was an entirely different, more unsettling thing to defend myself against the world inside my head.

I had the senseless idea that if I wasn't in control of myself, I might as well get drunk and enjoy a buzz while I was at it. Which is how I found myself sitting on a bar stool at Billy's with a bottle of tequila and a shot glass in front of me, well on my way to inebriated. I didn't feel like being with anyone except Dimitri but he didn't pick up when I called. If I were being honest, the idea of having the bottle to myself and forgetting my name for a while, didn't bother me.

By the time I made a nice dent in the bottle, a hand went to the back of my neck, massaging the sensitive skin lovingly. Chills covered my body. I hadn't seen Thomas since my dad tore him apart but by myself in the bar, I was afraid he had finally decided to come out of hiding.

"Hey happy-cheeks." I nearly fainted with relief when Dimitri whispered in my ear.
"You scare the shit out of me." I scolded him.
"Sorry, I thought you liked it when I touched you." He said flirtatiously, wagging his eyebrows. Seeing him in a good mood melted away the lingering fear.
"Oh, you know I like it when you touch me." I returned with a mischievous grin. "Why don't we go explore the ladies room?" I offered.
"Jesus Paisley." He chided, adjusting himself in his jeans while he sat down beside me.

"How did you know I was here?"

"Because though you are incredibly beautiful, you're predictable as fuck."

"Why do you say that like it's a shitty thing?" I asked, swallowing a shot of tequila.

"Well, I was in the shower and got a phone call. When I checked the call display, my favourite number appeared." He began, acting like he was telling me an amazing story. "I quickly dialed the number, holding onto the towel around my waist because I was bare underneath." He winked to which I rolled my eyes. "To my utter heartbreak, the stunning princess I called upon was no longer waiting eagerly by the phone for me to call her back."

"I wasn't waiting by the phone." I argued without thinking and bit my lip when hurt appeared briefly on his face.

"I know." He said with a sigh before returning to his animated story teller voice. "Which meant but one thing. The lady was bursting apart from her desires and would hunt for the body of a young man to soothe her." He looked around the bar. "At Billy's" I laughed.

"Not quite but a very captivating tale sweet Dimmy." I complimented him, kissing his cheek. I was hit with a sudden realization that made me feel sick to my stomach. "Dimitri..." I began cautiously, leaning back to see his face. "Why do you think so highly of me?" I watched fear cross his face as he tried desperately to find words.

"Because you're perfect."

"I am far from perfect, don't lie to me." I said bitterly, pouring myself another shot.

"You're perfect in my eyes Paisley." He insisted, staring at me, enamoured.

"Dimitri. Stop it. It's not funny." I demanded, convinced that he must be high.

"Happy-cheeks, I thought you were a goddess when I first laid eyes on you and things have only gotta worse for me since. I'm completely crazy about you." He told me sincerely. The hope in his eyes made me want to cry.

"Dimmy..." I was at a loss. I was struggling to figure out what was wrong with me. I was so empty; Dimitri didn't deserve the shit that was tied to me. "I've got nothing to give."

"I know." He reached over and squeezed my hand. "That's why I haven't pushed you. I know you just came out of a toxic relationship and aren't ready to get involved with someone." His hand slid below the bar, onto my thigh and crept up to touch the seam below my zipper. He ran his finger across my heat seductively. "As long as I'm the only one who gets to wrestle with you naked, I'll be one happy son of a bitch."

"I don't think that's a good idea anymore." I told him even though the words stung. "I can't take advantage of your feelings for me Dimitri." I took his hand from between my legs and kissed his fingers.

"Not having you at all will hurt me a lot more than only having a small piece." He trapped my hand between both of his. "I need you; I can't let this go. If down the road, you meet someone who makes you feel the way I feel about you, then I'll understand and let you go. I can't let you walk away just because I was stupid enough to tell you how I felt." He was very convincing and if I were a better person, I would have held my ground but I wasn't. I wanted the connection we had; it was the only good thing I had left. He could see my resolve disappear. "So can I be you boy toy?" He flashed me his most charming grin.

"Yes, I would very much like to have you as my boy toy."
"Thank fucking Christ." He breathed, pulling me forward by the front of shirt and kissing me roughly, claiming my mouth.
"You're welcome. Can I have your dick now?"
"Why don't you tell me what you really want and stop beating around the bush?" He asked sarcastically as he chuckled at my request.

A few uneventful days went by peacefully. Though fresh wounds decorated my forearm, nothing seemed out of the ordinary. I slept three to four hours a night, able to wake myself when the nightmares began, glad to have the ability to avoid seeing the ghastly old man. I was becoming accustomed to the constant state of fatigue. Where at first, I would get highly agitated when I misplaced things or forgot something, I now chalked it up to sleep deprivation, knowing the item or memory would turn up eventually.

I stopped going to school. After my attempt to write an exam ended disastrously, anytime I stepped foot into the building, I would hear ominous sounds and if I lasted long enough, I would see the old man. I admitted defeat, allowing him to chase me away from school. My parents didn't insist I go back, instead, they enrolled me in a program that allowed me to study from home. Normally, I would not have the self discipline necessary to succeed but if I allowed my brain free rein, it would go to a dark place that haunted me. Despite the sleep deprivation, my grades improved considerably.

I should have been ready for the calm to come to a crashing end but I was still as caught off guard as I had been the first time.

I don't know why but as I sat on my bed, working on an assignment, I caught myself gazing off in a daze. Even when I realized that I was staring at nothing, I couldn't stop, couldn't blink. My eyes burned with the need to moisten. I wanted to close my eyes with an intensity that was making me crazy. The more I tried, the more they bulged in protest from my useless effort.

There was an almost audible snap as when I felt myself break. Pages from my textbook were torn to shreds and went flying across the floor. I flew around my room, pulling pictures from my walls, pitching so that they crashed into pieces. Drawers were yanked from my dresser, the contents upended. My arm swept across the top, scattering all the contents that lived there. I hooked my arms under my vanity and flung it to the ground. Makeup palettes popped open, painting the floor an assortment of chaotic colour. With both feet, I stomped on the powder, smudging it further. I held the table of the vanity down with one foot while I tore off the legs one by one. I kept the last one, using it like a bat against the lamp on my end table along with the alarm clock then I launched it through my bedroom window. When my room was in shambles with nothing left to break, I pounded my fists against the wall above my headboard. Distantly, I could hear someone screaming but I didn't stop. I continued pounding my fists against the wall even when my knuckles were swollen and torn. Where they connected with drywall, they left behind splatters of blood and still I continued. Dents and holes peppered the wall from one end of my headboard to the other. Of its own volition, my body fell onto my back against the mattress. I squirmed and contorted like a tortured cat before my hips lifted so high that I was holding myself up by my shoulders and the tips of my toes.

Another scream broke through my trance and I collapsed. I began to sweat profusely, my skin fevered. My eyes closed and I fell asleep to the sounds of someone sobbing.

It was another two days before I woke up. My room was bare. Nothing but my bed remained, reminding me of my mental break. I couldn't find it inside myself to care.

My body was stiff as I stood. Stretching loosened some of the taught muscles but the rest were too tightly wound to be relieved so easily. I limped to the bathroom as quickly as I could, barely getting my pants down on time to empty my bladder. An unfathomable amount of fluid flooded out and I was shocked that I was able to carry such a vast amount without exploding. My stomach cramped as I imagined my bladder contracting to its natural size.

The house was frighteningly quiet when I went downstairs, as though I were left in a deserted house. Shella, John, mom and dad all sat around the table, each of them looking pale and afraid. When I entered, they all looked up and stared at me with a mixture of fear and concern. Thy most likely expected me to start throwing things and pitching a grand fit. The looks on their faces irritated me.

I went to the cupboard for a coffee mug. Giving in to the urge to fuck with them, I turned and pretended to pitch the mug. I laughed riotously when they all jumped, John knocking his chair to the floor.

"What is wrong with you?" Mom demanded, livid.
"Johanne!" Dad barked.
"Don, why is it okay for her to scare the wits out of us?"
"Because it's funny mother. That's why." I told her with a chilling smirk.
"It is not funny!" She slapped the table.

I slowly prowled to the table, watching as her confidence wavered. When I reached the table beside her, I leaned forward, getting close enough to make her uncomfortable. When she looked away from me to give my father a look, asking him for assistance, I smiled.

"It is." I said, slapping the table and mocking her childishly.
"Paisley, is this necessary?" My father asked, coming to her defence.
"I'm sorry dad." I apologized, wiping the amusement from my face.

The quick change in my demeanour confused the lot of them. I paid no attention while I turned back to the coffee machine to pour myself a cup. I didn't wait before taking a sip, burning my tongue and the roof of my mouth in the process.

"What happened the other day P-Baby?"
"I don't know, was I not asleep?" I asked, playing dumb.
"When you destroyed your room. What happened?"
"I honestly haven't got a clue. One minute I was staring off into space, the next I was trapped inside a tornado."
"So, you lost your temper?"
"No. I wasn't mad."
"That makes absolutely no sense. Your father paid a lot of money for the furniture you so carelessly tore apart. Now stop your lying and

tell him the truth." Mom demanded; her anger returned now that I was away from her. I slowly turned a glare her way. Sending icicles her way.

"Trust me mother, I know damn well who *paid* for the furniture and I'm sure as shit not a goddamn liar." She was taken aback by my tone. I dismissed her, turning back to my dad.

"I am very sorry for breaking my things. If I knew what happened, I would tell you, so that I would hopefully be able to prevent any further outbursts." Looking at him, I felt terrible for what I had done. I knew how hard he worked, day in and day out to support his family. "Do you think we could visit the lake sometime soon?"

"I'd love that." He smiled, very pleased that I sought his happy place in my time of trouble.

      The next morning was much of the same. Anytime my mother spoke to me, I would retaliate with quick tempered irritation. The same held true for the morning after that. She was just stubborn enough to keep trying, frantic to make our relationship healthy again. She didn't realize that my eyes had been opened and I couldn't regard her with any modicum of respect and her efforts did more damage than good in my current state of mind.

"What's wrong Paisley? Why do you despise me so much lately?" She pleaded with me.
"If you would leave me the fuck alone there wouldn't be a goddamn issue! Instead, you choose to nag and nag. You make me fucking insane!" I yelled fisting my hands in my hair to drive my point home.
"If you would just talk to us, we could help you!"

      I stood at the counter, swaying with fury. If she didn't stop soon, I was going to leave the kitchen, filled with regret.

"Paisley, please. What's going on?"

My heart pounded, muffling her words.

"Do you think seeing a doctor would help?"

Thump. Thump. Thump.

"Will you look at me? You can't keep living like this!"

Snap. I gripped the full pot of hot coffee and heaved it. It flew past her, narrowly missing her head as it exploded against the wall behind her. She screamed, caught off guard by my outburst though I had warned her that she was pushing me too far.

"Enough!" Dad stood from his chair, set off by my actions. "You will not continue to disrespect your mother this way!" He pointed an angry finger at me.

For the first time in my life, I was not afraid of my father in a bad mood. Maybe I *had* completely lost my mind. Watching him fume only brought my fury to a new level. I grabbed the edge of the table and flung it up sending it and everything on it to the floor. Plates and cups shattered; cutlery clattered against the tiles. Shella and John fell out of the way just in time, avoiding a collision with the table. I spun on my heel, intending to empty the nearest cupboard of all its contents and mom wrapped her arms around me, trying to restrain me. She was no match for me and my adrenaline. I ripped her hands off of me, taking a sharp step back, shoving her back.

Realizing my mother was out of her depth, dad stepped in, holding my arms at my side. To everyone's shock, including my own, I raised my arms and used my nails to dislodge his grip. I bent at the waist and used my shoulder to push him off, letting out a battle cry. I reached out and grabbed the toaster, smashing it to the floor.

Again, dad gripped my biceps, squeezing to keep a strong hold on me. Like a monkey, I planted my foot just above his knee. With my foot planted, I raised the other one and stepped on his stomach. One more step on his shoulder and I was able to push off of him and flip back, forcing him to let go. Free from his hold and on my own two feet, I smirked at him. The mason jar of sugar was next to meet its end, followed by mom's ceramic tea pot.

"John, give me a hand." Dad commanded.

John was afraid while he crept up behind me. Together they pounced on me. John wrapping his arms around my neck in a sleeper hold and dad grabbing my wrists, binding them together in one hand and hugging me with the other one, locking my hands at my chest. I used their hold to raise my knees and plant my feet against dad's hips, pushing with all my might. Off balance, he stumbled back, releasing me. With the force from my legs, John and I fell back and I landed on top of him. I rolled back to my feet, crouched and ready.

"Oh God Don, what do we do?" Mom cried.
"You leave me the fuck alone!" I screeched, sweeping the serving bowl from the counter where it broke apart with the rest of the glass. "Johanne, Shella, she can't hold off the four of us."

Watching Shella stand tall and confident made me want to punch her in the face. I wanted her to fear me. I wanted her to dread the thought of restraining me. The fact that she was neither of those things infuriated me. I stepped towards her and spit a mouthful of saliva into her face. When the other three were within arms reach, I fainted.

I regained consciousness in my bed. The stiffness in my body was gone. If felt well rested, rejuvenated. I was started by movement in the corner of my eye. I turned to see dad sitting in a chair just inside my bedroom door, watching me. When our eyes met and his looked so unsure, I burst into tears.

"I don't know what to do for you Paisley." He told me; one arm crossed over his chest supporting the elbow of the other one as he rested his chin in his upturned palm.

"I don't know either dad. Maybe I really am crazy." My chest heaved with my sobs.

"What's going on inside that head of yours?"

"Fear." I answered vaguely, not having a clue how to explain the turmoil I was in.

"What are you so afraid of?"

"Myself."

He thought deeply about my answer, knowing there were no words to comfort me. Without knowing what was happening, there was no way to know if I would eventually find my way out.

"You have to stay strong baby girl. It's the only way to make it to the other side of this. Just know, everyday that you suffer, I'm suffering with you." He stood and came to the side of my bed, leaning over to place a gently kiss on my forehead. "Sleep. I'll be back to check on you in a bit." He ran a hand over my head just like he used to at bed time when I was really young.

I didn't sleep. I laid on my bed and cried until my eyelids felt like sandpaper. I wanted to disappear. If I wasn't such a coward, I would have taken drastic measures to make it all stop. It wasn't the potential pain that held me back, it was the fear of the unknown, the thought that I might succeed and be trapped in limbo. What then? What if I killed the part of my brain that was still mine and I was left living in a body that no longer belonged to me?

When the tears dried, I decided that the fight wasn't over. I would take dad's advice and stay strong. I would get through these crippling episodes one at a time and when they were over, I would live my life the way I wanted until the next one came along. I would force myself to accept the blips of time I lost and take full advantage of the rest. I couldn't spend my life dwelling on the things I had no control over.

First thing to do, was to apologize for what I had done. I held my head high when I descended the stair. Mom, dad and John sat in the living room. When I came in, mom closed her book and looked watched my approach. I almost laughed at the fact that just the sight of her almost turned me around, swallowing my words of regret but I was determined. Instead, I focused on John and dad.

"I'm really sorry for the way I treated you guys. I don't know what's wrong with me but you didn't deserve any of it." I let my remorse show on my face, hoping they would believe me.

"Paisley, you have got to learn to control your temper." Mom told me in a stern voice. I could feel my blood pressure begin to rise.

"As I said. I am sorry." I insisted, refusing to look at her.
"Don't let it happen again."
"I'll try to walk away if I feel my control slipping." I tried to compromise. I couldn't believe after everything that happened, she still thought confronting me was the route to take. Why would you push someone who openly admitted they couldn't control themselves?

"Don't just *try* Paisley. If you think that we're all here to cater to your moods, you're mistaken. If you're in a bad mood, keep to yourself." With the snotty tone in her voice, my eyes snapped to hers.

"I came down here to apologize *mother,*" I said with a snarl. "You would think that after what happened this morning you would just shut your mouth and let the dust settle. But *no,* you can't bite your tongue for the moment and give me this bull shit speech another day, when I wouldn't be as likely to blow a fuse." I took a deep calming breath. "I do *not* expect any of you to cater to my moods. Truth is, my mood is irrelevant. I could be in a great mood but then the sound of your voice takes a shit on it and I'm ready to throw down my gloves." My voice was quiet and ice cold. "To avoid outbursts, I'll have to avoid you. So, stay the fuck away from me and I will be damn sure to keep you out of my sight." I turned and stomped to the front door. The windows shook when I slammed it closed behind me.

I walked blindly for a long time. My feet hurt and the night air was chilly on my bare arms. I didn't want to go home, didn't want to go to Billy's or to stop in on Laurie. I still felt restless, even though my calves burned. With nowhere to go and no desire to be around people, I walked into the next gas station I passed.

"Can I use your phone please?" I asked the attendant.

"Sure." He turned to grab the cordless phone from the counter behind him.

"Thank you, and can I get a pack of Pall Mall cigs please? King size."

"You got some ID?" I pulled the well used fake one from my pocket and handed it to him. He barely glanced at it before reaching under the counter and grabbing the cigarettes. I dropped a lighter on the counter to add to the bill and paid for my purchase.

I walked to the corner of the store, out of earshot to dial a number from memory. I listened as it rang once, twice.

"Hello?" He answered groggily.

"Hey Dimmy."

"What's going on happy-cheeks? What are you doing calling me so late?"

"Oh, I'm sorry. What time is it?" I asked, looking around to try and find a clock.

"It's one in the morning."

"Oh shit. I'm sorry." There was a pause before he spoke.

"Where the hell are you? I don't know this number."

"I'm at Max Convenience on fourth ave."

"What the fuck are you doing so far from home at this time of night?" I could hear him shuffling around while he worried about me.

"I was walking off some steam and found myself here. Would you mind coming to get met?"

"Of course. I'll be there in ten minutes. Just wait inside, God only knows what kind of weirdos hang out on that side of town." I could hear him pulling on clothes.

"Thank you, Dimitri. I really appreciate it."

"Anytime Paisley, you know that."

I listened to him breathe for a moment before hanging up. I brought the phone back to the clerk and stepped outside, ignoring Dimitri's warning. I went around the corner of the building and lit a pall mall. I leaned against the brick wall while I smoked. The first one burned out before I was satisfied so I lit another one.

When headlights pulled into the gas station, I recognized Dimitri's pickup truck and walked towards it. Opening the passenger door, I hopped in with a smile on my lips, ready to greet him. The cross look on his face caused me pause. He never looked at me that way before. I hesitated to buckle my seat belt, unsure whether or not I should get out of the truck.

"Are you upset? I'm sorry, if I'd have known what time it was, I would never have called." I rushed to explain.

"I love that you called me when you needed someone." He began, loosening his grip on staying angry with me. "I told you to stay inside the store. You're in a sketchy part of town, alone, in the middle of the night. Do you want to get jumped? Raped?" He questioned, his hands holding onto the steering wheel with such a tight hold that his knuckles turned white with the strain.

"Oh baby, were you scared for me?" I asked, using a patronizingly sweet tone, leaning across the centre console and pulling his earlobe between my lips, nibbling the sensitive skin and making him shiver.

"Paisley, I'm being serious." He struggled to remain unaffected.
"I'm here now. My big hero saved me from all the bad, bad men out there." I rubbed my breasts against his bicep, enjoying the game I played.
"Come on, cut it out." He leaned against his door, trying to break the contact.
"Oh baby, will you not forgive me for being a bad girl?" I pushed out my bottom lip, pouting at him.
"You scared the shit out of me Paisley. I knew you wouldn't listen and would stand outside like the stubborn-ass girl that you are."

"You're right. I don't know what came over me." I looked down at my lap in mock shame. I surprised myself when I was able to force tears to my eyes before I looked back at him. He was horrified when he saw the moisture pooled on my bottom lid.

"No happy-cheeks, don't cry. It's okay. Really. Just... don't do it again. That's all. No need to be upset." He grabbed me, pulling me back across the console and hugging me to his chest.

"Will you spank me?" I asked, adding a hiccup to drive the act home.
"What?" He was thrown off by the question but his voice was husky with the visual of bending me over his knee.
"Will you spank me?" I repeated, looking him in the eye. "Please."
"You want me to spank you?" He asked, unable to believe what I was asking him.

"Yes. Spank me, then fuck me senseless." I requested, sliding a hand over the front of his jeans where his arousal was making itself known. His mouth crushed onto mine, taking it with a kiss that starved for more.
"Paisley, you make me crazy." He said against my lips.
"Good. Now take me to your place."

It didn't take long to make it to Dimitri's apartment. Especially since the only traffic laws he obeyed on the way, were the traffic lights. When we got out of his truck, he grabbed my hand and dragged me along behind him as he ran to the entrance. His lips never left mine on the elevator as we rode to his floor and he had my shirt off before we were closed in the apartment.

His hands eagerly groped at me, tearing at my bra, seeking their soft weight in his palms. I ripped his shirt over his head running my hands over his hard stomach and taunting him with my fingers sliding just below the waistband of his pants. I pulled his hips into me and could feel his erection straining to be set free. My hands shook with impatience as I undid the front of his jeans. As usual, he was without underwear, leaving no barriers between his thickness and my greedy fingers. I grabbed him in a firm grip. His head fell back as I stroked him and a moan whispered from his parted lips.

He enjoyed my touch for a minute or two before pushing me up against the wall. He yanked my pants off and shredded my panties with his hands, no longer able to restrain his need to be inside me. I hooked my calf around his hip and gasped when he filled me in one quick thrust. With a maddeningly slow movement, he withdrew, watching the disappointment on my face. I screamed when he slammed back into me. With increasingly violent thrusts, he brought me to the edge of ecstasy and I cried out when I fell off. He didn't stop and my pleasure mounted again. He slowed his pace, changing tactics, from an angry fuck to sweet love making. I was dazed, staring at his parted lips as he panted. When the second orgasm hit me, my legs shook. His hips sped up with his impending release and he quickly followed me to bliss.

When he caught his breath, he lifted me into his arms bridal-style and carried me to his room. Laying me down on the bed and pulling the covers over my naked body before going around the foot of the bed, sliding in and curling himself around me. Holding me close, he breathed against the back of my neck and I marvelled at the comfort I felt with him. I wasn't shy about my nakedness, I wasn't stiff, overly conscious of him being so close. I was completely at ease and I relished the feeling.

I awoke the next morning, with a hairy leg tangled between mine, a hand on my ass cheek and warm breath against the top of my head. I smiled into Dimitri's chest when a mischievous idea came to mind and I wondered if I could do it without waking him up before I was in position. Slowly, I shimmied down until I was face to face with his member, already standing at attention. Tentatively, I ran my tongue across the head and grinned when I heard him moan in his sleep. I swirled my tongue around the crown before wrapping my lips around him and gently sucked. His hips bucked forward with another moan. I looked up and his head was turned into the pillow I had just vacated.

"Pais...ley." He groaned, still fast asleep. I smiled around his dick, pleased that he thought of me while unconscious.

Rewarding him, I swallowed him deep into my throat and went to work, focused on getting him off.

"Oh fuck." He gasped, opening his eyes halfway, drowning in the sensation of my mouth on him. I met his eyes and kept at it.

When he nudged my shoulders, trying to make me stop, I sucked harder, refusing to back of.

"God Paisley. Stop. I'm gonna come." He warned. I cupped his soft sack in my free hand, swiping my tongue across the crown before taking all of him again, relentlessly bringing him to the brink. "Ah... Fuck!" He yelled as he exploded. I drained every drop from him before letting him go.

I leaned back on my feet, watching him drag his hands over his face and into his hair, his world thoroughly rocked. I bent forward and planted a kiss on his pubic bone before rolling from the bed.

"Where are you going?" He asked, scrambling to try and catch my hand to stop my retreat.

"Well Dimmy, however scrumptious you are, I'm still hungry." I smiled at him before strutting from his room, completely naked, feeling his eyes on my ass on my way out.

His kitchen was pretty scarce. I smiled looking into his fridge. A case of beer, still in the case, a carton of milk left open and an almost empty jug of orange juice. The crisper didn't house vegetables, instead I found an unsealed package of bologna and a full sleeve of hot dogs. I poured two cups of milk and found bread in one of the cupboards to make us some peanut butter toast.

When I returned to the bedroom with our breakfast, Dimitri was sprawled on the bed with his hands behind his head, staring at the ceiling.

"Breakfast is served." I handed him his milk and toast, which he accepted with a big smile.

"A guy can get used to this."

"Toast crumbs in your bed?" I asked with a smirk, sitting cross legged on the floor beside the bed where I could still see him.

"Being served by a gorgeous girl wearing nothing but her birthday suit." He wiggled his brow salaciously.

"You're terrible." I laughed.

We ate, exchanging smiles every now and again. When we were both finished, I took our dishes back to the sink, intending to wash them and put them away. I had the plug in the sink, turned the water on and squirted in some soap when long arms wrapped around my waist from behind and lips nibbled the skin under my ear. I giggled and leaned my head back onto his shoulder. He started swaying against me and I realized there was music playing. This beautiful man put a love song on his radio and wanted to dance with me, naked, in his kitchen. I turned in his arms and wrapped mine around his neck, following his lead. The moment couldn't be more perfect.

"You are something else Dimmy." I sighed, blown away by his sweetness.
"What can I say happy-cheeks, you make me feel all warm and fuzzy inside." He smirked before leaning forward and giving me the softest, most loving kiss, I had ever felt. No tongue just warm lips full of tenderness.

Twenty minutes later. The slow song was long over and the two of us bounced around his kitchen to high energy music. We laughed and danced to the happy beat. When our eyes locked, we became entranced by each other. Slowly we moved closer until our bodies became glued to one another and we continued moving. Grinding quickly led to stiffness pressing against my stomach. Inevitably, we fell onto each other like starving animals.

Dimitri and I never got dressed that day or the next. By the following day, when Dimitri was getting ready for work, I shared the shower with him and dressed to go home. I didn't want to leave but I knew that he would witness the crazy that waited in the shadows, ready to destroy the wonder we had lived the few days we spent together.

"You can stay Paisley. I would love to come home to you waiting for me." He told me as we walked to his truck.
"I can't Dimmy. I need to go home. Plus, I'd really like to put on

some clean clothes." I grinned.

"You don't need clothes here but if you insist, I have a closet full, probably a bit too big but they would be comfortable."

"Tempting but I don't want you getting sick of me. Maybe I'll call you from a gas station sometime this week and have you come and rescue me in the middle of the night." I baited him.

"You better not go wandering around town all night again Paisley." He admonished with a serious expression on his face. "But if you can't help it, don't ever hesitate to call me. Even if I'm at work, I'll come and get you." He grabbed my hand and turned me to face him. "Especially if it means I'll have you to myself for a couple days." He winked before kissing my cheek and opening the passenger door for me.

We held hands while he drove me home. The closer we got to the house, the more I could feel the dark clouds creeping in over my head. When he pulled in front of my house, I could almost choke on the dread in my throat. There weren't any signs that something was coming but somewhere in the back of my mind, I knew that it was and whatever had my hairs standing on end, wasn't good.

I turned to Dimitri and leaned over to kiss him one last time before being away from him for the first time in days. The idea of being away from him, brought a deep-seated sadness to the pit of my stomach.

"Have a good night at work." I rubbed my thumb over the stubble on his cheek.

"I will. I'll miss you Paisley. Can I call you on my break?" He asked, reluctant to leave.

"Of course. I'll look forward to it." One more kiss and I stepped out of his truck.

I waved him off before I turned to the house. Steeling myself with a deep breath, I walked to the front door. I could hear the TV through the front door before I opened it. Dad sat in his chair, sipping his Pepsi and watching a hockey game. He looked up when I walked in and a smile brightened his face. I was relieved to find him happy to see me.

"Hey P-Baby. Long time no see. Have a good weekend away?" He asked.

"Yeah, it was nice. Felt good to get out for a while." I sat on the couch beside his chair.

"I bet. How are you feeling?" He searched my face to gauge my mental state.

"I'm good dad. I feel... revived?" I asked, feeling like it wasn't the right word.

"I'll take it." He stated with a smile. "Who is this boy who has you feeling *revived?*"

"His name is Dimitri. He's a great guy. Maybe if he wasn't so perfect, I could love him." I said out loud for the first time.

"It sure seems like you love him, maybe it's just not the forever kind of love but not all relationships need to be for a lifetime. Don't dwell on it kiddo, just enjoy it." He advised, understanding my predicament.

"I plan on it." I smiled. "It feels too good to let it slip away just yet."

"Good. I like this kid already." He stated, to which I laughed.

"Dad, you would love him. It's impossible not to be drawn to him like a fly is drawn to a pile of dog shit." Laughter erupted from him. He was in a great mood and I wondered if it was because he had me back at home.

"I'm ordering pizza for supper; your mother is out with her girlfriends. You sticking around?" He asked when he regained his composure.

"What kind of person turns down pizza?"

"Johanne Coleman turns down pizza." He replied with a smirk.

"I rest my case." I chuckled, standing from the couch. "I'm off to get my pyjamas on. Can we watch a movie while we eat Galeano's pizza?"

"Who said I was ordering from Galeano's pizza?"

"Dad, please. Don't scare me like that. There's no pizza like Galeano's pizza."

"I remember someone saying the same thing to you not that long ago." He grinned.

"You trained me well oh wise one."

I jogged up to my room and tears came to my eyes when

I saw the new vanity and dresser sitting in my room. He replaced my furniture even when I didn't deserve it. They were simple but beautiful and so suited to me with their dark antiqued wood and black metal handles. I took a moment to admire the new pieces before rummaging through the dresser to find the well-worn t-shirt my dad gave me for a nightshirt and a pair of pyjama shorts. I scooped my hair up into a messy bun on top of my head and hurried back downstairs to rejoin my father for pizza and a movie.

John was by the shelf when I came back down, looking for something for us to watch. I usually hated his taste in movies but at that moment, I didn't care what he chose. When he pulled down a slasher flick, I realized that he had dad and I in mind when he made his selection. We loved horror films while it would have been the last thing he would choose for himself.

"Holy shit Johnny, have we converted you into a horror movie junkie?" I asked him in surprise.
"No way. I don't understand why you guys like this stuff. It's so gross." He said gross but I knew he meant scary. He didn't exactly have nerves of steel.
"That's half the fun!"

The doorbell rang and dad handed his wallet to John so he could answer it and pay the delivery driver. He came back with two white boxes and a smile.

"This is going to be so good." John said, sniffing the air as the mouth-watering aroma of cheese and pepperoni floated in the air.
"Wanna grab the paper plates from the kitchen?" Dad asked me.
"On it." I jumped up and grabbed three plates and some juice for John and I.

It wasn't an exciting evening but I loved spending time with John and dad, worry-free. We hung out and polished off both pizzas. When the first movie was over, John popped a second one in, none of us in a hurry to call it a night. I huddled down on the couch with a blanket wrapped around me, watching people get torn apart on TV.

It was just after eleven when mom came through the front door. I debated staying where I was but decided not to take any chances and potentially ruining the evening. Standing from the couch, I folded up the blanket. She came into the living room as I was leaning down to kiss dad's cheek.

"Good night dad." I looked at mom, praying she wouldn't question me. "Good night mom."

"Nice of you to turn up." I ground my teeth but chose to ignore the comment and walk around her to go upstairs. "She turns up and you reward her with pizza?" I heard her ask dad as I made my way upstairs.

"It's food Johanne. I was having pizza regardless." He stated, irritated with her tone.

I smirked when I heard her huff and stomp across the room and to the kitchen. I pulled the blankets down and curled up in bed. My eyes were just starting to drift closed when a knock sounded at my door.

"Yeah?" John popped his head in.

"Phone's for you."

"Thank you." I got up and took the phone from him, yawning while I put it up to my ear.

"Hello?"

"Hey happy-cheeks, tired or something? Someone wear you out?"

"Very tired and deliciously worn out."

"Whatcha wearing?" He asked and I could hear the wolfish grin in his voice.

"My dad's shirt and ratty old shorts." I answered honestly.

"You really suck at this. Coulda lied and told me you were naked."

"You've seen enough of my nakedness the last few days; you can visualize me in my comfy clothes." I teased.

"Oh, how deluded you are sweet girl. There is no such thing as seeing enough of you naked." To this I laughed before letting out another yawn. "When will I see you again?"

"You free Thursday?"

"Paisley! That's five fucking days!"

"I know how to count."

"You want to send me into withdrawal?"

"You'll survive you big dork."

"Let me see you tomorrow."

"I can't. I have a lot of assignments I need to catch up on."

"Then Tuesday." He persisted.

"We'll see."

"Say yes."

"I'll try. I promise."

"All right. I suppose I can live with that. Go get some sleep beautiful."

"Good night Dimitri."

"And Paisley?"

"Yes?"

"If you have sexy dreams about me, touch yourself then you can tell me all about it on Tuesday." I laughed.

"Good night."

"Good night happy-cheeks." He kissed the phone, loud enough for me to hear it and I smiled when I ended the call.

I did not have sexy dreams that night. The old man came back with a vengeance. The nightmare returned and when my eyes flew open, I was paralyzed. Unable to move, words trapped in my throat. Only my eyes were free to look around the familiar sight of my bedroom. I tried so hard to keep my eyes open but they were too heavy. I fell back asleep and started the nightmare from the beginning. Three times I woke. Each time I lay in bed, paralyzed. The last time it happened, I managed to keep my eyes open long enough to feel my fingertips start to tingle. I focused on the pins and needles to stay conscious. Finally, after long minutes of fighting sleep, I was able to move again.

I sat up in my bed, panting in terror and gripped my chest where my heart furiously pounded. Much like the last time, I caught myself staring at the wall, in a daze. I heard myself whimper, unable to blink and feeling the horrible burning in my eyes. I tried to focus on my breathing and desperately hoped I could just wait it out.

When my feet slid out of the blanket and onto the floor, my heart dropped. Once more I was paralyzed, only able to watch as my body moved on its own. I stood from the bed and pulled off my shorts, my underwear going with them. I wanted to scream, terrified of what my body was doing. I gripped the hem of my shirt and stood completely naked in front of my vanity mirror. I watched my face break into a wide grin that made the corner of my lips sting in protest from the unnatural expression. The grin was all too familiar and I was horrified to see the old man's smile on my face. Another whimper managed to squeak out.

I turned to my door and ambled down the hallway, my limbs moving in an odd, creepy way as I continued toward my parents' bedroom door. My hand wrapped around the door knob and without a sound I walked up to their bed where they were both fast asleep. I crawled onto the bed and straddled my mother's hips, naked and staring down at her resting face. I gripped the blanket on either side of her neck and pushed it into the mattress, trapping her and limiting her airflow.

Her eyes whipped open as she struggled to take in a full breath. She looked at me and I knew that the grin was still plastered on my face. She was terrified at what she saw. She squirmed beneath me, trying to buck me off of her without success. Her struggling startled dad awake. It took him a moment to understand what was happening. He tried futilely to pull my hands off of the blanket and allow mom to breathe properly. When that did work, he came behind me and tried using his whole body to pull me off of her. I didn't budge.

"Paisley, get off! She can't breathe!" He yelled, yanking the hair at the back of my head in an attempt to break my concentration. "Paisley! Let! Her! Go!" Still, I held my position.

I could feel him move off the bed but didn't look away from mom to see what he was doing. Something whacked me on the side of the head and finally I let go of the blanket, looking over at dad, still wearing the evil grin. I could see the same horror on his face that I felt when I had seen it in the mirror. He held a curtain rod in his hand, which must be what hit me on the head. A deep, malevolent laugh came from my mouth, vibrating against the walls. I felt my bladder empty on my mother's blanket and I instantly felt my face relax. Then, there was nothing.

# Chapter Eight

Doctors. Pills. Numbness.

*Tricia Warnock*

When I woke up, I was in a hospital bed. Assuming it was a dream, I screamed, terrified. When the door flew open and three nurses came rushing in, my screams reached another level, echoing in my eardrums. I kicked and thrashed around on the bed when they grabbed a hold of my arms and legs, pinning me to the bed. A needle pricked my arm and within seconds, I was subdued. My eyes grew heavy forming tight knots in my stomach.

"No, no, no. Please. I can't sleep." I cried, begging them to make it stop.

They ignored my pleas, the three of them looking relieved that I stopped fighting them. I couldn't stop myself from succumbing to my body's drug-induced need to sleep. I was headed to a meeting with the old man and no one could save me.

I walked towards the black door, already in tears. Unlike every other time I had the nightmare, I didn't turn the knob, I knocked. The door opened slowly and the old man appeared. Only, he didn't wear the creepy grin, He looked like the kind of sweet old man you would find sitting in the park, tossing bread into the pond for the birds. He wore a denim bucket hat and overalls, completely out of character.

"Come in sweet girl. Come in." He stood back and gestured for me to enter the black door.

Though it felt wrong, I was relieved to see the change in the old man. I couldn't take my eyes off his face, waiting to see if morph.

"Sit child." He gestured to a wooden picnic table surrounded by emptiness. "I'm sure you have many questions for me." He sat across from me, leaning forward on his elbows and tenting his fingers.

I noticed a word carved in large, bold letters, carved on the table top. Tracing them with my index finger unconsciously, I wondering what it meant. B-R-A-X-E-U-S

"Brax-ee-us?" I said, unsure of the pronunciation.
"Brack-zeus." He corrected, a corner of his mouth lifting in a smirk that showed a hint of the face I was accustomed to. There was something in his eyes that kept my guard up, like he was trying to manipulate me into thinking he was safe.

"What does it mean?"
"It's my name sweet child. Just as you are called Paisley Louise Coleman, daughter of Donald and Johanne Coleman formerly Finch, I am called Braxeus."
"Of course, you know my name, you live in my sub conscious." I snipped.
"You will be wise to watch your town with me." He warned, coldly.
"Or else you will continue driving me mad?" I asked, unphased.
"Firstly, I live in more than just your head. Secondly my goal is not to torture you."
"Well then, what the fuck do you call the nightmares you've caused? The sleep deprivation? Showing up at my school? Was that just you inviting me to drink fucking tea?"
"I said," He began calmly. "Watch your tone!" he yelled and the table vibrated with the deep bellow of his voice.

I jumped and froze. I shut my mouth and stared, shocked and afraid. Watching him compose himself sent chills down my spine. The anger that had appeared so suddenly, evaporated in a breath, returning to the calm smile of an easy-going old man.
"I sit before you with the intention of helping you overcome your troubles."
"How the fuck--." I stopped, catching myself. "Sorry. How would you do that? I don't even know what's wrong with me."
"I've lived a long time little girl. There aren't many things I haven't come across and what's happening to you is fairly common with

young people."

"Well, what's wrong with me?"

"The mind is an incredible thing. It can do so much more than what people would expect. Sometimes, a certain kind of mind comes along that rebels against its restraint and causes a lot of grief. If you want me to, I can make it stop."

"How?"

"Give yourself to me."

"I'm not having sex with you."

"Not sex," He said crossly. Give me control. I will fix this for you."

"Control of what? My head?"

"No, you can keep that. Heal. Let me have control of your body."

"Do you know how crazy that sounds." Briefly, that creepy grin of his appeared but he quickly toned it down when I pulled away.

"I'm asking you to let me fix the mess you have made of your life."

"You say that like I did this on purpose."

"No child, I know you didn't but I also know how much strain you're putting on your loved ones." I could feel my heart restrict with guilt. "I can fix it for you. The relationship with your mother that will soon be beyond repair? I can make it right. You just have to trust me."

"If I don't?"

"If you don't, then life will continue much the way it has been. I can't tell you if it will ever go back to normal. Chances are, you will quickly become too much for your family to handle or someone will be seriously injured and you will spend the rest of your days in a padded room."

"How can I trust you?"

"I am the only one willing *and* able to make this right, set you back on track to live a peaceful existence." His confidence was laced with unappealing cockiness.

"I'm not sure I believe you."

"I can understand your hesitation. Let me make you a deal. Let me take the wheel for twenty-four hours. If I do not improve your situation drastically in that short amount of time, then you don't have to accept my offer. If I do, then you can hand over the reins, sure of your decision."

I thought over what he offered me. I was desperate for a way out and was drowning in the fight for sanity on my own. I badly wanted to jump on the opportunity to take a step back but something in my gut was telling me to run. Run to the nearest church and pray until my knees bled. When I pictured myself, crawling on top of my mother, strangling her with her blanket, the decision was made.

"All right. I'll give you twenty-four hours." With those words, a sinister smile appeared.
"I look forward to walking in your shoes." He said.
"To help me." I was inclined to remind him.
"Of course, child, of course." He stared at me, his eyes burning terrifying holes into my soul. "Give me your hands and let us begin."

When I woke up again, I felt no different and I the disappointment stole my breath. I had to chuckle at myself for being so ridiculously naive. I squeezed my eyes closed, mourning the loss of what little hope I had left. I wanted to slap myself for believing I could ever learn to live like this.

I resorted to my usual punishment, scratching a chunk out of my forearm. It did nothing to ease my mental anguish and I punched the mattress beneath me in frustration.

When the nurses came into my room, my anxiety melted away and I was filled with a sense of calm. They came to the side of the bed, tentatively checking my vitals.

"How are you feeling today miss Coleman?" The older nurse with glasses asked.
"I'm good." My mouth answered, surprising me.
"That's wonderful dear." She said with genuine kindness.

"Sure is. It's been a long time since I felt good." More words came from my mouth and a smile curved my lips.

"That's great news." She returned the smile. "We're just going to wheel you down the hall for your MRI. The doctor wants run a few tests and make sure everything is all right." She explained, raising the guard rail on one side of the bed while the other nurse did the same on the other side.

I laid back on the bed while they rolled it through the doorway. My brain checked out while the test ran. When the platform pulled me out of the machine, different nurses rolled me back onto my bed and wheeled me to an exam room. I was alone for a couple minutes before the doctor came in.

"Good morning Paisley. I want to take some blood samples to check a few things then we will get you back to your room." He informed me, focused on the file he held in his hands.

I let him poke me with his needle, filling four vials with my blood before taping a cotton swab to my arm.

"A nurse will be in to take you back to your room, you have an appointment with the hospital's therapist this afternoon who will make recommendations for a plan of action moving forward. Once the blood tests come back, I'll check those results along with the ones from the MRI and let you know if I find anything."

When my mom walked in with a woman who looked like she could act as undercover student in a middle school later that afternoon, I wasn't overcome with irrational anger. I sat up in my bed and waited patiently for the two of them to settle themselves into chairs close to my bed. Mom looked like she hadn't slept in days and her neck still showed evidence of my attack.

"Hello Paisley. My name is Daniella Hall, I'm a registered therapist

for the hospital. Dr. Forsen referred you to me. I've been talking with your mother and she told me what happened the other night. Do you remember any of it?" I nodded; still unsure she was old enough to be a therapist. "What was going through your mind when you did it?"
"Nothing."
"You weren't thinking about what might happen to your mother." I shook my head. "Were you afraid?" Nod. "Were you in any kind of pain?" Shake. "Did you hear anything?" Shake.
"She was like a different person." Mom stated, frustrated with my lack of answers.
"What do you mean exactly?"
"The expression on her face... It wasn't a Paisley face." Mom tried to explain.
"As is she appeared angrier than she normally did? More aggressive?"

"No, like she was a completely different person. One I didn't recognize." I realized then that mom was more afraid of the way I looked than what I had done to her and I was hit with a new wave of guilt. Hearing her speak didn't grate on my nerves the way it had just days ago and that too, surprised me.

The rest of Daniella Hall's assessment, I sat and listened while mom told her about my depression which seemed to stem from Thomas and kidnapping me. She went on to explain my behaviour at school and how I was no longer willing to step foot in the building. I was stunned that she seemed to have noticed so much more than I thought she had.

"It seems you've been through the wringer lately." Daniella told me with a warm smile and eyes filled with pity. "Getting to the bottom of something like this takes time, it's a lot of educated guess work to find something that's going to work for you." She was scribbling furiously in her notebook. "It sounds to me like you're suffering from something called schizoid personality disorder. I'm going to suggest Doctor Forsen write you a prescription for a medication called Zyprexa. This is just a quick diagnosis but I think that something needs to be done now. I strongly believe that waiting will do far more harm than good."

I felt wonderful. The medication was a miracle drug as far as I was concerned. I hadn't seen or heard from Braxeus in weeks. Daniella and I met once a week and it didn't take long before I started looking forward to seeing her. Her genuinely kind nature reminded me that there were still good people in the world and I embraced it wholeheartedly.

There were side effects. I gained weight but that wasn't a bad thing, I needed to fill out again. I had trouble staying focused and some days, I felt dopey but it was a small price to pay.

My biggest accomplish thus far was inviting Dimitri out on a double date with Laurie and David. I heard all the emotion in Laurie's voice when I asked her. That was four days ago and she's called me everyday since, filled with contagious excitement. I was looking forward to introducing Dimitri to my best friend. Even though Dimitri was nervous, I knew they would hit it off.

I decided to take it one step further and asked my mom to take me to the mall to pick out an outfit for the big night. The minute the words were out of my mouth, her hand covered her mouth as tears filled her eyes instantly. She was speechless for a few minutes which was very awkward for me. I shifted my weight on my feet, debating whether or not I should leave her alone.

"Let's go." She grabbed her purse from the counter and went straight to the front door.
"I didn't mean right this minute." I said, hurrying to catch up.
"We gotta go before you realize what you're doing and take it back." She wiped her eyes and smiled at me. I laughed.
"Okay, let's go but I wouldn't have changed my mind." I pulled on my shoes and followed her to the car.

I swear she beamed the whole time. In and out of the stores as she suggested the next one we should check out. She would grab things from the racks and tell me to try them on and then she would wait for me to come out and model them for her. She was in her glory. A cute jean skirt with patches on the back pockets, a pair of grey capris, a pair of jeans that fit me perfectly were the items she insisted I *had to have.* According to her, the three blouses were also necessary so that I left with complete outfits. My cheeks ached from laughing at her enthusiasm.

"We've got to his up that cute dress shop downstairs for your date." She said, almost skidding toward the escalator.
"Mom, I can choose any one of the three outfits you just bought me!"
"Oh come on Paisley. Those are not date worthy!" She insisted, turning back to grab my hand and drag me along behind her.

She was very serious while she looked through the dresses, as though finding the perfect one was crucial. A couple of times she would pause on a dress and look up at me with a very serious look on her face. She would either pull the dress out and lay it across her arm out shake her hand and keep flicking through hangers.

After we picked out the perfect pair of red pumps to match the black dress with white polka dots, she was finally satisfied. We sang along to the radio on the ride home.

When we got home, I ran upstairs to hop in the shower. I was humming while I washed, feeling like I was riding the clouds. There was still a part of me that thought the floor would fall out from under me at any moment but I pushed the worry to the far corners of my brain, unwilling to dwell on the idea that I was walking a thin line. Going into my room, wrapped in my towel, I sat at my vanity to blow my hair dry and apply some makeup for the first time in ages. The last step was applying a thin layer of gloss and I smiled at myself while I twisted the lid back on. I had never thought of myself as pretty but looking at my reflection and seeing clear eyes without shadows underneath them and the same cheeks I used to despise for being round back in place, I could never have been prettier.

I hadn't seen Dimitri since my stay in the hospital. We talked on the phone almost every night and he begged to see me several times. I didn't know what to tell him, there was no way I was going to tell him the truth, I couldn't stomach him looking at me like I was crazy or fragile. At the same time, without telling him the truth, I couldn't think of a valid reason to tell him why I was avoiding him. For now, he was accepting my excuse of being ill.

I was nervous but mostly excited to see him. I wondered what he would think about the drastic change in my appearance. Maybe now that I had flesh on my bones, he would think I was fat and not want me anymore. Even knowing that it would hurt if he rejected me, I would accept it. I was thrilled with the way I looked and his opinion wouldn't change that.

I looked at the clock and my timing was spot on. Dimitri would arrive in fifteen minutes to pick me up so I went downstairs to show mom my final look. Dad, John and Shella sat at the table while mom plated their supper. Dad saw me come through the doorway and his smile was blinding.

"Jesus Christ P-Baby, you clean up real nice!" He complimented and when mom heard him she whirled around to have a look.
"Oh Paisley, you look gorgeous!"

I blushed at the attention and saw Shella curling her lip at me from the corner of my eye. I ignored her and spun around for mom when she spun a finger in the air.

"It's a very pretty dress." John smiled and my heart melted. John was usually very quiet but he was always sincere when he did.
"Thank you John."
"Are you gonna sit with us until the lucky bastard gets here?" Dad asked, still smiling.
"That was the plan." I answered pulling out my chair and having a seat.
"Where are you kids going tonight?"
"We're going to head over to that new Chinese place downtown and probably go to the indoor mini putt afterwards."

"Mini putt is so lame." Shella put in snobbishly.

"Good thing you weren't invited." I told her, smiling because even her sourness couldn't dampen my mood.

"You couldn't pay me to go."

"Shella." Dad warned, giving her a cold glare. "There's no need to piss on your sister's mood."

"I'm sorry." She said, always compliant when he spoke to her.

"When do you see Daniella again?" Mom asked, offering another topic to avoid tension.

"I'm going to see her Monday, she's really happy with the way things are going, she can't believe that we had so much success on our first try."

"It's been incredible seeing you blossom again." She smiled and I knew she was relieved to be able to talk to me without an outburst.

"Who would have thought that such a little pill could make such a big difference." Dad added.

The doorbell rang and when I jumped from my seat, dad held out a hand to stop me. *Shit.* I never considered the fact that he might want to meet Dimitri. I was not at all ready to introduce them. He slid his chair back and went to get the door himself. I waited, not moving a muscle. I heard muffled voices by the front door but couldn't make out the words. I could feel the panic building in my chest and did the best I could to breathe through it.

When dad came back through the threshold, Dimitri followed him, his beautiful lips curled into a charming smile. I stared, struck by the joy just seeing him brought me. Time apart had definitely made my heart grow fonder of the man standing beside my dad. I went to him and took his hand.

"Guys, this is Dimitri. Dimmy, this is my mom, Johanne, my little brother John, my sister Shella and I assume my dad already introduced himself." I pointed them out as I introduced them.

"It's so nice to finally meet you." Mom rushed over and grabbed his hand between hers, squeezing while she stared at him like he was her hero. "You've been so good for our little girl."

"Mom." I hissed, embarrassed.

"Well Misses Coleman, your daughter has been so good for me too."
He told her while he stared at me as though his eyes couldn't look
away.

"You best take the girl and run boy, otherwise my wife'll start
weeping on ya." Dad laughed.

"It was nice meeting all of you. Misses Coleman." Like a cheesy
gentleman, he kissed her hand. "Mister Coleman." He shook dad's.
"I'll let it slide this time but moving forward call me Don or I wont
answer you."

"I'll keep that in mind Don." He smiled at my dad before leading me
to the door.


   As soon as we got to his truck, Dimitri pinned me against
the passenger door, assaulting my mouth with his own. His hands
pulled my hips against him, desperate to be as close to me as
possible. The kiss was full of heat, radiating in the most intimate part
of my body. I smiled against his lips.

"Someone's happy to see me." I teased.

"You have no fucking idea." He leaned his forehead against mine.
"You look absolutely gorgeous Paisley. Whatever the hell you've
been doing, keep doing it and you're going to have me on my knees,
begging you to marry me so I can lock you down and keep you
forever." I giggled, before giving him a quick peck and pushing him
back a step.

"We need to get going prince charming. If we make Laurie wait to
long, she'll hunt us down."

"If you insist." He sighed in mock disappointment before going
around the hood of the truck.


   Laurie and Dave were already seated in a booth when we
walked into the restaurant. As soon as her gaze landed on me, she
jumped from her seat and charged at me. The extra weight that I
gained came in handy otherwise she would have knocked us both to
the ground when she jumped into my arms.

"Paisley! Christ, I missed you, you gorgeous lump of lady meat!"
She squealed, leaning back and looking me over to be sure it was

really me. "You look fantastic!"

"So do you. Man, it's good to see you." I pulled her back in for another squeeze.
"You must be the lucky Dimmy." Laurie said, openly checking Dimitri out when I let her go. "Yeah," She nodded to herself. "You are just as sexy as Paisley said you were." She told him, without an ounce of self consciousness.

"Well thanks. Nothing better than being admired by pretty girls." He answered, a slight blush colouring his cheeks.
"That girl doesn't know the meaning of girl talk." I explained, laughing.

"Does that mean I can ask her all your dirty secrets and she'll tell me?" I paled, thinking about all the things Laurie has seen and heard. I knew she would never tell him anything that might hurt me but the idea that she *could,* was unsettling. "Chill out, I'm not that kind of guy." He seemed insulted by the look on my face, obviously offended that I didn't trust him with certain things.

"Come, let's not leave Dave all alone or he'll feel left out." Laurie interrupted, pulling us both towards their booth. "Dave this is Paisley's boyfriend, Dimmy. Dimmy, this is my heart, walking freely, Dave." Laurie introduced them when we were all seated at the booth. Her and I on one side, Dimitri and Dave across from us.

"So, what's new and exciting?" Laurie asked, nearly bouncing in her seat with excitement.
"Well, being called Paisley's boyfriend is pretty new and exciting." Dimitri answered, looking at me with a smile that didn't reach his eyes. Laurie glance between the two of us with widening eyes.

"I am *so* sorry. I shouldn't have made that assumption." She said to Dimitri. "When she asked me to invite Dave out on a double date with her I just kind of thought that meant..." She trailed off uncomfortable with where her sentence was going.

"Don't worry about it. Paisley's made it very clear where I stand with her." He tried to smile at Laurie to reassure her but even she could see the sadness it was failing to hide.

With his comment, Dimitri managed to do something I never would have thought possible for him to do. He infuriated me. I watched our waitress place our drinks in front of us and before I spoke, I took an extra moment to take a sip of my cocktail in an attempt to compose myself.

"I am very sorry you two stumbled into this but I seem to have made a very big mistake." I told Laurie and Dave then turned my angry glare on a Dimitri, looking like a deer in the headlights. "You're right, I did make my intentions *very* clear. I cannot give you something I don't have and I seem to remember you telling me you didn't have a problem with that. Now I see that you very obviously *do* have a problem with it and instead of bringing it up in private, you've decided it would be okay to spit out in front of my best friend and her boyfriend." I squeezed the booth under the table, forcing myself to remain seated. "How lovely of you to make them feel so at ease." I added sarcastically.

Everyone sat in uncomfortable silence. Even though Dimitri's eyes were lowered, watching the bubbles run through the beer in his glass. I could see the tears making them shine. In the aftermath of scolding him, my anger was dispelled and I was ashamed of myself.

"I'm sorry." I told the table, standing. "This was my fault. I knew better than to let things continue with Dimitri but I did it anyways because I was selfish." I grabbed my bag from under the table. "I'm just going to walk home."

"Sit down." Laurie said is a soft, stern voice.
"Laurie, I can't stay." I insisted.
"I said sit down." She repeated and this time I did, leaving my bag in my lap.
"Why are you being so fucking stupid?" No one could say that Laurie wasn't forward.
"I'm not being stupid."
"Paisley. You've been fucked up for months and the only one you would allow near you was Dimmy. When you cut the world off, you

still had room for him. What does that tell you?"

"Laurie, it's not what you think it is."

"It most definitely is my friend. You're just too *stupid* to realize it. He's clearly a good man or he wouldn't still be sitting here with us. Stop being such a bitch and give the poor guy a fucking chance."

"I can't." I whispered, feeling defeated.

"Yes Paisley. You can."

"Laurie, listen to what I'm telling you." I grabbed her by the shoulders. "I really can't." I willed her to understand but she shook her head at me.

"Laurie," Dave interrupted, pulling her attention away. "This seems like a conversation for Paisley to have with Dimmy." He suggested.

"I know but she isn't going to have this conversation with him. She's going to run and..." She looked to Dimitri apologetically. "Probably disappear on you." He cleared his throat and took a sip of his beer.

"No one can force her to stick with me. The last thing I want, is for her to be with me because she feels guilty." He turned to me and reached an arm across the table to caress my cheek. "Let's just enjoy our evening and let whatever happens after that, happen."

"For fuck's sake. You my boy, are a hell of a lot better than I am." Dave stated, patting Dimitri on the back. "If this were Laurie and I, I'd handcuff her hand to mine and melt the key."

"You would be so lucky to get rid of me that easy." Laurie laughed.

Throughout dinner we avoided serious topics, keeping conversation lighthearted and the four of us laughed so much our cheeks hurt. The three of them got along famously and the tension from early on in the evening was forgotten.

"Has Paisley told you about the time she started her period during gym class?" Laurie asked, laughing hysterically before she even started to tell the story.

"What the fuck?" I asked, amused and slightly embarrassed. "What made you think of that?"

"Raspberry truffle." Was all she could manage, holding up her dessert.

"That's disgusting!" Dave complained, pushing his dessert away.

"That is pretty gross." Dimmy agree. "But I'm dying to know what happened.

"You guys are right, it's gross. Laurie's the only one who finds it funny."

"Well, we were playing touch football and there's this really cocky guy who was driving Pais and I up the wall. Anyway, this ass-hole got so into the game that he forgot that we were playing *touch* football and decided to tackle me for real. His head ended up hitting me in the nose and making it bleed. Paisley lost her shit! She came charging over and threw her whole body into him, knocking him off of me. She had him pinned to the ground while she straddled his chest, pounding him in the face like it was a speed ball. I pulled her off but she left him a surprise!" She burst out laughing again.

"Oh shit! You lost your tampon on him?" Dave asked me, horrified.

"No!"

"She fucking bled all over his white t-shirt!"

"I did not bleed all over him! It was a little smear of blood." I argued, remembering the palm sized smear just below the guy's chest.

"What did he do?" Dimmy asked, laughing along with Laurie.

"He screamed like a little bitch and ran to the changing room."

"That part is true." Agreeing through my own chuckles.

We ordered another round of drinks and enjoyed each others' company, exchanging more embarrassing stories. We were just catching our breath after hearing about Dave's mom showing him how to use a condom on the leg of his sister's baby doll. According to him, she went through two of them before managing to get one on without tearing it.

"Hey, isn't that Shella's boyfriend?" Laurie asked pointing to a table across the room. I looked to where she pointed sure enough, Nathan was sitting with a few of his friends and he was looking right at me. When he caught my attention, he wagged his fingers at me in greeting.

"Ugh, time to go folks, otherwise he's going to come over here and ruin our night." I warned.

"Why would your sister's boyfriend come over here?" Dimmy asked.

"'Cause he's got the hots for our girl here." Laurie explained, wrapping her arm around my shoulder.

"That so?" He looked over and caught Nathan's eye and the look on his face was far from friendly.

"He's a fucking creep." I curled my lip in disgust at Nathan.

"Well let's bust outta here. You girls wanna go dancing?" Dave asked, pulling bills from his wallet and putting them in the cheque's sleeve.

"What kind of question is that?" Laurie asked, taking the hand he offered.

"Come on man, watching these two, wiggle their asses on a dance floor is the hottest thing you'll see in your life." Dave told Dimmy, dead serious while he smirked.

"Damn right it is, me and my girl are man killers on the dance floor." Laurie hooked her free arm through mine on our way out of the restaurant.

We danced until our feet hurt and then we danced some more. Laurie and I were both pretty drunk and had lost our shoes not long before the bar closed. The boys found them and sat at a booth dutifully guarding our things. It was a wonderful evening and it ended too soon.

Laurie gave me a warm lingering hug in the parking lot before leaving with Dave. I was a little sad watching their car pull out of the parking lot. I didn't want the night to be over already, it had been too long since I had enjoyed myself as much as I had. Only when Dave's car turned the corner out of sight did I hop into the truck with Dimitri.

"Afraid of being alone with me?" He asked when I buckled my seat belt.

"'Course not. You're too handsome to scare me." I told him with a slur to my words and a smirk on my face. He chuckled and turned over the engine.

"You're fucking adorable when you're drunk."

"Pfft. Who the hell wants to be adorable when their older than five?"

The truck was running but he made no move to pull out of the lot. In my drunken state, it took me a few moments to realize we weren't moving yet and I was confused when I did. He was watching me expectantly so I leaned over and kissed him. He didn't pull away but he didn't give in either. When I opened my lips, his hand gently nudged me on the shoulder in a gesture to stop me.

"That's not what I was waiting for Paisley."
"Well then what's the holdup?"
"Am I driving you home?" His rejection stung deep but I understood.

I was embarrassed for kissing him once I thought it through. Why would he want me to kiss him after what I said in the restaurant? How could I be so careless? *Again?* Suddenly, I wanted to escape. I wanted to crawl into a hole by myself and disappear. This wasn't something I could fix. Especially in the state of mind I was in.

I reached for my buckle and pulled the belt off, making a quick exit. I swallowed the lump in my throat when he didn't make a move to grab my arm before I hopped out and I nearly ran from the truck in my hurry to get away. I didn't look back, didn't have the nerve to even try.

I squealed when a pair of hands hauled me off of my feet and threw me over a broad shoulder. If I didn't already know who it was, I would recognize the jean clad ass swinging right in front of my face anywhere. A hand slapped my bottom sharply.

"Why the hell are you running from me happy-cheeks?"
"Because I kissed you."
"You've kissed me plenty of times and never bolted like a scared cat before."
"This time was different. You wanted to drop me off at home."
"I wanted to know if I was bringing you home or two my place. Dork."
"Oh."
"That's right. Oh. You and your damn assumptions."

"Me and my damn assumptions." I agreed fully.

"Well?"

"Well, what?" He set me on my feet and held me steady while I got my balance.

"Keep up." He demanded. "Where am I taking you?"

"That's up to you."

"No, it's not. Both of us know that if it were, you would be living at my place. Where am I taking you?" He repeated.

"Your place. Please." I smiled, going to my toes and kissing him again, relieved.

"Good." He said against my lips.

"You know, Laurie was right."

"About what?"

"I *am* stupid for not giving you a chance."

"You're not stupid." He cupped my cheek, running his thumb over my bottom lip. "You have your reasons."

"Can I change my mind?" His hand froze and he stared at me.

"About us." I added.

"You want to marry me?" He asked with a cocky grin.

"Whoa, whoa. Not that far. I was thinking you could be my boyfriend and I won't be such a pain in the ass about it." He picked me up again and swung me around.

"You just made my week happy-cheeks!" He yelled excitedly then slammed his lips against mine before putting me back down. "Let's go home and celebrate!"

"You got anything other than beer at your place?"

"I didn't mean that kind of celebration." He chuckled, pulling my hips into him so I could feel just how happy he was.

Dimitri and I played house for a week. He would go off to work and I would hang out in his apartment and wait for him. Being a bartender, he didn't get home until well after two in the morning so I was usually asleep when he got back. He would snuggle into bed with me and wake me up with loving kisses that would end with me screaming his name.

I loved being with him but towards the end of the week, when he left for work, I would feel very restless. Thursday, I cleaned his apartment from top to bottom. I was still wiping down the walls when he came home from work that night and we made love in his living room.

By Saturday, I couldn't stand it anymore. I asked him to drive me home on his way to work. Though he looked upset, he understood my need to get out of the apartment.

When we pulled up outside my house, I lingered in his truck, not wanting him to leave. He took my hand and placed his lips on my knuckles in a loving gesture.

"Don't miss me too much happy-cheeks." I smiled.
"I will miss you like crazy, no doubt about it."
"Want me to pick you up on my way home?" He offered.
"No, my dad would have a stroke if he caught me sneaking out at such an ungodly hour."
"Be quiet and he won't even know."
"I can't Dimmy. I don't want to risk scaring them."
"Pussy." He teased and I slapped his shoulder while I laughed.
"Don't be a jerk. We've survived being apart before, I'm sure we can manage."
"You weren't my girlfriend before." He pointed out.
"Who's being the pussy now?" I returned.
"I am most definitely whipped by this." He slid a hand between my legs and squeezed, instantly setting a fire he wouldn't be able to put out this time. "And it's all mine."
"That it is. I may borrow it tonight though." I hinted, my voice thick with desire and amusement.
"Oh God. How the fuck am I supposed to concentrate at work thinking about you at home doing unholy things to yourself?" He asked, reached down to adjust himself in his jeans.
"Be a good boy. Don't think about me using my hand to get myself off while I remember how good it feels when you're inside of me." I leaned over and whispered in his ear, knowing it would make him

crazy.

His hand whipped out, wrapping around the back of my neck and pulling me to his lips. It was far from a gentle kiss. It was desperate and filled with hunger. I was half out of my seat when a knock on the window broke us apart. Dazed, I looked over to see my dad grinning at me.

"I'll talk to you later." I told Dimmy with glowing cheeks.
"Miss you already." I smiled at his cheesiness before leaving him.

I stood on the sidewalk, watching his truck drive away while dad stood beside me, still looking like he was on the brink of laughter.

"Glad to see you still remember where you live." He stated sarcastically. I turned and surprised him by wrapping my arms around his waist and hugging him close.
"I missed you too dad." His strong arms squeezed back just as hard.
"I'm glad you're home."
"Me too."
"Didn't look like it from what I saw in that truck." He snickered.
"Yeah, I don't like being away from him." I agreed.
"I can understand that." His eyes were distant as he took a stroll through memory lane. "Don't worry, that feeling only gets worse with time."
"Thanks for the reassurance dad." I joked, playfully punching him in the arm.

I followed dad into the house. He took sat in his chair while I ran upstairs to jump in the shower before supper. Feeling sentimental, I put Dimmy's sweatpants and t-shirt back on after my shower, feeling the need to be wrapped in his scent.

After dinner, I sat on the couch and watched TV with dad, not really paying attention to what was happening on the screen, just trying to avoid being alone. I stayed put even when dad started snoring softly, passed out in his chair. When mom yelled down for him to go to bed, dread filled my stomach. Instinctively, I knew that it was going to be a long night for me. I had gone too long living a peaceful existence, one I never fully believed was really mine.

I got into bed and wrapped myself in my blanket. Paranoia kept my heavy lids from sliding closed for while until my brain was unable to focus and I slipped away. I didn't immediately fall into the dream with the long hallway leading to the black door like I expected to. Instead, I wandered around a dilapidated house with boarded windows and holes in the floor. There was a staircase off to the right but many of the steps were missing and looking down, the only thing you could see was an endless pit of darkness.

It was as I was looking down into one of those pits that a pair of hands pushed me from behind and I fell in. I fell for so long I wondered if I would ever hit the bottom. As my doubts set in, my body connected with the hard surface of a wooden floor, knocking the wind from my lungs in a startled gasp of pain. When I looked around, I saw the familiar black door and I wanted to climb the walls to get back into the house. Like every other time I found myself in this place, my body didn't give me a choice and I headed for the door.

Before I could reach out and touch the knob, the door swung open. Braxeus stood in front of me looking very pleased to find me there.

"Paisley! What a pleasure it is to see you!" He said and I couldn't help but hear a hint of malice in his voice.
"Braxeus." I greeted simply.
"Come in, come in." He led the way to his picnic table where we sat.
"So, how have things been going?" He asked pleasantly.
"Good." I wasn't sure if I should tell him the truth so I decided to downplay it.
"So, I've been doing a good job then."
"What do you mean?"
"I've been working around the clock to make sure I held up my end of the bargain."
"You said twenty-four hours. It's been a hell of a lot longer than that." I said, feeling the bubble of my newfound joy burst into pieces.

"Well." His expression was nowhere near close to being friendly. He looked angry. "When you decided to doubt me that first day, thinking some useless tablet was your cure-all, I thought it was in my best interest to keep going and prove without a shadow of a doubt that it was indeed I, Braxeus, who solved your problems. Not some fucking doctor or useless cunting nurse!" When he finished the volume of his voice had increased to an angry bellow and he slammed his fists against the table in frustration. "See what you've made me do?" He asked, running his hands over his shirt to straighten it back out. "You have me acting like a spoiled toddler. You would think that with all the effort I've put into your well-being, you would at least give me some fucking credit, yet you sit here and continue to doubt me." His black, soulless eyes pinned me with a look of disdain. "Do you know how aggravating it is to put so much effort into something only to be dismissed like a soiled band-aid?"

"I'm sorry." I didn't know what else to say.
"No, you aren't but you will be soon enough."
"What's that supposed to mean? You gonna cut me off from these stupid meetings?" I asked, irritated with his over inflated ego. He laughed. It wasn't a sound born from humour. It was a terrifying noise of foreboding.
"You'll see you little witch. You'll see." He predicted, the unnatural grin spreading across his face.
"Whatever, I've been through enough shit. Not like I can't handle a little more." I challenged.
"The difference child, is that eventually, even the strongest people break under the weight of all their shit. When that day comes, you will beg me to save you." He laughed, so sure of himself that I wanted to gouge his eyes out and stuff the down his throat.
"I don't know what you expect me to say." I told him honestly. "Do you want me to cry and ask that you not let your wrath loose on me?"
"It wouldn't hurt." Hide overly exaggerated grin impossibly widened.
"Not fucking likely to happen."
"Do you want to know what the best thing is with stubborn little girls like you?"
"I'm dying of curiosity." I lied, knowing that his answer was going to piss me off.

"When they finally give up and come crawling to me for relief, it's so much more gratifying."

I didn't get the opportunity to answer him because my eyes flew open and sunlight flooded my bedroom. I looked to my clock and was shocked to see that it was past noon. I slept for eleven hours but felt like I only slept for two. I didn't feel the slightest bit rested, if I closed my eyes, I was sure to fall right back to sleep.

I rolled out of bed and plopped myself in the chair by my vanity. I watched my reflection as I ran the brush through my dark hair. Surprisingly, there were no shadows under my eyes and my cheeks still had a healthy glow. The encounter with Braxeus hadn't sucked the life out of me like I thought it had. I was still healthy and alive.

I tried to brush off my niggling worries and move on with the start of my day. I could hear movement downstairs and assumed mom was busy with her afternoon chores. In hopes of distracting myself, I made my way to the stairs.

I froze on the spot, looking down at my mom who was sweeping the entryway. Her face was turned towards me but her eyes were not their normal greyish blue colour. The more I looked, the more I realized that they were Brazeus's eyes, dark and surrounded with deep wrinkles that didn't normally tarnish my mother's face. I felt the urge to vomit when terror swallowed my heart. Before I could turn and run back to my bedroom, two hands pushed me forward violently. I was sent cartwheeling down the stairs. One hand caught between the posts on the banister and I felt the bone in my wrist crack. On the last step, I landed harshly on both knees with a sharp thwack. The two of us screaming brought dad barrelling in from the kitchen, frantic. Mom threw her broom to the floor and fell to her knees beside me, checking for more wounds while I hugged my throbbing wrist to my chest and moaned in pain.
"What the fuck happened?" Dad demanded as he joined her on the floor.
"I don't know! It looked like she just jumped down the goddamn stairs!"
"I didn't jump. Someone pushed me." I told them.

"You were the only one upstairs Paisley. No one could have pushed you." Dad reasoned.

"I felt hands shove me."

"You must have missed your footing or something." He insisted.

"I think my wrist is broken." When I took my unwounded hand away, the throbbing in my wrist made my vision blur but I could still see that it had doubled in size.

"Jesus, it's definitely broken." Dad lifted me from the floor. "Johanne, get the door. I'm gonna take her to the hospital and get it looked at." Mom rushed to open the door for us and followed so she could open the car door too.

A fractured wrist and effusion in both knee joints. When I watched the doctor sink a giant needle into my knee to drain the excess fluid, I fainted. I was relieved when I woke up and the second one was already done. With my recent history of mental illness, I was not allowed to leave the hospital without first speaking to my therapist. I was brought to a room where they laid me on a bed to rest while I waited for Daniella to finish her appointment. Dad stayed with me for a while but grew restless so he started pacing in the hallway outside my room. It was off having him with me. Usually, it was mom who always stayed with us at times like this. I assumed it was because with me, there was no telling what had happened or if it would set something deeper in motion and so he was more worried than he usually was.

I fell asleep while I waited. I didn't dream but I did hear sadistic laughter in the distance. Goosebumps covered my body because I knew exactly where that laughter came from. He was letting me know that he was the reason I lay in the hospital, waiting for permission to leave.

Heels clacking in my room pulled me from my restless nap. I opened my eyes to see Daniella's friendly smile. I had the sudden urge to throw something at her and if I didn't have the presence of mind to know it would prevent me from leaving, I probably would have done it.

"Hey Paisley. What's going on?" She asked as if she didn't already know.

"I took a swan dive down the stairs." I told her without emotion. Trying very hard to keep my sourness to myself.

"I know that part. Tell me what happened leading up to your tumble. Did you have a bad morning?" She asked as she sat in the chair by my bed and pulled out her notebook.

"I didn't have a morning."

"Care to elaborate?"

"I had just woken up. Was going downstairs to help my mom with her chores when this all happened."

"Oh no." Though I knew the empathetic expression on her face was more than likely genuine, I couldn't help but feel like she was mocking my misfortune. "How did you fall? Did you trip on something?"

"I'm sure my dad already filled you in." I stated, rolling my eyes at her question.

"He told me what he believes happened. I want to hear it from you."

"An imaginary man pushed me down the stairs." I told her deadpan, knowing she would never believe me.

"Does this imaginary man have a name?"

"Fred Flintstone."

"I would appreciate it if you could take our conversations seriously."

"What the fuck does it matter what his name is?" I asked, my temper slipping.

"It matters to me." She insisted, not really answering me.

"Braxeus."

"Braxeus." She repeated, thinking it over. "As in short for the demon Abraxus?"

"I have no idea. He just says Braxeus."

Ice ran through my veins. Was she onto something? Was Braxeus really a demon? No fucking way. Demons lived in the same realm as zombies, dragons and vampires. Stories told to scare the shit out of people. Not real life. Maybe Daniella was the one who needed to take medication.

"Have you done any research on demonology?" She asked, curious.

"No. The only thing I know about demons is what they tell you in the Bible." I couldn't believe she was entertaining this crazy line of questioning.

"Haven't given it any more thought than that?"

"Not until you mentioned Braxeus potentially being one! Now I'm pretty much ready to have a heart attack."

"Well, your dad says there was no one else on the stairs with you and you mentioned him intentionally causing you bodily harm. Braxeus is a common short form of Abraxus. It's not that far of a stretch."

"Have you considered the fact that you may be just as crazy as I am?" She laughed at my observation.

"Just because I'm a therapist doesn't mean I don't have outside interests. I've met several people who present atypical symptoms that couldn't be explained by a mental or personality disorder. Spirituality fascinates me." She explained.

"So, you think I'm being haunted by a demon?"

"I'm not sure what's going on yet. You seem to have symptoms indicative of schizoid PD, bipolar disorder and some that point toward borderline PD. Right now, we're working on the process of elimination."

"Well, that's a whole lot of mumbo jumbo to me and I'm not going to pretend to pay attention to any of it until we come to a conclusion. Otherwise, I'm gonna get a whole lotta confused and probably start seeing symptoms where there aren't any."

"That's very wise." She agreed.

"What's the next step?"

"I want to increase the dose of your prescription. I want to add Lorazepam. I don't want you to take it unless you need to. When you're feeling overwhelmed or like you're on the edge of losing your control, take one. It will calm you down."

"So, what you're saying is, you want me to take one everyday, several times a day."

"No. Only when you start seeing signs that you might start acting irrationally. If it's normal anger or excitement, ride it out."

"All right I can manage that."

"We'll get through this Paisley. It just takes time."

"I wish I could believe that. Nothing against you or anything. Just feeling a little hopeless at the moment."

"I know but just focus on the positive. We had a long stretch without issues! That's fantastic!"

"Yeah, that's true." I smiled at her, even if I didn't feel it.

"Don't hate me but I think you should stay the night." She said, looking contrite.

"What the hell for?" I screeched, feeling my blood pressure rise.

"I think that being home right now might set you off again. I want you under close supervision. If everything goes smooth tonight, I promise you can go home tomorrow."

"Going home is not going to set me off." I argued.

"I just want to play it safe. Just one night."

"I swear to Christ, if I have start having hospital sleepovers every time something happens, I'm going to jump out the fucking window."

"Are you feeling suicidal?" She asked, full of concern.

"Not yet! I said *if* Daniella. *If*. Mostly I was being dramatic."

"Okay. That's good." She breathed a sigh of relief. You would think that someone in her line of work would be used to people talking before thinking and that she would be able to decipher the difference.

"Is that all?" I asked with a snarky tone.

"Are you kicking me out?" She smiled, thinking I was joking.

"I'd like to go to sleep so that it can be tomorrow already."

"All right. I am sorry Paisley. I just want to be sure. If I sent you home now and something else happened, you would be admitted to the third floor indefinitely and I wouldn't be able to stop them."

"I know, I don't blame you. I'm just pissed off and bitter at the world right now."

"I want you to know that I am on your side one hundred percent of the time. Even when you, yourself... Are not." She closed her notebook and stood. "Have a good night. Call me if you need anything."

"Have a good one."


I turned my back to her and curled into a ball, waiting to hear her shoes on the linoleum as she walked out of the room. When she did, I flopped onto my back and stared at the ceiling. I wanted to scream but if I did, someone would surely come running. Instead, I pulled the pillow over my face and yelled out every bad word I had in my arsenal. It helped a bit but not enough so I went through the list a second time and then a third.

How much of this shit could I take? I knew for a fact that I didn't *want* to deal with anymore. If only they still did lobotomies, I would gladly sign up for one.

# Chapter Nine

No One But Him and Me

_Tricia Warnock_

I woke up in the middle of the night. After several attempts to sleep, I gave up. When I tried, hearing Braxeus's laughter echo the darkness would startle me awake. I was frustrated and bored. When the nurse would come to check on me, I would pretend to be fast asleep. I didn't want them to question why I was awake and potentially forward their findings to Daniella, who would inevitably keep me longer.

When sunlight finally broke through the window, I got out of bed and awkwardly dressed with one arm wrapped in a cast. I couldn't do up my jeans so I pulled my shirt down to hide the open button. I sat in the chair, tired of being stuck on the stiff bed. It felt like hours before someone came to my room. As soon as the nurse came in, I jumped up.

"Am I being discharged?" I didn't give her a chance to make it all the way into the room before I asked. "We're just waiting for the doctor to sign off on your new prescription then you'll be on your way." She explained, gesturing for me to take a seat so she could check my blood pressure.
"I'm fine, what do we need to do this for?"
"It's just procedure miss Coleman." This nurse was clearly coming to the end of her shift or she was not a morning person. She had no patience and her shortness irritated me.
"Procedure is bullshit." I mumbled.
"Just because you think it is, doesn't mean you're special enough to break protocol."

"It was a comment, not a request." I snapped at her. Fatigue and her attitude leaving me lacking in tolerance.

"Good morning P-Baby!" Dad came in the room, interrupting our dispute.

"Good morning. Come to bust me out of this prison?" He chuckled.

"They said you weren't quite ready to leave yet."

"That's why I said *bust* out. Help me escape."

"You're on a secure floor. I strongly advise you don't make any attempts to leave without permission." The grumpy nurse warned.

"That's how *prisons* usually work."

"And giving attitude to the people trying to help you doesn't help expedite the process either."

"Maybe I'm tempted to hang around a little while longer since I seem to be making you really happy."

"Paisley. There's no need to be difficult." Dad chided.

"You're right. I am very sorry for disrupting your morning by why you needed to check my blood pressure."

She kept her mouth zipped while she finished checking me over. She didn't bother telling me what was in the needle she stabbed into my arm and I didn't ask her what it was, I was happy with her silence.

It didn't take long for the doctor to arrive after she left and I wondered if she had anything to do with it. He was nice enough as he handed me a sheet of paper for my prescription and signed my release form with a follow appointment. I didn't really listen to what he told me; I was too eager to get out of there.

I hated the increase in dosage. There were no repeat outbursts but I was always drowsy. I couldn't sleep because I didn't have the energy to do anything during the day and the lack of sleep didn't help the side effects. I was always in a foul mood but thankfully, being so out of it all the time, I couldn't muster the urge to argue with anyone. No one else seemed bothered by my zombie-esque state of existence.

Dimitri didn't last very long without hearing from me. I spoke to him on the phone the second night after my discharge and told him I fell down the stairs. He called a few more times but I always pretended to be asleep when whoever answered told me to get the phone. By the end of the first week, he showed up at the front door. Mom answered and brought him up to my room where I was curled on my bed staring out the window.

I was surprised to see him and was embarrassed that he was looking at me while I looked like garbage. I pulled the blankets up to my chin to hide my ratty pyjamas.

"What are you doing here?" I asked, happy to see him even if I hadn't been ready.
"You've been avoiding me." He stated simply, pulling my vanity chair up beside the bed.
"Look at me. Of course I've been avoiding you."
"You look beautiful."
"Don't lie to me, I know how to look in a mirror."
"There's no way for you not to be beautiful to me Paisley. Even if you caught a skin disease that ate half your face."
"Shit, I knew I looked bad but not *that* bad." He chuckled, shaking his head at me.
"You're gorgeous. But you should stop fishing for compliments."
"I am not." I stuck out my tongue at him.
"Wow. In a girl's room for five seconds and she's already propositioning me." He raised his eyebrows in mock surprise. "I don't think I have it in me to defile you in your father's home."
"Oh, shut up. I was not propositioning you. Weirdo."
"Yes, but this weirdo is all yours and starting to forget how his dick works."
"Well, when you start to feel a tingle, it's your body's way of telling you that it's time to use the bathroom."

"Oh, if it were only that kind of tingle, I would be all right." He leaned over the bed and kissed me, pulling back but staying close enough that the tips of our noses rubbed against each other. "I've missed you so much, I thought I was going to start climbing my walls if I couldn't see you."

"I'm sorry. I've been in rough shape." I told him vaguely.
"What's wrong?" I struggled with wanting to answer him and being afraid of how he would react.
"There's something wrong with me... Mentally." I began, looking him in the eye, wanting to watch his reaction.
"Okay. I'm listening."
"Think about it really good before you ask me to go on. What I tell you might change the way you feel about me." I warned.
"Don't be ridiculous. Go on." I groaned, my stomach doing flip flops.
"It's still early on and they're still trying to figure it out. Right now, they're leaning towards me having a schizoid personality disorder but they threw out a few other possibilities too."
"What does that mean exactly?" There was nothing but curiosity on his face.
"It means I'm nuts."
"Fuck Paisley. Stop putting yourself down. There's shit you're dealing with. That's it. Now what does that mean?"

"I don't really know what it means. They think I push people away and do things so that I don't have to get close to people. Like social anxiety but to the extreme. I don't think that's what my problem is but the medication they prescribed me worked in the beginning. After I took the tumble down the stairs, they increased my dosage and now it's doing nothing but making me feel like shit."

"Have you talked to your doctor recently and told her that it wasn't doing you any good?"
"No."
"Don't you think that you should?"
"I'm kind of afraid to. She said if I had another outburst, they might admit me to the psych ward. If they take me off of the medication... I may freak out and then what?"
"Then they might find another drug that actually works? Oh God, whatever would you do then?"
"No need to be an ass." I reached over and smacked his arm.

"I'm not being an ass; I'm playing your assumption game."

"It's a lot more complicated than that."

"Or maybe it's not as complicated as you're making it."

"I don't think you understand."

"Kind of hard when all you're telling me is what the doctor *says* is wrong with you. What *may* happen if you stop taking medication that makes you miserable. You're not telling me what you're thinking or feeling."

Where would I start? Everything in my head was a mess. Nothing really made sense and it scared me. I thought about the conversation with Daniella and how she thought Braxeus might be a demon. Was that possible? Could I believe something like that? It was unsettling to realize that I found Daniella's theory a relief. If Braxeus were a separate being and not just in my head, then my brain wasn't broken.

"I caught my ex having sex with another girl so I broke things off with him. He started talking to me, then one day he decided to grab me and lock me in his basement. I was trapped for three days before his parents found me. Nothing was the same after that. I started having these nightmares where an old man was tormenting me. Then I started hearing weird noises and seeing flashes of him while I was awake. I've been all kinds of fucked up. When I fell down the stairs? I felt someone push me."

He didn't say anything. He got onto the bed beside me and pulled me into his arms, hugging me close. It felt so good to be close to him, especially now that he knew everything.

"Thank you for trusting me with this." He whispered against my ear.

I was in an empty room. Wood panelled walls.

Hardwood floor. High ceiling with an antique crystal chandelier. One window looking off into nothingness and the ever-present sadistic laughter echoing off of all the dead trees.

Though the sound no longer gave me crippling fear, it still succeeded in chilling me to the bone. It was the telltale sign that *he* was coming for a visit. Avoiding him was out of the question. The first time, I tried relentlessly to escape. I even jumped through the window, landing right back in the middle of the empty room, where he stood waiting for me.

I didn't understand the purpose of these visits. He never said a word. He would stand there and stare at me through dark eyes with his grin firmly in place, watching as I crumbled.

What was worse, I spent the majority of my time asleep, unable to stay awake. An hour of consciousness was exhausting and wherever I was, whatever I was doing, I would fall asleep and be back in the empty room.

After missing a few appointments with Daniella because I couldn't drag myself out of bed, she decided she would do a home visit. Mom let her in while I slept on the couch. I managed to tear my eyes open after listening distantly to mom tell her what has been going on.

"Oh no, so the medication has been having some serious side effects. Why didn't she tell me?"
"I don't know but we need to do something. This cannot be healthy."
"I thought sleep healed the body." I stated groggily, looking at them through heavy lids.
"To an extent. Hypersomnia can be just as dangerous as insomnia. We are going to wean you off of the Zyprexa. Cut back to the old dosage for ten days and then cut it right out completely."

"What if it all goes back to the way it was before?"
"It might but we will be ready for it this time. We know what to expect and we can intervene before things escalate beyond our control."
"I don't really think that's possible Daniella."
"We will put an action plan together. Keep you under observation--"

"I'm not staying in a fucking hospital!"
"No. Your mother will keep an eye on you and I will come here for our weekly meetings."
"What if this is something that can't be fixed?"
"It can't. It can only be managed."

So, there it was. I would spend the rest of my life *managing* something that I didn't really understand. A lifetime of terror. A lifetime with *him* waiting around every corner, hiding in every shadow, always looking for new ways to torment me. With those thoughts lingering in my brain, my eyes grew heavy and exhaustion won once again. Lights out.

Slowly coming off the medication was not nearly as bad as I had anticipated. I started coming back to life which was a huge relief. I was able to participate in life without falling asleep. I still felt dopey at times but it was not unreasonable.

It was very difficult to explain to the outside world what it was like living with Braxeus inside my head at all times. I had no secrets from him. I couldn't block him out and knowing he was ever present was very much like having someone constantly looking over my shoulder, gloating.

I hated him but I hated myself more fore being unable to fight him. It seemed as though lately, he was burrowing himself deeper into my life which I never thought would have been possible. The same odd noises I heard during my exam, could now be heard in my bedroom, late at night. The sounds of mice scratching the inside of the walls. I set traps in the corners of my closet but I knew there weren't any.

That night while I waited in the empty room, there was no laughter, just deafening silence. I waited for my host to arrive while I glanced around the room to see if there was anything else that was different.

"Are you ready to bed?" I jumped at the amused question from behind me.
"I'm sorry for doubting you."
"Apology accepted. Are you ready to beg?" He repeated.
"Why me?"
"I told you. You're stubborn, watching you break is entertaining."
"You have to stop."
"No." He said simply.
"How do you expect me to trust you to help me when *you* are the cause of all my problems?"
"I'm not the cause Paisley."
"The laughing. The noises. I know that's you."
"I get bored in here. I have to find ways to amuse myself."
"It has to stop. I can't keep playing this game."
"I told you how to make it stop."
"That's right, you want me to beg you to take over, let you deal with my problems."
"Precisely. It's a simple fix but you seem quite willing to continue suffering."
"I can't fucking hand myself over! You're the one causing the problem!"

"Listen closely Paisley. I will only repeat myself once." He said, ice dripping from his voice. "I am *not* the cause of your issues. I'm just taking advantage of them to entertain myself. The depression, anxiety and all the rest of the psycho-babble bullshit is all you." His eyes bore into me with fury. "While I am being generous, I'll also remind you to watch your tone, girl!" I flinched when he raised his tone.

"You need to find yourself a new plaything."
"I quite like my current bauble but thank you for your concern."
"Can I ask you a question?" I asked when a memory floated through my brain.
"You can."

"Are you Abraxus?" Before the name finished leaving my lips, Braxeus was keeled over with laughter.

"You shouldn't listen to that idiotic therapist of yours. She smoked away her brain cells in high school. Barely even old enough to be menstruating."
"Daniella has been nothing but kind to me."

"She's kind because you pay her salary. She couldn't care less about you. She goes home and complains about you to her husband. As a matter of fact, they all do. Your parents think you're out of control and are tired of being on their toes around you. Your sister thinks you're playing a game to get attention and I'll bet you haven't even noticed the fact that your brother has avoided being in the same room as you for weeks." It was true, I couldn't remember the last time I had seen John for longer than a few seconds while we crossed paths. Could what he was telling me really be true? "And that little boyfriend of yours?" He chuckled heartlessly. "He's been getting enough tail on the side that he only hits you up when he's in a dry spell. You annoy him more than a rash on his undercarriage."

"That's ridiculous. You're just searching for reasons to hurt me."
"Oh no darling. I can do that just fine without bringing others into it."

I don't have a rebuttal for him. I couldn't disprove his statements because they all made sense. If I were on the other side, I would certainly feel bitter. I was a nuisance to all those closest to me and there was no end in sight for any of them.

"I'll see you around Paisley. It won't be long until I have you in the palm of my hand. You're on the brink and the only way to survive is to give me what I want or to jump off a jagged cliff."

The sound of his laughter followed him out. Moments later, my eyes flew open and I was coated in sweat. I ran my fingers over my face and pinched the bridge of my nose trying to ease the tension behind my eyes.

This time when my lamp when flying, it was out of

hopelessness. Every muscle in my body was tense and twitching with bottled desperation. I wanted to lash out, throw myself against the walls in hopes that I may crack and let the negativity pour out.

I went to the bathroom and turned on the shower. I stripped down and sat down under the spray, letting the water pound against my back. When the water ran cold, I shivered but stayed put. My teeth chattered violently, making my jaw cramp but it wasn't enough to motivate me to move. My joints became stiff as my body fought the cold. I turned the water off when a knock sounded on the bathroom door.

"Paisley?" Mom called.
"Yeah?"
"Everything all right?" Her question brought a new flood of tears to my eyes.
"I'm fine." My voice was thick through the tightness in my throat.
"You don't sound all right." She opened the door enough to poke her head through.

When her eyes landed on me, my forehead was resting against my bent knees while my arms hugged them to my chest. She sat on the edge of the tub and gently ran her hand over the top of my head trying to comfort me the only way she could.

"I know it's tough. The only thing we can do right now is fight so we can come out of this stronger than ever."
"I don't want to fight anymore mom."

"Oh Paisley." She choked, going to her knees and pulling me into her arms as much as possible with the wall of the tub between us. "You can't give up. There's so much more life has to offer you. If you give up now, you'll miss the best parts."

"Like what? I might miss the part where I lose the rest of my sanity? Go completely bat shit crazy and force you to put me in the crazy house?"
"No, like grow and discover who it is you're meant to be. Maybe get married and have babies of your own."
"Now you're the one who sounds crazy."

"Stop it." She smacked my arm. "You have to find a reason to keep going Paisley. Hold on to something that's going to make you want to pull through."

"I'll try." I told her just to put an end to the motivational speech. It was all a bunch of bullshit anyway.

      The strange noises persisted, occurring regularly throughout the day. I no longer only heard them while I was alone, now I could hear them when I was around other people. I watched their reactions and no one else seemed to notice. The few times I asked mom or dad if they could hear it too, we would sit in awkward silence for a moment and nothing would happen. I was then forced to watch them shrug and look at me with pity. They never questioned what it was I heard and I didn't elaborate. When I managed to ignore it, the noise would get louder, drowning out everything else. My parents just assumed I was spacing out and would wait for me to refocus before continuing their train of thought.

      When I refused to allow the sounds to dictate my every action, things seemed to escalate. I started catching movements out of the corner of my eye. When I would look, there wouldn't be anything out of place. Soon, what began as blurred glimpses turned to shadows on the walls. On more than one occasion, I would hear heavy footsteps running towards me and they would stop as soon as I turned in the direction of the noise. Up until that point, the footsteps were the most terrifying.

      It was very early in the morning; the sun was just starting to make an appearance. I stood by the sink in the kitchen filling the coffee carafe, rubbing the sleepiness from my eyes. Two and a half hours of sleep the night before wasn't enough to feel refreshed but I couldn't convince myself to push for more. I started the coffee machine and watched the dark liquid drip into the carafe. I kept my focus on the hot beverage until the pot was half full then I shook myself out of my daze and turned to grab a mug.

When I had the cupboard open, I reached for a blue mug but jumped out of my skin when I heard the sound of exploding glass. I grabbed my chest where my heart pounded violently and turned to see the black steaming liquid mixed with shards of glass puddled on the counter and splashed across the floor. It was strange but not uncommon. The pot could have weakened with age.

My feet were glued to the floor and my jaw went slack when the remaining cupboards flew open. I could only let out a little squeak, it was the only noise I was capable of making in the moment. Mugs, plates, bowls went flying across the room, smashing into the opposite wall. I struggled to breathe through my sobs of terror, still rooted in place, unable to run. I couldn't believe the amount of dinnerware that was housed in the cupboards.

When the pieces of the last bowl clattered to floor, I was finally able to move and I fell to my knees in the middle of the kitchen, shards of ceramic digging into my skin. I heard someone gasp and looked up to see both of my parents standing in archway.

"What in the hell did you do?" Dad demanded; eyes slightly bulged at the sight before him.
"I didn't do it." I sobbed, knowing that there was no way to explain what happened and that they would inevitably believe I had caused the destruction around me.
"Don't fucking lie to me Paisley! You're the only one in here!"
"I don't know what happened. I didn't do this!" When I heard the familiar scratching noise on the floor beside me, I flinched and screamed the way I wanted to when all of it had started.

I used my hands for balance while I pulled my feet under me, causing scrapes and cuts on my palms and knees. I bolted from the room and out the front door as fast as I could, desperate to be as far from the chaos as possible. I ran until my stomach cramped and my calves felt like they were on fire. I bent forward, squeezing my sides as I struggled to catch my breath. When I could breathe again, I was surprised with how far I made it, I was far from home and didn't recognize the neighbourhood I was in. I looked at the beautiful houses with the perfectly manicured lawns. This was a different world than the one I lived in. I could just imagine the kind of uptight ass-holes who would live in houses like the ones I was looking at.

I circled the neighbourhood twice, spending more than two hours wandering down the sidewalks and through the public park. I was sitting on the swing watching my feet dig into the rocks when flashing lights caught my attention. I looked up to see a police cruiser parked in the lot beside the park. I watched as an officer stepped from his car and put his hat on before making his way over to me.

"Are you Paisley Coleman?" He asked when he reached the side of the swing set.

"Yes." I answered, confused as to how he knew who I was.

"You need to come with me."

"Why? What's going on?"

"Your parents called; they are very worried about you. There are officers all over town looking for you."

"I don't understand why they would be worried. I'm capable of going out on my own. I do it all the time."

"They said you've been struggling with a mental disorder and it's not safe for you to be out on your own right now."

"Oh, that's bullshit. Yes, I have a bunch of crap going on but they've never given me a fucking curfew or limited my freedom because of it."

"They told dispatch you broke all their dishes and then bolted. Doesn't sound to me like you're in the right state of mind to be out wandering the streets."

"I didn't break their dishes." I argued, irritated.

"I was at the house Paisley. I saw the damage."

"It wasn't me!"

"They said everyone else was still in bed."

"It wasn't me." I persisted, without a logical defence to provide.

"Are you going to come with me willingly so I can take you home or are you going to make me cuff you and take you to the station?"

"Why would you arrest me?"

"You're a danger to yourself and to others." At his response, I laughed humorlessly.

"Whatever." I shook my head, defeated. "I'll go with you." I hopped down from the swing and followed him to his cruiser.

He opened the back door and stood back while I took my seat. We didn't talk on the way to my house. There was no way for me convince anyone that it wasn't me who caused the damage so fighting them was pointless.

The officer escorted me to the front door and when my mom answered, I didn't wait to hear what they were going to say to each other, I walked past her and went straight to my room. I stood by the window and watched cars drive by, waiting for the officer to leave. I knew that once he left, my parents would have words for me. Sure enough, no sooner had the cruiser pulled out of the driveway, there was a knock on my door.

They didn't wait for me to answer before they came into my room. Dad took a seat on my vanity chair and mom sat herself on my bed. They both looked at me, waiting for an explanation.

"Don't you have anything to say?" Dad asked when I didn't break the silence.
"No. There's nothing for me to say."
"What the hell happened?"
"I don't know."
"Well, you were there when it happened, you have to know how the floor got covered in broken glass."
"I can't explain it."
"Yes, you can Paisley. Tell me what the hell happened in that Goddamn kitchen!"
"Braxeus fucking happened! He emptied the cupboards! He made the coffee machine explode!"
"Who is Braxeus?" Mom asked softly, fear filling her eyes.
"He's the old man who entertains himself by ruining my life!"
"What do you mean? Where does this guy live? Why haven't you told us about him?"
"Because he isn't real! He's in my fucking head."

They were speechless. Silence followed my confession but for a horrified gasp from my mother. Dad was looking at me, waiting to see if there would be a punch line. He saw the anguish on my face and knew that I wasn't lying.

"How long have you been seeing him?" He asked.
"I don't even remember the first time anymore. It started with nightmares but has just gotten worse since. Now I don't even know what it would be like *not* seeing him all the time."
"Does he want to hurt you?"
"He says he wants to help me."
"How?"
"He says that if I let him take control, he can fix all my problems."
"What do you mean by taking control?"
"He wants me to let him control my actions. Like take over being me." It sounded worse when I tried explaining it to someone else.
"But you said he was ruined your life? He's ruining it so you will let him, have it?"
"He says it's me who's ruining it, he just wants to fix the mess I've made."

They looked at each other, a mix of worry and fear plastered on their faces. They had no idea how to process the new information I threw at them. We were all in silent agreement that what they said next could very well sent me to meet my end or encourage me to find my way out.

"I'm going to call Daniella. I honestly have no idea what to think about all of this." Mom said as she stood from my bed.
"Daniella knows about Braxeus."
"She does?" Mom plopped back down; the wind sucked out of her sails.
"I told her when she came to see me in the hospital."
"And what did she have to say about it?"
"Not much. She seems to think that Braxeus is short for a demon named Abraxus."
"Demon!" Mom screeched.
"Why in the fuck would she think it was okay to tell you something like that?" Dad exclaimed.
"She was trying to make me understand that the cause of all my issues could be an assortment of things. I asked Braxeus about it and he laughed in my face so I'm fairly sure that theory goes out the window."

"What a fucked-up situation. Our daughter's therapist tells our daughter she could possibly be possessed. Where the hell did she get her diploma? Rome?"

"What if she was right? Would you still think she was being ridiculous for mentioning it as a possibility?" Mom asked him, irritated with his closed mindedness. "I think we should consider *all* avenues right now. There has to be a way to help Paisley."

"I just think she should be careful what she says to a young girl who is facing a mental collapse."
"So should you!" I yelled, exasperated.

"Paisley, listen to me. You're suffering enough. Bringing up something as dark as demon possession to someone who is already struggling to find a way to cope with their mental illness is reckless and insensitive. If she thought it was a possibility, she should have mentioned it to me or your mother. We could have looked into and kept a close eye on your symptoms to decide if the theory had enough legs to stand on."

"You honestly believe in that hocus pocus?" I asked, stunned that he would consider such a possibility.

"You know your mom has always been a religious woman. I may not be a very good Catholic; I do believe in God. If I believe in God, then I would logically believe in the Devil and all his minions."

"Well, that theory is off the table anyway, Braxeus isn't a demon."
"Do you honestly think that he would tell you if he was?" Mom asked, her eyebrows dipping with her seriousness.
"Who the hell knows?"
"He wouldn't. Why would he give you the upper hand in knowing the cause of your torment?"

"I don't know. I'm flabbergasted that this is even a serious conversation. Dad, can you pinch me? I think I may be hallucinating again." Then the scratching noise started in my closet. For the first time, mom and dad both froze and stared at the door to the closet as though they could hear it too. "Do you hear that too?" I mostly whispered; afraid I was mistaken. They both nodded in unison. What that could mean was even more frightening than being the only one able to hear the strange noise.

The noises went on for most of the night. Despite my exhaustion both from the lack of sleep the night before and the days events, I was unable to sleep through the disturbance. I tried going to the living room and curling up on the couch but just as my eyelids grew heavy, the noise would follow me and begin it's song behind the TV. To see if I could still hear it outside, I wrapped myself in the blanket and huddled in the corner of the porch, out of sight from any night time wanderers. After hearing the running footsteps race toward me, I bolted back into the house and locked the door behind me.

I decided to go back up to my room. There was no point hanging out anywhere else if I wasn't going to find peace. Before I made my way up the stairs, I grabbed one of mom's romance novels to take with me.

I sat against my head board with my blanket and opened the book to the first page. I tried to focus on the words despite the scratching noises getting louder. Some time while trying to read the same sentence for the fifth time, I must have dozed off because I found myself in the middle of Braxeus's empty room.

"How nice of you to join me." A familiar voice came from the corner of the room.
"If you say so." I muttered, unphased.
"You wouldn't imagine my surprise when I overheard you talking about me today." The look on his face said it wasn't a pleasant surprise.

"Right. You just happened to *overhear* a private conversation I was having with my parents."
"I don't appreciate being the centre of gossip Paisley."
"It wasn't gossip. We were brainstorming."
"There was no need to mention the name of a demon when discussing me. I clearly told you that idea was preposterous."
"Brainstorming involves putting all ideas on the table and exploring every possibility."
"Waste your time as you wish. Just know that the more you smear my name, the more I will smear yours." He threatened.
"I thought your goal was to help me? Not to make my situation worse."
"You stupidly refuse to accept my offer. If you won't take my help then I might as well do as I wish."
"Which would be to put me through hell. Much the same as a demon would." I pointed out.

"Take it whatever way you want to. If I want to make you completely crazy, you can be damn sure that I will do exactly that. That episode in the kitchen?" He chuckled darkly. "That was merely a parlour trick child. It barely scratched the surface to what I am truly capable of." He crept closer. "You think your parents were upset seeing their shattered dinnerware? What would they think if they found you holding a hammer that was used to nail your little brother to his ceiling?" Vividly, my mind projected the sight of John's body hanging from the ceiling, covered in bleeding wounds where nails prevented gravity from pulling him to the floor. His face contorted in agony. "Or how about walking in on you playing surgeon with your sister? You think they would enjoy the sight of you cutting into your sister's stomach and holding her large intestine in your bloody hands?" Again, I could see Shella's pale, dead face, sliced open from the centre of her chest down to her pubic bone. "I haven't decided where I'm going with this yet. Rest assured, it will be something traumatizing enough to secure a long term stay in a padded room for the lot of you." His confidence in the outcome turned my sweat ice cold. My stomach dropped to my feet. I had no doubt he would be able to follow through with his threats.

"No."
"Oh yes. Those are just two of my favourite ideas but there are

several others. I will toy with you until I decide which one to choose."

"No. Please."

"I am giving you fair warning Paisley. It *will* end badly."

"Please. I'll do anything." I pleaded and he laughed.

"Don't be dramatic. We both know you wont. I told you to give yourself to me and I would rectify this situation of yours. Hell, I was patient and offered out of sheer kindness but you declined. Repeatedly."

"I will! I will! You can do whatever you have to do to stop this. Just don't hurt them." I begged, desperate tears spilling over my cheeks.

"What if I changed my mind? Maybe I've got my heart set on your demise?"

"Please, don't. You can walk around in my meat suit and fix this mess of mine. Please, just reconsider." He looked at me as though he were weighing his options, running a long bony finger across his lips.

"You need to learn to live with your decisions."

"No! Please! Just help me. Please." I fell to my knees, feeling my whole world come crashing down around me. I could barely handle my own torture, there was no way I would survive watching my family get dragged further into the hell I was in.

"Fine. I'll do it for a couple days but I won't make any promises. If I don't get your full submission, it won't work and we will be back to discussing ways in which I plan to bring you to your end."

"All right. I promise. I will do whatever you need me to do."

I felt like I was falling off a cliff. My stomach twisted with uncomfortable flutters as I sailed downward. I jolted awake when my body hit my mattress. It felt so real, I wondered if I had been hovering above my bed.

I lifted my head and looked around my quiet room. Nothing seemed out of place and relieved, my head flopped back onto my pillow. I let out a horrified gasp when Braxeus's face appeared above me on the ceiling. I stared at the projection as my body trembled in terror.

His eyes were locked onto mine as he gripped his jaw bone through his sagging cheeks. The skin stretched as he slowly pulled down. He continued pulling with very little resistance and when the sides of his lips could no longer withstand the force of his hands, they began to tear into his cheeks. The sickening sound of his bones separating from their sockets pulled everything in my stomach up into my throat. Still, I was unable to look away even while I had no control over the bile pooling in my mouth. I reached up and in horror, realized that my jaw had mirrored his and the contents of my stomach overflowed out of my torn lips. The sting from the stomach acid hitting the open wounds on my face struck me before the blinding pain in the junction below my earlobes where my jaw used to be.

Tears streamed down my temples and when the pain became more than I could bear, my eyes rolled to the back of my head and everything went dark.

The bright red of my eyelids was the first thing my mind registered before my heart jumped back into my throat. I ran my tongue over my bottom teeth, nothing hurt. Confused, I tentatively ran my fingertips over my face to ensure everything was where it was supposed to be. I slowly gripped my chin and moved my jaw back and forth very carefully. The only remnants left from the experience was the lingering taste of vomit on my tongue.

I turned on my side and curled into the fetal position. I cried with relief but also because the fear still held a tight grip deep in my core.

When my tears dried, I felt oddly calm, as though my mind had needed the release and was now ready to function as it should. I got out of bed and dressed in an old pair of jeans and a comfortable t-shirt. I brushed my hair out of my face and looked closely at my reflection. My eyes were clear, my cheeks rosy. No one would be able to tell I woke up in a sorry state. Satisfied, I made my way to the kitchen.

A new coffee machine stood where the old one was. I filled it with water and sat at the table to wait. I smiled brightly at my mom as she joined me in the kitchen. She hesitated for half a second, surprised by my mood before she returned a smile of her own.

"You seem to be in a pleasant mood this morning." She commented.
"I feel good this morning. Like it's going to be a great day."
"Good! What a great way to start your day."

She went to the coffee pot and poured us each a cup before sitting at the table with me. We chatted and made plans to go to the hairdresser's together later that afternoon. I decided it was time to freshen up my look, take a few inches off of my long hair, maybe add some layers around my face. When dad came in, he was greeted with a smile from both mom and I.

"Wow. A man can definitely get used to waking up to two of the prettiest girls smiling at him." He couldn't repress the grin that automatically pulled his lips upward. Mom and I giggled.

"Especially when one of them is usually scowling or throwing things right?" Shella jabbed as she followed him into the kitchen.
"Well, at lease two out of the three ladies in this house are in a good mood." Dad stated, pinning Shella with a look of irritation.

"I'm in a great mood." She disagreed before turning to give me a look filled with contempt. "I'm just not willing to push all her shit under the rug and let her get away with everything just because she decides to act like a normal human being."

"Shella, if you've come in here to stir up trouble, you can turn around now." Dad warned her, not at all impressed with her attitude.

"Don't worry dad, I understand where Shella's coming from and she has every right to feel that way."
I smiled at her without an ounce of warmth. "It's too bad she couldn't use the same sense of self preservation where her two-timing, dickhead of a boyfriend is concerned."

"Oh, shut your mouth. We all know you're just jealous of my relationship with Nathan. No decent man would stick with a nut case like you." With that I laughed.

"Nathan doesn't even swim in the same pond as decent men." I continued to chuckle. "That *boy* would fuck anything with a hole he could get off in. But to each his or her own. If you want to settle down with a *good* man like Nathan, then all the power to you."

"Just because he turned you down when you hit on him--"
"Let me stop you right there." I held up a finger at her as I cut her sentence short. "I would sooner sleep with the rotting corps of a woman before I would make any kind of sexual advance on Nathan's nasty-ass so you can forget that idea. I don't mean to offend you; I simply have a very poor opinion of him. That's it. This discussion is over, I don't want thoughts of him tainting my day."

When I ignored all further comments she had on the topic, she huffed and stomped out of the kitchen.

"So, what are your plans for the day dad?" I asked, unwilling to dwell on Shella's interruption.
"Gotta go to work P-Baby. Gonna be a short one though. Just finishing a roof."
"Thank god it's a short one, it's supposed to be crazy hot out today."
"I'm used to the heat. How else would I get such a good tan?" He wasn't exaggerating, his skin darkened five shades throughout the summer.
"That's very true. You studly manly man you." I winked at him and he chuckled.

It was a great day. My hair looked great. It no longer reached the belt of my pants but it was still long enough to tickle my elbows and the hair dresser did a great job with the layers, they framed my round face just right and I now had bangs for the first time in my life. My look matched the refreshed feeling I felt deep in my soul.

I was still floating in the clouds after supper when the phone rang. Mom stood to answer it but I had a feeling it was for me. I was already walking through the threshold when she turned to hand me the receiver.

"Hey Dimmy."

"Happy-cheeks! How did you know it was me?"

"Only two people call me these days. The other person only calls during business hours."

"Well, that's good to hear. At least I know there aren't any other dogs sniffing around my girl."

"Ain't no dogs sniffing this bitch." I giggled. I knew what I had to do but I struggled to bring the words to my lips.

"What are you up to beautiful girl?"

"Not very much. Just finished supper. How bout you, handsome boy?"

"I'm working my way towards asking you to go to Billy's with me tonight."

"I can't"

"I thought you said you didn't have anything going on."

"I don't."

"Then why can't you come out?"

"Dimitri, listen..."

"No Paisley."

"No what?"

"I know what that tone means."

"It's over Dimitri."

"No, it isn't Paisley."

"It is. I'm a dark pit and it's time for you to climb out."

"You are not. You're an incredible--"

"Stop. I'm not gonna string you along, let you believe there's hope because there isn't. It shouldn't have gotten this far."

"Don't give me that bullshit again, we already went over that."

"Well, it never disappeared for me so I'm calling it quits now."

"You're gonna regret this Paisley." He said in a choked voice.

"Is that a threat?"

"What?" He was shocked. "No! That sounded bad but it was not at all what I meant. I'm not going to *make* you regret it. You're just going to regret throwing this out the window. We fit together."

"You're right. Being with you feels good but it's going to end badly and I'm saving us both from a world of hurt."

"How altruistic of you. Not everything ends in doom."

"This will."

"You can't possibly know that unless you plan for it."

"Dimitri. We're done. This conversation is done. I want nothing but the best for you." I didn't wait for a reply, I hung up and put the phone back in its cradle. When it rang a minute later, I didn't hesitate to reject the call.

I took a deep breath, feeling like I emptied boulders out of my purse, lessening some of the weight I carried around. Letting Dimitri go meant I had one less person to worry about. One less person in Braxeus's radar.

# Chapter Ten

## May I?

*Tricia Warnock*

I didn't see Braxeus again until a week later. Throughout the week, my mood was immensely improved, and it was evident that he was the cause. Something so deep and dark couldn't change so drastically overnight.

Waiting for him in the middle of the empty room, I decided to be grateful. I prayed he wouldn't decide to turn away and pursue my torture.

"Hello." This time, he appeared right in front of me with a smile on his lips.
"Hey."
"Have a good week?"
"It's been a great week. Thank you."
"You're very welcome."
"Have you made a decision?"
"I've made a few decisions this week."
"I meant the one about me."
"Care to elaborate?" He pushed with a knowing smirk.
"You gonna let me off the hook or turn tail and torture me?"

"Let me be straight with you." He held his hands behind his back as he circled me like a shark. "I'm not sure this is something that we can fix temporarily. I think that the moment I sort this mental disaster out, something new will come along and put you right back here."

"So, you're saying I'm fucked either way." I deflated.
"No. What I'm saying is that you are not going to like the solution."
"What's the solution?" I asked suspiciously.
"Let me have control indefinitely." He stated, wrapping his index finger under my chin and preventing me from looking away from his intense gaze.
"Indefinitely?"

"Until we can be sure the problem is solved in its entirety and we won't have a repeat."

"As long as I can come back if I change my mind."

"No."

"What do you mean *no*? I'm not going to let you have complete control *forever.*"

"I need total control. If I let you have an inch, you will slowly creep farther and farther back in and all my efforts will be in vain."

"I can't do that." I told him, afraid of what his response was going to be.

"Well, it's either that or I leave and you can drown in the disgustingly depressing mind of yours."

"I can't do that either." My lip quivered, struggling to hold back the tears.

"Those are your options. I'm not your toy. You can't keep me in your drawer to take out and play with when you feel like it."

"I know. I'm sorry. I really appreciate everything you've done for me."

"This is a limited time offer. I'm not going to wait around for you to make a decision."

"How much time do I have?"

"Thirty seconds."

"*Thirty seconds?* Are you fucking kidding me?" My eyes bulged.

"Watch your mouth." He warned through a clenched jaw. "We've been playing this game for months little girl. It's about time to pull the goddamn trigger."

"That's one hell of a decision to make in thirty seconds."

"I've been patient enough. It's time we shit or get off the pot."

"I don't know what to do."

"Well, what has the last year been like for you?" My gut reaction was to laugh at his ridiculous question.

"Miserable."

"And the two times I stepped in?"

"Reminded me what normal felt like."

"Then I think it's a fairly simple decision."

"Yes, but I don't like the idea of not being able to pull the plug."

"That's a risk you'll have to take."

"Can't we agree to revisit the indefinite part in like a month?"

"That's not enough time."

"Well two months then."

"Six."

"*Six months?*"

"You're lucky I'm agreeing to this at all. Six months." He insisted.

"All right. Six months and we will discuss continuing our *therapy.*"

"Fine. Shall we shake on it?" He smiled victoriously.

"Are you going to show me that scary face again?" I asked, worried.

"Not unless you want me to." He chuckled.

"Not the slightest little bit." I shook my head for emphasis.

"I can refrain from frightening you this once."

"It's very much appreciated."

Nothing seemed to change. I could breathe comfortably without having to keep an eye on dark corners. I was no longer neck deep in sinking sand. The best part, everyone around me seemed to feel the same way. I never thought that having people picking at me would be a relief but knowing that they did it because they no longer felt the need to tip toe around me, was wonderful.

After two weeks, I was ready to celebrate. I called up Laurie and the girls and we were on our way to dance the night away at our favourite hangout, Billy's. I felt great in my short leather skirt and tank top. The long silver chain and matching earrings were the icing on the cake. I wore flats so that blisters wouldn't dampen my evening.

We were having a blast. We were wrapped up in our own world, swaying to the music and laughing when Gemma busted out her crazy old school moves like the funky chicken or the shopping cart. She was so smooth that even when she was acting like a dork, she made it look sexy. Claire's hair was shorter than I remember, she was rocking a cute pixie cut. I hadn't seen the girl in ages but she was still the same easy-going Claire she always was.

"Paisley, have I told you how fantastic you look these days?" She asked, throwing her arm over my shoulder. The way she leaned into me was her tell that she was feeling a pretty good buzz.

"Only forty times or so."
"Have you lost weight?"
"You saying I was fat?"
"Not even close. I just can't put my finger on what's changed."
"Well, I lost a lot of weight, then I gained some back, now here I am."
"I heard you had a lot of shit going on."
"Yeah, you can say that."
"I'm really useless in those kinds of situations Pais. I'm sorry I wasn't around as much as I should have been."
"Don't sweat it lady. I wasn't a very nice person to be around anyway. Ask Laurie, I pushed everyone out."
"Yeah, she told me that. It's the main reason why I never even tried. I figured if Laurie wasn't allowed, there's no way I would be." I turned to her and pulled her into a tight hug.
"Honestly. Don't worry about it. I was dating a super sexy dude while I was MIA." I threw her a bone and she perked right up.
"Oh? How sexy?"
"Like… Sexy enough that even your grandma would cream in her pants if he winked at her." I smirked when she fake gagged.
"That's so disgusting. Nana doesn't have parts that cream. She's a saint."
"Exactly. He's *that* sexy."
"Then why the fuck aren't you still dating him and why is he not here for the rest of us to gawk at?"
"She cut him loose." Laurie answered, handing out a fresh round of drinks.
"What?" Claire asked mouth agape.
"Yeah, he was too perfect."
"What in the hell is wrong with you?"
"She doesn't think she's good enough for a guy like him."
"Has she been doing drugs?"
"I thought the same thing." They both stopped and looked at me like I was a five-year-old caught picking her nose.
"Oh, stop it you's two."

"Well, what the fuck Paisley! We need more asses to look at! Dave's is going to disintegrate soon if we don't give it a rest!" Gemma put in as she wiggled hers in emphasis.

"So much for having your girls' backs." Now the three of them pointed insulted looks at me.

"Well, today is his day off but if you come here almost any other night, I'm sure you'll see him."

"He works here?" Claire was shocked.

"Yeah, he's a bartender."

"No way! How have we not seen him then?" Gemma asked.

"Cause he's a bartender not a server. He stays behind the bar."

"Claire and I have spent many nights sitting at the bar."

"Then you've more than like seen him." I shrugged.

"Hey, I bet it's Dimples." Claire smacked Gemma on the shoulder as the idea struck her.

"Oh yeah, dimples does have a great butt."

"Dimmy does have great dimples."

"Dimmy *is* working tonight." Laurie grinned, tipping back her drink, emptying it and handing me her empty glass.

"No, he's off every other Friday. It can't be Dimitri." My heart dropped. I was not ready to face him.

"Trust me. That's him." She turned me by the shoulders and pointed to Dimitri, serving a group of girls at the opposite end of the bar. I was shocked that I hadn't noticed him sooner.

"How did I miss that?"

"He is gorgeous. Bitch." Gemma snickered. "Keeping him all to yourself."

"I hate you." Claire shoved me playfully.

"Yeah, it's your turn to get the next round." Gemma took Claire's empty glass along with hers and handed them to me.

"No fucking way! I'm not going over there! Are you guys nuts?" I dug my heels in when Laurie shoved me towards the bar.

"Either you go over there or we go tell him to come over here." She threatened.

"You wouldn't do that to me." I looked at her and her intentions were clear. She would definitely follow through. "Laurie. I can't." I pleaded.

"You can. I'm not saying you need to get him back into your bed. I'm saying you need to repair a sore spot."

"You are such an asshole." I gripped all four glasses in my arms and

stomped to the bar like a scolded child.
"You love me."

       I took several deep breaths before stepping up to the bar. I put the glasses downs quietly, trying to avoid drawing his attention toward me for as long as possible. I silently prayed the other bartender would see me first. No such luck. He turned away from the group of girls to scan the bar and make sure he wasn't neglecting anyone when his eyes landed on me. I saw the hurt before he could hide it. There was a hesitation before he started towards me and I hated myself for putting him in such an awkward position.

"What can I get you?"
"Four rum and cokes please." If he wanted to act like he didn't know me, so be it.
"Having a good time with your girls?"
"Yes. I didn't realize you were working tonight."
"Yeah, I've been taking extra shifts. Saw you girls come in."
"I wasn't expecting you to be here."
"Otherwise, you wouldn't have come?" He asked, looking me in the eye for the first time.
"I would have gone somewhere else." I admitted.
"Why?"
"To avoid this." I wagged a finger between the two of us. "I don't want you feeling uncomfortable at work."
"Seeing you doesn't make me uncomfortable."
"Well, it can't possibly make you happy!"
"It does. Even if I can't have you, seeing you smiling and having a good time, makes me happy."
"Oh, shut up Dimitri. Stop feeding me your bullshit charm." I spit out, irritated that he was being sweet when I wanted him to be angry with me. Anger would make it easier for me to stick to my resolve. He gave a soft chuckle.
"I miss you happy-cheeks. Not having you around has been a shock to my system."
"I miss you too but it'll get easier." I patted the hand he had resting on the bar which was a mistake because before I could pull away, he turned his hand over and held mine in a firm grip, preventing my retreat.
"Come outside and have a smoke with me." He requested, still

holding on to my hand.

"I can't. My friends are waiting for me."

"I'm asking for five minutes not the rest of your night." He insisted.

I looked over at my friends and they were all watching me with grins plastered across their faces. I flipped them off before turning back to Dimitri and nodding my agreement.

"I'm stepping out for a break." Dimmy told the other bartender as he passed him to go through the swinging bar door.

I didn't protest when he threw his arm across my shoulders to lead me out the side door where he took his smoke breaks. I knew it was wrong and that I shouldn't lead him on but it felt good. Once outside, he leaned his should against the brick wall and offered me a cigarette.

"How have you been lately?"

"I've been all right. Feeling a lot better. You?"

"Good." He purposely avoided answering the question, taking a long drag and blowing the smoke out through his nose. "You *do* know that ending things with me is bullshit right?" He asked, no hint of a smile to take the edge off his question. He was serious and clearly had given it a lot of thought.

"It's not Dimmy. I can't do this with you right now."

"This conversation or this relationship?"

"Both."

"You know, I would have given you my heart on a silver fucking platter if you'd have asked me to. I've never asked you to change for me, I understood your need for space, followed along when you wanted me around and when you didn't. Never once have I given you a reason to doubt me. Pulling the rug out from under my feet just when things seemed to be going great is unfair." His cheeks were red, the anger I wanted earlier was making an appearance and suddenly, I didn't want it anymore.

"Stop. I know it isn't fair."

"Then why the fuck are you doing this?" He slapped the bricks beside him out of frustration.

"I don't know!" I shrugged, unable to find a way to make him understand. "I'm unstable. I can't give you a healthy relationship. That's just a fact. I'm cutting you loose before we have too much invested."

"It's too late for that."
"No, it isn't. Dimitri, stop. I've made up my mind and I'm not going to change it." I crossed my arms over my chest.

I should have left it at that and walked away but I didn't. I should have said good-bye when he flicked his cigarette to the ground and ran back inside to my girls with my tail between my legs. Most of all, I should never have come outside with Dimitri in the first place.

He pulled me behind the building by the elbow and I didn't struggle against him. Initially, I had no idea what he was doing but when we turned the corner and he shoved me up against the building, I got the message. Still, like an idiot, I didn't run.

He leaned into me, framing my face with his hands while his lips claimed mine with an urgency I felt under my skirt. I wanted to punch myself in the face when my lips opened for him. When his hands slid into my hair and squeezed into tight fists, I whimpered with need into his mouth which elicited a hungry growl in response.

One his hands slid down my arm, grazing the side of my breast on its way to my thigh. He took a firm grip and hiked it up to hook over his hip. His action forced my skirt up my legs, leaving nothing but my panties covering me. He pushed himself against the warmth of my underwear, teasing me with his hardness. Of its own volition, my other thigh wrapped around him, locking my ankles behind his back.

I don't know how he did it without my notice but suddenly his cock was free and rubbing against me with nothing but thin cotton preventing it from getting where it wanted to go. I couldn't stop the moan of pleasure that came out of me. Dimitri had always felt good, just because he wasn't mine anymore didn't mean my body didn't still enjoy his. He reached down between us and squeezed me, applying pressure where I desperately needed it. I sucked on his bottom lip to keep myself quiet, even when I felt his fingers curl around my panties to pull them out of his way. My brain was so filled with lust that the idea of hitting the brakes was laughable.

I pushed my hips forward in invitation and he didn't disappoint. My whole body quivered with relief when he filled me. It was incredible. Only a few thrusts and I was ready to explode. When I tensed with my climax, he didn't slow down, instead, he gave me more. I bit his shoulder, muffling my scream and he did the same to mine.

He didn't let me go when we were both spent and trying to catch our breath. His arms held me close as he laid kisses along my neck. I unhooked my feet, letting them slide back to the ground. Like a gentleman, he adjusted my skirt first before putting himself back into his jeans and zipping up his pants.

"That was... amazing." I told him, running my fingers through my hair.
"That's putting it mildly." He smiled and ran his thumb across my bottom lip gently. I took the hand by my face and placed a kiss on his knuckles to soften the blow.
"This doesn't change anything Dimmy."
"I know." He leaned in and kissed me. "But I'll happily be your booty call any day of the week."
"I can't promise a repeat."
"Just promise that when you feel the urge." He wiggled his eyebrows. "I'm the one you'll call."
"All right. I can agree to that. Just don't wait by the phone."
"God you're sexy." He smacked my ass when I turned to head back inside.
"Let's go Romeo. People are going to start searching for us soon."
"Just one more." He pulled me back around for a kiss before taking hold of my hand and leading us back to the door.

Laurie, Gemma and Claire were all sitting on bar stools watching the door when we came back in. The second they saw me, mischievous grins appeared on all three of their faces. I smacked my forehead, knowing they were going to embarrass the hell out of me. Dimitri pinched my backside when we split at the swinging door, making me laugh. Still smiling when I reached the girls.

"So, have fun out there?" Gemma asked with a wink.

"Meh, it was all right." Dimmy walked up in front of us as I answered and laughed which set the girls off in a fit of giggles.

"Can I get you ladies something to drink? It's on me."

"Oh shit. Are you gonna lay on the bar and let us drink from your belly button?" Claire asked, licking her lips before snorting out more guffaws.

"Not quite what I meant." He smiled; cheeks flushed. "I will buy you girls a round." He turned to get four fresh glasses.

"You two have a nice breath of fresh air outside?" Laurie snickered.

"Paisley didn't go out there to breathe." Gemma leaned against Laurie, making sure she had all our attention. "She rode the bologna pony." She sniffed the air in front of me. "You smell like cock." And we all bent over, busting a gut.

When Dimitri turned back around to place our drinks in front of us, he was a beautiful shade of burgundy and trying hard to avoid making eye contact with any of us.

"Skank." Claire teased, shoving me playfully.

"Hey, Paisley deserves to have a good time. If anyone has earned it, she has." Laurie was quick to come to my defence.

"Oh, don't worry. I'm the last person to slut shame a girl. I'm just jealous." She held up her glass to Dimitri. "Thanks for the drink handsome. Got any cute colleagues due for a break?"

"Unfortunately, Ty is the only other one on tonight and he's happily married with a bun in the oven."

"Well shit. I can never catch a break. My girl parts don't even remember what it's like to be loved."

"Oh, shut it, Claire. We all know it gets plenty of love from mister jelly."

"Mister jelly?" Dimmy asked, naively setting himself up for more awkward girl talk.

"Her magical silicone cock." Gemma explained, grinning when understanding crossed his face.

"Mister jelly is getting old."

"Time for us to take a trip to the adult superstore?"

"Fuck that. Billy's is usually good for a fix." She turned on her stool and searched the crowd for a target.

We all turned to scan the crowd. I swear I could feel my heart stop when I spotted an old man sitting alone in the corner booth, staring at me. He looked so much like Braxeus that all the hair on the back of my neck prickled. I forced myself to move my line of sight to the other side of the room. I gasped when again, another Braxeus look-alike was sitting alone, staring me down. My eyes shot back to the first one and no one was there. There was no way he could have made it through the crowd to the other side of the room that fast. When I couldn't find the second one, I shook my head, trying to shake the crazy out. It didn't work. The next person my focus landed on, was smiling at me in that creepily wide smile that Braxeus used. I watched, transfixed as wrinkles started forming across their forehead and around the amused eyes. Braxeus's face slowly took over and I could see his shoulders vibrate with suppressed laughter.

"Him." Gemma pointed toward a guy standing with four of his friends drinking a beer while one of them held the group's attention, telling them an obviously exciting story.

"Oh yes. He's crazy cute." Claire agreed.

"You gonna go chat the poor unsuspecting boy up?" Laurie asked with a grin.

"Bet your ass I am." Claire grabbed her drink from the bar and emptied it for extra courage.

I tried to keep myself under control, to push my delusions aside. We all watched Claire comb her fingers through her hair and smooth a hand over her shirt. It was like watching a soap opera, we were all glued to the show, Gemma even passed me the bowl of peanuts she was munching on.

She had her strut down to perfection, her hips swaying just enough to draw attention to her tight round bottom without being obnoxious. I envied her confidence as she walked right up to the boy in her sights and touched his arm to draw his attention to her. I watched as he smiled at whatever she said before handing his bottle off to one of his buddies. He took her hand and led her to the dance floor. She looked over her shoulder to send us a wink, we laughed and clinked our glasses to celebrate her victory. Poor guy didn't even know it yet but he was in for one hell of a night if she got her way.

**"How disgusting."** I heard Braxeus in my hear. I quickly looked at Laurie and Gemma to see if they heard it too but they were still watching Claire. **"Only prostitutes chase men."** I heard his indignant growl.

"Stop it." I whispered but Laurie heard my voice.
"What?" She asked.
"Oh nothing. Thought I saw a spider." I lied.

**"And that one is dumb, you're a terrible liar. How can you debase yourself by associating with such filth?"** It took everything inside of me to bite my tongue. I repeatedly told myself it wasn't real, no one was talking to me. **"Turn around, Dimitri is looking at you. Give him a smile."** I looked over my shoulder and sure enough, Dimmy was leaning against the bar, watching me while he dried a glass. His smile was impossible to resist and had me smiling back instantly. **"Good girl, now pull the front of your top down a bit and give him a glimpse of your tits. He didn't get to see those earlier."** I broke eye contact with Dimitri, feeling dirty knowing that Braxeus had watched. **"Don't be upset child, sex is perfectly natural. He came onto you and you followed through. Nothing to be ashamed of. I'm proud of you, you did so well that the boy can't stop thinking about it."**

"Earth to Paisley!" Gemma yelled, reach over Laurie to slap my arm.
"Sorry, I spaced out."
"No shit. That was impressive! I wish I could tune the rest of the

world out like that."

"What were you saying?"

"I was trying to get you in on our little wager."

"Yeah, Gemma says they don't make it back to his place and will probably end up fucking in the bathroom. I say they cut the night short and head out any minute now." Laurie elaborated.

**"Claire's a whore. There's no way she'll make it out the door. She will probably jump him in his car right outside in the parking lot."** Braxeus stated in revulsion. His input pissed me off and the girls looked at me, confused by my expression.

"What's wrong? We're just having fun with it. If I was in the mood, I would be right over there with her, groping one of his friends."

**"That's because she's just as disgusting as her dear friend *Claire.*"**

"Gemma? Not in the mood for a roll in the hay?" Laurie pressed her hand to Gemma's forehead. "You feeling okay?"

"Oh, don't be a bitch." Gemma smacked her hand away. "I don't need dick to have a good time."

"You sure about that?" Laurie grinned. Gemma pretended to consider the question seriously while she examined the group of guys Claire had picked from.

"You're right. I bet that sexy piece of man meat doesn't nag as much as you do." Gemma emptied her glass and hopped down from the barstool.

**"Fucking abhorrent! How do you waste your time with such vile creatures? How can you sit there and watch such repugnant behaviour?"**

"What happened to sex being natural?" I asked out of frustration but only caught myself when the words were already out of my mouth.

"Nobody said that it wasn't." Laurie said, looking at me in confusion.

"I was being sarcastic." I said, attempting to disguise the words. Laurie laughed.

"Yeah, those two definitely act on their *natural* instincts."

**"There's a difference. You don't have to put your pussy on a silver platter. Combined, those two girls have spread their legs for dozens of males. I'm shocked neither of them have contracted a flesh-eating disease between their legs. You, my child, have made Dimitri crawl through obstacles to get into your panties. He earned it. Your friends have had a threesome together, did you know that?"**

"No fucking way!" Laurie jumped at my outburst.
"What?"
"Have those two had a threesome together?"

"Yeah, more than once." She looked at me, searching my face, trying to figure out where my head was at. "I'm not going to bed with you and Dimmy. I'm in a committed relationship. Even if I was single, not my cup of tea."

"What? No, no. I'm not interested in that kind of shit either. It just popped into my head and I wondered if they had. As if they would fucking do that!"
"Paisley. Have you not met them? Seen them together? Sometimes I wonder why they aren't *together,* together."
"Seriously?"

I looked over to the two of them on the dance floor. They were facing each other and laughing while they danced with their conquests at their backs.

**"Fucking dykes."**

I was speechless. I never noticed a closeness between them that seemed more than just a close friendship before. I usually saw Gemma and Claire as having the same kind of relationship that Laurie and I had, closer than sisters.

"Well shit." I leaned back, resting my elbows against the bar.
"You don't remember them telling us about it, almost a year ago?"
Laurie leaned back with me, sipping her drink.
"Here you go ladies." Dimitri reached out and placed fresh drinks between us.

"Thanks, handsome." Laurie gave him a grateful smile.
"Why do you two look like your up to no good?" He asked us and
when Laurie and I locked eyes, we both giggled with mischief.

"Well… we were thinking…" I trailed off, Laurie and I spun around
to watch as the wheels turned behind his eyes.
"How *adventurous* are you?" Laurie asked, cocking an eyebrow
suggestively.

A flush darkened his cheeks as he caught on to what
we were hinting at. He looked between the two of us, waiting for one
of to crack and laugh. After several uncomfortable, for him, seconds,
he cleared his throat.

"I uh, I'm uh, not sure. I uh, don't know." He grabbed a rag under
the counter and started scrubbing the bar.
"So, you've never thought about spicing up the bedroom?" Laurie
pushed.
"Not really no. I've always been more than happy with what went on
with me and Paisley."
"Aw really?" I reached over and squeezed his hand, smiling when he
looked up at me.
"Yes really. I thought you were too."
"Oh handsome, this has nothing to do with your sexual prowess.
Paisley and I were just considering what it would be like to share."

He tugged on the neck of his shirt, unable to look at
either of us. He clearly had no idea what to make of our
conversation.

"It doesn't necessarily have to be Laurie and me. We could invite
Dave if you want, Laurie can watch. Or hell, we call have a little
orgy with the four of us."
"Oh yeah! What a brilliant idea!" Laurie exclaimed excitedly.
"I uh, I don't think I'm uh, the right fit, maybe." Dimitri
stammered, still scrubbing the same spot on the bar.
"Dimmy?" He froze his scrubbing hand. "Dimmy, look at
me." I requested, when he looked up, I smiled brightly.
"We're pulling your leg."

"Paisley and I were talking about how neither of us were interested in inviting a third person into the bedroom." She giggled when relief melted across his face.

My stomach hit the floor when a maniacal laughter sounded in my ear, before either of them could react, I scooped up my bag and bolted for the door. Whatever the reason was for the ominous sound, it was not a good sign and I wasn't ready to sit still and wait to see what would happen next.

I ran. When I heard the door open behind me, I didn't look back, I kept running. It could have been Laurie or Dimmy or it could have been another Braxeus look-alike, I didn't want to know.

My lungs were on fire when I ran up the front steps, relieved to finally be home. I didn't make it to the front door, I collapsed outside, on the porch, struggling to breathe. The world around me was spinning and I couldn't find a spot to focus on. With the lack of oxygen, over-exertion, and the inability to regain my bearings, my stomach began to heave. I squeezed my eyes closed when burning liquid rose into my throat while I gagged, and it was so much worse than the normal sting of bile. It kept pouring out of my mouth even when my body stopped trying to empty its contents. When whatever faucet inside of me turned off, I had emptied an unimaginable amount of fluid. When I opened my eyes, I was horrified at the sight of all the thick black tar-like substance in front of me. The black substance was pooling around my fingers and I could feel how sticky it was. It wasn't normal for a body to eject such putridness.

While I examined the odd excrement, I heard the front door open.

"What the fuck is that?" Dad asked, rushing to pull me onto my feet and away from the mess in front of me.

"I was sick." My voice was raw.

"You were sick?" He asked, stunned. "That looks like something from a construction sight. Did you shit yourself?" He spun me around to see if I had any on the back of my skirt.

"No. I threw up."

"That came out of your mouth?" He struggled to process what could have happened.

"What in the hell did you eat?"

"I had supper with you guys and that's it. I had rum and coke at the bar."

"That doesn't look anything like pot roast, potatoes or coke." He chuckled, trying to pull our attention away from the shock of what came out of my body.

"Not unless mom slipped some asphalt into the food."

Dad wrapped an arm around my shoulders and led me into the house. In the living room he gestured for me to lay down on the couch and I complied. He left and came back with a glass of water and a cold cloth.

"Take it easy kid. It was probably just a mix of something that your body didn't like." He put the cloth across my forehead before picking a movie off of the shelf and plopping into his chair.

"Let's watch an old slasher movie." He suggested, hitting play.

I pulled the blanket off the back of the couch and snuggled in. I appreciated my dad's comfort. He seemed to understand that I didn't want empty words or theories, just his presence and a movie I didn't have to concentrate on. I fell asleep at some point during the movie.

It wasn't something I ate. Every night for a week, I was bent over the toilet, expelling the black tar. I now sounded like a heavy life-long smoker. I worried that the damage would be permanent and I would never sound like myself again.

The vomiting was the only strange occurrence in my life and I happily accepted it because all the crazy from before no longer had a hold of me.

I was working on an assignment in my room and contemplating whether I was ready to return to school or not. It was something I planned to discuss with Daniella when she arrived for our meeting. I felt like I was ready, that I was well enough to take a step toward returning to normalcy. I hoped that my recent progress mentally and being caught up on my assignments would play in my favour where Daniella was concerned. When I heard the familiar knock on the front school, I crossed my fingers.

"Hey Daniella." I greeted when I opened the door for her.
"Good afternoon Paisley. How are you doing?" She asked as she walked in and bent down to pull off her shoes before following me to the kitchen.
"I've been great actually. Ask mom." I gestured toward my mom who was sitting at the table with her crossword puzzle.
"Misses Coleman, nice seeing you."

"Hello Daniella. Would you like a cup of coffee?" Mom asked, standing to grab a couple mugs from the cupboard.

"That sounds fantastic. Thank you."

"What did you want to ask me?" Mom asked, placing our coffee cups on the table for us.

"I was telling Daniella that I've been doing great. Haven't I?"

"She really has been. Her mood has done a three sixty. She's been pleasant to interact with, she's taking care of herself. It's been wonderful." Mom gushed, smiling at me the whole time.

"That's great news! I'm so happy to hear that." She seemed genuinely excited with the update. "How are things outside of the house?"

"Good, I've been talking to my friend Laurie again, I even went out with her and our friends Claire and Gemma."

"That's phenomenal. Good for you Paisley." She patted my hand. "Any concerns? Anything you want to improve?"

"Not really no. I mean the only negative would be the fact that I've been throwing up this thick black gunk but otherwise, I feel like I'm back to normal. I was hoping to go back to school." I held my breath, nervous of her reaction.

"You've been throwing up black gunk?" She asked, worried.

"Yes."

"How often does this happen?"

"Nightly."

"*Every* night?"

"For about a week, yeah."

"Oh." She seemed to be at a loss for words.

"About school…"

"I know you feel like you're ready but I'd like to give it some more time just to be sure." She looked at me, worried she would hurt my feelings.

"Okay." I said internalizing my disappointment so that it wouldn't make her feel worse.

"We'll talk about it again when we get together next week." She promised.

"Okay." I repeated.

"I know this will be gross but the next time you're sick, can you get a sample for me? I'd like to have a look and see what it is that you're throwing up."

"Ugh, yeah I can do that I think." The thought of scooping up vomit made me want to gag right there on the spot. Maybe, she would get her sample right away.

"Thank you. I don't think it's anything to be too worried about, I just want to make sure it isn't blood or signs of a deeper issue."

"Oh, it's not blood. It's like thick, black slime. It's disgusting. Dad has seen it."

"He has?" Mom asked, surprised that he never mentioned it.

"Yeah, the first time it happened was on the front porch and he helped me into the house. We thought it might have been a bad reaction to something I ate."

"You don't feel sick or anything otherwise? You're just vomiting?" Daniella asked, making notes in her notebook.

"No, otherwise I feel fine. Usually, I take my shower then I sit on the floor because the room starts to spin, I throw up, brush my teeth and call it a night."

"Strange." Daniella commented, tapping her pen against her chin as she thought about potential causes.

"Tell me about it. I never would have thought puke could look like that."

"From the sounds of it, neither have I." Daniella's admission startled me. She worked in a hospital, surely, she's seen everything. Then again, she did work with mental issues rather than physical ones so maybe not. "But I'll take a look at the sample and show Doctor Spence to see what he thinks just to be on the safe side."

"We certainly appreciate it." Mom told her.

"I'm really glad you seem to be doing well though Paisley. You've made a remarkable recovery and I'm so proud of you." My face heated.

"Thanks. I was starting to think it was never going to get better."

"Oh, it might have taken time but we were bound to find a way to make things better for you." She smiled.

If only we had known that what we thought was the start of a strong recovery, was actually the beginning of a terrifying battle of wills. One that would leave deep scars on all those who witnessed it.

# Chapter Eleven

Just Take Me.

I was exhausted. I've been on the go all day long. Mom brought me shopping this morning because we were both bored and wanted to get out of the house. When we got back home, dad was just getting into his car to go to the lake, so I hopped in with him. I joined him every chance I got; it was an opportunity to enjoy the peaceful outdoors, the quiet, the beauty. Every time we sat together by the water, our bond grew stronger and I could tell that he appreciated it just as much as I did. The only positive thing I found throughout the mess I had become, was the strong relationship that bloomed between myself and my father, something I never would have thought was possible. Thinking back on my early childhood, I saw him as a monster. In the past, it was always the four of us living under his iron fist. I couldn't excuse his brutal parenting methods, but I now understood that he was doing the best that he could. He had a violent temper, and not only did he not know how to control himself, but he also didn't know any other way to cope with what he saw as disobedience. It could be that he grew throughout this experience, but I saw him differently now, he was an ally and I loved him so much more than I ever have before.

On our way home, we swung by the pharmacy so that I could pick up the refill for my medication. Dad let me out at the front door before parking the car to wait for me. The usual cashier stood at the counter, wearing her perpetually friendly smile.

"Good evening, how can I help you?"
"Hello, my doctor was supposed to have faxed in a refill for me."
"Your name ma'am?"
"Paisley Coleman."

"Let me have a look." She stepped to the side behind a glass wall and began ruffling through paper bags. When she didn't find it, she went through the door behind the counter and returned a moment later. "They're putting it together for you now, it'll only take a minute or two."

"Thank you."

I plopped myself into one of the chairs nearby, leaning my head back against the wall while I waited. I couldn't have taken more than a few breaths before I heard an all-too familiar mischievous laugh. Much the same as the snap of an over extended elastic band, my body jolted upright. In a panic, I looked around to see if any of the customers wandering around showed any signs of having heard the evil mirth or my knee jerk reaction to it. Tears filled my eyes as terror weighed heavily in my stomach. He was coming and there was nothing I could do to block him from making an appearance.

"Miss Coleman?"

The moisture in my eyes evaporated instantly, my head made a slow but purposeful turn to meet the eyes of the pharmacist. I locked gazes with him and sank my teeth through the thick muscle of my tongue. I stood and walked to the counter; my mouth steadily filled with the coppery taste of my own blood. Without breaking eye contact, I slid the dangling piece of flesh from my mouth, caressing my upper lip with the fresh wound. As my chin showered in the warm flowing blood, I smiled wickedly at the look of complete horror on the poor man's face.

"Thanks Henry, tell that slut daughter of yours to keep sucking her teacher off after classes. I like the show." Before turning to leave, I sent a mouthful of plasma into the mouth he had hanging open in a mixture of terror and utter shock. When he screamed, I howled with laughter and strutted away, pleased with myself.

Stepping out of the pharmacy, the fresh air cleared the fog from my brain. I covered my mouth, trying to catch the blood so that I wouldn't make more of a mess. The pain was excruciating and once I was in the safety of the car beside my dad, my body shook with the sobs I could no longer hold back. There was too much blood, my hands couldn't hold it so I pulled the hem of my shirt up to help contain the flood.

"What the fuck happened?" Frazzled, dad leaned over to the glove box to pull out napkins he kept stashed there.

"I bi oth my pungue." I struggled to tell him with my mangled tongue.
"You what?" He pulled my shirt back and paled when he saw the damage. "Jesus Christ." He yanked the shifter and peeled out of the parking lot, screeching his tires.

When dad carried me into the hospital, the triage nurse took one look at me and rushed us to a bed. Dad laid me down on the stiff bed while the nurse pushed a button on the wall before putting a metal bowl under my chin to catch the blood and rushing around to gather medical supplies.

A doctor came running into the room moments later, heading straight for me.

"What happened?"
"She bit off her damn tongue!" Dad screeched.
"Was she having a seizure? Did she fall and hit her chin?"

"I don't know, she went into the pharmacy to pick up her medication and came out with a mouthful of blood."

"What kind of medication is she taking?"

"Zyprexa. She's been weaning off of it so I'm not certain what dosage she's been taking."

"Lana, get me two and a half milligrams of morphine please."

I couldn't hear a word they were saying over the loud ringing in my ears. Not long after the nurse poked me with a needle, the pain disappeared and for that I was grateful.

It was impossible to avoid watching the doctor stick a needle into my tongue. I was too nervous to keep my eyes closed and the only other option was to watch him sew the pieces back together. The flesh was numb but I could still feel the popping of his needle breaking through the thick skin and it wasn't a pleasant experience. When he was finished with the stitches, he had me rinse my mouth with a foul-tasting liquid that made me gag. Talking was out of the question, my tongue felt like it was three sizes too big for my mouth and too numb to operate.

"The stitches will dissolve in about seven days. Only soft food like jello or soup broth and I'm going to send you home with a rinse I want you to use anytime you put anything into your mouth other than water. Use Advil for pain management. Two capsules every four hours as needed. If the pain is still unbearable after a week, come back in so we can make sure there's no signs of infection."

My throbbing tongue woke me from a deep sleep. When I cracked open my eyes, the sun was already bright outside my window. I took my time getting out of bed, I knew that an interrogation would be waiting for me in the kitchen. When the noise downstairs got louder, I knew that my time was up, Mom wasn't going to wait much longer. I stumbled my way down the stairs, rubbing my stiff jaw.

I barely made it through the threshold before she was on me. She was squeezing me and kissing my cheeks. When she settled down, she held me at arms length to look me sharply in the eye. Dad watched on from his seat at the table, sipping his coffee.

"What the hell did you do?" She asked but my response was so jumbled that neither of us understood the words that came out of my mouth.

Frustrated, she went to her junk drawer and pulled out her pad of paper and a pen, slapping both on the table in front of me.

"What the hell did you do?" She repeated.

*I bit my tongue.* Her eyes scanned the words.

"You bit it?" I nodded. "Why in the hell did you bite it?"

*I don't know.*

"You didn't think to stop when it started to hurt? You had to bite right through your fucking tongue?"

*I couldn't control it.*

"You expect me to believe that? Are you not taking your pills regularly?"

*Yes.*

"What the hell are we supposed to do Paisley? How can we be comfortable leaving you by yourself?"

*I don't know what to tell you mom. There weren't any warnings, it just happened.*

She gripped my chin and yanked my mouth open to have a look at my tongue. She cringed when she saw the purple muscle covered in black stitches.

"That looks awful Paisley. I don't understand what could have gotten into you." She released me to run her hands over her face.

*Neither do I.*

"Well Daniella is on her way over here."

*I don't want to see her.*

Just as mom finished reading, a knock sounded on the front door.

"Too bad she's already here. It would be rude to turn her away."
Once she was through the threshold, I threw her notepad against the wall. Daniella could say whatever she wanted but I was not about to say or rather *write* a goddamn word. I didn't appreciate being cornered and I certainly wasn't happy about being left without a choice. I was in no mood to feign friendliness.

"Good morning Paisley." Daniella greeted when she entered the kitchen. I nodded. "I hear you're in pretty rough shape." Without telling it to, my mangled tongue jutted out of my mouth in a childish gesture. "Oh my, that must be terribly painful."

"No, it feels wonderful. Nitwit." I responded in a voice that wasn't mine but that I recognized instantly. Mom, dad and Daniella gasped when they heard the guttural sound.

"How did you… A minute ago, you couldn't talk." Mom said unsteadily.

"I had no desire to have words with you. You irritate me to no end. Now be a dear and keep that useless mouth of yours shut before I bite your tongue off too." I warned, the surprised horror on my face at odds with the words I spoke.

"You watch the way you speak to your mother Paisley." Dad said crossly, standing from his seat to exert dominance.

"I will mind you this once because I like you, however, keep in mind that you have no authority over me." My response to him was strong and assertive when all I wanted to do was run and cower.

"She isn't herself at the moment Donald. She won't process anything you tell her right now." Daniella held out her hand to stop dad from pursuing an argument.

"Well, look at the little girl using her head. Isn't that cute." My lips curled into a menacing grin, aimed at Daniella. "Let's play nice with the little girl Paisley. We don't want to make her cry in front of her *patients*." She raised her eyebrows in question when I said it in plural.

"I only have one patient here."
"That's right. My mistake." My hand hid my mouth in a mockingly coy movement as I giggled sadistically.
"Paisley *is* my only patient. Right?" She asked in third person, acknowledging the fact that it wasn't me who spoke.
"I don't know, is she?"
"Is there anyone else here besides Paisley, her parents and myself?"

"Wouldn't you like to know?" I rolled my eyes at her and turned to grab the pot of coffee, pouring myself a cup and filling my mouth with the steaming beverage. My eyes teared with agony when the hot, bitter liquid swished against my wounded tongue. "Paisley likes this shit. I don't understand why. Maybe she'll change her mind when blisters pop up around the stitches." Another mouthful of coffee and the tears spilled out.

Daniella reached to take the cup from me but I slapped her hand away, holding the cup closer to my body defensively.

"Try and take what's mine again and I will cut off the lids from your eyes and chew them like bubble gum." I threatened her and I could feel my face twist into a hateful expression. She snatched her hand back.

"Who are you?"

"Daniella, don't be ridiculous." Mom told her, annoyed with the way she was talking to me.

"I told you to shut your mouth!" I yelled at her, feeling just as irritated by the sound of her voice as I used to.
"Look at her eyes Johanne. Tell me those are your daughter's eyes." Daniella suggested. When mom focused, colour drained from her cheeks, whatever she saw, left her speechless and terrified.
*to*
"Who are you?" Daniella repeated.
"None of your fucking business." I snarled.
"Who are you?" Again.

"Christine Wilson-Perdy." Her jaw dropped, stunned. The name meant nothing to me but clearly it held significance to her. "It pleases me to see that you remember."

"How do you know Christine?"
"What makes you think I'm going to tell you that?"
"Stop messing around!" Daniella raised her voice, losing the composure she kept on a tight leash.
"Don't get all frazzled Daniella. It doesn't become you."
"How. Do. You. Know. Christine!" She asked again, annunciating every word slowly.

"Well, Christine and I had a long talk before she took her swan dive." When her bottom lip quivered, a cruel laugh burst from my chest. "You really hurt her feelings. You should consider taking classes on showing empathy."

"It wasn't my fault." Daniella's hands balled into fists at her sides.

"Oh no, of course not dear. She never told you she wanted to end her life. She didn't show you the noose she kept hidden in her closet. She didn't cut herself right in front of you. If she had done these things, you might have showed a little more compassion. You probably never would have told her to stop acting so dramatic." The smirk never left my face while I overloaded Daniella with the sarcastic words that were clearly causing her a great deal of pain.

"Her mother told me she played the pity card and not to give in to it. She *told* me coddling her would only make it worse!"

"Right, and I'm sure she shared the same things with her mother that she shared with you. I'm sure her mother is a registered therapist who is adequately educated to make those kinds of assumptions."

"Her mother knew her better than anyone." As she spoke, I crept closer to her. I put myself so deep into her personal space that our noses were only a whisper away from touching. I had to give her credit for not backing away from me.

"You know for a fact that her mother had no idea that she had self harmed. Her mother was oblivious to the steps her daughter had taken to end her own life several times before she managed to succeed. You can lie to yourself and you can bullshit the people around you but there are *no lies* where I am concerned. I know about poor little Christine Wilson-Perdy. I know about Jacob Thompson and Lisa Judd. I can even tell you about the pitifully shy David Strict who hung himself in his parents' garage when you told him you weren't interested in dating a boy who couldn't look you in the eye." I watched tears fill the bottom of her eyes and begin to spill slowly down her cheeks. A heart-breaking sob
escaped before she grabbed her purse and turned to run from the house.

I didn't move until I heard the sound of a car peeling out of our driveway. When the sound disappeared down the road, the air left my lungs and my whole body went limp. I crashed to the floor, narrowly missing the table with my forehead on my way down. I was still conscious but I wasn't able to move. It took several moments before my parents snapped out of their stunned dazes and realize I wasn't getting up. They bumped into each other in their hurry to reach me.

"P-Baby? Can you hear me?" Dad asked, kneeling beside me and shaking my shoulders.

"Oh God. What the hell just happened?" Mom frantically paced the kitchen, unable to focus. "There's no way Daniella told her all of those things. It would be unprofessional not to mention completely inappropriate."

"Johanne, now's not the time to worry about it. Get me a wet cloth." Dad ordered.

She kept quiet while she pulled a clean cloth from the drawer and ran it under the faucet. She didn't say another word but her mind was elsewhere when she handed him the sopping wet rag.

"Yeah, don't worry about wringing it out or anything." Dad told her sarcastically but she wasn't listening. He twisted out the excess water right on the floor beside him before placing it gently across my forehead.

"Something is seriously wrong with her Don. How the hell did she know all those things?"
"Something's been seriously wrong with her for a while now." He muttered.
"I should go see Daniella. Make sure she's all right."
"You should leave that poor woman alone." Dad said before she made two steps.
"She's probably really upset."
"Exactly. She doesn't need you hovering around asking her all kinds of questions. Leave her alone."
"What are we going to do Don? Daniella was the only one who seemed to get anywhere with Paisley."
"I don't know right this second. I'm sure Daniella just needs to regain some composure."
"I've got to do something. I have to make sure she's all right and is still willing to meet with us."
"Johanne! Shut the fuck up! Daniella is the last thing I'm worried about! Our daughter is p
assed out on our goddamn floor, get your head out of your ass and help me for Christ sakes."

I could feel pins and needles in my fingers and toes as though circulation had been cut off for too long and was finally returning. Seconds late, feeling returned to the rest of my body and I was able to move again. My emotions were chaotic. I was ashamed of myself for what I had done to Daniella, terrified that I had no control over my words or my actions and I was worried because it had happened so suddenly, giving me no warning as to what was going to happen. There was no way for me to protect myself or those around me if I didn't know when to leave the room and hide.

"You ok P-Baby?"
"I don't know." I answered, unable to lie so that he wouldn't worry.
"Do you remember anything?"
"Unfortunately."
"How did you know all those things about Daniella?" Mom asked.
"I have no idea. Words were just coming out of my mouth." Neither of them knew what to say so no one said anything.

Dad helped me to my feet and I went upstairs to shower, hoping hot water would melt away the lingering numbness in my skin. I stood under the spray until the water ran cold and sat on the edge of the tub, wrapped in a towel. Eventually the steam in the bathroom disappeared and I started to shiver. I dressed in my comfiest jogging pants and worn-out t-shirt, cleaning up the bathroom before locking myself in my bedroom. I didn't leave my room for the rest of the day other than quick trips to the bathroom. If I didn't think they would send the police after me, I would have left the house to further isolate myself. As it was, I knew that it wouldn't take long before I was hauled back home in the back of a police car.

My eyes sprung open to complete darkness. It took a moment for my pupils to adjust and when they did, my legs swung out from under my blankets, over the side of my bed. I rose and slowly limbered across my room and out the door. My limbs moving on their own made me want to scream, to warn my parents that something was going to happen. All I could manage was a choked whimper.

I went to the door next to mine and my hand reached out to turn the doorknob. John was surely fast asleep and unaware of the terror he was about to experience. I could see the faint rise and fall of his steady breathing under his comforter. I desperately fought with myself to turn around and leave him in peace but I could feel the anger my lack of submission caused. Fighting was not only useless, it was dangerous.

Once I reached the side of his bed, I shoved a corner of his blanket into his mouth through his slightly parted lips. He startled awake but before he could get out of my reach, I straddled him and held both of his hands in one of mine and kept them trapped above his head. I laughed when his body shook with fear.

With my free hand, I dug my nails into his bare chest. His muffled scream made me laugh even harder, making my stomach cramp with my amusement. I dragged my nails across his chest, leaving deep gouges in their wake. Suddenly, the light in John's room flicked on.

"Paisley no!" Dad yelled when he took in the sight of John gagged with me on top of him, clawing his chest. "Get off of him!" He grabbed me around the waist and hauled me off of the bed.

Mom came running into the room, pulling a terrified John into her arms and rocking him back and forth, trying to soothe him as he cried. Thin lines of blood ran down his chest where my nails broke skin and the maniacal laughter continued while dad used his arms to keep mine pinned at my sides. My parents looked at each other, unsure of what they should do so they just waited in hopes that it would soon pass.

For the second time in twenty-four hours, my body went limp. Dad caught me and maneuvered us so that he could support me with an arm across my back and the other behind my knees, lifting me off the floor. He carried my lifeless body back to my room and laid me on the bed. He stepped out quickly and returned with a blanket and pillow.

He spent the night sprawled in front of my door. If I tried to leave, I would have to roll him away from the door so that I could pull it open. So began a new routine. Dad would sleep at my door, protecting the rest of them from any harm I might inflict and keeping me safe in my own room. For the first time in his life, John began experiencing night terrors so mom spent her nights with him.

The dust settled. Tension seemed to lessen and smiles returned to our faces. John still refused to be near me and I didn't blame him, if the roles were reversed, I would feel the same way.

I appreciated being around my family. With them, I was able to pretend that I was all right. I could ignore the fact that Braxeus was peeling away at my resolve, he was burying me under layers of dark thoughts. If other people were talking, it brought me back to the surface.

Alone, Braxeus bombarded me with hateful words. It was constant.

**You're disgusting.**
**You're weak.**
**You're useless.**
**You drive people crazy.**
**You're such a pain in the ass.**
**No one is comfortable with you around.**
**They wish you would disappear.**
**Your mother wishes she'd lost you as a fetus when she fell down the stairs.**
**Your father used to beat you because you make him sick.**
**Your sister would burn you alive if she thought she could get away with it.**
**John thinks your parents need to lock you away and throw away the key.**

**Jump out your window.**
**Hold you head under the water.**
**Go to your mother's medicine cabinet and swallow every tablet**
**in there, you'll be doing them all a huge favour.**
**Remember that bridge where you found Thomas fucking that**
**stupid slut? It would be the perfect bridge to jump from.**
**Go to the garage, in the third drawer of your father's tool box**
**there's a X-Acto knife, use it to cut across your throat. Make**
**sure you get the jugular.**

All day. Every day. Over and over and over again. He was relentless and I could feel my resilience faltering. I started to believe the things he was telling me. He would say them in such a way that they made sense and I could see proof in the way my family acted around me. I couldn't begrudge them because if the roles were reversed, I would have turned tail and ran a long time ago. They stuck around and wanted to see me come out of whatever psychosis I was in.

It was a gloomy day. Dark clouds painted the sky all day long. A storm was brewing and I could feel my mood mirroring it. I stood on the front porch listening to the rumbling of thunder in the distance. When I felt my throat rattle with an answering growl, I knew without trying to move that I was no longer behind the wheel.

The front door opened and I wanted to badly to warn whoever it was to turn around and go back inside. Instead, a delighted grin curled my lips and I turned to lean against the porch railing to watch my dad approach.

"Gonna be a good one tonight." He said, referring to the storm headed our way.
"It most certainly is." He froze at the sound of the voice coming from my mouth.
"Paisley out for the night?" He asked, cautiously testing the waters.
"She has better things to do this evening."
"Such as?"
"Keeping her mouth shut and being a good girl."
"That so? Mind if I talk to my daughter?" My grin widened at his request.

"I mind."

"Why?"

"Because I don't feel like cooperating." He looked over my face and could clearly see that he wasn't going to change my mind.

"All right then. Guess I'll just hang out with you then." He conceded, sitting on the porch swing in front of me. "So, what's your name then?"

"Why do you want to know?"

"Braxeus." I was shocked that I actually answered him truthfully.

"Braxeus." Dad repeated the name, looking uncomfortable with its strangeness. "How old are you?"

"Old."

"That's kind of vague. I consider myself old."

"I'm older than your mother's incestuous rapist father." Dad's eyes widened with shock.

"That's quite the allegation." I laughed.

"It isn't merely an allegation Donald. I watched your history unfold. Hell, I enjoyed a bowl of popcorn while I watched."

"So, were you haunting someone else back then?"

"No, I was in between gigs at the time."

"You know everyone's back story?"

"No, don't be ridiculous. I only pay attention to the entertaining ones."

"I guess that makes sense. It would probably be awfully boring otherwise."

"Precisely." We both fell silent and I watched him through burning eyes because Braxeus refused to let me blink.

"So how long do you plan on sticking around to torture my daughter?"

"Funny that you should phrase it like that."

"Why is it funny?"

"Well, you tormented the child for her first sixteen years. Why should I not torture her for the next few?"

"I didn't torture her."

"My apologies. You *disciplined* her." I barked a humourless sound sarcastically. "Some say discipling is a swat on the bottom, maybe a smack on the mouth for poor manners. Some parents choose to use liquid soap to have wash out a potty mouth. Don't get me wrong, I'm a firm believer in corporal punishment. Broken bones and bruised organs are usually considered excessive but I myself see nothing wrong with being sure a child know their place."

"I didn't go overboard purposely." Dad looked both ashamed and insulted.

"Oh no of course not. You just have a nasty temper. No one expects you to know how to control yourself at your age. It's not like you could have walked out of the room to cool off before reacting too harshly." My tone was sharp and accusing. I could feel the switch in Braxeus's mood. There was no longer a mischievousness behind his words, fire took its place. I could see the same fury building in my dad's eyes.

"Quaint, coming from whatever the fuck you are, using my daughter like a goddamn puppet!" I could see the vein in dad's forehead bulge.

"I'll remind you to watch you tone."
"You're not my fucking mother!" Dad yelled, standing from the swing. My smile stretched, adrenaline beginning to pump through my veins.
"You should consider that a blessing." He took a step toward me, making me chuckle with his attempt at intimidation.
"Do you think you scare me?" I straightened from the banister.

I could feel my face contort and it must have been drastic because dad gasped and stumbled back a step. I caught my reflection in the window over his shoulder. Braxeus didn't have control of my bladder because what I saw, sent urine trinkling down my leg.

As a lover of all movies in the horror genre, I had become desensitized to seeing frightening faces. The one looking back at me was the exception. My warm brown eyes were gone and in their place were cold metallic grey irises with dilated pupils and a ring of yellow around the black pits. The rim of both my eyelids were a blood red colour that seemed to be melting into the whites of my eyeballs, staining them to look inordinately bloodshot. The eye sockets themselves were sunken in and surrounded by deep purple and blue bruises. My brow bone was more prominent, stretching my already thin eyebrows to near extinction.

I couldn't think of anything that would be more frightening than what my face had turned into. My demonic eyes turned back to my dad, cheeks wrinkling with a malevolent smile.

"What did you do to Paisley's face?" Dad barely managed to ask between tight lips.

"Oh, I'm sorry. Does it bother you?" Impossibly, my smile widened further, feeling like it was getting uncomfortably close to my disappearing eyebrows. "I thought you were a big brave tough guy. You aren't afraid of a little teenage girl, are you?"

"I'm not looking at a teenage girl." Dad crossed his arms over his chest. "I have no idea what the fuck I'm looking at."
"Your daughter."
"You are not my daughter!" His angry tone tickled laughter from me.
"I am now. Don't you love me anymore daddy?" My eerie voice mimicked a girlish tone.
"That's not funny Bracky!" I didn't know if my dad erred purposely or if he genuinely couldn't remember but Braxeus's smile snapped into a bilious sneer.

I didn't feel my knees bend but before either of us could blink, I launched myself at him, clinging like a spider monkey. He stumbled back a step but caught himself before falling. His hands balled in the back of my shirt, trying to pull me off but getting nowhere. I grabbed a fistful of hair on the top of his head and pulled it back, giving myself enough space to cuff the side of his cheek. The impact made his eyes lose focus and he blinked furiously to clear the fog. Two more shots followed in quick succession, bringing him to his knees and still, I held on, my legs wound tightly around his waist.

He struggled futilely to get me off of him but I wouldn't budge. I could sense his growing panic; he was desperate to put space between us. His knuckles connected with my mouth, busting open my bottom lip. When I barked a crazed laugh, he groaned. He tried again and all he got was more of the same demented sounds from me. He bellowed with frustration, moving his hands to block his face from my further assault.

Mom and Shella must have heard the struggle because they came barrelling through the front door, wearing twin expressions of fear.

"John! Get out here! Help!" Mom screeched over her shoulder.

Shella and mom each grabbed one of my arms, putting all their weight into trying to pull me off of my battered father. A very pale John ran over to join the fray. He forced his arm between my dad and I and around my waist. When the three of them paused to adjust their grip, my body crumpled. Before they realized there was no longer any resistance, they pulled. Mom and Shella both lost their balance and fell back. John rolled onto his back and I went cartwheeling down the porch steps.

I felt my heart clench when my dad, with his busted face, pulled himself up and rushed to make sure I was all right. I was sinking in my shame. I desperately wanted my limbs to work so that I could run to my room and hide. No one deserved to be punished with my presence.

I must have lost consciousness because the next thing I knew, I was waking up in my bed. I tried to roll onto my side and would have cried if I wasn't still riding backseat in my own body. My parents must have assumed they were safe for the time being because there was no one guarding my door.

My limbs began to move, pulling me off the bed and to my

dresser. I pulled out a pair of jeans and a bright red halter top. I carried both to my vanity and grabbed the scissors from the drawer. I cut the legs off of the jeans right at the crotch, angling upward toward the hips. I changed into my top and altered jeans, running the brush through my hair before sliding my feet into a pair of black open-toe stilettos. I stuffed my ID between my breasts and made my exit. I went straight out the front door without stopping to tell anyone where I was going.

I walked for a few blocks, deep into the grungier part of town. When I came to a stop outside of a biker bar, known for its ill-reputed patrons, I prayed that we would keep walking even though my toes were throbbing with fresh blisters. No such luck. I made my way into the bar and parked myself on a stool between two big, leather clad biker boys with long greasy hair and matching beards.

"What's your poison?" The bartender, an overly made-up redhead, asked.
"Can I get a double rum and coke and a shot of tequila please?"
"Not going to ease into it?" The burly biker to my left asked with a smile. He was missing his two front teeth and his mustache was stained yellow from smoking cigarettes.
"No reason to waste time." I smiled.
"You give it hell. I gotta go drain the snake." He stood from his stool and stumbled away, taking most of the pungent scent of body odor with him.

When the bartender placed my drinks in front of me, I swallowed the tequila and chased it down with the rum and coke.

"Mind if I sit with you?" I turned, smiling brightly when I saw a handsome dark-haired man with piercing blue eyes. His hair was slicked back and he wore a leather vest over a white t-shirt.
"You think I would mind having a gorgeous guy sit beside me?" He grinned at my reply and sat down.
"Darla, can I get another beer? And the lady would like another drink too please." He asked the bartender.
"First name basis with the bartender?"
"I should hope so, it is my bar after all." He chuckled.
"You own this place?"

"Well, my dad does but he doesn't want to run it any more so here I am." Darla placed our refills in front of us.

"Married? Kids?" I asked.

"No and no." He smiled. "You?"

"I'm the fourth wife in a polyamorous relationship and I'm currently pregnant with my fifth child."

"Well shit, you look pretty damn good for a pregnant mother of four." He laughed sipping his beer.

"Well, my husband is very *active*." I wagged my brows at him suggestively. "A wife has to cater to his needs you know."

"Did you drink throughout all your pregnancies?"

"Only rum and tequila. Something about the hCG hormone makes me crave the harsh taste."

"How old is your husband? One lucky son of a bitch to have a wife who looks like you."

"Twelve." I answered deadpan and he bursted with laughter.

"Name's Mark." He held out a hand.

"Brutus." I took his hand and shook. He laughed at my reply.

"Your name is Brutus?" I made a show of looking around the bar at all the tough-looking biker-types.

"I figure I need a tough name to be in a place like this."

"Nah, they look mean but they're all a bunch of pussies."

"Watch it boy." Came a rumbling warning from my other side. ."

"Point taken." Frank answered and refocused on his drink.

"What's your real name?" Mark asked.

"Paisley."

"That's much prettier than Brutus." He nodded in approval.

"Well thanks, mom thought it suited the mucus covered, screaming monster she pushed out."

"Jesus." He muttered through laughter. "Quite the little clown, aren't you?"

"Hey, nothing little about me. I'm five foot seven inches tall and all muscle." I flexed a bicep for added proof.

"Well, my six feet four inches, appreciates every bit of your *hugeness*."

"Pfft. Six feet four inches, you're a goddamn sasquatch!"

"Well, I don't know about that but I am a sasquatch where it counts." He winked an eye at me suggestively.

"Where's that? Your feet?"

"Hah, well, I do have sasquatch feet." He agreed, grinning while he sipped his beer. "But big feet mean big… other things."

"Ah yes, big earlobes." I nodded, finished my drink. Again, he laughed.

"Yes, earlobes, toes, nipples, dick. All bigger on men with big feet."

"Oh my." I fanned my face sarcastically. "You have big nipples? That is so sexy."

"Bet you've never seen nipples as sexy as mine." He challenged.

"Well, you haven't seen mine." I returned.

"Touché." He flagged Darla for another round.

"Would you like to?" I asked when Darla walked away. He coughed on his mouthful of beer.

"See your boobs?" He asked when he cleared the liquid from his throat.

"No, my toes." I rolled my eyes.

"I'd love to see your toes, along with the rest of you." I smiled brightly before guzzling down the drink Darla just brought and grabbing his hand.

"Let's go." He let me lead him through the bar.

"Where are we going?"

"Bathroom. Mind you, you run the joint, you probably have a better idea." I glanced over my shoulder at him but didn't slow down.

"Bathroom works."

I pulled him into the ladies' room and shoved him into the first stall. I squeezed in with him, using a hand to nudge him to a seated position on the toilet. He reached out and pulled me onto his lap by my shirt and once I was straddling his hips, he yanked the shirt up, exposing my breasts to his hungry gaze. He put his mouth on me and I moaned, fisting my hand in his dark hair.

Braxeus was enjoying himself immensely, listening to my screams of protest in my head. It was hopeless, there was nothing I could do to stop him from using my body. I couldn't even look away because Braxeus kept my eyes locked on Mark. When his hand reached into my makeshift shorts and cupped my most intimate place, I cried. No one but Braxeus and I knew the despair I was in but it didn't matter. I felt violated both physically as well as mentally.

"Fuck me sasquatch." I whispered in his ear in a voice laced with desire.

"Yeah? You sure you wanna do this here?"

"Am I not wet enough to answer that question?"

"Fucking right you are." He unzipped his jeans and forced them down as much as he could with me in his lap. It was enough for him to reach in and free his manhood. "You're going to have to take those off short stack." He grinned as he nodded towards my shorts. "You think so?" I reached between us and ripped the strip of fabric between my legs, turning my shorts into a skirt.

I didn't wait to see his reaction; I lifted my hips and with a hand around his hardness and placed it at my entrance. I rode him until we were both panting and on the brink of orgasm. I slowed my pace momentarily to pull his vest and t-shit off, dropping them on the floor beside us. I ran my hands over his chest, making him shiver with my light touch. I didn't have to lean down very much to run my tongue around his nipple, tasting the saltiness of his skin and moaning when my nose filled with the manly scent of him. His hands wrapped around my hips, lifting me up just enough so that he could thrust deeper into me.

Once he took control of our pace, I quickly reached my climax and moaned into his chest, digging my nails into his ribcage. When he groaned, my teeth clamped down on the sensitive peak of his nipple. I tasted blood and increased the pressure of my jaw. His pleasure was cut short by the pain I was inflicting and he tried to push me off of his lap but my teeth held on.

"What the fuck! Let go!" He screamed with rising panic when he saw the blood running to his navel.

With a quick jerk of my head, I tore the pink flesh from his chest, spitting it in his face and letting it bounce to the floor. I laughed maniacally as he cried and pushed me to the floor before running from the bathroom.

I was still curled on the floor, gasping for breath between fits of laughter when two police officers came running into the ladies' room. One of the officers forced me onto my stomach and pressed a knee to the middle of my back. He yanked my hands behind me to put hand cuffs around my wrists.

"You are under arrest."
"I assumed that's what you were doing when you put the bracelets on." I answered sarcastically, still smiling.
"You have the right to remain silent—"
"Save it dickhead. I don't give a shit what you have to say. He raped me. I was trying to defend myself the only way I could."
"That's why you were laughing like a fucking lunatic?"
"It's called shock. Ever heard of it in your line of work?"

He pulled me to my feet and the second officer led us out of the bathroom. I didn't struggle, following willingly until we got out to the bar.

"Ow, stop! Please." I begged in a pained voice. "I think I rolled my ankle, just let me take these heels off."

The officer huffed but let me stop. I leaned against the bar to toe off my shoes. When he bent to retrieve them for me, I whacked my head against the top of the bar. The loud bang startled him and jumped to his feet. I smiled when his gaze landed on me with the cut I just caused starting to bleed. Before he could process what had happened, I slammed my head against the bar-top three more times as quickly as possible, making myself see stars.

"What the hell is wrong with you?"
"Police brutality!" I screamed, throwing my face against the back rest of the nearest stool, catching my brow bone. "Stop, I'm not resisting!"

The handful of people still sitting in the bar had been watching the officers escort me through the bar. They witnessed my erratic behaviour and knew that the officer hadn't laid a hand on me. The crazy laughter started again as I flung my throbbing eyebrow against the stool a second time.

The officer who led the way out of the bathroom snapped

out of his shock first and reacted. He wrapped his arms around my waist from behind and pulled me away from the bar, almost carrying me the rest of the way out of the pub. His partner ran to open the back door of the cruiser for him so that he could push me onto the bench seat. When he closed the door behind me, they both leaned their backs against my window to take a minute to calm themselves down.

"Dispatch? This is officer Clemens." "Go ahead officer." "Suspect is mentally unstable. Officer Brown and I are going to transport her to Saint Matthews Psychiatric Institute. We're going to need a doctor to meet us outside to subdue her." "Copy that. I will call ahead and let them know. Thank you, officer Clemens."

By the time we pulled up outside the hospital, my body was paralyzed once again. When Officer Brown opened the door, the doctor looked in at me, confused when he saw me laying motionless across the seat.

"I thought the patient was out of hand?" He asked.
"She was acting very strangely, hitting her head against wooden furniture at Player's Tavern, screaming police brutality. We're going to go back and get statements but there is definitely something wrong with her doc."
"All right. Hang on, the wheelchair I brought isn't going to cut it. I'm going to send out a couple nurses with a gurney."

Three days later, Braxeus had all the nurses afraid of coming into my room. The first morning in the hospital, my face had morphed into the demonic mask that appeared on the porch with my dad and stayed that way. The nurse who watched it happen never came back and I heard the other nurses say that she was on sick leave.

The second morning, while my new nurse was taking a blood sample from my forearm, I popped my elbow. She froze, eyes fixed on my arm bending the wrong way. I laughed, pulling her focus to my face and from the corner of her eye, she saw my second arm do the same thing. She screamed and ran from my room while I laughed hysterically.

Word spread quickly. Between the scary demon face, broken limbs and croaking masculine voice coming from a teenage girl, the nurses refused to come into my room alone. I could feel Braxeus becoming bored and restless being stuck in a hospital bed.

When two nurses tapped on my door to announce their presence, I smiled at them. It wasn't a pleasant smile, cheeks spread unnaturally wide and evil eyes would never be considered anything but eery.

"Come in, come in," I greeted them in my cracking smoker's voice. "We just came to give you your medication and check your blood pressure." The younger one stated.
"No need to be afraid child. I'm in no mood for games today."
"Uh, okay." She said hesitantly before dragging her feet into the room and dragging the other nurse behind her.

When they got to the side of the bed and she held the medication in front of my mouth, I opened obligingly and swallowed the tablets before opening wide and wiggling my tongue to prove they were gone. She threw out the cup in the garbage and wrapped the cuff around my arm to count my heartbeats.

"Still extremely high." She told the other nurse. "One eighty over one twenty."
"That's crazy. I've never seen anyone with blood pressure so high before."

"Have a seat ladies. Let's chat a bit." I requested and both nurses looked at one another with fear and uncertainty. "Sit!" I ordered crossly and both of them instantly dropped into the seats left for my visitors. "Brenda. How is your young man treating you these days? He still sneaking around with that little slut while you're at work?" I asked the older nurse who gasped in shock while her colleague let out a squeak of terror. "Oh, I do apologies, I forgot I wasn't supposed to know that." I said, pretending to be contrite. I turned toward the younger one. "And you Lisa? Still worried about that lump you found on your cunt?" Her face turned red as she covered her mouth with her palm. "Don't worry about it. It's just a boil but you really should stop spreading your legs for every man who looks your way. One day you *will* catch something serious."

"How did you know that?" She asked, too curious not to ask. "Oh, you naïve little twit. I know a lot of things." My smile returned. "Like that time when you gave your daddy's best friend a blowjob in your parents' bedroom during their anniversary party. Weren't you about fifteen at the time?" She choked on a horrified sob before she bolted from the room, Brenda hot on her heels.

I laughed for a few minutes when they left, wishing my little trick had done more to cure my boredom. My laughter stopped abruptly when I realized that they had forgotten to close the door behind them when they left. I didn't wait to see if they would come back, I jumped from the bed and stood at the door, looking both ways before stepping out. The coast was clear.

I went towards the exit sign, ignoring the cries and moans coming from behind the other doors. I pushed open the door to the stairway and looked back to make sure I wasn't being followed before jogging down the stairs. On the bottom floor, I smiled at my luck. An emergency exit. I didn't have to sneak through reception.

It was late afternoon and I decided to wait and see if there would be a show when they realized I was no longer in my room. I made my way to the end of the employee parking lot, leaning my butt against the trunk of a car similar in colour to my hospital gown. It took a while but eventually, a loud alarm sounded, alerting the staff that there was an emergency. A handful of nurses came out through the front door, searching around frantically. I laughed as they ran around like a group of chickens with their heads cut off.

I wandered around town until the sun went down and the moon lit the darkness. I could hear sirens approaching from behind me and when I looked over my shoulder, a police cruiser was slowing down by the curb. I didn't have to wait to know that I was their target. I ran down the nearest laneway to the backyard and climbed over their fence. I kept running. I could hear the sirens flying down the street, surely headed around the block to keep searching for me. I kept to the shadows, hiding in hedges and gardens until I was satisfied that they wouldn't be able to find me. I crossed the street and realized that I was close to home and decided to make my way there.

When I turned the corner on my street, I could see two more cruisers parked in front of the house. Going home was no longer an option so I turned and headed towards the park instead. It wasn't far and when I crossed the lot, I could see a group of five teenagers hanging out around the swing set. I smiled, deciding to have a little fun with them.

"Hey guys!" I called out when I was within earshot. The three boys stood in a semi circle around the two girls on the swings.
"Hey, do we know you?" The boy closest to me asked.
"Nope. I was just out and about on my own and figured I would introduce myself."
"Out and about on your own in a fucking hospital gown?" One of the girls asked, looking down her nose at me.
"She's fucking scary looking." I could hear the second girl whisper to the boy closest to her.
"You got that right. Her face looks like a Halloween mask." He answered.

"Nice manners." I stated sarcastically. "You make a habit of talking shit about someone when they're standing right in front of you?" I watched as all five of their spines stiffened at my tone.

"I'm sorry, did we hurt your feelings?" The first girl taunted.
"Not in the slightest." I sent her my creepy smile. "In any case. I was wondering if you guys would like to see a trick?"

"Does the trick involve you fucking off?" The third boy asked and I laughed humourlessly.

I ran at them, making all five of them jump at my sudden movement. When I was within reach, I jumped up, grabbing the top of the swing set, pulling myself up like a gymnast. With a foot beside each of my hands, I squatted on the bar, looking down at the teenagers who watched in disbelief and fear.

"How the fuck did you jump that high?" The first boy asked.

"Skills little boy." I croaked, turning around and swinging forward so that I hung upside down in the same position but right in the middle boy's face. I was close enough to smell the sweat coming from his hairline. "I'm pretty sure this qualifies as the opposite of fucking off." I grinned.

He stared at me, speechless. I didn't move and he started to fidget with discomfort. Just before he cracked and took a step back, I opened my mouth and bit his cheek hard enough to break skin. He screamed and his *friends* took off running. When I let him go, he fell on his butt. I dropped from the swing set and crept closer to him while he scrambled to get up. As soon as his feet were under him, he bolted. I chased him to the fence but instead of going over, I dropped to all fours. I knew he would look back before he was out of sight so I wanted to give him a visual to feed his nightmares.

I gripped the chain link fence with my toes, using them like fingers to climb. I spread myself out on the fence like a spider on its web, my hair dangling against the grass. When the boy looked back, I slid my tongue out through a hole in the fence, flicking it like a lizard. He stumbled but caught himself before falling again. He didn't take a second look.

I stayed on the fence, waggling my impossibly long tongue. I hung there so long that my head started to pound from the pressure of my blood being unable to fight gravity.

"Paisley?" Someone asked from beside me. I turned my head, tongue still dancing. "Oh my God." Mom gasped, covering her mouth in horror.

I heard her sob then everything went black.

# **Chapter Twelve**

Is it Over Yet?

My parents were furious with the hospital for their carelessness. They refused to send me back and to avoid a lawsuit, the hospital agreed to send a nurse to the house daily while I remained in the care of my parents.

Mom and dad remained vigilant, my dad took leave from work and kept me under constant supervision. After several physical altercations with Braxeus, they decided that the best course of action was to tie me into a straight jacket and keep me in my room. If we were having a good day, they would belt me into a wheelchair and bring me out onto the porch with a blanket disguising the restrains on my upper body.

My parents and siblings were afraid to engage in conversation with me. Not only would they hear Braxeus' voice, they would hear his hair-raising laughter and be taunted with his knowledge of their darkest secrets. I was completely isolated with

Braxeus. They could all walk away and hide but I was locked in a cage with the monster living in my head.

I was laying on my bed, staring out the window one morning, waiting to hear everyone wake up and come out of their bedrooms. Dad was asleep on the cot right inside my door, soon enough mom would come and knock on the door to wake him.

I could feel tingling on my knee caps. It was a strange sensation. It started with a light tickling and progressed to pins and needles. It didn't stop there, it evolved into an uncomfortable stinging and eventually it started to burn. I tried to squirm and shake my legs to ease the pain. It didn't help. It felt like I was kneeling in a fire pit, letting the flames burn away the skin. With my arms wrapped in my jacket, I couldn't rub my knees to make the hurting stope and the helplessness was feeding my sense of panic. I thrashed my legs around, screaming in agony.

Dad jumped so much that he fell off the cot.

"My legs! Me legs! Oh God it hurts! My legs!" I screamed over and over.

Dad rushed over and unravelled the blanket from around my legs. Once freed, he pulled up the leg on my pyjama pants in search of the cause of my agony. Once he reached my knee, he had to be careful because the cotton was sticking to the skin. He managed to peel it off and expose the bubbling blisters underneath.

"Jesus Christ! What the fuck happened?" He gasped, taking the second pant leg and pulling it up to see that it was in the same condition. "Johanne!" He yelled at the top of his lungs. "Johanne! Get in here!"

I heard running footsteps outside my door before it was pushed open, knocking the cot over. Her hair was all over the place and her nightgown was rumpled. She went to my dad's side, where he gestured for her to look down at my legs.

"What the fuck did she do?" She stared down at the burned flesh on my knees.

"I haven't got a clue! I woke up to her screaming her head off and when I looked, this is what I found!"

"It looks like some kind of chemical burn." Mom noted, taking a closer look. "Go get a clean wash cloth and the gauze pads from the medicine cabinet."

When dad left the room, Braxeus started to laugh uncontrollably. Mom jumped back, putting herself at a safe distance from me.

"Fucking idiots! The lot of you!" Braxeus screamed at her, pinning her with a look filled with contempt and disgust. "Get your head out of your ass! You're not going to win this battle Johanne."

"What battle?"

"The battle for your daughter. Thus far, I've only been toying with you."

"So, this is all a game for you?"

"Is that what I said?" I yelled, irritated. "I said I've been *toying* with you! Meaning I've been letting you think it was possible to get your daughter back." I growled, like an angry dog, making her eyes bulge. "It's not going to happen Johanne."

"We're not going to get Paisley back?"

"Are you fucking stupid! That's what I *just* said." I seethed through bared teeth. "You need to get the hell out of my face." I warned.

"Or what? You going to make the straight jacket disappear?" She asked, challenging me and making Braxeus seethe.

Dad came back into the room, interrupting the angry atmosphere. He came to the bed and handed mom the cloth to clean my wounds. She dabbed at the blisters as gently as she could but it was still torture, feeling the terrycloth against my open wounds. I laid back on my bed and stayed still while they did what they could.

I remained quiet for the rest of the afternoon. Mom and dad took shifts sitting by my bed, reading or doing crossword puzzles. The thought of the two of them spending their lives babysitting me was heartbreaking.

*We agreed on six months.*
**We did.**
*Then they will get me back. Why did you tell my mom they wouldn't?*
**No. What you fail to realize is that when the six months are up, you will be too broken to ask me to leave.**
*No. I want you gone!* His laugh echoed in my head.
**You have no idea what you want. When the time comes, you will beg me to put you out of your misery.**
*Fuck you Braxeus.*
**Watch what you say Paisley. Getting rid of me will not make the torture stop. I either remain with you or I am loose to drive the rest of them mad. Your sister would be the easiest, especially after witnessing your demise. Your brother's fear makes him an easy target. It wouldn't take much to push his boundaries. Your mother is stubborn but she's so in love with your father that it gives me a weakness to take advantage of. Your father would be the toughest but also the most satisfying. He would be my favourite. Next to you of course.**

I screamed in frustration and was surprised to hear it outside of my head. Dad jumped in his chair beside me and flew to my side, afraid that more damage was being inflicted to my body.

"Where does it hurt?"
"No where. Sorry dad, I guess I had a nightmare." I whispered, surprised that it was myself speaking, feeling like Braxeus was going to jump in at any moment.
"Paisley?" Dad took a closer look at my face, skeptical.
"It's really me dad."

"Oh, baby girl." He breathed, choked with emotion. He pulled me into his arms and hugged me so tight that it was hard to pull in a full breath. "God, I missed you." He leaned back and looked me in the face. "Are you okay?"

"No." I managed to get out before my body shook with a sob. "I'm not okay dad."
"Are you in there when all these things happen?"

"Yes. It's like watching a movie in first person." Tears poured from my eyes, it felt like I was crying from the wounds in my heart. Hysterical hiccups rocked my shoulders, I was broken.

He sat on the edge of my bed, holding my hand. He was at a loss. There was nothing he could say to make me feel better. Nothing he could do to make it better. We were both trapped in the prison Braxeus had put us in.

"I'm drowning dad." I told him when I could get the words out. "I don't think I'm going to make it out of this."
"Don't go down that road Paisley. You need to be strong."

"Dad, I'm not being dramatic. I'm not strong anymore. I'm being buried alive inside my own head. I'm all alone in this. I'm alone in my head to listen to all the horrible things he says. I can't fight him on the inside and on the outside. This is the first time I've been allowed to make an appearance in so long that I don't even know what to think. You can't help me. Daniella can't help me. I can't save myself. I'm in the middle of the fucking ocean, I'm getting too tired to swim and nobody can throw me a goddamn life preserver!"

"Paisley…" He knew I was right. He badly wanted to argue but he was out of ammunition.
"Dad. Can I just be alone for a little while?"
"You know I can't leave you alone…"
"Please dad? I never have a minute to myself to just breathe." I pleaded. What he saw in my eyes broke through his resolve.
"Ten minutes, P-Baby." He conceded, standing to leave my room. He looked at me for a long second before closing the door.

I looked down at the hand I had hidden under my blanket. The truck keys weighed heavily in my palm. Slipping them from dad's pocket while he was hugging me had been too easy. I knew I didn't have much time but I took a minute to go to my vanity and scribble a quick note.

*I'm sorry.*
*I know you wanted me to get through this but the truth is, I can't.*
*This isn't a battle that can be won. Even if Braxeus left today, I'm a*

*broken person. There's no coming back for me and I can't keep waiting for him to hurt one of you. I'm not willing to stick around in hopes that I make it out of this*
*when being here puts you guys at risk. It's only a matter of time before things go too far.*

Don't ask me what hurts the most,
I am too ashamed to say.
Don't ask me what I fear the most,
The answer is the same.
They say don't let your bottle fill,
One day it will spill out.
It doesn't really matter much,
Mine is broken anyway.
Crazy lives inside my head
And I just can't get away
Don't ask me what hurts the most
I'm too ashamed to say
Don't ask me what I fear the most
The answer is the same
I can't escape the evil one
Who breathes inside my brain

*Love you for always,*

*Paisley Coleman*

I placed my good bye on my pillow and went to open my window. I heard footsteps coming up the stairs and, in my panic, fumbled with the latch. I managed to pull the window open and climb outside. I had to hurry because I knew it wouldn't take dad long to run back down the stairs. If he found me, I wouldn't get another chance. I placed one foot in front of the other until I got to the front porch and could hop down onto the slanted shingles. I crab walked down to the edge and rolled onto my stomach. I dangled my feet over the side and lowered myself until I felt my feet on the banister. I barely caught my balance on the grass before I was running. I could hear raised voices inside and I knew they were on their way.

Mom and dad tore out the front door as I was pulling the truck out of the driveway. Both of their mouths hung open in shock. Mom's hands balled into her hair, holding my note and dad was frantically searching his pockets to find his keys were gone.

I only needed three minutes. They would recover soon and start using their heads. It would take them at least a minute to find mom's keys in their panic and by the time they decided mom would stay home, call the police and wait, dad would be about five minutes behind me. I only needed three. I was headed in the direction of Player's tavern, where no one would think to look for me.

I wasn't going to the bar, my goal was farther than that, to the old number 2. The old highway led out of town where houses were set far back from the road, often separated by pine forests. Once I was satisfied that the houses were far enough apart, I pulled over to the side of the road. I cleared my mind and put on my favourite playlist. It was time.

I unclipped my seat belt and pulled back onto the road. Pushing the accelerator, I quickly picked up speed. When I hit a hundred kilometres and hour, I picked the biggest tree in my line of sight and aimed the front end in its direction.

I closed my eyes and braced for impact. Before all noise was drowned out by the sound of crunching metal, Braxeus' evil, full-belly laugh echoed in my ears. Tears of defeat trailed down my cheeks. It would all be over soon.

The collision was unbelievably loud, like thunder going off right inside the cab of the truck. I felt the back end of the truck bounce off the ground a half of a second before I was thrown from my seat, head first into the windshield and it was lights out.

I didn't feel a thing. For the first time in over a year, I felt at peace, weightless. Finally, all the negative emotions, the dark clouds, it all poured out and my soul felt cleansed. I was giddy. My body couldn't move but I was laughing internally from the sheer joy and relief of freedom.

I watched from the sidelines as a car screeched to a halt by the mangled truck being worn by a tree trunk like a skirt. A young woman ran over to the driver's side, leaving her door wide open in her hurry to assess the situation.

"Oh God. Jesus." She cried when she saw my lifeless body on the dash, blood pooling under my face. "Can you hear me sweetheart?" She asked from the open window. When I didn't respond, she reached in and patted the hand I that was flopping around by the steering wheel. "Shit. If you can hear me, don't worry. I'm going to go to the house just up the street and call for help. Don't give up honey, the world needs you."

She was so genuine that it warmed my heart. She was a much-needed reminder that true kindness still existed in such a cruel world. I watched her drive away and new without a doubt that she would do everything she could to help me.

She was back in under ten minutes and she stayed by my side, waiting for help to arrive. Her hand held mine while she prayed that I would be all right.

Her warm hand stayed on mine until the paramedics took over and asked her to take a step back. The younger male paramedic pushed his upper torso through the window to check my vitals.

"Low heart rate but she's still with us. How far is fire rescue?"
"Two and a half minutes. Door jammed?"
"No way we're getting that thing open, it's completely mangled."

The second paramedic handed the first one an oxygen mask and he pulled the elastic around the back of my head. Their hands were tied until the firemen arrived to cut the door off and get me out of the mess of a truck.

"See any ID or anything?"
"No, I don't see a purse or anything, could have fallen onto the floor. Won't know until we can get in there."

Sirens came flying up the road. Three police cruisers pulled up to join to fray, followed by a big red fire truck.

They quickly got to work and though the tools they used to pry the door open looked scary, they were comfortable using them and had the job done in what felt like minutes. They helped the medics remove my body from the truck after they checked me over to make sure it wouldn't cause more damage. Onto a gurney I went and into the back of the ambulance.

I wondered how long it would take for my body to shut down and let go of the last threads of life. I didn't think there was anyway for me to survive such a wreck but it was taking longer for them to pronounce me dead than I expected.

When we arrived at the hospital, I watched a bunch of people rush around, plugging me into this machine and that machine. Everything seemed to be beeping and I wondered how these people didn't go mad listening to the irritating noise all the time.

I had no idea what they were doing. I couldn't even begin to wrap my head around any of it. They seemed to be satisfied with whatever they did because they rolled me from one bed to another and four of them started running the wheeled bed down a hallway and through a swinging door.

A doctor was ready and waiting for me, looking like he was ready to go to war. A needle was pushed into my arm and for the first time since I was separated from my body, I felt it. Just as I registered the fact that I felt the prick of the needle, the rest of my body screamed in agony. I let out a blood curdling scream making everyone jump, even the doctor.

Then I blacked out. Completely.

I couldn't open my eyes but I could certainly hear the incessant beeping from somewhere beside me. If nothing else, I wished I could throw a boulder at whatever was making the noise. Did it really need to go on and on forever? Whoever turned it on deserved to have their ears boxed.

"Paisley? Can you hear me baby?" Dad's voice. It sounded so far away. "It's been too long sweetheart. You have to wake up. Your mom and I are losing our minds over here." His raspy tone was evidence that he had been crying or screaming for an extended period of time. "I don't know if I can survive losing you kid." His voice thickened and when he squeezed my hand, I could feel that his was shaking. "I know it's selfish of me to want you to stick around considering all the shit you've been going through but, damned if I can help it." I felt moisture running onto my knuckles and my chest tightened. "You're the only thing I've ever done right in this world. If you leave, you'll be taking the best part of me with you."

"Paisley." Mom. She could barely speak through her sobs. "Wake up." She demanded, taking hold of both my hands. "How could you do this to me? You really thought this would solve everything? Your father and I could have lived with the sporadic bouts of craziness, as long as you were with us." I could feel a finger against my cheek. "We really miss you, Paisley."

"Hey beautiful. How's it going up in this bitch?" Laurie asked, sounding completely deflated. "Pretty fucked up situation you got yourself into... I wish you would have felt comfortable enough to talk to me. You're like my soul sister. With you in this bed, I'm flying without my wings. I'm gonna fucking crash and burn! No offense." She gently patted my shoulder. "You're such a bitch for doing this to me." The sound of her voice did not match the attitude in her words. She was hurting. "You're my sidekick." I heard a sniffle, which she tried to mask with a sad chuckle. "Or I was yours. Whatever. You get my drift. We're lifers and you are not allowed to drop out yet! I swear, if you don't wake up soon, I'm going to tell everyone you're a transgendered lesbian with a fetish for bestiality." She was quiet for a minute, waiting for a sign that I heard her. "Wake up you bitch!" She cried.

"Hey Pais." Well. This was a surprise. "I'm sorry I haven't been there for you lately." Sniff. "You know I run from confrontation and I was just so afraid of you." It was the first time John willingly spoke to me in months. "I just… I just didn't understand what was wrong and if things would ever get better." He blew his nose. "I was going to swallow a bottle of pills a while ago but then you came back and I was so happy to see the real you that the pills took a backseat and I forgot all about them. Since then, I've just been waiting for you to come back for good. I never would have dreamed you would do something like this. I always thought you were too strong to give up. You were always like Wonder Woman to me. Invincible. I can't tell you how many times I wished I could be like you." I heard a whimper and my heart cracked for my little brother who kept everything bottled up. "Whatever happens Paisley, I'll never forget you. I get it, it must have been unbearable if you felt you needed to end your life. I love you Paisley." He kissed my cheek softly.

"Mom and dad told me to come in and talk to her because the doctors said it might help encourage her to come around." Shella told someone, sounding irritated. "I think it's all a bunch of bullshit. She's a goddamn vegetable. She did all of this to herself, clearly she doesn't want to be around anymore."

"Shell, cut her some slack. Your parents should have had her in a home. They knew she was a fucking nut case." I couldn't believe she would bring *him* here.
"Cut her some slack? Are you kidding me?" Wow, I've never heard my sister sound so... resentful.
"No. What the hell is wrong with that?"

"I've been through the same shit she has. Cut *her* some slack? She acts like her life is such shit but people worship the fucking ground she walks on. I'm so sick of her poor me attitude! Everyone is playing into her game like losing her would be the beginning of the apocalypse but what about the hell she's put the rest of us through?"

"Oh, stop it Shella. You're acting like a brat and it's not very attractive." He told her in disgust.
"Fuck you, Nathan." I hear her shoes stomp out of the room and there was silence for a minute.

My stomach started to knot when I didn't hear a second set of footsteps follow her from the room. He needed to leave. He couldn't be in the room with me, alone, when I couldn't defend myself.

"God I'm glad she left." He came closer to the bed. "I didn't think I would get the chance to be alone with you." I felt his fingers moving up my leg. "You're so sexy when you're complacent." He was right in my face and I could smell his breath. "This is better than all my fantasies. You're always such a fire cracker, having you in front of me, so submissive… you've got me rock hard." His lips pressed against mine and I actually felt my stomach roll. When I heard him groan, it rolled even more. "Fuck. I'm almost ready to cum in my pants." One of his hands rode up my rib cage and squeezed my breast while he kissed me a second time, stuffing his vile tongue past my lips.

Voices in the hall startled him and he jumped away, putting a respectable distance between us before he got caught violating me.

"Nathan? What are you doing here? Where's Shella?" If only dad had been more quiet, he would have seen what Nathan was doing and beat the hell out of him.
"She was here but she got so upset that she had to leave. I was just saying goodbye."
"She's not going to die." Dad told him and I could hear that Nathan had struck a raw nerve.
"Oh no, no Mister Coleman. I didn't mean goodbye like that…"
"Just shut your mouth and get out of here."
"Yessir." He nearly ran from the room, afraid of dad's temper.
"Fucking creep." Dad mumbled when we were alone.

My body was stiff. I pulled my feet up to my bottom, stretching my calves and knees. I tried to stretch out my arms but when my right hand caught on a wire, I froze. Suddenly I remembered where I was. The accident, the out of body experience, the hospital, all the tears came flooding back.

"Paisley?" Mom and dad said at the same time when they saw movement.

"Yes?" I answered in a faint, weak whisper.

"Oh God." Mom rushed to the bed and dad fumbled with a switch beside my bed, to call the nurses.

Mom was crying, throwing herself on me to hug me and smother me with kisses. Dad's hand squeezed mine.

A nurse knocked on the door and the three of us looked over at her. Her eyes bulged with surprise when she realized that my eyes were actually open.

"Patient in twenty-two forty is awake! Call doctor Gauthier!" She yelled down the hallway before rushing to the bed to check my monitors. "Good morning sweetheart. How are you feeling?"

"Fine."

"No pain? We have you on a morphine drip but if anything hurts, I can top you up with some Tylenol."

"No, nothing hurts, I'm just stiff."

"Well, you've been out for thirty-four days. A stiff body is to be expected." She smiled kindly at me, seemingly pleased to see me coherent. "You are one lucky girl."

"Thirty-four days?" I screeched in my weak, raspy voice.
"Longest month of our lives." Dad muttered from the foot of
my bed where he moved to give the nurse some space.
"How long has she been awake?" A man in a white jacket
asked, putting a stethoscope to his hears as he approached the
bed beside the nurse.
"Forty-two hours." I answered, deadpan. His eyes widened
and he froze on his way to press the metal of his stethoscope
to my chest. "I'm pulling your leg." I explained when I
realized he believed me.
"Awake and cracking jokes already?" He smiled. "Impressive.
He nodded, listening to my heart beat.
"Impressive, right." I mumbled sarcastically.

When he finished checking my blood pressure, he sat
on the edge of the bed and looked at me with eyes filled with
compassion. He was definitely in the right line of work.

"Does it hurt anywhere?"
"No."
"Not even a little?"
"No. I just feel like I haven't moved in a while." I grinned and
he chuckled at my nonchalance.

"You were in a medically induced coma. There was
hemorrhaging in your brain that should have killed you but
we managed to get it under control. You have three cracked
ribs and a lot of cuts and bruises. I understand that you did
this to end your life but apparently, you have a guardian
angel that wasn't ready to let you go yet." My heart sank with
his words and the fear on my face startled him. "What's
wrong?"

"Braxeus." I answered.

"What's that?" I realized my mistake and shook my head. I forced a smile that seemed to appease him.

"When can I bust out of here doc?"

"Let's not rush anything. I want you under close observation for at least a couple of days. We'll see how it goes and if we don't hit any bumps in the road, you can go home."

"What if I throw you a twenty?" He laughed at my bribery.

"I don't think so. I'd rather be sure you're in good shape." He smiled. "Get lots of rest, it will help your body heal."

"No offense but I think I've gotten enough of that."

"You'd be surprised." He turned towards mom and dad.

"Mister and misses Coleman, nice to see you again."

"And neither of us are screaming at you this time." Dad joked, smiling sheepishly.

"Don't worry about it. Your heart was in the right place." He patted my dad's shoulder reassuringly before leaving the room, the nurse at his heels.

No one spoke. My parents stared at me like they were both star-struck. I squirmed uncomfortably under their gazes.

"Uh so… What's up?" I asked.

"It's hard to believe you're finally awake." Mom whispered, swallowing another urge to shed tears.

"You scared the hell out of us P-Baby."

"I know dad." I didn't offer an apology because I didn't feel sorry about what I had done.

"Is he still in there?" Mom asked, needing to know but I could see that she was terrified of the answer.

"I don't know." I told her honestly.

"You don't hear him?" Dad asked, coming over to hold my hand.

"No. I heard all of you talking to me while I was… uh…. Sleeping? But I haven't heard Braxeus."

"That's good. Maybe he's finally gone." Mom breathed a sigh of relief.

"I doubt it. You hear what the doctor said? It wasn't a guardian angel. It was Braxeus."

"No. He wouldn't have given you back to us, knowing how happy it would make us." Dad insisted.

"Maybe not but he would certainly like watching us all rejoice just to crush us all when he came back."

"Fuck him. I'm not going to let him have another win. I'm going to enjoy having you back. No need to dwell on what might or might not happen."

It was graduation day. I stood in line at my old high school, waiting to cross the stage and receive my diploma along with the rest of my classmates. Laurie and I held hands. She was supposed to be farther at the back of the line but she snuck over to stand with me. Since leaving the hospital, she was glued to my hip and I didn't mind in the slightest. I was afraid of being alone so her need to be with me was not one sided.

"You ready bitch?" She nudged me with an elbow to my ribs, still holding my hand.

"Ready as I'll ever be."

"I'm so fucking happy we get to do this together."

"Me too." I smiled at her.

"I'm so proud of you." She choked while her eyes filled with tears.

"Stop that sappy shit or you can go stand at the back of the line with the rest of the riff raff." I warned. She wiped her eyes with the sleeve of her burgundy gown. "I'm proud of you too Laurie. For graduating and for being an amazing person."
"Jesus Christ. You expect me to keep my shit together when you say things like that?"

"Paisley Coleman." Mister Shaeffer called into the microphone placed centre stage. Three rows back, mom, dad and John stood to cheer.

I made my way onto the stage. I was so proud, taking the rolled diploma from Mister Schaeffer and shaking his hand.

"Congratulations." He smiled.
"Thank you."

I felt light as a feather as I walked across the stage. I was happy, a feeling I was just starting to be familiar with again after living in the darkness for so long. Braxeus hadn't returned after the coma and I was finally able to become reacquainted with who Paisley was. I thanked God daily for allowing me to survive the car wreck and free me from my tormentor.

# Chapter Thirteen

My Angel

I brushed my hair in front of my vanity mirror. Months had passed since the last time I saw my face distorted into terrifying features that were not my own. Yet still, I would sit in front of my mirror and stare at myself, waiting to see them come back. They didn't. My own brown eyes stared back at me.

I kept my face bare, brushing my hair back into a high pony tail, ready to start a new chapter in my life. Culinary school. I spent my summer working in a kitchen, discovering that I had a knack for cooking and I thoroughly enjoyed it. I was thrilled with the idea of college and moving on with my life.

I practically skipped into the kitchen, a ball of excitement and nerves. Mom and dad were already seated at the table, sipping coffee from their mugs.

"Good morning beautiful people." I greeted them.
"Good morning. Someone's in a good mood." Dad smiled.
"I'm ready to explode with joy." I agreed, filling my own cup of coffee and returning to sit with them.
"I can't believe my baby is going to college today." Mom said, voice full of pride, making me smile.
"I cannot wait." I checked the clock, anxious to get started.
"Get any sleep last night?" Dad asked.
"Well, I had a bitch of a time falling asleep, that's for sure but I feel good."
"Am I allowed to drive you to school?"
"Don't you have to go to work today?"
"Yes, but I told my boss I would be late because I was dropping my little girl off at school."
"I'd love a ride to school dad." I gave him a heartfelt smile. It meant the world to me that he was trying to maintain a close relationship.

I made my way through the hallways, searching for room 2030. I had butterflies in my stomach and my hands shook with the school map in my hands. I was nervous but I felt amazing.

"Hey, you look familiar." I turned and my jaw dropped. He was smiling at me, one hand in his pocket, the other holding a binder at his side.

"Connor? What are you doing here?"

"Well, I'm here to further my education. How about yourself? You look a little lost."

"Same. I am lost." I conceded, looking down at the map.

"Where are you headed?" He asked, coming closer to look at the paper in my hand. "Nice, Mister Grady. Follow me."

"How long have you been going to school here?" I asked, noting his comfort in the halls of the school.

"First day." He grinned.

"Seriously? How the hell do you know where to go?"

"My best friend started here last year and I came to visit him a few times. He showed me around." He led the way down the hall. We walked in silence for a moment. "You never called." He stated.

"I didn't."

"Why not? Not interested?"

"I… I had a lot going on."

"I see. So…" He trailed off, waiting for an answer to the second question.

"I was interested, yes." He grinned but kept his eyes on the floor in front of him.

"You *were* interested." He reiterated, stopping in front of a door.

"Here we are." He gestured to the 2030 marked on the door.

He opened the door for me and stood back for me to walk through, following behind me. I picked a seat in the second row and he continued toward the back of the room. I was surprised he didn't sit beside me but appreciated the space.

"Good morning class." A man stood in front of the classroom and pulled our attention.

I stood in front of the main building, waiting for my dad to pull up. It was the end of the school day and I was in an even better mood than I had been that morning. Every class I went to, reaffirmed my belief that I was making the right decision.

"Hey, are you stalking me?" Connor came up behind me. I laughed when I looked at his smirking face.

"Of course. I can't help it."

"Thank God. I thought I was the only one."

"The only one I stalk?"

"No, the only one doing the stalking." He answered with a chuckle.

"Oh." I laughed when I caught his meaning. "You're a stalker!"

"I'm just playing around." He grinned. "Where are you headed? Feel like celebrating our first day?"

"I was going to call my girlfriend and see if she wanted to go out tonight."

"Oh." He looked like I had dumped a bucket of ice water on him. "I'm sorry I didn't realize."

"What?" I was confused by obvious embarrassment.

"I didn't know you uh… well that you… I don't know the proper way to say it."

"Just say it. You won't offend me." I pressed.

"I didn't realize that you were into girls."

"Huh?"

"That you were a lesbian." He said in barely more than a whisper.

I couldn't help it. I laughed hysterically at both his assumption and his discomfort. The poor boy looked like he was asking me for a tampon, he was so embarrassed. He looked at me with raised brows, smiling at my uncontrollable laughter.

"Glad you think I'm funny."

"You, are fucking hilarious!" I answered when I could breathe. "I'm not gay."

"You just said you had a girlfriend."

"I meant a girl who's a friend. She's more than just a friend so we call each other girlfriend. I certainly don't get off on muff diving."

Dad pulled up to the curb and I waved to let him know I saw

him. I smiled at Connor, buying myself some time while I debated taking him up on his offer.

"Well? Can I get your number?"
"My dad's waiting, I gotta go." I deflected, stepping away from him.
"I'll walk with you and you can give me your number on the way."
"You're willing to risk an encounter with my dad?"
"Why not? I should thank the man for blessing the world with such a beautiful woman."
"Jesus Christ. Give me a pen." I chuckled. He quickly pulled a pen from his pocket before I changed my mind. I scribbled my number on the back of his hand. "See you later Connor."
"Looking forward to it Paisley." His smile widened when he said my name.

I jogged to the car and waved at Connor once my door was shut and dad was pulling away. A smile still plastered across my face.

"I take it you had a good first day?" Dad asked, giving me a side-eyed half grin.
"I had a great day. It was even better that I thought it would be."
"Good. How about the school part?" He laughed at his own jab.
"The school part was the great part." I smirked, blushing.
"You're unbelievable, you know that?"
"What are you trying to say dad?"
"I'm saying you need to stop growing up Paisley. While you're at it, stop drawing boys in like flies to fresh shit." His simile made me snicker.
"Are you calling me a pile of shit?"
"Not at all. Though at times I wish you were, then I wouldn't have to worry about some guy coming along and stealing you away from me."

I leaned over and wrapped an around his shoulder in a sort of half hug.

"Oh dad. Don't get your hopes up so soon. It's going to take a lot more than some random dude to get rid of me."
"I hope so P-Baby." He reached up and squeezed my hand.

"I feel like I'm on top of the world dad." I smiled at my dad, filled with elation.

"You are kid. Enjoy your youth. It goes by way too fast."

I didn't wait for Connor to call. As soon as Laurie showed up at my front door, I was ready to leave.

"Don't you want to get ready first?" She asked, rushing to keep up with me as I headed to her car.

"Fuck that. Let's go!" She laughed at my enthusiasm.

"Jesus Paisley, there's no rush, the bar's not going to run out of booze before we get there."

"Maybe not but I'm feeling all kinds of amazing right now and I don't want to waste it."

"All right. Let's do this then!"

We didn't go to Billy's; I didn't want to see Dimmy and have my guilt dampen my mood. Instead, we went across town to a club called Patchuly's. My lightheartedness was contagious and the bouncers didn't charge us the door fee or card us before letting us in.

"If I wasn't already taken, I would jump you." Laurie flirted with one of them as we walked by. I laughed and pulled on her arm to keep her moving.

We got drinks for both our hands before making our way onto the dance floor. We sipped our drinks while we danced and gossiped about couples around the bar who were all over each other. One couple in particular, was sitting in a booth and the girl's hand was down the guy's pants where she openly jerked him off.

"I think they had some drinks." Laurie commented and we both giggled.

"Bet they feel great in the morning."

We watched as the guy's hand flew to hers to halt her movement. He whispered something in her ear and they both got up and left in a hurry.

"Gee, I wonder what they're running off to do." I said to Laurie with a smirk.
"Probably going to church." We both roared at the idea.
"It's been too long since their last confession." I managed between breaths.
"Oh, stop it Paisley." Laurie struggled to mock seriousness. "They're probably cousins that came to catch up over cocktails." We held our sides as we cramped from all the laughing.

"You two have a very fucked up sense of humour." Someone piped in from behind us, making both Laurie and I jump. Of course, that set us off again and we both clung to each other for balance.

"Connor. You really are stalking me, aren't you?" I asked, unable wipe the smile from my face. He chuckled and the smile on his face hit me right in the gut. I barely knew him and already, he put what I felt for both Thomas and Dimitri to shame. I swallowed the lump of nerves in my throat and gave my head a shake.

"Hey, aren't you the Pussy-God?" Laurie asked. Connor spit out the sip of beer he just poured into his mouth, pinching his nose as the amber drink dripped from his nostrils.
"Yeah Laurie. This here is the Pussy-God." I answered for him, hooking an arm through hers as we both stared at him.
"Wow. He's even better looking up close."
"I know right? It shouldn't be legal."
"Uh... Did you girls want me to step away so you can talk?" Connor asked, his blush reaching his ears.
"Are you uncomfortable having two girls check you out?" Laurie asked with a grin.
*"No?" He said sounding more like a question than an answer. "You aren't very shy, are you?"*
"Paisley and I are both shy when we're alone but get us together and our shyness disappears. We're like each other's courage." He smiled.

"So, this is your girlfriend?" He asked me.

"My one and only." I bumped her with my shoulder.

"And she knows you better than anyone?"

"Yes…" I trailed off, trying to guess where he was going.

"Hi, my name is Connor." He held out a hand.

"Laurie." She shook the hand he offered.

"Laurie, tell me something would you?"

"Depends." She narrowed her eyes at him but the smile on her face counter-acted her intent.

"It won't break girl code." He promised.

"What would you like to know?"

"Why won't Paisley go out with me?"

"Well…" She looked me over, considering her reply. "She told me she thinks your gay." She said, and we both laughed. I made sure to tell Laurie about Connor's assumption after school.

"I'm not gay." His voice rose an octave, defensive.

"It's okay sweetheart. Your sexual orientation is your business." She rubbed his arm in reassurance.

"I'm not gay." He quickly looked around, searching the crowd.

"Hey! Brad! Come here a sec!" He yelled to a group of guys. A tall blond turned and sauntered over.

"What's up? Need a wing man?" The new girl took his time looking us both up and down. Connor smacked him behind the head.

"Shove it man." He demanded without humour. "This is Paisley and her friend Laurie." He gestured to us.

"As in *the* Paisley?" He asked, slack-jawed. "The imaginary girl you've been talking about for *months*?" Connor's face brightened.

"You're such an asshole." He punched his friend on the shoulder, hard enough that Laurie and I could hear the thud. Brad rubbed his arm and bit his lip, obviously sore.

"Aw, you've been talking about me?" I teased.

"No." He denied, too quickly. Then, feeling guilty for lying, he rolled his eyes. "Maybe."

"That's so cute." Laurie commented, playfully shoving Connor on the arm.

"You guys are getting way off track." He said, rubbing his hands over his face. "Brad, tell them I'm not gay."

His friend didn't answer right away. He looked back and forth between the three of us. He looked offended and hurt but Connor's request. When his eyes landed back on Connor, his bottom lip quivered.

"What do you mean Con? I thought you and I had something real?" His voice had deepened. "You told me that if I let you have your way with me, we could be together."

Laurie and I both stared at Brad, stunned. I couldn't believe my ears. Connor was gay? And he was playing with this guy's feelings? How could he be so heartless and cruel?

"Fuck off Brad! You're not funny!" Connor didn't look guilty at all, just annoyed. Brad started laughing, bending over at the waist to brace himself with a hand on his knee.

"Sorry man." He said when he stood back up and wiped his eyes. "That was just too easy." He turned to Laurie and I. "No, this guy is most certainly not gay." He flipped a thumb in Connor's direction.

"We were just messing with him but you definitely had us thinking we stumbled onto something." Laurie told him.
"Nah, he likes pussy *way* too much to be even remotely gay."
"That's not any fucking better!" Connor yelled. "Get out of here." He shoved him back in the direction he had come from.
"Jesus. Come here, go away. Bossy prick." Brad mumbled with a mischievous smirk.

Connor shook his head before turning his attention back to us.

"So?" He persisted.
"So…" Laurie cocked a brow inquisitively.
"Why won't she go out with me?"

Laurie didn't answer right away. She looked at me and thought about how to answer him. Folding her arms across her chest, she looked him in the eye, serious and willing to give him honesty.

"Paisley has had a rough past." She began, taking my hand in both of hers to offer me reassurance. "She's still healing." She looked at me with a sad smile. "She's worth the wait though."

"I'm sure she's more than worth the wait." He nodded in agreement. "Should I keep trying or give her some space?"
"You should definitely keep trying." I answered for Laurie and he smiled.

"All right." He took a step toward me. "I can do that." He leaned forward and kissed me lightly on the cheek. "I'll leave you girls to go on with your evening. It was nice meeting you Laurie." He shook her hand again. "I'll see you in class tomorrow Paisley." Again, the way my name sounded in his mouth, made butterflies flutter in my stomach.

He was waiting for me in the hallway the next morning, leaning against the wall. As I approached, he stood straight and smiled at me.

"Good morning." He greeted.
"You're awfully chipper in the morning." I commented. He chuckled.
"I'm a morning person."
"That's a sign of a being a psychopath." I grinned.
"Being a morning person makes me a psychopath?"
"It's a check mark in the that category."
    He slung his arm around my shoulders, trying to act like it was unconscious but he was too stiff to pull it off.

"Are you trying to get fresh with me?"

"Well, I'm trying but I don't think I'm doing a very good job."
"You're doing great." I told him, leaning into his warmth, making him smile.

He sat next to me that day, spending more time glancing my way than listening to the lesson. I covered my mouth to muffle the giggle at his grade school antics.

*I can't get over how beautiful you are. If I'm the Pussy-God, does that make you the Cock-Queen?*

I couldn't stop the laugh from busting out when I read his note. The startling noise in the silent classroom made several students jump as well as Mister Grady who was seated behind his desk. He gave me a dirty look.

"Something funny miss Coleman?"
"Sorry sir. I thought of something that happened last night." I fibbed.
"Maybe you should be concentrating on the paper in front of you."
He suggested and when I looked at the paper on my desk, I snickered when my eyes fell on Connor's handwriting.
"Yes sir." I saw Connor's shoulders shaking with laughter from the corner of my eye.

*Thanks, I guess... Are you always so romantic? Cock-Queen?*

I tossed the paper back to him and tried to focus on my quiz. Anyone looking at me would think I was crazy, grinning at my paper.

*I figured if you had a cool nickname for me, I needed to have one for you. I think you might be the prettiest girl I've ever seen. Think I could take you out some time?*

*You have my number.*

*Let me take you out after school.*

*I don't think going out for drinks again tonight is a good idea.*

*I was thinking bowling or mini putt and then maybe some food.*

*Wow, you're talking about a real date?* I heard him chuckle quietly, reading my response.

*That's the idea.*

*I'd really like that.*

I was on cloud nine for the rest of the day. I enjoyed the rest of my classes but at three forty-five, I rushed to get outside and meet Connor.

He wasn't there yet but my dad was waiting by the curb. I took another look around to see if Connor was nearby before going to the car. I opened the passenger door and bent over to see my dad.

"Hey dad, I'm going to go out with a friend. Is that okay?"
"Who's the friend?" He asked, smirking with mischief.
"Connor." I rolled my eyes.
"Connor? Is that a boy?"
"Yes dad."

"Hi mister Coleman." Connor appeared beside me, reaching into the car to shake hands with my dad. "I'm Connor and yes, I am a boy."
"Where are you taking my daughter?" Dad asked, the smirk gone, a stern expression on his face instead.
"I was going to bring her to Patty's Putt-putt. Then get some pizza."
"You're going to have her home at a reasonable time?"

"Is nine good?" I lowered my brows at him like he was nuts. I wasn't twelve.

"Nine is acceptable." His smile returned. "Have fun kids."

"See you later dad."

When dad pulled away, I turned to Connor to look at him like a second head sprouted from his neck.

"Nine? Really?"

"Well, it *is* a school night." He grinned, slinging his arm over my shoulders again and leading me to the parking lot.

"Unbelievable." I shook my head but chuckled while I did.

We walked over to a small, blue pickup truck and he opened the passenger door for me. I watched him circle the hood and get in beside me. When he started the truck, I decided to slide over on the bench seat and snuggled up closer to him. The smile on his face made it clear that he was thrilled having me close to him.

We walked side by side to the cash hut, smiling at each other but saying nothing. We split inside the hut while I chose a putter and he got our golf balls. When he came back holding one pink ball and one blue one, I grinned. He chuckled when I took the blue one.

"Willing to make a bet with me?" He asked with an impish smirk.

"Sure. What's the bed?"

"If I win, you have to kiss me."

"And if I win?"

"I don't?"

"Those stakes suck." I complained.

"Well, if I win, I want a kiss." He pouted.

"How about if I win, you have to keep me out until at least ten thirty.

"I told your dad I would have you home by nine." He reminded me.

"Well, you'll just have to win then, won't you?" I giggled.

"I never would have taken you for a bad girl. You seem close to your dad."

"Oh, I'll call him when I win, don't have a hissy fit."

"Shake on it?"

"You don't trust that I'll call home?"

"For the bet Paisley." He exaggerated rolling his eyes at me.

I took his hand to shake it and he used it to pull me up against him. His hands wrapped around my waist and he was close enough to touch the tip of his nose against the helix of my ear.

"I can't wait to get my prize." He whispered. The butterflies in my stomach went ballistic.
"Dream on lover boy." I playfully shoved him back a step.
"One day." He answered with a grin.
"One day?"
"I'll be your lover boy." He winked, and his boyish grin and flushed cheeks knocked the wind from my lungs.
"You sure about that?" I teased.
"In my dreams I am. Maybe if I keep saying it, it'll come true."
"Oh Jesus." I said, laughing while I turned to make my way to the first hole.

I had so much fun playing mini putt with Connor. A game I normally found boring and monotonous was a riot with him. We laughed so much that midway through the game, my stomach was so sore, I was sure I had a six-pack. Like a brat, he would be quiet and then randomly say something right before I hit my ball, trying to throw me off of my game. When it was his turn, I made a point of standing by the hole, bending over to give him a nice view of my ass or running my fingertips over my bottom lip. Every time I did it, he struggled to keep his eyes on his ball. His reaction made me feel beautiful and encouraged me to keep teasing him.

On the second last hole, I was ahead by three swings. I debated which outcome I wanted. I didn't want the night to end early but I wanted him to get his kiss at the end of the game. He made it easy for me to decide. When I stood on the green, he strutted over to the hole. He bent over to 'tie his shoe', wiggling his butt at me and making me laugh until tears filled my eyes. In my fit of laughter, my putter knocked the ball, making it roll about half a foot from the green. We both laughed when I struggled to get the ball towards the hole. Thus, Connor shot to the lead.

At the end of the last hole, Connor danced around with his arms in the air, celebrating his victory.

"You're a cheater." I grumbled lightheartedly.

"Say whatever you want, I still won." He winked and pinned me with a look that made my knees weak.

"You won." I agreed. "Think they'll let me use the phone in the hut to call my dad?" I teased.

"You gonna call your dad and tell him I'm going to kiss you?"

He dropped his putter and stalked toward me like a cat after a mouse. The only thing that wasn't predatory about his appearance was the smile on his face. I didn't move. I was dying for him to close the gap between us. When there was only a whisper left between us, his hand reached up to tuck a lock of hair behind my ear.

"Can I kiss you Paisley?" He asked, all humour erased from his face.

"Yes." I whispered and braced myself for impact.

When his lips touched mine all the cheesy lines in my mom's romance novels didn't seem like a load of bullshit anymore. I felt his kiss all the way to my toes. He pulled away too soon. When I opened my eyes, I could see that his were wide open and surprised.

"Wow." He whispered before his mouth crashed back against mine.

The second kiss was even better than the first one. I leaned into him, wanting more. His lips were soft and he tasted like peppermint gum. My hands balled in his shirt by his hips, just as much to keep him close as to hold myself up.

"Kissing you is so much better than what I imagined." He whispered against my lips.

"Yeah." Was all I could manage at the moment. My head was in the clouds.

"We should get out of here before someone comes along and busts our chops." He suggested but made no move to step away.

"Yeah." I wanted to slap some sense back into my head.

I took his hand into mine and forced myself to turn towards to the cash hut. We walked in silence, both of us flushed and wrapped up in thoughts of each other. My feelings for him were blooming far too fast for my comfort. An unsettling thought wormed its way into my head. Maybe I was getting attached because of some lingering effects from what I had gone through. Braxeus could have left me with lasting emotional damage or maybe the car accident had caused some kind of brain damage.

I didn't scoot into the middle on the way to the pizza parlour, choosing to stay on my side of the bench. Connor looked over at me questioningly but didn't ask. He reached over and pulled a hand from my lap so he could hold it while he drove.

"If the kiss made you uncomfortable, we don't have to do it again." Connor said, peeking at me from the corner of his eye.
"What makes you think the kiss made me uncomfortable?" I asked, feeling guilty for making him second guess something so amazing.
"Well, you seemed to have pulled away. Literally." He said, nodding towards the empty space between us.
"I... I'm just... confused." I didn't know how to ease his worry without making myself look needy or spilling out my recent history and making him think I was crazy. Especially since I couldn't dispute it.

"Confused?" He grinned. "Let me clear it up for you then." He parked the truck in the parking lot of the pizza parlour and turned to face me in the truck of the cab, patting the hand he held with his free one. "When a boy is attracted to a girl and that attraction is mutual, they usually press their lips together to see if there's any sparks. In some cases." He took a deep breath to keep himself from cracking up. "there's major sparks. Almost like fireworks." He smiled. "In our case, there was an atomic bomb."

"I'll say." I agreed, unable to keep myself from smiling back at him. Knowing he felt strongly about it, eased some of my fears.

"Now that you understand the dynamics, can we go back to the lighthearted Paisley who didn't look like she was trying to solve the world's problems?"
"But I *am* trying to solve the world's problems." I told him, deadpan.
"Well how about we start with solving *my* problem?"
"Which is?"

"I'm starving." He whined.

"That's an easy fix." Feeling frisky, I leaned over and kissed him, trying to prove to myself that it was okay and I was overthinking the situation. The sparks were still there and it felt amazing.

"Damn Paisley, you sure know how to make a guy's problems disappear." He smiled with his eyes still closed. "One more." He requested. I happily obliged.

"Come on Lover Boy, it's time for food."

We drank beer with our pizza and the laughter from Patty's Mini Putt, followed us to the restaurant.

While we were finishing our drinks and digesting, something caught Connor's attention and he jumped out of his seat like his pants were on fire.

"What's wrong?" I asked, feeling my anxiety rise. He didn't answer. Instead, he pointed his chin towards the wall. I looked to see a clock. When I saw that it was five after nine, I laughed out loud.
"You're in a frenzy because it's after nine?"
"I told your dad I would have you home by now." He ran off to the counter where our waitress stood.

He was in such a hurry; I was surprised he didn't throw me over his shoulder and run to the truck. As it was, he held my hand and pulled me along to his truck. I laughed when he took a moment to pull me over the bench to the middle beside him before I could buckle myself into the passenger seat.

"You can't tease me by doing it once and then taking it back. This is your seat now."
"All right." I smiled and rested my head on his shoulder while he peeled out of the parking lot.

He raced to get me home, swearing every time he got a red light. When he pulled into my driveway it was 9:22. I laughed at the look of guilt on his face.

"Don't sweat it. Dad won't geld you." I kissed his cheek to offer some comfort.

I was surprised when he turned the truck off, unbuckled his seatbelt and got out. I watched him come around and open my door for me.

"What are you doing?" I asked, confused.
"Walking you to your door and apologizing to your dad." He explained.
"Seriously, Connor. Don't worry about it. I've stayed out for weeks at a time before."
"Seriously?" His brows shot up.
"Yeah."
"Where did you go?"
"I was at an ex's house."
"Okay. I don't want to know." He shook his head to dislodge any visuals my explanation put into his head. "I'd feel better just apologizing. I gave him my word."
"Yeah Paisley! Let the boy do things his way." Dad said from his spot on the porch swing, clearly amused by our exchange. Connor jumped, caught off guard.

He took my hand and walked me to the porch. Once he was in front of my dad, he leaned his butt on the rail across from him, wearing the same guilty look he had on in the truck.

"I'm sorry Mister Coleman. We were at the pizza parlour and lost track of time."
"Pizza parlour or your bedroom?" Dad asked, looking serious but I knew him better than that, he was pulling Connor's chain.

"No sir!" Connor's face turned beet red. "We went mini putting and then went to the pizza place across town. We didn't do anything you wouldn't have approved of." He coughed before confessing.
"Except, I did kiss her." He admitted sheepishly.

"You kissed my little girl?" Dad repeated.
"Yes sir."
"Oh dad, cut it out." I warned, going to Connor's side to take his

hand. Dad howled, not feeling bad at all for making Connor squirm.

The front door opened and mom came out with two steaming mugs. When she looked up and saw Connor and I, she smiled. She joined us, handing dad his cup.

"You must be Connor." Mom greeted, holding out her hand.
"Yes ma'am." Hearing him using his manners with my parents melted my heart. I never realized that respectful men were a turn on for me.
"It's so nice to meet you. Can I get you a cup of coffee?" She offered. Before he responded he looked at me and I could tell that he wanted to accept the offer just to linger a little longer.
"I'd love one." He graced her with his gorgeous smile.
"Don't worry mom, sit." I gestured to the empty space beside dad. "I'll grab it."

For whatever reason, I was comfortable leaving Connor alone with my parents. I knew that dad would probably do his damnedest to make him uncomfortable but I was confident that Connor would handle himself just fine.

When I returned with our coffees, the three of them were laughing, Connor looking more at ease than when I left him. My heart skipped a beat, seeing him getting along with my parents. This boy was pushing all the right buttons.

"What's so funny?" I asked, handing Connor his cup.
"Your dad was telling me about the time he came home from work and found you on the front lawn." He grinned wickedly. "Naked." My face flamed.
"Dad! Why would you tell him that?" I scolded.
"Your mother already told him about the time you chased the little boy in daycare and cried when he wouldn't kiss you." He shrugged, pushing the blame to mom.
"What the hell! I leave you alone for a minute and you jump at the opportunity to embarrass the hell out of me?"
"Oh, don't be embarrassed." Connor told me, pulling me to rail beside him by the hand and holding me around the waist. "I think it's endearing."

"Endearing, my ass." I muttered sulkily.

"Don't be such a sour puss." Mom said, smiling happily at the sight of Connor and I cuddled close.

"Yeah, we all do dumb shit as kids. Your grandfather told me that your mother used to take her diaper off and pee on the couch." He laughed when mom smacked him on the arm.

"Donald! No one needs to know that!" Connor and I both laughed.

Things with Connor were going extremely well. We had our own little routine and I loved seeing him outside of Mister Grady's classroom, waiting for me every morning. After school, we met outside the main entrance and he would drive me home or take me out. He regularly came over for dinner and when he didn't, he made sure to call me before bed. I looked forward to every minute with Connor and could never get enough. He made me feel like I was on top of the world and my parents seemed to really like him and told me several times that they were glad I'd found a man who knew how to treat me well.

It was a Friday afternoon; classes were done and I was on my way out the front door to meet Connor. He was already waiting for me by the sidewalk and I smiled like I always did when I saw him.

"There's my gorgeous girl." He greeted, pulling me into his arms and planting a kiss on my lips. "God, that gets better every time." He remarked.

"It really does." I agreed wholeheartedly.

"I have to ask you something." His serious look froze me in place.

"Okay."

"My mom wants to meet my new girlfriend." My heart soared hearing him call me his girlfriend for the first time but the thought of meeting his mom flooded me with nerves, making me want to puke.

"Meet your mom?"

"Yeah." He brushed my hair back from my face and cupped my cheeks to hold eye contact with me.

"When?"

"Sunday?" He asked, trying to read my expression.

"Okay." I conceded, terrified.

"Are you okay?"

"I'm fine. I'm just scared." I admitted.

"Don't be. She's a cool old bird." He assured, hugging me close to him while he let out a deep, relieved breath. "I'm so glad I was able to distract you with the idea of meeting my mom."

"Distract me?"

"Yeah, from calling you my girlfriend." I giggled against his neck.

"I'm your girlfriend now?"

"Well, I figured if you weren't you would have corrected me when I said that."

"No. We can be girlfriends." I teased, looking up at him. "Just don't tell Laurie, okay? She gets jealous."

"Paisley, be real. Do you and Laurie do this?" His lips came down to mine and he kissed me deep and slow, teasing my tongue with his. I moaned against his mouth, loving the taste of him.

"Get a room!" Someone yelled, we looked up to see a group of girls walking by and giving us snotty looks.

"Sorry girls. Sometimes I can't control myself around her!" Connor yelled back, grinning when one of them snorted their disgust.

"They're just jealous they aren't in my shoes." I told him, smiling up at him.

"God you're beautiful."

"Let's go Lover Boy." I took his hand and barely held myself back from skipping to his truck.

# Chapter Fourteen

I Fantasize About You

I was on edge all weekend, waiting to meet Connor's parents. I barely slept and struggled to focus on anything other than the fact that Sunday was drawing near.

I waited on the porch for him to pick me up. It was a beautiful, sunny afternoon and the sun felt wonderful on my skin. When Connor pulled into the driveway, my smile was automatic and seeing him put me more at ease. He hopped out of his truck and his smile was just as instantaneous as mine.

"Hey beautiful."

"Lover Boy." I stood on the second step, putting us at equal height. I wrapped my arms around his neck and he wrapped his around my waist, swinging me in a wide circle.

"I missed you."

"We were together yesterday!"

"That was twenty-four hours ago."

"Oh my." I rolled my eyes sarcastically. "I missed you too." I admitted, kissing him lightly.

The kiss wasn't as quick as I had intended. Instead of pulling away, he leaned in, holding me against him. My body went up in flames, wanting the moment never to end. He nibbled my bottom lip and let out a groan.

"You're wrecking me woman." He grinned. "I can't stand around and kiss you all day like I want to. Mom's waiting to meet you. Not very patiently I might add."

"No?"

"No, she's been hounding me all morning."

"Why?" I asked, getting nervous again.

"She's just excited." He smiled, taking my hand and leading me to the passenger door of his truck.

I scooted to the middle and waited for him to hop in beside me. I rested my hand on his thigh while we drove in silence. I felt guilty dreading the visit when he was noticeably excited about introducing me to his parents. I did my best to hide my reservations with a smile.

He pulled into the driveway of a modest brick house on the nicer side of town. There was a well-kept garden on either side of the front door and a dog leash tied around a tree in the yard. He led me to the side door and held the door open.

A dog ran right up and yipped happily at my knees. His entire back end wagged with his tail. I bent over to scratch his ear and fell in love immediately when he pushed his head against my hand. His black and white fur was like silk against my fingers.

"Rex is a terrible guard dog. If anyone ever broke in, he would be thrilled at the idea of making a new friend." An older woman commented as she smiled and shook her head at the dog's easy acceptance of a stranger in his house. "Hi, I'm Noella." She held out her hand and when I took it to shake, she covered it with the other and held on sweetly while she gave me a smile filled with kindness.

"Paisley." Her warmth dissolved my nervousness and I smiled easily in return.
"Give her some space mom. Let her in before you smother her." Connor joked, coming up behind me and putting a hand on my hip.
"I'm sorry sweetheart, I don't mean to make you uncomfortable." She let my hand go and took a step back. "Come in."

Connor and I followed her into the kitchen where a man was sitting, reading a newspaper. He didn't hear us come in and when Noella coughed to get his attention, he jumped. She giggled at his reaction.

"Paul, this is Connor's girlfriend, Paisley. Isn't she just the prettiest little thing?" She asked, standing by her husband's side with a hand resting lovingly on his shoulder.
"She is certainly a looker." He winked at his son in approval.
"Please, have a seat. Pete should be home soon to have dinner with us." Noella pulled out a chair and gestured for me to sit down.
"Pete's home every night for dinner." Connor rolled his eyes, plopping down beside me.
"Boy can't cook." Paul chuckled.
"Or wash his own laundry." Noella added, smirking over her shoulder from the stove. "I hope you're a meat and potatoes kind of girl Paisley. The boys requested pork chops."
"I'm not fussy."
"You make that strawberry shortcake for dessert?" Connor asked.
"Sure did."
"Paisley's gonna love it. She's got a sweet-tooth that could challenge yours." Connor grinned.
"I don't know about that kid, that's a pretty high bar." Paul chuckled and Noella turned to smack him behind the head. "Oof."
"I enjoy dessert. Nothing wrong with that. You boys pack it away

just as quickly as I do."
"If you say so mom." Connor told her sarcastically.

"S'up gang?" Holy *shit.* Connor's brother could be his twin. I looked
back and forth between them and if Connor hadn't already told me
that Pete was a year older, I would think that they were identical.
"Hey honey. Did you bring those jeans that you needed me to hem?"
Noella asked, kissing him on the cheek once he was sitting down
across from Connor.

"Yeah, I forgot em in the car. I'll grab em before I leave." His eyes
landed on me. "Wow, since when do we have eye candy for
supper?" Just like she did to Paul, Noella smacked him behind the
head.

"Don't be rude Peter Michael Rousseau."
"Yeah. And she's *my* eye candy ass-hole. Keep your damn eyes to
yourself." Connor warned, anger shining in his eyes.
"Oh, calm down. I'm not gonna move in on your little girlfriend."
He balled up a sheet of paper town and threw it across the table at
Connor.
"What happened to Jessica?"
"Didn't work out. She wanted to settle down and I'm not there yet."
"Yeah, she seemed pretty clingy."
"Hah, that's putting it lightly. Beer dad?" Pete stood and pulled open
the fridge.
"What kind of question is that, boy?"
"Just using my *manners.*" He said, winking at Noella. "Con?"
"Yes please. You want one Pais?"
"Yes please."
"She drinks beer? Better lock her down." Pete handed out the bottles
and returned to his seat.

I felt a wet nose nudging my elbow and looked down to see
Rex begging me for attention. I ran my hand over his head,
scratching behind his ears. He took my gesture as an invitation to
jump up and plant his front paws on my lap. I giggled.

"Oh Rex. Go lay down. Not everyone comes here to visit you." Paul
scolded, sounding more jovial to be taken seriously but Rex listened

and trotted over to lay by his feet. "Sorry Paisley, he can be very needy."

"I don't mind. I love it. He's the sweetest pup I've ever met."

"Sh. Don't say that too loud or he'll hear you and fuse himself to your hip." He warned in a stage whisper.

"I wouldn't mind, he can come home with me." I smiled. Connor gripped his chest like his heart hurt.

"Ouch. Jesus Rex, you dick. She hasn't even invited me to go home with her yet." Hearing his name, Rex ran over and plants his chin on Connor's lap.

"You've been to my house many times." I argued.

"Not what I meant." He winked lasciviously.

"Connor!" Noella scolded. "Am I really going to have to smack all three of you in the same evening?" She huffed.

"No mom. I can behave." He crossed his fingers when she wasn't looking and Paul, Pete and I chuckled.

I adored Connor's parents. They were so loving and easy-going. Dinner went so much better than I could have imagined and I left their house feeling like I was already part of their family. His mom even insisted I go back for dinner again the following Sunday.

Two days later, I was lounging on the couch reading over my class notes while dad watched a hockey game when the phone rang. I quickly hopped up to pick up the receiver.

"Hello?"

"Hey girl! What are you up to?"

"Just brushing up on some school crap. You?"

"I'm just touching up my makeup."

"Oh? Going out tonight?"

"Sure am. Be there in ten."

"Wait? What?"

"Ten minutes Paisley."

I didn't know what the hell Laurie was up to but I knew that she wouldn't let me out of whatever she had planned. Why she felt the need to stress me out was beyond me. I rushed upstairs to change out of my pyjamas.

I just finished tying my hair up in a high pony when I heard her boots bouncing up the steps. She didn't knock, just let herself right in.

"What the hell are you up to Laurie?"
"Nothing." She said, feigning innocence.
"Oh bullshit."

"Okay, okay." She let out a breath, eyes rolling as she tried to find the words to explain. "Dave… has been acting really strange lately. Distant, distracted. I found a note in one of his jackets." She hesitated and I finally noticed the pain on her face.

"What was on the note?" I asked, dreading her answer.
"It just said eight o'clock, Billy's."
"Laurie… that doesn't mean anything. Do you think you might just be jumping to conclusions?"
"I really hope I am. I just need to make sure."
"Okay." I squeezed her. "Let's go play detective."

We didn't spot Dave right away. We grabbed a couple drinks to blend in while we circled the bar. I caught sight of the top of his head, sitting in a corner booth and I jabbed my elbow into Laurie's side. I pointed and when she spotted him, her face dropped in disappointment.

"He really did come here to meet someone." She whimpered in agony and my heart broke for her.

We watched as a tall blond in thigh highs and a skin-tight, strapless black dress strutted over to his table and slid in the booth across from him.

"Oh God." Laurie covered her mouth. "I'm going to be sick."
"No, you're not." I held her shoulders and willed her to be strong with my eyes. "We are going to go over there and confront him."
"I can't." She moaned, barely controlling her tears.
"You have no choice." I wrapped my arm around her shoulders and supported her while I pulled her to the booth.

As we approached, Dave looked up and to my utter surprise, he smiled brightly. When he registered the look on Laurie's face, his smile disappeared instantly and he shot out of the booth.

"Babe?" He pushed the hair away from her face, keeping his hands on her cheeks to hold her eyes. "Why do you look so upset?"

The two of us were caught off guard by his reception. We were expecting a confrontation.

"I thought—I thought that you—you were maybe—going to—to meet someone." She stammered through deep breaths, struggling to stop the tears from breaking free.

"I am here to meet someone but I don't understand—" He shut his mouth when realization donned on him. "You thought I was *cheating* on you!" If Laurie hadn't been so deeply wounded, the offended look on his face told me he would have blown a fuse. Instead, he bit his tongue and looked away for a moment to gather his bearings. "I would *never* do that to you Laurie. You know how much you mean to me."

"I found a note saying to meet you here at eight and you've been acting so strange lately… I really didn't know what to think."
"Well, your friend Dimitri," He nodded towards the bar where

Dimmy was taking off his jacket, obviously getting ready to start his shift. "Got me an interview with Georgia." He gestured to the woman still sitting in the booth. Up close she was a lot older than the three of us and very clearly bored while she waited for us to sort out our business. "He wrote it down for me so I wouldn't forget."

"You're trying to get another job?" Laurie asked, trying to process the new information.
"Yeah… I'm trying to save up to buy you a ring and Dimmy said I could make really good money here so…"
"A ring?"
"Yes babe. A ring."

"Well shit." Her cheeks reddened with embarrassment. "I really fucked all of that up. Didn't I?" He held his index finger and thumb an inch apart and squinted his eyes.

"I'm sorry I worried you." He pulled her into a tight hug. "Can I do my interview now, please?"
"Yes, oh shit. I'm so sorry." She pushed him to the booth. Before he sat back down, he kissed her and smiled.
"Thanks. We can have a drink after I'm done."
"Sounds like a plan." She smiled; eyes still shiny from unshed tears.

We turned away and walked to the other side of the room. Neither of us said a word for a moment then both of us cracked simultaneously and laughed.

"Fuck… Only you and I would get ourselves in such ridiculous situations." I sighed, holding my ribs.
"I'm sorry Pais. I don't know what came over me." Laurie said, when she was able to speak.
"Nothing to be sorry about. If we didn't come and see for ourselves, it would have nagged at you and probably turned into something a lot worse than it was."
"Yeah, you're right. I don't mean to be a jerk but finding Thomas with that girl was horrible and I'm terrified of going through something like that." I wasn't offended, if Dave ever did anything like that to her, I would castrate him.
"It was crazy, that's for sure but Dave has a heart. There was

something wrong with Thomas."
"No doubt." She nodded. "Let's get go get a drink."

I looked over at the bar where Dimitri stood, talking with customers. I didn't feel the same way towards him that I used to. Part of me wondered if the feelings I did have were real or exacerbated by the situation I was in. I felt guilty being in the same bar as him, like I had used him or lead him to believe something that wasn't real.

"I don't want him to know I'm here."
"Oh yeah." She looked over to Dimmy, then back to the booth where Dave was talking with Georgia. She was clearly torn. "You want to go somewhere else?"
"Why don't you go and get us a drink? I'll wait here." I suggested.
"You sure?"
"Yeah, just go get us a drink. Maybe two." I grinned.
"Okay…" She agreed but didn't appear confident in the decision.

I watched her walk over to the bar and Dimitri's face brighten when he saw her. My heart panged with compunction when his eyes scanned the bar, obviously looking for me. I watched as they exchanged small talk. Something caught Laurie's attention because she looked over her shoulder to the opposite corner of the bar. She half turned to wave and even from where I stood, I could see her stiffen. I looked over to see who it was but the crowd blocked my view. I wasn't willing to get any closer and risk catching Dimmy's eye.

Laurie thanked Dimitri and scooped up the tray of drinks. She returned as quickly as she could without spilling anything.

"Drink up bitch. We gotta bust outta here."
"Why? What's going on now?"

I glanced back at the bar and my heart dropped. Dimitri was looking right at me. I smiled politely and watched his face split into a grin. When he dropped his rag on the bar and said something to the other bartender, I wanted to bolt.

"He's on his way over." I mumbled as he wound through the crowd.
"He saw you?" Laurie turned to look behind her. "Oh, you mean
Dimmy."
"Who the fuck else would I be talking about?" I asked, choking on
my panic.
"Well—"
"Hey Happy-Cheeks! How are you doing?" Dimitri asked, smiling
from ear to ear.
"I'm all right. You?"
"Better now that you're here." He openly flirted, ready to pick right
up where we had left things.
"She started college." Laurie told him, trying to supply a safe topic.
"Is that right? What are you taking?"
"I'm in the culinary program."
"Good for you!" He took advantage of an excuse to lean over and
wrap me in a hug.
"Thank you."

I thought I was uncomfortable in his arms at first, when I
looked over his shoulder and saw Connor leaning his back against
the bar and watching our interaction, I got *really* uncomfortable. If
he joined us, things couldn't possibly go well, no matter how he
reacted.

I stepped out of Dimmy's embrace sooner than he wanted me
to, his hands lingering on my hips for a moment before falling down
to his sides.

"I've missed you." He said, voice full of sincerity.
"It has been a while…" Avoidance was my best friend in this
situation.
"Haven't you missed me?" He pushed.
"I uh… Well… I…" I stammered, feeling stupid for blanking on
something to say.

"She's been very busy lately." We shared a look, I realized that she
was trying to warn me that she had seen Connor. "Between school,
her new boyfriend and of course me, she hasn't really had time to
spare." I felt like a terrible human being when he flinched at the
mention of a boyfriend.

"You're seeing someone?" He asked, hoping to have misunderstood.
"Kind of." I glanced at Connor, still leaning against the bar. "No. I definitely am." I corrected.
"Well, ain't that a kick in the pants." He chuckled to mask his hurt, running a hand through his hair and stepping back to put more space between us.
"I didn't do it to hurt your feelings."

"I know. It's just that I've been waiting around like a loyal dog, waiting for you to come around. I guess I thought we could have more than we did and eventually you would feel the same way I do."

"Dimmy… I told you I didn't feel the same way." I was starting to feel defensive because I *did* warn him repeatedly that I wasn't ready to commit. I was wrong for taking advantage of his emotions and it was past time I pay the price.

"I know. I'm not blaming you. I just… I guess it was just a fantasy I built in my head." He looked down at his feet, deflated.
"I'm sorry. I shouldn't have let anything happen between us." My words seemed to do more harm then good because it his brows lowered as his eyes closed and his Adam's apple bobbed like he was swallowing a sour candy.
"Did you not enjoy *any* of the time we spent together?"
"I did…"
"Then why the hell would you be sorry you let it happen? What little time I had with you, means a lot to me. It kills me to know that it meant nothing to you, even if it wasn't *love*." His emotions were going south, quick. He was angry.
"You know what I meant. I wish you didn't get hurt because of me."
"It is what it is." He took another step back. "You girls have a good night."
"Dimmy wait." I pleaded. "Let's talk about this. I want us to be friends."
"I can't talk right now Paisley." I waved a hand, dismissing the idea. "I just can't do this."

I watched him go back to the bar and grab his cigarettes from his jacket pocket before pushing out the side door.

"Girlfriend, you and I are on a fucking roll tonight." Laurie said, throwing her arm around my shoulders.

"We aren't even done yet." Connor was no longer at the bar. I looked around, trying to find out where he went.

"Yeah, Connor didn't look very impressed."

"All right. All done. What are you ladies drinking?" Dave joined us as we were looking through the crowd.

"Two shots of tequila." Laurie answered.

"Each." I added.

"Oh, so that's where this night is going?" He looked between the two of us, trying to figure out what we were up to.

"Oh baby, you have no fucking clue." Laurie said, leaning her back against Dave's front.

"You gonna enlighten me?"

"We came to see if you were fucking around on me and then Paisley's boyfriend left thinking she's fucking around on him."

"Why does he think she's cheating?" His brows lowered in confusion.

"Well Dimitri came over to give her a hug and say hello, meanwhile, Connor was watching."

"I don't get it."

"I told Connor I was staying home tonight." I explained. "Then he catches me at a bar, with some other guy's arms around me."

"Oh shit." Dave whispered as the missing pieces shed light on the situation. "Tequila." He agreed, going to get us some shots.

"What the fuck do I do now?"

"Beats me."

I was nervous as I walked down the hallway to class. I didn't know if Connor would mention seeing me at the bar, if he was going to be upset or if he would pretend nothing happened.

When I turned the corner and didn't see Connor waiting for me, my heart ached. It was so much worse than I thought. I took a deep breath for courage and went into the classroom. I tried not to look but I couldn't help myself, Connor was slouched in a desk at the back of the classroom, head against his chair and staring at the ceiling. I didn't take the seat next to him even though I desperately wanted to. I prayed all he needed was some space and that he would come around.

For the first time since starting college, I couldn't focus on any of my classes and just wanted the day to be over. I spent more than half of my last hour watching the clock above the door and didn't finish any of the work sheets, meaning I would have to take them home and get them done for the next day. When the professor finally dismissed us, my bag was already packed.

I waited by the front door for Connor to come out. I figured that I was probably one of the first ones to leave but when more and more students piled out and Connor hadn't yet appeared, I started to worry. I sat on the curb and watched as the parking lot emptied.

When the professors started milling out, my heart ached. Connor was gone. He was hurt and he had every right to be but I wish he had given me the chance to explain what happened.

I could have gone to the main office and used the phone to call my dad for a ride but I chose to walk instead. It was a brisk afternoon and I was glad I wore my hoodie. I couldn't help but appreciate the power of karma. Dimitri had been so good to me and I didn't appreciate him as much as I should have. I hurt him deeply. It was only fair that I tasted the same pain he did.

It was after dinner when I finally got home. I grabbed an apple from the fridge and went up to my room in hopes of distracting myself with my assignments.

It didn't work. Rather than get anything done, I sat at my vanity and wallowed in self pity. When someone knocked on my door, I jumped.

"Yeah?" John popped his head in.

"Phone's for you." He held out the cordless.

"Thank you." I took the phone and put it to my ear.

"Hello?"

"Hey sexy bitch."

"Hey gorgeous. What's up?"

"Not too much, kind of bored and figured I'd call and see what Connor had to say."

"Oh well gee, nice to know my drama is a cure for your boredom." She laughed at my sarcasm.

"Don't be a baby-la-la."

"Don't be a bitch then."

"So?"

"So what?" I asked, knowing full well what she wanted to know.

"Who's being the bitch now?"

"He didn't say anything." I told her, saying the words brought a fresh sting of pain.

"So, he just pretended he didn't see anything?"

"I mean he didn't say *anything*. He didn't meet me before class and he left without me. He pretended he didn't see *me*."

"You're fucking kidding me." She gasped, sounding offended by the idea of someone ignoring me.

"Not even a little. I don't know what to do Laurie."

"Don't worry. I got your back." Her angry tone did anything but calm me down.

"What's going on inside that head of yours?"

"Well, I'm grabbing my keys and heading to his fucking house. You didn't do anything wrong and that ass-hole is going to get a piece of my mind for being such a narrow-minded prick."

"Laurie, I love you. He is not an ass-hole or a narrow-minded prick. Quit being a hypocrite. We were ready to beat Dave's ass for the same damn reason."

"We're allowed. Connor is not." She insisted stubbornly.

"Oh, shut up." I chuckled. "I appreciate your willingness to defend my honor. Let's just hope he comes around."

"And if not?"

"If not, I'll take you with me when I go and slap some sense into him and make him realize he didn't see what he thinks he did."

"You promise?"

"Absolutely."

"All right then." She was quiet for a moment. "Shit. I don't know what to do with myself now. I want to do something but I don't really wanna do anything." I laughed at her ridiculousness.

"Go take a hot bath." I suggested.

"Brilliant. Hot baths fix everything. Love ya girlfriend."

"I love you too Laurie."

I flopped back on my bed and knew exactly how Laurie felt. I wanted to call Connor but I was afraid of what he would have to say. In the end, I dialed his number and chewed on my thumb nail while I listened to it ring.

"Hello?"

"Hey Noella. Is Connor around?" I listened to a heavy silence. "It's Paisley."

"I know who it is." She did not sound friendly at all. "He's not around at the moment."

"Okay, can you tell him I called?"

"No Paisley. I will not tell him you called." I was talking to a very angry mama bear. I fumbled for words that would help diffuse her fury.

"Okay." My voice was thick as the dam holding back my tears grew weak. "I went to the bar with my best friend last night because she thought her boyfriend was there with another woman. I ran into my ex who was an amazing man but I treated him poorly. He told me he hoped that we would get back together and it killed me to hurt him but I told him I had a boyfriend that I was very serious about." I sniffled as the tears broke through. "I really care about your son Noella. He has every right to be upset with me, I just wanted to explain what he saw. That's all." There was an awkward silence and I debated whether or not to hang up.

"Was he cheating?" Her question confused the hell out of me and I wondered if she heard a word I said.

"Pardon me?"

"Your friend's boyfriend. Was he cheating?" She elaborated and I could hear the pity in her voice.

"No. He was there for an interview. He got a second job so that he could buy her a ring."

"What a sweet boy."

"He is the perfect guy for her. I was so relieved when we realized that we were wrong." I wiped my tears on the back of my sleeve but they kept coming.

"I'll let him know what happened Paisley. He's out with his brother but I'll talk to him when he gets home."

"I appreciate it. Thank you for hearing me out."

"You didn't really give me a choice." She chuckled.

"Well thank you for not hanging up on me."

"Thank you for telling me even though it wasn't my business. I was seething and I hate being angry."

"Have a good night."

"You too sweetheart."

I fell asleep with the phone in my hand, hoping Connor would call me back but the phone never rang.

The next morning, I was sure Connor would be waiting for me outside of Mister Grady's classroom. I was even more disappointed to see the hallway empty than I had been the first time. I couldn't bring myself to go through the door right away. I backtracked and stepped into the bathroom to get myself under control.

When I my breaths were no longer quivering, I swallowed my pain and went to class.

"Miss Coleman, nice of you to join us." Mister Grady greeted me while I took my seat.

"I'm sorry for the interruption."

When he resumed his lesson, I glanced over my shoulder. Connor was in the back row, scribbling on a piece of paper. Part of me wished he wasn't there, then I could deny the fact that he was still ignoring me.

I took my time gathering my things when class was over. I watched Connor follow the crowd out of the room and part of me wanted to confront him but I didn't have the nerve. My hands were shaking as I zipped up my bag.

I was the last one to leave the room, keeping my eyes on the floor while I made my exit. I yelped when a finger tapped me on the shoulder. Connor was waiting just outside the door.

"Connor." I whispered, relieved that he remembered my existence.
"This is for you." He handed me a sheet of paper.
"Uh, Okay." I unfolded the note, nervous because I couldn't read the expression on his face.

*Paisley*

*You're still the most beautiful girl I've ever seen.*
*I missed you like crazy. Kiss me before I pass out.*
*I'm going through Paisley-withdrawal and I*
*Am dying for a fix.*

*Pussy-God.*

I laughed hysterically. Folding the note, I placed it in my pocket, intending to cherish it forever. When I looked up at Connor, the blank expression was gone replaced by his gorgeous smile. I took a second to savour the moment and the smile that was all for me. My heart did a cartwheel and I jumped into his arms, kissing him with everything I had.

"I'm so sorry Connor."
"Shut it. I'm not done yet." He ordered, muting me with his lips.

The sparks caused by Connor's kiss melted every bone in my body. Like a smoker taking their first drag after a long cigarette-free day, I drank him in.

# Chapter Fifteen

Please Believe Me

There was a part of me that still expected to see Braxeus when I looked at my reflection in the mirror. I tried to reassure myself that he was gone for good but no matter how many days passed without a visit, I couldn't swallow my anxiety. Without closure, it was impossible to close the door on that chapter of my life.

I needed to talk to Daniella, I wasted enough time avoiding her. It was time to apologize for everything I said and make sure she was doing all right. I dialed the number for the hospital, going through the automated menu to direct my call to the department of psychology.

"Good afternoon, how can I help you?"

"Hi, is Daniella Hall available please?"

"Please hold." Music came through the speaker while I waited for Daniella to answer. It took a few minutes, they needed to track her down in the hospital.

"Hello?"

"Hey Daniella. It's Paisley Coleman."

"Paisley! It's so nice to hear from you!" She sounded genuinely pleased. "How are you doing?"

"I'm doing really good. How have you been?"

"I'm all right. I've been working with our younger patients so it's been a welcome change of pace."

"That's great. If your seeing younger patients, I take it you wouldn't have a slot available for me?"

"I'll always have time for you Paisley. How's this afternoon? I have an opening in about an hour and a half."

"That would be awesome! I'll see you then."

"Sounds good."

I sat in an empty waiting room, waiting for Daniella to return from her appointment on the pediatric floor. I stood to greet her at the door when she stepped off of the elevator.

"Hey Paisley. You look fantastic!" She looked thrilled at my recovery.

"Thank you. I didn't think I could be normal again."

"Now here you are." She smiled and in my normal state of mind, I could see her inner beauty.

"Here I am." I agreed with a chuckle. She gestured for us to take a seat.

"Listen, I'm just struggling with a few things."

"I'm sure you are. You've been through significant mental trauma."

"Yeah… about that…"

"What's going on?" She asked, concerned.

"It doesn't make sense. What the hell was wrong with me and why did it just suddenly disappear after the accident?"

"Your mom told me about your accident. You're very lucky to have survived. You really did it on purpose?" She looked saddened by the idea that I could have wanted to end my own life.

"Yes. I couldn't take it anymore. Braxeus was hurting my family just as much as he was hurting me and I couldn't let it continue. What if he killed someone? It wasn't worth the risk."

"I understand."

"When I woke up, he was gone. No fading away, just gone. I keep thinking he's going to come back any minute. I won't survive another round with him."

"You're a lot stronger than you give yourself credit for."

"It doesn't make any sense Daniella. I can't come to grips with everything that happened because I don't know what caused it, what made it stop?"

"Paisley, I think you experienced a psychotic break brought on by trauma. You were stalked by your ex-boyfriend, then he kidnapped you. Your mind couldn't process the stress so it initiated psychosis."

"What about all that demon stuff you were talking about? When you said Braxeus was short for Abbraxus?"

"I'm not a priest. I can't say whether or not your experience was a spiritual encounter. I think that it's possible but there's never a way to say with certainty which one it was."

"If it was a demon, won't he come back?"

"I don't think so. When you chose to end your life, you took control and forced him to step down. When someone is strong-willed, the fight isn't worth it for the demon. They want to win, not fight just to stay on top."

"Temporary insanity or demonic possession. Ever have another patient with such range?" I asked, making her chuckle.

"Not exactly. You're definitely a once in a career kind of patient."

"Bet your glad my file landed on your desk." I remarked sarcastically.

"I am Paisley. You're a good kid. I witness a lot of terrible things in my line of work. Sometimes it can be difficult to see the bright side. Seeing you healthy and mentally stable is something I'll cherish forever." She smiled, showing her sincerity.

I nearly ran when the front doorbell rang. When I whipped the door open, my excitement turned to instantaneous aggravation.

"What do you want?" I asked, crossing my arms over my chest and not bothering to hide my displeasure.
"Paisley, is that any way to greet a dinner guest?" Nathan asked, smiling despite my lack of welcome.
"You're not my fucking dinner guest. Take a hike ass-hole." I shut the door in his face, satisfied with the brief glimpse of surprise on his face.

"What the hell Paisley!" Shella shoved me aside to let Nathan in.
"I'm so sorry babe. I don't know why she has to be such a bitch."
She spared me a dirty look before pulling Nathan into the kitchen.

"Paisley?" I turned to see Connor in the doorway. "I was on my way to the door when it closed so I figured I'd just open it. I hope that's okay." I giggled at his unease.

"Of course, it's okay. You're always welcome here."
"Well, that's good. I'd hate to get the same reception the last guy did." He closed the door behind himself and pulled me in for a kiss.
"That other guy is a dickhead." I explained.
"Oh?"
"Yeah, you'll see."
"Why don't we just ditch this joint?" He grinned mischievously.
"Can't. Mom's making you meatloaf 'cause you told her it was your favourite."
"Shit. What the hell are we waiting for then." He stepped around me to go to the kitchen but turned back at the threshold to wait for me to

join him.

"Guess you're a jerk too, abandoning me for my mom's food." I pretended to be insulted.

"No way." He nuzzled his nose against the side of my neck. "I could live without meatloaf. We both know I can't live without you."

"All right, chill out there on the cheesy lines." His stubble tickled the
        sensitive skin beneath my
earlobe, making me giggle and squirm.

"I can't help it; you make me cheesy."

"Okay love-birds. Cool it." Dad said with a chuckle, busting our bubble on his way to the kitchen.

"Sorry dad. He *can't help it*." I mocked Connor.


We followed dad to the table, sitting across from Shella and Nathan. John was away so mom took his seat at one end while dad sat at the other. Our plates were already on the table, steaming.


"Thanks for supper Misses Coleman. Looks and smells like heaven." Connor told mom who smiled at the compliment.

"Hopefully it tastes just as good." She said, cutting into her beef.

"If you covered it with tin foil, it would hold a lot more moisture, then you wouldn't need to coat it in so much tomato sauce." Nathan suggested, putting on his cocky, know-it-all look.

"If your dad had used his fucking head and covered it, the rest of us wouldn't have to suffer your ignorance." I told him, feeling my temper rise.

"Paisley…" Dad warned before turning his angry eyes on Nathan. "It would be appreciated if you could keep your opinions of my wife's cooking to yourself this evening."

"I don't mean to be rude Don. I'm just trying to help her improve, that's all." Nathan explained, unphased, filling his mouth with the food he was critiquing.

"I'm just trying to help you improve your table manners, that's all." Dad replied, mimicking Nathan's patronizing tone.

"Dad, we all find mom's meatloaf dry; he's doing all of us a service." Shella said, defending her boyfriend's lack of consideration.

"Actually, I think it's perfect so technically he's doing *me* a *dis*service." Connor argued, his meat almost completely gone already.

"Thank you, Connor. Let's just eat in peace. There's no need to argue." Mom said, willing everyone to change topics. "How did the interview go at the DMV?" Mom asked Shella.

"It went well. She said she'd call me by the end of the week one way or the other."

"I told her not to get her hopes up. She doesn't have any experience in an office setting." Again, Nathan's unwarranted opinion grated on my nerves.

"Does your mouth ever have anything positive to say?" Dad asked through gritted teeth.

"I'm a realist. I think that she should have applied for a job she's qualified for."

"Such as?" Dad asked, knowing that the answer was going to light his fuse.

"Well, she would make a suitable waitress or cashier. I found an ad looking for a house cleaner that I thought would be a good opportunity for her as well."

"You have got to be fucking kidding me!" Dad's fist slammed down on the table top. "Shella, what the hell do you see in this clown?" He demanded.

"Well, I'm so sorry." She bristled. "Maybe if I spent time in a goddamn loony bin like your other daughter, I could be perfect too!" She shoved her chair back and stomped out of the room, Nathan at her heels.

We all sat in awkward silence, no one eating or making eye contact. Despite the outbursts, I was glad Nathan was no longer in the same room.

"What the hell does having shitty taste in men have to do with me being perfect?" Dad and Connor burst out laughing, mom just shook her head and smiled.

"I think she had that bottled up for some time now." Mom reflected.

"You spent time in the loony bin?" Connor asked, catching the part I was hoping he wouldn't have.

"I did." I admitted, my smile disappearing.

"Is there something wrong?"

"You never told him what happened?" Mom asked, surprised.

"No. I've been avoiding it. Along with thinking about everything else that happened."

"Don't have much of a choice now." Dad said, between mouthfuls.

"We could all just forget that Shella opened her stupid mouth." I suggested, knowing we couldn't get the cat back into the bag.

"You don't have to tell me if you're not ready Paisley." Connor put a comforting hand on mine under the table.

"See? Why can't Shella have found herself a Connor?" Dad asked mom who laughed.

"No way! There's only one and he's all mine."

We were curled up on Connor's bed, the movie forgotten. We managed to make it through an hour before our focus lost its innocence.

It started when I kissed his strong jaw and continued when I moved down to his collar-bone. Connor wasn't content following my lead, he rolled onto his side, forcing me onto my back and kissing me until I couldn't think straight. His mouth set my body on fire. I wrapped my legs around his hips and used my calves to pull him on top of me, wanting to feel his weight.

His hand crept up the bottom of my shirt and rested on my ribcage, just below my breast but his manners stopped him from going any further. Frustrated, I rocked my pelvis against his, desperate to be as close to him as possible. The friction against the bulge in his zipper made him groan against my lips. His kiss turned savage as he struggled to keep himself under control. I was done trying to be patient and move at the pace he set. I unwound my hand from the back of his shirt and moved his hand farther north, under the cup of my bra. I used his hand to massage the tender mound of my breast.

His control snapped and I finally got what I wanted. His mouth moved over my chin and went down to meet his hand. He teased the pink nub with his tongue and my hips bucked against his. I felt myself clench with need. I wished the barrier of clothing between us would disintegrate so that I could feel every inch of his skin against mine. When he pulled away from me and pulled my shirt up and over my head, I wondered if he could read my thoughts. He unclipped the front clasp of my bra and exposed my chest to his hungry gaze.

Before he could resume his exploration with his mouth, I stopped him to rip open the button up shirt he was wearing, sending several black buttons flying to his floor. I wasn't finished, my hands found his belt and with shaking fingers, I pulled the leather strap open to get to the button and zipper holding him back from me. When my hand closed around him, he curled into me, as though my touch eased a nagging ache. He allowed himself to enjoy the feeling of me stroking him for a moment before rolling off the side of his bed so that he could free me from my leggings and look down at my naked body, sprawled across his bed.

"Goddamnit, you're gorgeous." He breathed, appreciating every inch of my flesh.
"Are you going to join the party or just stand there and look at me like a creepy voyeur?" I asked, grinning mischievously.

I watched his eyes follow my hand down my stomach to the warmth between my legs. I ran a finger between my folds, pressing against my pulsating arousal. I wanted to close my eyes and find my release but I was too wrapped up in watching Connor. A low growl rumbled from his chest before he tore his pants off and joined me.

He pulled my legs apart and placed himself between them, laying himself back on top of me, letting his lips return to mine. He gently moved my hand out of his way so that he could take over teasing my sensitive nub. It was only a couple mind blowing seconds before my body erupted and I sucked on his bottom lip to muffle my moans.

"Please Connor. Oh God please." I begged, pushing my hips forward

to persuade him to give in.
"Are you sure?"
"Please!" I insisted and cried out his name when he pushed forward
and broke through my opening.

Connor was an incredible lover. He made me see stars over
and over again before he finally permitted himself to join me in post
orgasmic bliss.

We lay naked, a sheet covering our tangled limbs as we
watched the end of the movie. With my head on his chest, I listened
to the beating of his heart and felt myself letting go. I stood on the
edge of a cliff, watching my heart fall to into the bottomless pit. It
was long gone and it was up to Connor to save it.

"Are you going to tell me what happened?" Connor asked and
instantly, my body went cold.
"What do you mean?" I knew exactly what he meant but I was
hoping I was wrong.
"How did you end up in the hospital?"

I turned away from him and sat on the edge of the bed while I
dressed. He didn't say anything, he didn't pull me back. He gave me
space and waited.

"Can you take me home?" I looked over my shoulder at him, trying
to put the words together to explain everything.
"You don't have to leave. We can stay here. If you don't want to tell
me it's okay. I'm just curious." He reached over and took my hand.
"No, I need to tell you. I just… I want to go home." If I tried now, it
would make it more confusing and come out as a jumbled mess.
"All right." He conceded, getting up and going to his dresser to pull
out a t-shirt.

I led him up to my room. When I had the door closed, I turned back to him and needed the closeness back before I could unload my secrets. I wrapped my arms around his neck and kissed him. Wasting no time, I pulled his shirt over his head. He didn't argue.

We quickly did away with the rest of our clothing. I used his body to ease my anxiety. Our love making was more urgent the second time. I needed to feel him inside of me and I didn't want to wait and take our time to enjoy foreplay.

Laying a light kiss on the back of my neck. The rough stubble on his chin tickled the nape of my neck making me giggle and pull my shoulders up to break the contact. I felt his lips curl up into a knowing grin against my shoulder blade.

He raised himself on an elbow to lean over me.

"Don't like my kisses? That's kind of rude you know." He stuck out his bottom lip in an exaggerated pout.
I raised a hand to run my fingers against his cheek and he took the opportunity to pounce. Straddling me and grabbing both of my hands to hold over my head, he touched the tip of his nose to mine. "It's on now lady!" When I squirmed, he kissed me under my earlobe, forcing more giggles to escape. The kisses around my neck did not stop until tears rolled down my cheeks and both of us were out of breath.

He plopped back down beside me and his smile melted my heart. Slowly I watched as his smile faded and a serious expression replaced it. Worry filled my chest, unsure where his thoughts had gone.

"I love you Paisley."

I was lost. Completely caught off guard. I sat up, holding the sheet to my chest, trying to buy time to catch my scattered thoughts. He sat up beside me, running a hand gently down my back.

"It's okay, you don't have to say anything. I just wanted you to know." He didn't need to add that he was hurt. The forced smile he was giving me quivered and I was certain his heart ached as much as mine did.

"Look Connor, you know I love you too." He moved to pull me into his arms but I held up a hand stopping him in his tracks. He covered the hand I held on his chest with his own and looked at me, more hurt than before and silently pleading. He thought he knew where I was going with this but he could not have been more wrong. I would not be the one to end any hope I had to a happily ever after. It would be up to him. He would have a decision to make and the only prayer I had left was that he had meant it when he said he loved me.

I took his hand and used his fingers to trace the scars on my body. His eyes softened and though he was still confused, the fear subsided.

"Do you want to know what ruined me before we met?"
"You're far from ruined. You're perfect." He kissed me and the guilt in the pit of my stomach did a somersault.
"Connor you need to listen to me. I'm going to tell you a story and when I am done, you won't see me the same way." His grip on my hand tightened and I returned a gentle squeeze. "I need you to keep an open mind and know that the past 6 months with you has done more to heal my soul than any kind of doctor ever could have."

"You don't have to tell me anything. Some people face traumas and spend their lives fighting the demons that those traumatizing moments leave behind. I get it. I love you and I want to help you fight your demons moving forward."

"You think you love me but... you don't *really* know me."

I stood from the bed and went to my closet to retrieve a box I kept hidden under a pile of blankets. Butterflies filled my stomach as I sat back on my bed facing Connor, holding the box tightly against me. Taking a deep breath, I removed the lid. Inside were notes I had taken while I was still able, pictures my parents had taken to document the progression of my 'ailment' and a battered copy of the Holy Bible that I only recently stopped sleeping with.

Then I placed a picture of me, prior to my ordeal, in front of Connor. The second picture was one my mom had taken of my distended stomach, swollen like a woman who was moments from going into labour. Healed bruises in a sickening shade of green and fresh purple bruises covered the mound like a child's painting. The third picture was a close up of my battered face. Dried lips with 2 deep splits on both sides of the bottom one. One eye was swollen shut but the other was just black with a sliver of white circling it. My cheeks were turned up into a smile of sheer delight. The last picture I placed in
font of him was a picture of me climbing a chain link fence upside down. My matted hair hung by my face. My mother took the picture from the other side of the fence, capturing the evil look on my face. The last picture made my skin crawl. My hands were wrinkled, swollen and broken, my feet were bare and my toes clung to the fence like a second set of hands. I was smiling in the picture, rotting flesh left exposed between my teeth. The sides of my mouth were cracked open, making my smiling mouth unnaturally wide.

"What the fuck is all this?" Connor leaned away from the pictures like the subject would jump out at him.
"This is Braxeus. A demon who supposedly took over my body for a year and a half." I dug a little further in the box and pulled out a research paper with a black and white picture of a demon who had a striking resemblance to the one of me on the fence. He took the sheet of paper to have a closer look at Braxeus.

He looked up to make eye contact, searching my eyes for more answers.

"You're not kidding." He concluded and I shook my head. He put the paper back on my bed and took a moment to work through his

397

thoughts.

I watched him pick up the pictures and put them back in the box before closing the lid. He leaned over and pulled me into his arms before laying us both back down on the bed. He held me close and I felt his lips on my forehead.

"I love you Paisley." He said again and the tears of relief flowed freely down my cheeks.
"I love you too Connor." He kissed me before taking my hands into his and giving them a reassuring squeeze.
"Now, from the beginning Paisley, tell me how it started."

"I have a therapist named Daniella who says it could have been a psychotic break. I don't know the exact moment it happened but a lot of doctors seem to think it started when I was really little, I'll start there and let you decide whether or not they are right." I looked into a dark corner of my memory, a place I avoided like the plague. Without any difficulty, things I had been trying so hard to forget, all came flooding back.

~***~

"It's so ironic. At eleven years old, I had perfected the resting bitch face. People didn't approach me unless they were left with no choice and that's just the way I liked it. The irony laid in the fact that in reality, I was a weak, terrified little girl who was lost in a world that just couldn't be bothered.

I had no control at home. None. You could be damn sure that outside of the house, I had full control. The other kids at school feared me, shit, even some of the teachers did. Nobody needed to know that they only got a small taste of the terror I felt when I got back home." ….

The fair was in town. Laurie and I decided that we were going to drag the guys on a double date to go on all the rides and eat cotton candy.

The fair was so much more fun at night. The bright lights and music came alive in the darkness. Laurie and I walked arm in arm, laughing and drinking beer from travel mugs while Connor and Dave trailed behind.

"Bitch, we are getting our asses on that thing!" Laurie squealed, eyes like saucers.
"I'm not sure you're tall enough for that bad boy." I smirked, looking up at the pendulum rude.
"Shut your face." Laurie chuckled, pulling me to the back of the line.
"Babe?" Dave called out.
"Yeah?"
"Con and I are gonna go and play hoops." He gestured toward a game a few stands down the path.
"Have fun. Don't come back until you win me something." He rolled his eyes as they walked away.
"Damn, he has a nice ass." I remarked, eyes on Connor's butt in his jeans.
"Get your eyes off his ass. That's all mine and I don't share." Laurie warned, narrowing her eyes at me.
"Not Dave's. Connor's." I argued. "Though Dave's does come in a close second." I added, glancing at his bottom to compare.
"You're such a jerk." Laurie laughed, almost bouncing in place as the line started to move.

Laurie and I sat side-by-side, thighs touching as the guy running the ride locked the protective bar across our laps. I felt the familiar excitement fluttering in my stomach. The ride slowly started swaying, building momentum. We got higher and higher and soon we were high enough to see across the park. Laurie and I screamed in exhilaration as we swung to the other side. When the ride began to slow down, we were both laughing like lunatics.

As the chair was coming to a stop, I happened to glance at the exit gate and my blood ran cold. What I saw made me want to vomit.

"Shit." I mumbled.
"What?" Laurie asked, still catching her breath from all the laugher.
"Get ready, shit is about to hit the fan." I told her, looking her in the eye to make sure she understood the severity of our situation.
"Why?"
"Look who's standing by the fence." I kept my eyes on her as she looked around.
"You have got to be fucking kidding me!" I watched her knuckles turn white on the bar across her middle. "I'm gonna fucking murder that ass-hole." She swore through a tight-lipped snarl.
"What do we do?" I asked, panic rising.
"Hold my stuff while I kick his ass!"
"No, seriously! What are we going to do?" She grabbed my arm and squeezed, forcing me to focus only on her.
"We are going to walk through the gate and pretend he doesn't exist."
"There's no fucking way." I muttered, watching the guy unlock the bar and raise it over our heads.

Laurie took my hand and held me steady as we hopped off the ride. She led the way to the gate and she played her part well, she didn't acknowledge Thomas whatsoever.

"Fancy meeting you here." I heard him say and tried to keep walking even though every hair on my body stood on end.
"Come on, the guys are just over there." Laurie told me, pulling me along, ignoring him completely.
"Now wait up a second." His hand wrapped around forearm, stopping Laurie and I in our tracks.
"Get your fucking hand off of her." Laurie ordered, sounding vicious.
"Move along Laurie, this has nothing to do with you." He spat, giving her a look of disgust. He was angry.
"No Thomas. Nothing about Paisley has anything to do with *you* anymore."
"Laurie, I don't have the patience to pretend to tolerate you. I'll give you five seconds to get the fuck out of my sight." He threatened.
"Fine by me." She tugged on the hand she was still holding. "Let's

go Paisley."

"No. Just you." He clarified, pulling sharply on my arm, making my shoulder scream in protest.

"Dave!" Laurie screamed at the top of her lungs in the direction of the carnival game where Dave and Connor were playing.

There was no way they could hear her over the music and noises from excited fair-goers but something caught his attention and he glanced over to see her waving her arm at him. Instantly, the ball fell from his hands and he smacked Connor on the arm before breaking into a run.

"Tell your ass-hole cousin to get his fucking hands off of Paisley." She demanded when he was within earshot. His eyes landed on Thomas's grip on my arm.

"What's going on here?" He asked Thomas.

"I want to talk to Paisley but Laurie is acting like a fucking psycho."

"I wonder why?" He threw his arms up in exasperation. "She doesn't wanna talk to you bro, back off."

"She's going to spare me a couple of minutes." Thomas insisted. "Take your little bitch elsewhere before I knock her in the fucking teeth."

"You think you're going to put your hands on my girlfriend?" Dave asked, getting right in Thomas's face, dangerously close to losing the thin control he had on his temper.

"Hey man, everything okay?" Connor asked as he broke through the crowd. He didn't see everything that had happened, only that Dave had taken off. He was walking in on a tense situation between Dave and his cousin.

"Connor." I whimpered, desperate to be in the comfort of his arms.

He reached out for me and that's when he noticed that Thomas had a firm grip on my arm. He ripped Thomas's hand off and watched as I rubbed the soreness from my bruising flesh. I didn't get the chance to find comfort in his warmth because he pounced on Thomas, tackling him to the ground. They tussled on the ground, fists pounding into one another. Dave didn't step in right away when Connor straddled Thomas and pummeled him in the face, he waited until Thomas's hands fell limply to the ground, then grabbed Connor by the back of his shirt and hauled him off.

We managed to blend into the crowd before park security showed up.

A week later, Connor showed up at my front door with a bouquet of flowers. I was pleasantly surprised when I opened the door. The bruise around his eye was almost gone and the cut on his lip was barely visible.

"Hey, I thought you had plans tonight?" I asked, taking the flowers he held out.
"I do. Is your dad home?" He looked nervous and his question was unsettling.
"Yeah, he's in the kitchen with my mom." I stood back and gestured for him to come in.
"Does he have a minute?"
"Sure, they're just playing cards."

I followed Connor to the kitchen, not sure what I was supposed to do if he was paying my dad a visit. Was I supposed to give them privacy?

"Hey Connor, how are you doing?" Mom asked, smiling in welcome.
"I'm good, yourself?"
"Good. Can I get you a drink?"
"No thank you. Mister Coleman I was wondering if you had a minute to talk?" Dad looked between Connor and I, confused.
"Are you pregnant?" Dad asked me, narrowing his eyes in suspicion.
"No!" I shook my head vehemently in denial.

"Okay…" Dad dragged his eyes away from me and onto Connor, eyes still narrowed. "Did you want my wife and daughter to leave?"

"Uh, I don't think that's necessary." I took Connor's hand and felt that sweat from his palm.
"Is everything okay?" I asked, terrified of the elephant he brought into the room.
"It's fine." He insisted.
"Have a seat." Dad suggested.

Mom was wearing a grin like she knew exactly what was going on while dad looked nearly as uncomfortable as I did. Connor cleared his throat and I waited while he squirmed in his seat, determined to follow through with whatever he had set in motion.

"What did you want to talk about Connor?" Dad pushed, the words putting a sour look on his face.

"Well sir…" Connor forced himself to look my dad in the eye. "I love Paisley." My face burned as dad glanced in my direction briefly. "I think that her and I have something amazing and I…" He cleared his throat again and his Adam's apple bobbed. "I know we're young but I don't think either of us are stupid. I wanted to talk to you because I want to ask Paisley to marry me."

The only sound was a surprised gasp from my lips. We all sat, deathly silent. Connor glanced around at mom and I, begging someone to rescue him. He rubbed his damp palms on his pant legs and looked back at my dad for his answer.

"Are you asking me for my permission?" Dad finally asked.
"Yes sir."
"You want to steal my little girl?" Connor flinched, eyes widening in shock.
"No! Absolutely not! I could never take her away from you. I just want to build a life with her."
"That girl means the world to me, you know that?"
"She means the world to me too."

"Jesus Christ." Dad whispered, leaning his elbows on the table and running his hands over his face. When he looked up again, he looked like he had aged before our eyes. He looked utterly drained. "What do you think about all of this?" He asked my mom, who was still smiling as she watched everything unfold.

"I think ultimately it's up to Paisley but I would be thrilled if she said yes."
"Of fucking course, you would be." Dad rolled his eyes. "I supposed Paisley could do a hell of a lot worse." He mumbled.

"Does that mean I have your blessing?" Connor asked in a voice thick with nerves.
"Yes." Dad muttered, pouting like a scolded toddler.

Connor pushed his chair back and knelt on the floor in front of me. He pulled a black velvet box from his pant pocket and opened the lid. The ring was stunning. It wasn't big and gaudy it was small and sophisticated, one bigger diamond in the centre with two smaller ones on either side.

"Paisley, will you marry me?" He asked and tears of sheer joy poured down my cheeks. I fell to my knees in front of him.
"Of course I'll marry you!" I threw myself in his arms, making him drop the ring box to the floor.

Mom covered her mouth, tears overflowing from her eyes. Dad smiled begrudgingly, happy to see me find a partner in a world that had once seemed so determined to tear me down. I kissed him before I let him go so that he could retrieve the jewelry box. He took the ring and slid it onto my ring finger and I couldn't take my eyes off of the diamond that proved he wanted me forever, despite my history.

# Chapter Sixteen

I'm Yours

Things progressed quickly. Mom was on a mission to plan our wedding to perfection. Connor and I chose a date in early October, both of us loved fall and we agreed that it would be the perfect time to begin our lives together. Laurie was thrilled when I asked her to be my matron of honour. Gemma and Claire argued regularly over their bridesmaid's dresses but were ultimately just as happy to stand beside me on the big day.

My hunt for the perfect wedding dress was turning out to be a lot more difficult than I had anticipated. I always just assumed that I would walk into a boutique, see a white dress that looked nice and walk out happy. Not only did I have my mom and three best friends offering opinions, there were hundreds of dresses to look at. If I thought I could just dismiss the ones I didn't find appealing, I was sorely mistaken. They insisted I try *every* goddamn dress on because they looked different when you wore them than they did on the hanger. All four of them were in their glory, ooh-ing and ah-ing over white frills and lace. I was contemplating walking down the isle in my fucking birthday suit.

The saleslady must have seen the look of distress on my face because she came to my rescue.

"Hey sweetheart. You look a little overwhelmed." She commented, touching my elbow lightly and offering a look of sympathy and understanding.
"A little?" I chuckled, brushing my bangs back from my face.
"I don't want to add to it but come with me a minute. I have the perfect dress for you." She requested, leading me away from my over-excited possie.

She took me into a back room where racks of dresses hung in plastic coverings. She let my arm go when we were out of sight and wandered away to find what she was looking for. She came back with a glowing smile, full of confidence. As she lifted the plastic from the dress, my jaw dropped. She was incredible at her job because it was *perfect*. The bodice was covered in floral lace with capped sleeves and the skirt was flowy, loose ivory. Matching lace lined the hem of the dress, bringing the whole design together. It was simple but elegant and when I put it on, it fit like it was made for me.

"It's a pre-worn gown so it isn't brand new but that just means that the price tag is a lot easier to swallow." She was smiling and nodding as she looked me up and down. "I don't even think you'll need alterations."

"Can I go show the girls?"
"Of course!"

When I came back, they all stopped flicking through hangers and looked over. All four jaws dropped as they took in the sight of me, happily modeling for them.

"It's gorgeous!" Laurie exclaimed, clapping her hands.

Mom was speechless, she nodded her agreement as the water works kicked in.

"Now we pray that no one gets their rag on the big day." Gemma grinned.

Her words were meant to be a light-hearted jest. Unfortunately, they made me realize that I hadn't had a period since the week before Connor proposed. Frantically, I counted the weeks in my head. Eight. *Fuck.*

"Tell me it's the one. It has to be. It's so you, Paisley." Claire commented, sighing wistfully.
"It's definitely the one. I *love* it." I did a little twirl to emphasize my point and to hide the worry on my face.

Laurie and I dropped the other girls and my mom off on our way to the mall to search for outfits for my Jack and Jill the following weekend.

"You know, you should have told me you weren't in the mood to do more shopping."
"What makes you think I'm not in the mood?"
"I've been sitting with your surly ass since we left the boutique!"
"I am not *surly*." I argued, knowing that my face bellied my words.
"Oh, bullshit, Paisley. I know you well enough to know that you're not thrilled right now."
"No, I'm not exactly thrilled. I'm shitting my fucking pants!"
"Oh, yeah. I guess putting on a wedding dress would make everything a hell of a lot more real." She nodded in understanding as

she pulled in to an empty spot and put the car in park.

"That's not it… Laurie, I missed my period." I told her in an unsteady voice.

"Fuck off." She laughed. When I didn't join in, her chuckles died away. "You're not joking?"

"I really wish I was." I told her, rubbing my face, hoping it was all a dream.

"Could be stress…" She reached over and rubbed my shoulder in reassurance. "We'll run in and grab a test. You can do it at my place. No need to freak out until we know for sure."

"What if I'm pregnant, Laurie?"

"What part of, 'don't freak out', did you not understand? Are you not on the pill?"

"I am." I nodded.

"Then it's more than likely just stress. Chill out."

I felt like all eyes were on me as we looked through the pregnancy tests. Laurie didn't seem phased at all as she held up two boxes to compare them.

"This one's a little pricier but I think something like this deserves the name brand."

"I don't care which one we get, let's just get the hell outta here." I pleaded and she laughed at my discomfort.

"Jesus, Paisley. If you can spread your legs, you can buy a pregnancy test." She rolled her eyes and took the box to the cash register.

Laurie was sprawled out on her bed, reading a magazine while I paced, waiting for the timer to go off. When it started beeping, I froze, feeling like I could puke. Laurie sat up and took the hint. She went into the bathroom to grab the stick for me.

When she came back, I searched her face for the answer but she had no tell. Without a word, she handed me the test stick. There were two blue lines in the result window. A bun was most certainly in the oven.

"Fuck." I muttered, falling onto her bed.

Laurie sat down beside me and wrapped her arms around my shoulders. She didn't try to placate me with empty words.

I turned down Laurie's offer for a ride. I wanted to clear my head and walking seemed like a good way to do it. It took me an hour and half but finally, I turned onto Connor's driveway.

"Hey, Paisley, come on in." Paul answered the door and stood back to let me in. "Connor is in his room."

"Thank you." I gave him the best smile I could muster under the circumstances. Paul looked concerned but didn't ask any questions.

I went downstairs to the basement where Connor's bedroom was located. I knocked on the door but didn't wait for an answer before opening the door. Connor was sitting at his desk, a textbook open in front of him. He looked up as I walked in and smiled.

"Hey babe." He stood to give me a kiss. "I wasn't expecting to see you tonight."

"Yeah, we need to talk." His brows lowered in concern and he took my hand in his.

"What's wrong?"

"So, uh…" I dropped his hand and started pacing again. "I don't know how to tell you this." I had no idea how he was going to react to the news and it exacerbated my nervousness.

"Paisley, what's going on, you're freaking me the fuck out." He sounded just as terrified as I was and I felt guilty for being the cause.

"Connor… I'm uh… There's… Fuck…" I couldn't get the words through my lips.

"Are you seeing someone else?" He asked, hurt flooding into his eyes as his mind ran through every possible scenario.

"No! Of course, I'm not cheating on you!" Part of me was insulted that he would think I could do something so heartless but logically I knew, I was going about the situation all wrong. "I'm pregnant." I choked out.

"Oh, thank God." He breathed out a sigh of relief as he crumpled to the side of the bed. Then I watched as the lightbulb went off inside his head. "Wait. You're what?"

"I'm pregnant." I repeated.

"Pregnant." He whispered, tasting the word.

He shot off the bed so fast it startled me and I jumped. He lifted me off the ground and swung me around with excitement.

"This is incredible!" He exclaimed, kissing me loudly.

"Are you fucking serious right now?" I couldn't process his reaction; it made no sense.

"Of course. I mean, it's a lot sooner than I would have like but it's not the end of the world. I love the idea of you having my baby."

"You're sick in the head." I joked, feeling the tension in my body melt away. If he was happy with the news, I could come to terms with it myself.

"Yes, I am. You make me crazy Paisley Coleman and I love every damn minute of it."

Getting ready for the wedding was an all-day affair. Laurie, Gemma and Claire spent the night with my mom and I in a hotel room where mom woke us up ridiculously early to get the day started. I was the only one who seemed to be irritated with the lack of sleep as the rest of them hustled and bustled to make sure everything was perfect. The crazy bitches even giggled while they did it.

Mom drove us to the hairdressers and we all sat in our stools and gossiped while we had our hair done. When the stylist spun me around to see myself in the mirror, I was overjoyed with the look she had done. Most of my hair was curled and swept over my shoulder with a few strategically pinned pieces throughout, keeping it away from my face.

Then we carted off one by one to the makeup artist. She kept my face mostly natural, taupe around my eyes, a light highlight on the top of my cheekbones and gloss on my lips.

Mom and Laurie helped me into my dress so that I wouldn't ruin my hair or makeup. I slid a blue garter belt up my leg and mom finished the entire ensemble with her mother's pearls. I never felt more beautiful and the look on dad's face when he saw me, told me he agreed.

"You make a very pretty bride P-Baby." He said before kissing me lightly on the cheek.
"Thanks, dad."
"Shall we get this show on the road?"
"I guess we should get a move on. Wouldn't want everyone to think I bailed." He chuckled.
"You know, you'll always be my baby girl. Married or not."
"I know." I smiled up at him and whether it was pregnancy

hormones or the sentiments that went hand-in-hand with marriage, I felt tears fill my eyes.

"Don't you dare. You cry now, you'll ruin your makeup and your mom will have a fit." He warned, wagging his finger at me.

Waiting outside the church doors, my girls took their turns hugging me. Dad took a deep breath before hooking my arm through his.

"Here we go kid." When he smiled, the corner of his lips quivered. "Here we go."

When the big wooden doors opened, my eyes instantly found Connor's and my heart soared. He looked gorgeous in his tux, hair combed back and a sexy goatee around his full lips. I couldn't believe how lucky I was to be marrying such an amazing man.

I heard a sniffle and when I looked beside me, my stomach clenched. There were tears on my dad's cheeks. The closer we got to the altar, the more he sniffled and wiped his eyes with his sleeve. Stopping in front of Connor and the priest, dad lifted my veil and kissed my cheek.

"I love you, Paisley."

"I love you too, dad." And that's when I cracked and started to cry too.

"Who gives this woman to this man?" The priest asked in a kind voice.

"Her mother and I do." Dad answered the best he could before placing my hand into Connor's.

"Introducing, for the first time, Mister and Misses Rousseau!" The

415

DJ yelled into the mic and the reception hall filled with applause.

Connor led me onto the dance floor where he held me close while we had our first dance as husband and wife. His hand slid over the side of my swelling abdomen.

"How are you feeling Misses Rousseau?"
"Wonderful. How about you, husband?"
"Fantastic." He grinned and kissed me until I saw stars.

# Epilogue

### Who Would Have Thought?

**~ Nine months later. ~**

It was Connor's first day as executive chef at Bella's Fine Dining Restaurant and I loved the way he looked in his chef jacket and checkered pants. I managed to talk him back into the bedroom when he first put it on but was still ready to jump his bones when he put it back on the second time.

He went to the playpen and lifted Damien into his arms. Watching Connor with his son was one of my favourite things to do. He was such a good dad and the baby adored him. No one could settle him the way his daddy could. He would coo and smile at Connor and my heart would turn to putty.

"Hey big guy. I gotta get outta here or your mother is going to sexually assault me again. Damn woman can't keep her hands off of me." He was talking to the baby but grinning at me mischievously.

"Oh, poor you. Such a terrible life you live." I rolled my eyes at him but couldn't help but smile.

"He's so perfect. How in the hell did this little guy come from me?" He asked, looking down at our happy little boy in awe.

"I'm pretty sure he came out of me." I disputed sarcastically.

"You know what I meant." He grumbled, eyes still soaking in the bundle in his arms.

"Yeah, crazy, isn't it?" I walked up to them and ran my finger over Damien's soft cheek.

Six months of motherhood and I was still blown away by the amount of feeling such a tiny human could bring into my life. No matter how much time I spent holding him, rocking him, singing to him, it was never enough. The first few weeks, I struggled with post partem, I didn't want anyone else to touch him and barely slept because I didn't want to put him down long enough to rest. I spoke to my doctor and got some help but it was still hard. It didn't bother me as much when other people cuddled him but I still struggled when I wasn't in the same room as he was. Connor was impossibly patient through the entire adjustment period. He was made to be a family man and soaked in every minute of it.

"I love you so much Mister Rousseau." I leaned over the baby in his arms and kissed him.

"I love you so much more than that Misses Rousseau." He grinned.

"You wish." I smiled.

It was past three in the morning when I woke up. Normally, Damien cried around two thirty, ready to eat. My over-engorged breasts pulled me from a deep sleep, my nightdress wet and sticking to me. I groaned, exhausted. When my foggy brain cleared, fear set it. My baby wasn't crying. I whipped the blankets aside and ran to the nursery.

I threw the door open and was confused when I heard Damien coo-ing happily in his crib. I nearly collapsed when my eyes adjusted to the dim moonlight coming through the window. A familiar face stood at the head of my son's crib. A wrinkled face with a menacing grin, unnaturally wide with rotting teeth on full display. Braxeus was leering down at my son.

"No!" I screamed at the top of my lungs.
"You didn't think I forgot you, did you Paisley?" He asked before cackling evilly.
"Get the hell away from him!"

"Paisley? Paisley, baby? Wake up." My eyes flew open to see Connor leaning over me, shaking my shoulders. He was white as a ghost. "Are you okay? You were having a nightmare."
"Damien!" I yelled, thrashing around, desperate to get out of bed and run to my baby.

"Calm down, he's fine. I got up and fed him so that you could get some more sleep." He let go of my arms to run his hands through his hair, still breathing heavily. "Scared the shit out of me when I heard you screaming." He rubbed a hand over his chest where his heart was still pounding.

"I'm sorry." I tried to calm myself but I couldn't. I stepped out of the bed to check on Damien.

He was sleeping peacefully in his crib, his little hand curled beside his face. I leaned my shoulder against the door frame and watched his chest rise and fall with each breath he took.

"We sure make cute babies." Connor whispered in my ear, wrapping an arm around my waist and lifting me into his arms to carry me back to our room.
"It's our super power." I agreed.

We curled back up in bed together. I relished the warmth of my husband at my back and knew without a doubt, that I had finally found my happy place.